Jessica Adams is the author of *The New Astrology for Women*, *Single White E-mail*, *Handbag Horoscopes*, and co-editor of *Girls' Night In*. She is a Leo with the Moon in Aquarius and lives between Bellingen, Sydney and London.

Jessica Adams' website address is
www.jessicaadams.com.au

Praise for *Tom, Dick and Debbie Harry*:

'A sparky, entertaining book – I found it funny, surreal and poignant, all at the same time'
Sophie Kinsella, author of *The Secret Dreamworld of a Shopaholic*

'Jessica Adams has written an engrossing and utterly original tale which is both funny and frequently very touching'
Isabel Wolff, author of *The Making of Minty Malone* and *Out of the Blue*

www.**booksattransworld**.co.uk

Also by Jessica Adams

SINGLE WHITE E-MAIL

and published by Black Swan

THE NEW ASTROLOGY FOR WOMEN

published by Corgi Books

Tom, Dick and Debbie Harry

Jessica Adams

BLACK SWAN

TOM, DICK AND DEBBIE HARRY
A BLACK SWAN BOOK : 0 552 14721 4

First publication in Great Britain

PRINTING HISTORY
Black Swan edition published 2001

1 3 5 7 9 10 8 6 4 2

Set in 11pt Melior by
County Typesetters, Margate, Kent.

Black Swan Books are published by Transworld Publishers,
61–63 Uxbridge Road, London W5 5SA,
a division of The Random House Group Ltd,
in Australia by Random House Australia (Pty) Ltd,
20 Alfred Street, Milsons Point, Sydney, NSW 2061, Australia,
in New Zealand by Random House New Zealand Ltd,
18 Poland Road, Glenfield, Auckland 10, New Zealand
and in South Africa by Random House (Pty) Ltd,
Endulini, 5a Jubilee Road, Parktown 2193, South Africa.

Printed and bound in Great Britain by
Clays Ltd, St Ives plc.

For my Auntie Margaret, who liked The Hollies

Chapter One

Between his twenty-eighth and twenty-ninth birthdays, Harry Gilby was invited to fifteen weddings. 'And now there's another one,' Harry complained to his parents at breakfast. 'Plus this muesli's got dangly bits in it, has anyone noticed?'

'It's not just another wedding, it's your brother,' his father said. 'And it's happening in about three hours time, so prepare yourself. Can I have some of that muesli or are you taking out a mortgage on the box?'

His parents, Harry realized, were wearing identical white terry-towelling dressing gowns. How long had that been going on for? He realized it had been years since he'd seen them before 11 a.m. Trying not to look, he poured himself some black coffee, trying to wake himself up by breathing in the caffeine and the steam.

'All I ever do is go to weddings,' Harry complained, 'and I don't care if it is Richard.'

He had a bad hangover from his brother's stag night and he was still wearing the clothes he'd slept in. 'And can we turn that radio down?'

'The weather,' his father said, waving a hand at the blaring stereo speakers. 'We need the weather for the wedding.'

'Yeah, but it's the weather for every single town in Australia. Dunedoo, Gundagai, Kurri Kurri, Scone,'

7

Harry droned, 'Bacchus Marsh, Dimboola, Chinchilla . . . Do we have to know the rainfall of everywhere from bloody Woy Woy to Wee Waa, just so they can get married in the garden?'

'You only think everyone's getting married all the time because of your age,' his mother said, turning the volume down on the radio. 'And it's natural. When people start getting to thirty, they want to settle down.'

Harry made a face, both at her and the stale muesli. 'Debbie Harry was thirty and she never settled down.'

'Oh no, not Debbie Harry again, not this morning, I couldn't stand it,' Mrs Gilby said quickly.

Offended, Harry munched in silence while his parents passed each other bits of the newspaper. Every time he stuck his hand on the tablecloth, it started trembling slightly, he noticed with satisfaction. It was good to have solid physical evidence that he really was as ill as he felt.

'Oh look,' his mother said at last, staring at the front page. 'Bill Gates has given all his money away.'

'Oh, I see,' Harry said. 'I can't talk about Debbie Harry any more, but you can talk about *Bill Gates*.'

'Yes, but we don't talk about him all the time,' his father explained.

'And we haven't got a great big sexy photo of him licking his lips stuck on our bedroom ceiling,' his mother said, meaningfully.

Trying to ignore them, Harry poured himself another black coffee. His hangover was so bad that every crunch of muesli against his back teeth sounded like someone was doing home renovations in his head.

'Anyway, I don't think it's true that all you ever do is go to weddings,' Mrs Gilby said suddenly, giving Harry a look over the top of the milk carton.

'It's just that I thought people had got all their marriages over and done with when I was twenty-five,' Harry complained, with a mouthful of muesli. 'I thought people had got it out of their systems. But this year's been like a tidal wave. Everyone who didn't do it when they were twenty-five is doing it now. And now Richard's going for his *second* one. I mean, he's actually settling down *twice*.'

'Well, I've got to get to the hairdresser's,' his mother said suddenly, looking at her watch. 'Sarah's already there – she's been up since 6 a.m. poor thing.'

Harry tutted, making a half-hearted effort to sound sorry for Sarah – after all, she was Richard's new wife to be, he supposed, and consequently his kith and kin, not that he really knew what that meant.

'Anyway, feel free to join me at the salon, Harry,' his mother said, 'or are you going to turn up this afternoon with those things all over your face?'

'Those mutton chops you're growing,' Dr Gilby tutted. 'They're out of control.'

'They're not mutton chops,' Harry said, sighing.

'What?'

'They're sideburns. Mutton chops are those things you get on Charles Dickens on the ABC on Sunday nights. These are *sideburns*,' he insisted 'These are *groovy*.'

Harry wished his parents would go away. He wasn't used to having breakfast with them. Even though he lived in the log cabin in their back garden, he usually ate breakfast alone – when he could be bothered at all. And he was still trying to come to terms with the matching dressing gowns.

'Remember to sign the card for Sarah and Richard,' his father reminded him, 'and you owe me two hundred and fifty dollars for the fridge.'

'We bought them a fridge? Richard's already got a fridge!' Harry said.

'Well, Sarah and Richard said they wanted a new one,' his father shrugged.

'Smile,' Mrs Gilby declared, picking up her empty cereal bowl as they left the room. 'I want everyone smiling in the photos.'

9

When they had finally gone – to his horror, he could see his parents were also wearing matching white terry-towelling slippers – Harry drank the rest of the milk from the carton. It might help him sleep, he reasoned, and if he was going to get through the wedding this afternoon, he was going to need a nap – or preferably a coma. Richard's stag night had almost destroyed him, even if it had consisted of nothing wilder than drinking double scotches and betting everyone in the pub that they couldn't list the names of all Seven Dwarfs.

Moving his parents' cat out of the way, Harry made himself comfortable on the couch and closed his eyes. By the time his mother came back from the hairdresser's, he'd almost be ready to rock, he decided – possibly. As he wedged his head between cushions covered in ginger cat hair, Harry thought about the day ahead. It seemed morally wrong. While Richard was on his second marriage at the age of thirty-five, Harry hadn't even lived with a woman – although he'd once got drunk at a Christmas party and proposed to a sheep.

It had been so easy for Richard. He'd just walked into some conference in London, seen a blonde woman – who'd turned out to be Sarah – trying to measure a window, of all things, and then he'd just offered to hold one end of the tape measure. Then they'd had lunch together at some special kiosk in a London park, that only Sarah knew about, where the toasted chicken sandwiches were good – or something. And then Richard had asked Sarah to see *Titanic*, and . . . blah, blah, blah, Harry thought. Easy. Six months later, instant wedding. Why was it never like that for him?

Holding his aching head in his hands, Harry turned sideways on the couch, trying to get comfortable. He just did not believe in weddings, he decided. That was the whole problem – you just couldn't get any love from a woman these days unless you were prepared to put up with them, and he wasn't. There were about thirty weddings a year in Compton, which had a population of three thousand people, according to the Lions Club sign as you drove into town. Harry realized that these days, half of those weddings seemed to involve people that he had gone to school with, or been in a band with, or played cricket with.

He turned up because he had to. After all, at a Compton wedding people were always trying to make up numbers. But he always fell asleep, or lost his place in the hymn book, or found himself thinking all the wrong things, like – *how the hell is she going to stand looking at his hairy back for the next fifty years?* Sometimes, when he was really bored, he imagined the entire congregation in the nude.

Stretching out on the couch, Harry thought back to the two weddings he'd been to the previous weekend. At one of them, the mother of the bride had dyed her poodles pink. The bride, waving a gladioli, had turned up in a horse-drawn carriage with her boobs hanging out, and afterwards, they had served a giant lobster wearing a white top hat made out of a paper napkin.

At the other wedding he'd been to, someone's sister had played 'The Lady in Red' on a Hammond organ, and everyone had been given a glass beer tankard to take home, with love hearts and the date etched into the side. Harry had caught the groom vomiting into his in the car park afterwards when he'd thought no-one was looking.

Thinking about it now, Harry decided the worst part of both ceremonies had been the horror he'd experienced wondering what it would be like to have sex, for the rest of his life, with any of the four people who had just got married. He felt guilty because he knew he should feel happy for them, but their weddings just depressed him.

Wincing as the cat jumped up on his chest, Harry gave in and made room for it. Soon it was kneading away on his shirt, doing a claws-in, claws-out dance. For reasons lost in the mists of time, the Gilby family had invented a term for this – fring-fronging.

'Stop fring-fronging on my bloody nipples,' Harry growled, but the cat ignored him. He was so hungover, he realized, that he couldn't even remember its name, let alone be bothered to hurl it onto the floor. Soon, he knew, the cat would also start to dribble. *Just like me ten seconds from now*, Harry thought, shortly before he passed out head first into a cushion.

Two hours later, he was woken up by the sound of hooting laughter and what sounded like uncontrolled whooping in the kitchen. He wondered, yet again, why all his parents' friends were so loud – did people automatically lose their volume control after they turned fifty? The women were definitely worse than the men. When they laughed, it was like listening to the feedback at a heavy metal concert. *A horrible, nameless, squealing noise without shape, without form and without end*, Harry decided. His mouth tasted of old milk now, from the muesli, and he was dying of thirst.

Yawning, he moved the cat which, embarrassingly enough, had decided to tuck its head lovingly into his groin. As he threw it onto the floor, he realized that his parents must have been cleaning around him as he'd slept. The breakfast mess had been cleared away, and instead there were now piles of wedding presents forming a pyramid on the kitchen table. He couldn't believe the wrapping paper some people used – horseshoes and bells and little tiny brides and grooms. It was like something out of the 1950s, Harry thought, and not even the good part of the 1950s.

'You up yet?' his father said, sticking his head around the door. He was now wearing a suit and tie, and a pair of black brogues that Harry remembered borrowing once for a *Rocky Horror Picture Show* party.

'What time is it?' Harry yawned again.

'Time for you to get organized,' Dr Gilby warned.

'Your mother's dressed and ready, and your brother's just gone into town to pick up your aunt and uncle. He'll be back in half an hour. And by the way . . .'

'Yes?'

'What have you been drinking, plaster of Paris?'

When he had gone, Harry looked in the mirror on top of the dresser. He had a milk ring around his mouth that made him look like Marcel Marceau. And horribly, he had also developed a small whitehead on the side of his nose. Squeezing it would have to be his first grooming gesture for the big day ahead. Making a face at the mirror, he decided he'd leave it until the last minute. If his parents' friends came in now and caught him squeezing things on his face, there'd be yet more anti-Harry outpourings.

He couldn't believe how bad-tempered his parents were today – it had to be because of Richard, he decided. It couldn't be easy watching their eldest son getting married for the second time – especially when the first one had been such a balls-up. Wincing, Harry held both sides of his head in his hands. Whenever he had a hangover, he had a recurring fantasy about a specially designed iron head clamp. One day, he thought groggily, he would have to invent it.

Heading for his log cabin in the back garden, Harry suddenly staggered on the grass as he realized someone had also managed to put up two giant white marquees while he'd been asleep. It felt like an invasion of his space – he'd always counted the garden as his territory, mainly because the cabin was there.

Harry had been living there for five years, allegedly to save money so he could pay for his first house in cash, but the cabin was his home and he didn't like seeing it suddenly surrounded by white tents with ribbons all over them. It was like *Day of the Triffids*, he thought in disgust, except instead of huge, tentacle-waving alien life forms, he had been taken over by great big wedding marquees.

'In and out in ten minutes, Harry!' his mother shouted from the kitchen window.

'What?' he yelled back. It was unbelievable – he could still hear the heavy-metal feedback squeal of her friends laughing, even at twenty metres.

'HURRY UP!' she shouted again, and slammed the window shut.

If they'd tied white ribbons to the cabin as well, Harry thought, he'd just rip them off. But fortunately, they'd left him alone. Once inside, he shut the door, and locked it on the inside in case any of his parents' loud friends wandered in by mistake.

As usual, his parents had used up most of the hot water in the house. Running the shower and waiting for the heat to come back, Harry managed to rip off his clothes with one hand and get rid of the whitehead on the side of his nose with the other.

'You're a damn sexy beast,' he told the mirror re-asurringly. 'A damn sexy beast.' What did his father mean, mutton chops? In the right light, Harry comforted himself, he could still look like a young Nick Cave – although a Nick Cave who sometimes shopped at K-Mart.

Singing Blondie songs, as he always did in the shower, Harry let the water splash over his face and then attacked his armpits with a new bar of Imperial Leather soap. He wondered if Tom was ready – after all, he had best man duties to perform. The good thing about living in the cabin, Harry decided, was that he could basically have a shower, get dressed and walk straight into the ceremony in his own back yard. Poor Tom lived miles away.

Thinking back to Richard's stag night the previous evening, Harry laughed out loud as he remembered Tom trying to recall all the names of the Seven Dwarfs. He hadn't even managed one. The trouble with Tom, Harry decided, was that he was born vague. You could see it in his eyes. Women went mad over them because

14

they were so blue, but they were always out of focus, somehow, like a television tuned into the wrong station.

Tom wasn't really his friend so much – he was more from Richard's era. But they all played cricket together and, in the days when Tom still used to drink, he and Harry had often spent an afternoon on the river, knocking back bottles of Cascade lager and catching trout.

As the hot water started to run out in the shower, Harry wound the hot tap round to the left as far as it would go and turned the cold tap off. One day, he promised himself, he would have the kind of shower that didn't depend on complex tactics and manoeuvres. Just keeping the hot water going in the cabin involved as much effort as doing a three-point turn.

Finally, as the water ran cold on his back, he gave in. It was now freezing and he had to get out. Finding a fluffy pink bath towel that his mother had once donated, Harry dried himself off and began the enjoyable process of choosing his clothes. As he laid them out, rejecting one shirt after another, he wondered idly what Richard would be wearing. Probably something Sarah had chosen, he decided. Richard was hopeless when it came to clothes.

In the end, Harry rejected his purple pants, white vinyl belt and paisley shirt and settled for a brown polyester suit, that he'd bought from an op shop in Hobart for fifteen dollars, and an orange ruffled shirt. Although the suit looked fantastic – like something The Six Million Dollar Man might have worn to a cocktail party with The Bionic Woman, it also stank of Old Spice and cat urine. To compensate, Harry brushed his teeth again. At least he'd be minty enough to be sociable.

Eventually he felt ready to go. Stepping out of his cabin in his Doc Martens, he carefully locked the door and made sure the curtains were closed so that nobody could see all his Debbie Harry posters. Then he made his way across the grass and into the main marquee – only to discover that he was almost the last guest to arrive. The place was packed.

'Have you got the time?' he hissed to a woman at the back.

It turned out to be nearly noon – he'd only just made it.

Finding himself a seat and avoiding his parents, Harry leaned back in his hired plastic chair, trying to relax. It was no good, though – he was already sweating. He noticed too that his father had already started the music in his absence, which meant more Harry-bashing later in the day as the music was supposed to be his job. His parents had also decided to put down fake grass and now it was beginning to smell. Someone had forgotten to keep the flies out of the marquee, too, and there were now three of them, rubbing their legs at each other and sitting on one of the white ribbons tied to his chair. It was a stinking hot day, Harry thought, a typical Compton November Saturday. At this time of year, it could get as high as thirty degrees. Inside the marquee now, it felt like about forty.

Flicking through the wedding programme, Harry realized that the last time he had come anywhere close to believing in the institution of marriage was at the age of eleven. Almost every class in his school had been sent down the road to watch the Monday morning TV repeat of Lady Diana marrying Prince Charles on the giant video screen at the pub that was normally used to watch the football. Harry and his nine-year-old girlfriend had sat in the front row.

The nine-year-old, a Greek girl with buck teeth called Mariana Xanthexenides, had held his hand when Diana and Charles kissed on the balcony and at that moment, he'd even been able to imagine himself in a suit, in a church, with the woman of his dreams.

How times change, Harry thought now, feeling old and jaded, despite the fact that he hadn't even hit thirty. He remembered Princess Diana's funeral, which the whole town had also watched on the same giant video screen at the pub. Perhaps that's what had turned him into a cynic, Harry thought. You could blame the Royal Family for a lot of things.

Mariana Xanthexenides was at Richard's wedding today, although Harry hadn't realized his brother had invited her. Sneaking a look at Mariana from the other side of the marquee, he could see her sitting quietly with her husband and two children, with her hands folded in her lap. They often came into the bank where Harry worked. The kids had buck teeth too.

Harry didn't regret the end of his affair with Mariana Xanthexenides. Even at the age of ten, she'd been passive-aggressive and pathologically violent, he decided. Harry had been to Mariana's wedding too. In fact, he had probably watched most guests in the marquee today getting married. Life in Compton was so slow that people could book you for a wedding three hours in advance, never mind three months. There was no way you could get out of it either, Harry thought, even if you rang and said you were coughing up blood – a trick he had tried at least twice.

Even though the ceremony today was for his brother, Harry realized he was still having the usual problems. A sick dread of hearing the vows – he never trusted people when they promised to be faithful – followed by nausea at the thought of the marzipan on the wedding cake.

Harry was beginning to feel itchy inside his boxer shorts and wished he hadn't worn such tight pants. Could you walk out of your own brother's big day? He was longing to run back to the cabin and get changed again. His parents would never forgive him if he left now, but more importantly, he wasn't sure if he could stand watching Richard put a ring on his new wife's finger.

Sarah was quite nice really. A London girl with a

very English name – and probably the whitest teeth and blondest hair he'd ever seen. But he still didn't understand why Richard had to marry her. Why couldn't they just live together? It had been bad enough the first time, when Harry had been fifteen, and he'd watched Richard walking down the aisle with his first wife, Bronte. It had all taken place in a cathedral in Hobart, and there had been an organ player and bagpipes, and smoked salmon afterwards. That was the only proof you needed that marriage was a joke, Harry thought. Despite all the fuss, it had lasted only ten years.

Just like Prince Charles and Lady Diana, Richard and Bronte had promised each other all sorts of things, and God had also been involved if Harry remembered correctly. The wedding presents had been incredible too – everything from an automatic boiled egg maker to a waterbed. And now Richard was doing it all over again fifteen years later, but with a different ring and a different woman. Harry found it hard not to feel sceptical.

He put a hand under the armpit of his jacket to feel if the sweat was coming through his suit. It was. When no-one was looking, he peered down at his left armpit. The suit was an even shade of milk-chocolate brown, just the way he liked it. And he could see his orange ruffled shirt was holding up. But the dark stain under his left arm was definitely visible. Harry cautiously lifted up his arm, like a chicken raising its wing. Yes – there it was. Showing a nasty patch, as his mother would say.

It was hard being the coolest person at a wedding when you were actually the hottest person at a wedding. Turning around in his seat, he took a closer look at what Richard was wearing. It looked like Sarah hadn't been allowed to interfere because Richard was in what seemed to be the same black suit, white shirt and black tie that he'd come up with the first time round in 1985. The only difference was, back then Richard had looked almost exactly like Gordon Gecko from *Wall Street*. Now his brother looked a bit more like a normal human being. Probably because he hadn't used any hair gel, he thought. Hair gel had been the curse of the eighties.

For a moment, Harry focused on Mariana Xanthexenides, sitting on the other side of the marquee. In 1984, she had turned up to the Blue Light Disco in Compton with so much gel in her hair that he had nearly sprained his hand trying to stroke it. She had also worn a Madonna crucifix and shown her belly button. Harry frowned, trying to remember if it was an innie or an outie. An outie, he seemed to recall.

With a jolt, he realized he was doing it again. Thinking about other things – like Mariana Xanthexenides' belly button – when he should have been thinking about the wedding. Or everlasting love. Or even his own brother.

At the front of the marquee, Harry could see Richard squinting around him. Tom, by his side, was gazing absent-mindedly into the distance, as usual. Where was Sarah?, Harry wondered. She was almost certainly late by now.

Shifting uncomfortably in his plastic chair, Harry looked at the wedding programme to double-check when Sarah was actually due to make her grand entrance. It was too hard to read though – someone had sprayed something gold and glittery over most of the words. It looked like a fairy had spat all over it, Harry decided. He shifted position again. The chair was making him sweat and there was something lumpy underneath him. Squirming, Harry found he had been sitting on a Bible. He pulled it out and threw it onto the grass in front of him, then caught his father giving him a look.

Ignoring him, Harry stared at the white canvas walls of the marquee instead, and dreamed about Debbie

Harry. He didn't care if his parents had outlawed her at breakfast. He wasn't going to be black-banned from thinking about Debbie by middle-aged thought police in matching dressing gowns, he decided.

Debbie and Chris Stein had never bothered getting married – and look at them. Together, they had created Blondie, the greatest rock'n'roll band of all time. Together, they had also written 'Heart of Glass' – the greatest song in the history of the world. Of course, he was glad Chris and Debbie had split up now. It made her seem more available, somehow. Perhaps it was also time to try writing to Debbie. Again.

Harry had been reading on the Internet about how older, famous, rich American women were tapping a new social trend – Beyond Toyboy. He liked the sound of Beyond Toyboy. It basically meant, from what he could see, that someone like him, working in a bank in Compton, Tasmania, Australia could get picked up by someone like Debbie Harry in Manhattan, New York, America. It would be a relationship of mutual respect, of course, he thought. It's just that his annual income would probably be around two per cent of hers. He hoped, however, that the spiritual, sexual and intellectual stimulation that Debbie might gain would be worth it. Well, he could always try.

All of Harry's girlfriends – if he could actually call them girlfriends – had been younger than him. He felt ready for the challenge of Beyond Toyboy at the moment. He was fed up with the small bras that twenty-one-year-olds wore.

Richard was still hanging around looking like he was waiting for something to happen, Harry realized. He felt sorry for him. It was bad enough having half the population of Compton staring at you, without the embarrassment of a delayed ceremony.

Maybe it was something about Richard, Harry mused. Had Bronte also been late at the first wedding? From memory, everything had gone smoothly that day.

Bronte had been on time, everyone had remembered their words in front of the priest, and even the food had been good. The only thing that had really gone wrong was Harry's hair.

Because his hair had been down to his shoulders at the time of Richard's first wedding, his Uncle Frank, a retired hairdresser, had been dragged in by his parents to cut it before the ceremony.

The exact words Uncle Frank had used were: 'Let's take an inch off the ends and blow-dry it out of the way so it looks tidy.' But instead, his uncle had lovingly curled the whole thing under so that in all the photographs from the day, he looked like Bonnie Tyler. Bronte had made him wear a kilt too and a little sporran that looked like a weasel. Remembering this now, Harry shrank into his seat with embarrassment.

Looking around him a moment later, Harry wondered why Bronte hadn't turned up. He knew Richard and Sarah had invited her, but there was no sign of her. And Bronte was easy enough to spot in a crowd, Harry thought. She had an arse like a Teletubby.

It was a good thing Bronte wasn't here, Harry decided. She always turned everything into a drama. When Bronte had split up with Richard, it had been so over the top they could have screened it in glorious technicolour on the big wide-screen TV at the Compton pub with Dolby sound and free beer over three big nights.

After Bronte had officially left Richard, given him the ring back and gone back home to her parents in Melbourne, Richard had stayed with Harry for a month. Because the cabin basically consisted of one room, a toilet, a collection of Blondie singles and an electric kettle, Richard had been forced to sleep on the floor on a piece of foam rubber.

Quickly, Harry flicked the memory away and wondered who else was missing today. Apart from Bronte

21

and her strangely Teletubbyesque hips, everyone in Tasmania seemed to be packed into the marquee. He could see people who had driven from as far away as Stanley and Jericho for the day.

A lot of people had brought their dogs, too. Because most people in Compton knew Richard through his vet's surgery, they seemed to have assumed that their dogs – his patients – were also included in the invitation, and there were dalmatians and blue heelers, with their tongues hanging out, lolling about all over the place. Harry watched as their own family dog, Max, sat down at the front of the marquee with his furry legs wide open, vigorously licking his crotch.

'Max!' Harry hissed from the front.

But the dog ignored him.

With a start, he reminded himself that he was supposed to be in charge of the music and should probably take over where his father had left off. Because Sarah was so late, Richard's tape of *The Four Seasons* had been put on random play – and they were now hearing 'Autumn' again, after an endless repeat of 'Spring' and 'Summer'. It was like musical global warming, Harry thought.

Suddenly someone tapped him on the shoulder. It was Richard.

'Can you do me a favour?' he said in a low voice.

'Close the dog's legs?' Harry asked.

'No, find some more music. You're the man who's supposed to be looking after it.'

'Can't Dad do it?' Harry said. 'He looks like he's taken over.'

'Dad's gone out there,' Richard hissed, nodding in the direction of the garden. 'He's looking for Sarah. They're *all* looking for Sarah.'

And then he was gone. Just like that. Harry stared – along with all the other guests – as his brother tried to half walk, half run out of the marquee without actually looking like he was rushing. He looked ridiculous,

Harry thought, like a duck going for a jog. Tom quickly followed.

Behind him, he heard someone tut and say that the bride was now twenty-five minutes late. Where *was* Sarah, anyway?

Harry had never seen Richard look so nervous. Normally, his brother was so Zen about everything. Even when he was jamming a thermometer up a cat's bottom, Richard stayed calm and philosophical.

My brother is the Zen Vet of Compton, Harry thought, liking the idea. Perhaps he could write a song about it. He'd just have to find something to rhyme with Compton, which was always a problem.

He started fishing around in his pocket for cassette tapes to replace *The Four Seasons*. He was bound to have something suitable for the wedding and, with a bit of luck, he might even find *The Best of Blondie*.

They were all starting to gossip about Sarah and Richard now. Harry could hear it going on behind him. In front of him, the women were taking off their hats and scratching their heads, like gorillas.

Harry looked at the tapes in his pocket to see if anything would do as emergency wedding music. One was a home-made compilation with some old Tasmanian bands he liked – The Fish John West Reject, The Muffdivers, The Sneakers, The Deaf Lepers and The Ernest Borgnines. He couldn't see that going down too well with the crowd, though. The women with the hats looked more like a 'Lady in Red' audience to him.

With any luck, the last tape in his pocket would be Blondie. It was. Relieved, Harry got up from his seat, nearly tripping over the Bible on the grass, and found the sound equipment at the side of the marquee. There were two tape cases lying on top of the tape player. One read 'BRIDE ENTRANCE MUSIC' in his father's handwriting, and the second one said 'BRIDE AND GROOM EXIT MUSIC'. *Good one, Dad*, thought Harry.

The speakers were making terrible thudding sounds.

He had hired them from a smelly hippy folk band in Hobart at a discount and he was beginning to regret it. Would the acoustics be better in the open air?, Harry wondered, starting to panic. They were the only speakers he had, and he would be using them for more important things later – like for his own band.

We've Got Blondie's Drumsticks And We're Going To Use Them were due to play at the reception at four o'clock. It would be their second gig in eight months. Harry wasn't sure if he could actually call his brother's wedding a gig – but in any case, he didn't want anything to go wrong.

We've Got Blondie's Drumsticks And We're Going To Use Them was definitely his girlfriend substitute at the moment. All his passion went into it. Life would be easy for him if he could also put passion into Pippin, his drummer and partner in the band. But he found it hard to work up feelings for a bisexual woman with a woolly hat. Especially when she was such a bad drummer.

They were the real thing, too – Blondie's actual drumsticks. Clem Burke had thrown them into the crowd at Blondie's concert in Melbourne in 1978 and Harry had grabbed them, shoved them down the front of his school shorts and run squealing out of the hall, followed by his mother beating off the punks with her handbag. Harry closed his eyes and tried to relive his moment of glory. He had won the concert ticket on the radio and then, after school, he and his mother had flown on a two-hour trip to Melbourne – and he had even been given a TAA Junior Flyers Club Activity Pack. Harry had remembered all this so many times that now he was boring himself with it. Instead, he began to drift off to sleep in his chair.

Meanwhile, outside in the garden, Richard was thinking about Sarah. Scratching the back of his head – his new haircut was too short and itchy – he looked around him, but there was no sign of her. She was now half an hour late. She wasn't in the house. She wasn't in the orchard. She hadn't left a note. And even her own parents hadn't seen her since she'd set off for the hairdresser's. They'd been staying at a hotel in town and had arranged to have breakfast with her – but she hadn't turned up and nobody had seen her since.

'All in good time,' Sarah's father said placidly as Richard came up to them.

If he heard him say that one more time, Richard decided, he would swing at him with a piece of wrought-iron garden furniture. He couldn't work out if he was more annoyed with Sarah's parents for losing her, or his own parents for failing to realize that she had disappeared from their house.

'It's amazing,' Sarah's father said. 'It's nearly one o'clock in the afternoon here, but it's really two in the morning there.'

'Amazing,' Richard muttered in agreement, although he couldn't see why Sarah's father had to keep going on about it.

Back in England, when he'd first met them a few months ago, her parents had been normal enough. Maybe it was the heat, Richard thought. They just didn't seem to be on the same planet since they'd landed in Tasmania.

Suddenly Tom caught Richard's eye and smiled, giving him a half wink. Thank God for Tom, Richard thought. He was glad he'd asked him to be best man. His parents had been doubtful because Tom was always so vague about everything – but just seeing his friend around was enough for Richard. It made everything seem more normal, somehow.

Are you sure we've searched all round the garden?' Sarah's father asked. 'She might have fainted somewhere. In the heat.'

Richard's parent's, who had just joined them after searching the road, shook their heads.

'We've been all round,' Richard's mother said.

'She might have come back from the hairdresser's, ducked upstairs to get dressed and missed us while we were out in the garden,' his father said, trying to be logical.

'All that time her bedroom door was closed this morning and she wasn't even in there,' his mother sighed. 'I mean, we did keep banging but then we just thought, leave her alone.'

Exasperated, Richard shoved his hands in his pockets and made a face to stop himself saying anything.

'You see, we thought she'd been on the phone to *you*,' his mother said. 'We thought you might have known where she was.'

Sighing, Richard shook his head. 'Well, I left it up to you. I was busy picking up half the guests from town.'

'What about those blue loos you've got in the garden?' Sarah's mother asked. 'She might be stuck in one of them. You know, the ones that look like Doctor Who's police box.'

'The *tardis*,' her husband corrected her. 'I think you'll find that's Doctor Who's proper name for it.'

Richard's parents looked at one other. Sarah's mother and father seemed to have gone quite mad. When they weren't looking, Richard's father winked at his wife and made a tiny kangaroo-paws gesture with his hands. This was Gilby family code for 'They've got kangaroos loose in the top paddock', and Richard knew it. Trying not to smile, he stared hard at his shoes instead.

'I think Mrs Kennedy means that Sarah might be in one of those blue portaloo toilets you hired,' Richard told his father, who had stopped making the kangaroo-paw hand signal to his wife. 'The loos are right out near the second orchard. Where all the cars are parked.'

It wasn't such a stupid idea, he thought. Who knows? Sarah might be in there. She certainly wasn't anywhere else and, although the blue portaloos were miles away, he knew if he walked fast, he could be back in fifteen minutes. And it was better than standing around in the heat talking about the time difference in England.

'I'll go,' Richard said. 'You never know, she might have been feeling sick or something, and gone for a walk.'

'Want me to come?' Tom offered, pushing his hair out of his eyes and trying to be useful, but Richard shook his head.

'You look after the guests,' he suggested kindly, though he honestly found it hard to imagine Tom looking after anything.

'But what if she turns up here?' his mother interrupted.

'I'll be back in a minute,' Richard waved her away. 'Just get everyone a cold drink or something. Tom, I've just thought of something else. Can you check out what Harry's up to with the music?'

Tramping over the grass in his new black shoes – they were far too tight – Richard finally allowed himself to look at his watch. It would be 1 p.m. soon. People had been packed into the marquee for ages, waiting for Sarah to arrive. And now they were listening to Harry's old Blondie tape. What a disaster. He should have known better than to put him in charge of the music. *And* he'd turned up late, despite the fact that his cabin was practically next door to the marquee.

In the distance, Richard could hear the sound of Debbie Harry singing 'Heart of Glass':

Once I had a love
And it was a gas
Soon turned out
Had a heart of glass
Seemed like the real thing

Only to find
Mucho mistrust
Love's gone behind

Fantastic choice of wedding music, you idiot, Richard thought, gritting his teeth. It was easier to feel angry with Harry because he couldn't bring himself to feel angry with Sarah. His heart was twisting for her, and the thought of her being ill, or lost – or whatever else had happened to her – was unbearable. Ignoring his tight shoes, he walked on. He wished, in retrospect, that he'd forced her to have a bridesmaid after all. At least a bridesmaid would have looked after her properly. But in the end, Sarah had flown out from London by herself. She'd said the wedding video would be enough for her friends. Her parents were useless, he thought, and then tried to stop himself, remembering it was their big day as well.

Hearing a noise behind him, Richard turned. Sarah? No, Max. It was good to see him though. He had grown up with Max and having a dog by his side made him feel calmer. Who knows, he might even pick up Sarah's scent.

Richard and Max kept walking side by side. Any minute now, Richard thought, I'll hear someone yelling and they'll have found her. He couldn't allow himself to panic. For one stupid moment, he thought Bronte might have phoned and somehow upset Sarah with some kind of ex-wife, new-wife drama. Maybe that was the reason. For a horrible, heart-stopping moment he could even imagine Sarah at Hobart Airport with her suitcase, waiting for the first plane to take her back to England.

Chapter Two

Crouching on the floor, Sarah pulled her knees up to her chin and tried to breathe deeply to stop herself being sick again. Her wedding dress had brown marks on it where she had been kneeling on the floor of the strange, blue-plastic toilet that was doubling as her hiding place. At some stage, she decided, she was going to have to leave the safety of the portable loo and go back to the bathroom inside the house. She definitely had to brush her teeth – she had been sick three times and her mouth tasted like the bottom of a budgie cage. Or the bottom of a budgie, anyway.

She felt desperately alone and wished, more than anything else, that Liz was there. If Liz hadn't been pregnant, she would have been her bridesmaid – but British Airways wouldn't let her fly. Sarah sighed and rested her chin on her knees. There were other friends who might have come, of course, and coped with the air fare from London to Tasmania. She thought of a few names and faces. But when she had broken up with her ex-boyfriend a year ago – the last boyfriend in the history of the world before Richard – most of those friends had sided with him, not her, and she hadn't felt confident enough to invite the handful of them she still saw. Half of their friends hadn't even made it to her flat for a cup of coffee after the break-up. Asking them to fly to Australia on her behalf was something she hadn't been able to bring herself to do. If it had been too political for that divided bunch of friends to take the tube halfway across London to see her, she could hardly expect them to take a 23-hour flight across the world in her honour.

Her ex and the Battersea flat seemed like years ago now. Richard and her new life in Compton had wiped it all out, even though she had only been living in Australia for two months.

It was funny, Sarah thought, how there had been no bells clanging in her head when Richard had turned up in her life. The day they first met, at some boring conference on the banks of the Thames, she had been holding a tape measure and a clipboard stuffed full of insurance papers, trying to measure a window of all things. She had registered that Richard was nice and polite and Australian, but that was all. It was only a few days later, when Liz pushed her, that she rang him up and politely offered to take him out for lunch and show him round London.

'I recognize a dashing white knight in shining armour when I see one,' Liz had said at the time.

'Oh stop being so hormonal,' Sarah had countered, 'you're pregnant. And anyway, he can't be my knight, he's got to go back to Australia.'

And then I was gone, Sarah remembered. *Just like that.* It was an odd way to fall in love, but it hadn't taken long before she was standing in bookshops, poring over Australian guidebooks, and gazing at pictures of white sandy beaches and kangaroos and wondering if any of it was for her.

Because Richard was so doggedly Australian – he actually said things like 'She'll be right' – she quickly realized that it was impossible to separate him from the idea of moving to a new country. Her relationship with him, and the chance of a different life on the other side of the world, had become bound together very quickly.

And now here she was. Sarah thought she was almost used to the small-town Tasmanian way of life now – the way they only had one shoe shop in the town, selling identical pairs of wellingtons and flip-flops in the front window, and the way they all talked about the weather without actually realizing they were doing it. She was also getting used to the mosquitoes and the flies and the heat, and the way they called vests 'singlets' and waistcoats 'vests'. She was even used to the strange things in the corner shop like mutton-birds and Chiko Rolls and vanilla slices and lime spiders.

Quick, Sarah thought, as her stomach rolled to the left, *change the subject*. The thought of greasy mutton-bird and blubbery vanilla slices was making her feel sick again. She dropped her head down between her knees. She had no idea if it worked, but she knew it was what you were supposed to do.

She breathed in deeply and wished she hadn't. The air inside the toilet was hot, stuffy and tinged with pine disinfectant. Sarah rubbed at her eyes. She might as well, she thought. If she was going to make it into the marquee, she would have to start all over again with her make-up, anyway.

The fact that she had managed to have a thought – even a small thought – about the possibility of actually being in the marquee for the wedding, made her feel slightly more in control. If I'm thinking that, Sarah decided, then maybe I'm OK. Maybe everything is OK.

She had never, ever felt so clearly split into twin selves. When she had given up smoking, she had felt like two people – one evil Sarah, and one good Sarah – but this was even more extreme.

Crying, Sarah turned her hands over in her lap, staring at the silver engagement ring that she had wanted for weeks. It was a nightmare – all this, she thought. It had been like a mad kind of fairy story – until now. What bothered her most was that she could go over the past few months – since June, when she and Richard had first fallen into bed, and July, when it had started getting serious – and still feel so detached from it all.

'I never wanted . . .' she managed to say and then lost it completely, sobbing into her upturned hands. She had never cried like this, she thought. It was like kindergarten sobbing.

In the distance, Richard shielded his eyes from the sun and kept walking towards the car park with Max panting at his side. His point of focus had shrunk to only Sarah. Up until now, his main problem had been her parents, his parents and the worry of two hundred guests in a marquee with the same music on repeat and no prospect of a bride actually turning up. Now everything seemed very small and very clear to him. It was like turning a pair of binoculars around and seeing Sarah at the other end.

Richard stopped for a moment, while Max was distracted by something in the long grass. He could definitely hear her now – a strange mewing sound, heard clearly above the birds.

Half running, he got to the toilet door just in time to hear Sarah – or someone – it had to be Sarah, being sick.

'Honey?'

Hearing him, Sarah shrank back inside her wedding dress. It felt so tight now, and this morning it had been so easy to get into. Perhaps the heat had made her swell up like a balloon.

'Mmmm,' she managed, through the door.

Waiting patiently outside, Richard heard her get up and flush the toilet. He wondered where it all went, that portable toilet stuff – probably straight into the local ecosystem, along with a lot of bright blue disinfectant. Wriggling, Max beat his tail heavily on the ground and waited too.

And then the door opened and she was standing there. White, wasted and pale. It wasn't the Sarah that Richard had imagined when he'd thought about this day. Her lips were almost blue, she had dark circles under her eyes and half her hair was falling down over her face.

'I love you,' he said immediately. He had never been so sure of it.

'Oh, God,' Sarah said, and started to cry again.

Taking her in his arms, Richard could feel the tiny seed pearls on her dress under his hands. She had lost a lot of weight in the past few weeks and he still wasn't quite used to it. Her perfume smelled great though. Always the same perfume – Coco. He let her sink her face into his neck, while Max danced around them on the grass.

'I'm sorry,' she sniffed.

'It's OK. Are you OK?'

'No,' she shook her head. And she kept on shaking it into his shoulder until she finally had to move away from him.

'What?' he looked straight at her.

'Stupid,' she said, trying to speak.

'You're not stupid.'

Taking her hand, Richard pulled her down onto the grass with him and they sat there for a few minutes with Max in the middle – the standing joke for the past eight weeks had been that Max was always in the middle, even when they were in bed.

'I am going to do this,' Sarah said at last. And for the first time, Richard felt a definite edge of fear. No, it was beyond fear. What was this? His heart lurched down to underpants level, hitting his libido as it came up the other way. He examined the sensation. Lust – which he always felt for Sarah – mixed with sheer terror. That was it.

Sarah gripped his hand. At least her fingernails were OK, she thought, looking down. You can't cry off pink fingernail polish.

'I am going to do it, Richard,' she said again, looking at him with eyes that were half misery, half love. It reminded him of dogs he had seen out in the bush, who had been dumped by their owners and then rescued. It almost made him want to cry. Instead, Sarah cried for him.

She shook her head. 'I'm mad. I'm stupid. I'm sorry.'

'Just nerves,' he tried. Going at things from the medical angle made him feel slightly more secure. He knew medical. He knew physical. It was the other stuff that overwhelmed him.

'Where have you been all this time?' he ventured. 'Not in here?'

She sighed and shook her head.

'Just hiding out,' she said. 'I will tell you about this one day,' she tried to joke.

'Well, I do hope you will,' he said, trying to toss her joke back the other way. Max left them to it, sighting a rabbit hole in the distance.

'Tell me what time it is,' she sighed.

'It doesn't matter.'

'Are they all waiting? Are Mum and Dad OK?'

'They're fine.'

To make Sarah feel less rushed, Richard leaned back in the grass, supporting himself on his hands while he stretched out his long legs in his new black suit.

'I love your dress, by the way.'

She smiled at him. She had completely forgotten that this was *the* dress, the great unseen dress, the whispered-about dress.

Suddenly she became aware of her breath.

'I'm vomity,' she said.

Richard moved to help her up.

'No, I mean I'm just . . . vomity. I'm not going to be sick again. I just don't think I taste very nice.'

'Come and brush your teeth, then,' he said.

'Yes.'

'And don't worry about anything else. You look fine. You look . . .'

For a moment, Richard let the full impact of Sarah, in her tiara and long white gown in the sunlight, sink in. The sun was lighting up her blonde hair like a halo and even her shoes moved him to silence. What was it about the tiny bows on those shoes? There was such an incredible femininity about Sarah, and there always had been – even when he'd first seen her, in her black London suit, stuck in a giant conference hall on the banks of the Thames.

'You look beautiful,' he managed.

Sarah took his hand.

'Unbeautiful teeth, though,' she said. 'I think you're right. I do need to clean up. Come on, Max! Maxy!' she called to the dog.

Together they walked as man, woman and dog back to the garden. Soon it will be man, wife and dog, Sarah thought. She felt herself go cold again. Even better, she decided, soon it will all be over.

In the garden, they found both sets of parents sweltering under a tree, sharing cups of tea.

Sarah spoke first.

'I'm ready. I'm sorry. Really sorry. Sick . . .' she waved an arm at the portaloo. She could hardly speak.

'Food poisoning,' Richard's father said, 'we thought about that. The oysters from last night.'

'Tch, bloody oysters,' Richard said, joining in.

'Well, we thought it was because she normally wears glasses, and she'd switched to those contact lenses for the wedding,' Sarah's mother started. 'That can affect some people.'

Sarah sighed.

'Anyway, I'd better go to the bathroom,' she said. 'Fix my make-up.'

She set off for the house.

After several cups of tea and a big discussion outside the marquee, it looked like both sets of parents had decided there was a fairly high chance Sarah was going to do a runner, Richard thought. He tried to ignore the looks they were giving one another.

'See you in a little while,' he called after Sarah as the parents watched her picking her way over the grass towards the house. Then there was a pause, and everyone started talking at once.

'Better go back inside,' Richard's father said.

'I'll take the cups,' Sarah's mother said, picking them up off the lawn.

'See you in there, then,' Richard said.

'Tch,' Mr Kennedy said, looking at his watch. 'If we were in England now, we'd be fast asleep with the electric blanket on three.'

Minutes later, inside the house, Sarah found herself talking to the mirror in Richard's parents' bathroom. She normally had to be drunk before she could do that.

'I must put more foundation on my foundation,' Sarah said to her reflection.

Then she sprayed up the front of her dress with a bottle of duty-free Coco she'd bought at Gatwick and, just for good measure, sprayed the outside as well.

'That should impress Richard,' she told the mirror. 'He always says I'm too stingy with it.'

It was the first thing she'd said which sounded remotely coupley, even if she was addressing a mirror, a wall and a bar of soap.

Then she smoothed down her dress, tried to forget about the brown marks at the back, and set off out of the house and across the lawn for the wedding that nearly wasn't.

It was only when she was near the entrance to the marquee that it dawned on her that someone was playing 'Heart of Glass'.

Once I had a love
And it was a gas
Soon turned out
To be a pain in the ass
Seemed like the real thing
But I was so blind . . .

Sarah had grown up with that song because one of
the teachers at school used to play it in aerobics classes
in the gym, but she'd never really paid attention to the
words before. Now they seemed to float out of the marquee in big, black capital letters. Why were they
playing it? she wondered. Then it dawned on her.
Harry. Of course. They'd put him in charge of the
music.

Her father was at the marquee entrance now, looking
down at his shoes and trying to ignore Max, who was
bouncing around his legs. At the sight of him, Sarah
almost felt like grabbing his arm and sprinting down
the aisle, just to put him out of his misery. But in the
end, she took his arm, just as the books had told her to,
and began her slow walk up the centre of the marquee.

She'd practised before, of course, but now the
moment had come, it was nothing like her pathetic
trial runs to Mozart in the living room of her flat in
Battersea.

Out of the corner of her eye, Sarah saw people
fanning themselves with their wedding programmes.
Why had she let Richard's mother talk her into putting
gold glitter all over them? It looked all wrong, somehow, in the heat of the day. It's funny, Sarah thought, I
always had such big ideas about my wedding, and
because it has all happened so quickly I haven't
bothered with any of them. Staring straight ahead, she
tried not to notice that her father's fingers were trembling slightly or that people were whispering about
her.

And then she saw him. Tom.

He was the only person inside the marquee that Sarah really longed to see, and he was the only person she knew she couldn't look at.

Oh God, there he is, she thought, her stomach lurching as she saw the back of his blond head.

I want him, I want him, I want him, she thought.

Then she stopped herself. *You stupid cow, he's the best man.*

Chapter Three

For months afterwards, the only thing that Sarah could remember about her wedding was the fact that the celebrant looked like Hillary Clinton. It was a blessing, in a way. When the Shakespearean sonnet that she and Richard had chosen was being read, she could focus on the way the celebrant's sturdy legs were just like Hillary's. And when it was time for Tom to produce the ring, she could concentrate on the fact that the celebrant's thick eyebrows were exactly like Hillary's too.

There had been talk of Tom reading a poem at the wedding service, but he had decided to save it for the reception. Sarah was glad about that. Listening to Tom's poetry during the wedding would have been too much. It was overpowering enough to be near him, without hearing his voice as well.

Willing herself not to look at Tom, even though he was physically closer to her now than he had been for weeks, she stared hard at the flowers. They were amazing – the most heavenly tiger lilies she had ever seen. Before too long, though, she found her gaze sliding towards the back of Tom's blond head. *How did it get this far?,* she asked herself as the celebrant ran through the vows. But, like most of the really important things in her life, the thing with Tom had started quietly and almost without her noticing.

It had probably begun in her flat in Battersea, she decided, staring mindlessly at the huge bunches of tiger lilies set up at the front of the marquee. She and Richard had been having dinner with Liz, who had just found out she was pregnant. And after coffee, Richard had produced one of Tom's poems from the back of his wallet. It had been part of a long letter to him, written on blue airmail paper, and because Sarah had been complaining to Liz about a boring BBC2 poetry programme on television, Richard had decided to get Tom's letter out.

'Now read this and tell me you don't like poetry,' he had said to her.

And Sarah had rolled her eyes and heaved a sigh and started to read it. Then, she remembered, she had put it straight down again because it had almost made her teary.

'It's good,' she'd said. She hadn't known what else to say.

'Your face looked different when you were reading that,' Liz told her.

The poem had been all about wallabies waking up in the Tasmanian bush at dusk, and it had seemed achingly sad and sweet all at once to Sarah. It made her feel as if she were already in Australia, or had been there – even though the nearest she had ever got to it was a one-night stand with a barman from Sydney, and an addiction to *Neighbours* when she was at school.

That evening, Sarah had known that Richard was willing her to like the poem, firstly because it was a poem – and that was the kind of thing Richard thought she should appreciate – and secondly, because Tom had written it. But she hadn't expected it to hit her like that. It had been a shock.

And then Richard had shown Sarah a photo of himself, Tom and Harry in their cricket gear, taken at a match between Compton and some other Tasmanian town a few years before.

'Is that Tom?' Sarah had said, pointing to Harry.

'No, that's my brother,' he said. 'Look at the haircut, that's Harry.'

Thinking about it now, with Harry to the right of her with his sideburns and his brown suit and orange shirt, Sarah supposed that people had always said that about Harry, for his entire life.

'Look at the haircut, that's Harry.'

The photo of Tom had gone back into Richard's wallet the same night, but Sarah could still remember every detail of it, even now. It was the kind of photograph where Tom had not looked merely phwooar-gorgeous, as her friends used to say, he had almost looked divine. Not of this world – not remotely of this world, Sarah decided.

It wasn't just the long legs in white cricket pants, or the floppy blond hair, or the slightly unfocused blue eyes. In that photograph, Tom had practically been surrounded by a full-body halo. And the day of the poem and the photo had been the day when she'd probably fallen in love with him. It was as simple – and as bad – as that.

When she had finally arrived in Tasmania two months ago, and Tom had turned up with Richard and Harry and their parents to meet Sarah at the airport, she had been given a chance to match the poem and the photograph to something real. It had been fatal. The more she had spent the past two months trying to stop herself thinking about Tom, the more she'd thought about him all the time, every single hour of the day.

Remembering it now, as she stood next to Richard in front of the marriage celebrant, Sarah tried to compare her feelings to an illness like the flu or glandular fever, then gave up again. Part of her wanted to give in to her longing for Tom, and as much as she hated herself for it, the flu and glandular fever had never been like that.

After Tom had met her at the airport with everyone

else on her first day, Sarah hadn't seen him again until she ran into him on the main street of Compton one morning. He was coming out of the fishing tackle shop and she was looking for mosquito spray at the chemist. And they had ended up talking about fish and insects in that order – which seemed safe and boring – but then they had gone for a coffee, which actually ended up being quite dangerous. Dangerous for Sarah, anyway. Because it was at that point that she looked at Tom's face, swallowed hard and had her first real doubt about marrying Richard.

They'd had three coffees together. *And each time a new cup of coffee arrived, the invisible thing that was pulling us towards each other just got stronger,* Sarah thought miserably, staring at the crowd of wedding guests. She was unbearably aware of Tom now, standing to the right of Richard.

Standing at the front of the marquee in her wedding dress, with hundreds of people staring at her, Sarah could only think that what she had felt in London with Richard was new and exciting and strong. But with Tom, it was like coming home. Even though she hardly knew him, she felt that very definitely.

She had given up trying to analyse it – she had spent most of the past few weeks doing that, and it hadn't helped. There was no point in explaining Tom away by saying that the engagement to Richard had been too fast, or anything else, Sarah thought, feeling her heart hammering now as she stood in her veil and wedding dress. *Tom would have turned everything upside down at any time in my life*, she realized – in any circumstance, in any town, in any country of the world.

While the celebrant ran through the rest of the service, with Tom standing close by, Sarah allowed herself the luxury of remembering the coffee shop day again. They had sat there until the waitress started giving them looks, and their coffees started going cold, and it had begun to get a bit embarrassing. And then – at last – Tom had told her about Annie.

With a jolt, Sarah remembered to look around for Annie among the guests, but she couldn't see her anywhere. *Thank God*, she thought.

Annie was in her mid fifties, more than twenty years older than Tom – yet Sarah had instantly felt jealous of her. Annie and Tom had lived together for three years. She had saved him, Tom admitted, after he'd gone through a bad time, developing a gambling habit at the Hobart casino, drinking too much and losing his licence – along with his bank account.

According to Tom, when he first met Annie, she hadn't needed a man at all – she had enough money, dogs and horses on her Compton property to do without a human being as well. But something had happened between them, and Sarah could see why. Annie was beautiful. On the coffee shop day, Tom had shown her his notebook with a photograph of Annie stuck inside the back cover. She was wearing an old brown cotton skirt in the picture, with her hair up in a ponytail, and she had amazing green eyes, too – because she was a vegetarian, Tom said. Annie had been hard to forget and Sarah was feeling miserable now, just thinking about her.

Annie was a sculptor. She'd built her reputation by concentrating on horses, and by the time Tom met her, she was selling one or two horse bronzes a year to America and living off the proceeds. Some of the smaller dog statues were in her garden. Tom had told Sarah all about it. She always sculpted the same animals too – the three mares in her top paddock and the various retrievers, heelers and labradors she had running around on the farm.

Richard's parents had told her that in Compton, Annie Archer was not the kind of person you expected to see at a wedding. So, Sarah decided, she should not have been surprised that Tom was there alone today.

But it made her feel better that he was. *Much better*, she thought, as the marriage celebrant who looked like Hillary Clinton droned on.

And then, Nigel Kennedy's *Four Seasons* changed from 'Winter' to 'Spring' again and the service seemed to be over. Just like that. Whenever Sarah tried to remember her wedding day later, it always seemed that she had spent more time crying in the portaloo with Richard than saying her marriage vows.

The reception was inside another marquee at the side of the house and by the time Richard and Sarah had finished being photographed with various dogs, kids and parents, there were already huge plates of Tasmanian crayfish, Pacific oysters and King Island brie piled high on the tables. Now that his ordeal was over, Harry grabbed the first waiter he saw, found himself two champagnes and drank both of them, and then found the same waiter again and took his only glass of Riesling, immediately spilling half of it down the front of his orange ruffled shirt.

On the other side of the marquee, Tom drifted off to talk to Richard's father, while Richard handled a queue of animal patients and their owners, all wanting him to shake their paws or their hands, and a queue of people from the Compton cricket team.

'Congratulations, Dick,' the waiter said.

'He'll always get called Dick by the locals,' Harry told Sarah as he saw the expression on her face.

'Well, I suppose it's part of the territory,' Sarah shot back. 'When your name is Richard, your best friend's called Tom and your brother's called Harry.' She was amazed at herself being able to use Tom's name without stuttering, but she did it. She was also amazed at the fact that she was making jokes. Perhaps it was the feeling of relief that it was all over.

Harry grinned.

'You're quite witty, aren't you? For a London girl.'

Sarah made a face. She was getting used to Harry's banter. Half the time he irritated her beyond belief, but she was glad to focus on someone – anyone – other than Richard or Tom, in that order.

Then the waiter disappeared and, despite Harry hovering beside them, Richard and Sarah really did seem to be alone, finally.

'You're gorgeous,' he said, moving forward to kiss her. And for a minute, it was just the two of them. Then he turned to his brother.

'Harry, the music was . . .' he spread his hands.

'Well, I always say you can't hear *The Four Seasons* too often,' Harry deadpanned. 'Lucky I had my *Best of Blondie* tape to save the day. Hey, great dress, Sarah, is it Harrods?'

'Why does everyone here think that because I live in London, I shop at Harrods?' Sarah pleaded.

Harry shrugged. 'You look like a Harrods girl to me.'

'Gee thanks,' Sarah said, 'but I had it made for me. Actually.'

'I love the way those English girls say actually, *actually*,' Harry said to Richard.

'Are you OK with your band gear?' Richard changed the subject.

Harry nodded. 'Yeah, I'm ready. All we need now is Pippin, but she's bloody late as well. Why are women always late for everything?' Then he saw Sarah's face and rolled his eyes.

'I'm sorry, I'm sorry. Sarah, I'm sorry.'

'Pippin is your drummer, isn't she?' she said, ignoring him. She had already seen Pippin in her woolly hat, propped up at the bar of the pub the week before.

'Drummer, glockenspiel player, singer,' Harry said.

'And there's only two of you in the band?'

'Yes, just like Sonny and Cher. Just like Renee and Renata, even. Plus we have backing tapes, of course.'

'And who came up with the name, We've Got

Blondie's Drumsticks And We're Going To Use Them?'
Sarah asked politely.

'Pippin did. When she was pissed. Because we *have*
got Blondie's drumsticks. I put them down my shorts
at their concert when I was eight years old. My mother
can tell you all about it.'

'Is Pippin . . .' Sarah hesitated, 'Is she . . . ?'

'Into women. Yes. And men. Plays on both teams,'
Harry said.

'Oh, I love that,' Sarah said, 'playing for both teams.
Is that an Australian thing?'

'Actually, mate,' Harry said suddenly, slapping his
brother on the shoulder, 'I've got to talk to you. Secret
men's business. Is that OK?' he said, looking at Sarah.

She nodded and wandered off to find her parents.

Harry pulled Richard into a quiet corner of the
marquee.

'We've actually had some serious interest in The
Drumsticks,' he said.

'Oh it's The Drumsticks now, is it?' Richard said.

'Yeah,' Harry jutted his jaw out, sending himself
up. 'The Drumsticks. The Mighty Sticks. The
Stickmeisters. Anyway, I've been offered two gigs,
one at the pub, the other at the Compton Show. The
only problem is, they're both on weekdays. The Show
gig's really important and that's on the Friday
lunchtime.'

Richard sighed. 'You want a medical certificate.'

'I know I said I wouldn't ask again, but this is really,
really important.'

'Don't you think it puts me in a difficult position,
asking my friends just because they happen to be doc-
tors?'

Harry shrugged.

'Harry,' Richard sighed. 'I am at my wedding here.
Why am I talking about getting you a fake medical
certificate just so you can have Friday afternoon off
from the bank? Why am I?'

'Because I'm your brother,' Harry slurped back his drink – this one a beer.

'Only because this is the last time,' Richard warned. 'Only because of that. And if you become bigger than Elton John, I want shares.'

'Elton John,' Harry muttered. 'Good God Almighty, you're so hip, Richard, you slay me.'

Then he caught sight of Pippin, dragging her drums in with one hand and fiddling with her nose stud with the other, and Harry left Richard in peace so he could rescue the female component of We've Got Blondie's Drumsticks And We're Going To Use Them.

Tom pushed his hair out of his eyes and went over to talk to Richard.

'The day's a bit warm,' he said.

Something is wrong with this picture of Tom, he thought. What is it? Ah! The absence of Annie. More and more lately, she seemed to be avoiding anything to do with Tom's life in town. Even coming to the wedding, which Richard had to admit he was hurt by. Annie had always been strange, though. Years ago, Bronte had been pestering her to do a sculpture of Mickey, her horse. Annie had turned her down flat in the street. She was famously rude though, Richard realized, and probably always would be.

'I suppose Harry will be entertaining us soon,' Tom smiled.

'Sarah's parents aren't happy about it.'

'Oh well,' Tom shrugged. 'Other people like his band.'

'He said they'd been asked to play a couple of things in town,' Richard said.

'Well, that's good. I think he's getting bored at the bank. He filled in my bank cheque the other day and it had ideas for new band names crossed out all over the back,' Tom said.

'He's always coming up with new band names,' Richard smiled. 'Sometimes I think that's the only reason he plays music.'

Harry walked up to them.

'Won't be long before The Drumsticks are ready, chaps,' he said. 'Just a little problem with Pippin's snare.'

'You know I don't know what that means,' Richard said.

'I might go and find one of those toilets,' Tom said, and left them.

Harry lifted his arms and flapped them up and down dramatically.

'Sweating,' he said. 'How's the suit?'

'Hot,' Richard said. 'But I'd be hot in any case. I remember why I had my first wedding in a church, now.'

Harry grinned.

'The whole reason to hire a church — those cool marble floors. Hush your mouth, you pagan. If Bronte could hear you now!'

It had been Bronte's idea to have a church wedding because in her twenties she had still been a Catholic, of sorts. That time round, Bronte's brother had been the best man.

'No sign of Annie,' Richard said, feeling mean-spirited for a moment.

'Did you expect there to be?' Harry asked.

Richard shrugged. 'It's half an hour away. She knows most of the people here. She was invited. Tom's my best man. You'd think for Tom's sake . . .'

'Ah, but do we really want to go there?' Harry said.

'Maybe not,' Richard agreed.

'In my opinion, the moment Tom stopped needing her, she turned off him,' Harry said.

'But Annie's always been difficult,' Richard replied. 'Remember Bronte trying so hard with her at the beginning?'

'But Bronte had an ulterior motive,' Harry interrupted him. 'Bronte wanted to be friends with her because Annie had the New York art galleries sending

48

her invitations to all their Christmas parties. You can't blame Annie for staying clear.'

Even though his marriage to Bronte had been officially over for five years, Richard still felt loyal to her. She was, after all, Mickey's mother, and he loved their horse – it had become *their* horse after the divorce, even though Mickey used to be Bronte's once. And whatever his ex-wife's faults – and they did include being somewhat starstruck and superficial in a Sydney kind of way – he wasn't about to take criticism of her from Harry.

'You can't lay things on Bronte all the time,' Richard said. 'Annie's just a hard woman. No wonder they didn't get on. When Annie gets me round to look at her dogs, do you think she can come up with a cup of tea?'

'That's because when you go round, Tom always wants to talk to you and she gets jealous,' Harry said.

'How do you know that?'

'Because I know what she's like. You know what the price is for Tom living in that mansion and doing a bit of gardening? She's turned him to stone. He's a sculpture, mate.'

'Dramatic,' Richard made a face.

'I'm not being dramatic,' Harry insisted. 'She owns him. It's just that she doesn't want him any more. Or he doesn't want to be there. Something. It's been coming on for a while.'

Richard looked around for a waiter to take his beer glass, but found no-one.

'Anyway, congratulations to you,' Harry said.

'Thanks.'

'My own love life, of course, is in tatters,' Harry said.

'I thought the tatters happened six months ago. That girl with the lips.'

'Oh no, that was other tatters. This is a desert. A womanly wasteland. I've got to get out of Tasmania.'

'Getting out of Compton would be a start,' Richard said. 'What about Melbourne?'

'What is it with this myth about Melbourne? I'm telling you, there are no women in Melbourne.'

Sarah came over to see Richard and Harry.

'Sorry, I've just got to get some more photos done for the paper. And tell them my life story or something.'

'Ah, the mighty *Compton Gazette*,' Harry said. 'Tell them they got our name wrong again, for the third time.'

'You were in the paper?' Richard asked.

'We've Got Blondie's Drumsticks And We're Going To Use Them are in it all the time. You know the *Gazette Gig Guide* at the back? We *are* the *Gazette Gig Guide* at the back.'

Sarah laughed. 'I'll tell them. Consider it my first favour to you as your new sister-in-law.'

'See?' Harry said as she went to find the photographer. 'Bronte was never like that. This is definitely the woman for you.'

'Anyway,' said Richard. 'Back to your love life.'

'Well, there's nothing happening. I look, I don't see anything I like. When I do see something I like, I try – and I fail.'

'Well, here's someone you can't fail with,' Richard said, waving his hand at a potted palm tree.

'Yes, foliage. I could make it with foliage.'

'Behind the foliage.'

Harry edged around so he could see who Richard was talking about.

'Now, see that woman behind the woman who's talking to Dad?' Richard said.

'No. Good God, she's the Elephant Woman!'

'No, no, no,' Richard said patiently. 'The woman in the sort of 1940s dress. Red lipstick. Long dark hair. See her?'

'Oh, now I see,' said Harry. 'Witchy Wendy Wagner.'

'Why is she a witch?'

'When she brings her deposit slips into the bank, she draws pentacles above the date. Small, so she thinks we can't see them, but we can. She hands the money over the counter and she says just one word to you – "threefold".'

'Threefold?'

Harry put his beer glass down on the grass,

'We used to think she was saying "Thank you" and she had a speech impediment,' Harry went on. 'Then one day someone sussed it out. The witches say three-fold when they're handing over money so that it comes back to them in three times the amount. Anyway, you want to fix me up with her. Thanks very much.'

Harry scratched under the arms of his op shop suit.

'Hey, Sarah's going to be on the front page of the paper,' he said, looking across at Sarah being snapped by the local newspaper's photographer.

'I didn't want to say anything,' Richard lowered his voice, 'but I think Mum fixed it up.'

'Well,' Harry said, 'what other stories do they get? Woman in Lower Compton accidentally sucks budgie into vacuum cleaner while cleaning out cage? Teenage boy with long hair seen blowing his nose outside shoe shop?' He shrugged. 'You owe it to them to give them Sarah. The beautiful English bride in our midst, who shops at Harrods.'

'She already told you she doesn't shop at Harrods,' Richard sighed. 'I wish you'd actually go to England one day, then you'd see the women are just normal human beings.'

'No, they're not,' Harry objected, 'There are only two kinds of women in England – they're either like Princess Margaret or Sporty Spice.'

Richard turned around after that and bumped straight into Pippin.

'Hello!' she said, kissing him on the cheek. She was wearing a T-shirt with an octopus on the front, a white cotton and lace petticoat, stripy brown tights, Blundstone boots and her woolly hat.

'Excellent wedding,' she said.

'Richard's trying to fix me up with Wendy the witch,' Harry interrupted them. 'What do you think? I mean, how low does he rate me? What desperate depths of celibacy has this simple country boy reached, that his own brother is luring him into a sexual tryst with a devil-worshipper?'

'Shut up, Harry,' Pippin said, scratching her head under her woolly hat. 'Anyway, I saw her first.'

Richard stared.

'Pippin,' Harry said, 'in the animal world, there is no playing for the other team. Consequently you have shocked my brother.'

'No, no,' Richard interrupted, trying to be tactful and failing. 'Seahorses,' Richard said quickly, trying to cover up his embarrassment. 'Seahorses play for the other team.' He tried to remember other sexually confused animals from his university biology class and failed.

'Wendy once told me she thought you were cute,' Pippin said.

'Ah, well that changes everything,' Harry replied.

And the strange thing is, Richard thought, it actually does. For all his endless torrent of words, Harry basically only needed one small vote of approval to shut up and actually feel something for a change.

'Another beer, *garçon*!' Harry called to the top of the tent. But the waiters were invisible now, jammed in by the crush of hundreds of invited guests and the late arrival of people who'd missed the Hobart–Compton bus or missed their planes from Melbourne.

Harry took his jacket off, revealing dark patches under both arms.

'I like the shirt,' Pippin said. 'Where?'

'Liverpool Street,' Harry said.

From long experience, Richard knew this meant the Liverpool Street op shop in Hobart, and that when Pippin admired one of his brother's shirts and asked 'Where?' it usually meant, 'Which particular branch of

St Vincent de Paul or the Red Cross did you pick it up from?'

Harry and Pippin are never going to make it together, Richard thought. You need mystery for love to develop, and there is no mystery here. Automatically, he turned to look for Sarah. The local paper had finished with her and she now had a little group of locals around her.

'I have to rescue my wife,' he said, using the word to describe her for the first time since she had actually become his wife. He relished the way it made him feel, especially since his years with Bronte had almost killed marriage for him.

Harry and Pippin watched him go.

'You're not really interested in Witchy Wendy Wagner, are you?' Pippin said.

'I'm so single I'm interested in anything which is moving about and uses deodorant.'

'Well, that's why you're single,' Pippin said mildly. 'When are you going to realize that women are not objects?'

'When you give me back that copy of *The Female Eunuch* I lent you six months ago!' Harry yelled as Pippin stomped off in her Blundstones.

From a distance, he looked at Wendy again. It might be true that she'd said something to Pippin about liking him. He knew he could get away with certain things when he was on stage, and she had enough of an alternative edge – witchcraft aside – to probably find him interesting. Appearance-wise, anyway. Let's face it, he was the only man at the wedding in a chocolate-brown polyester suit and an orange ruffled shirt. If Witchy Wendy Wagner got a bit closer and really got to know him though . . . Well, that would be a different story.

Stop beating yourself up Harry, he told himself, automatically reaching for a cigarette, even though his father had been wandering around all day telling people there was no smoking in the marquee.

'It's not a marquee, anyway, it's a bloody tent,' he said out loud, feeling fed up and drunk at the same time.

He was fed up with Pippin, too. How many men, women and beasts in Tasmania had she slept with, exactly? He narrowed his eyes, still looking at Wendy. He doubted Pippin liked her at all. It was just one-upmanship. Pippin always competed with him – not just over women, over everything.

'One-upwomanship,' he said out loud again, starting to feel drunk. *Bloody pseudo-feminists*, he thought. Then he wandered off to find some food.

The marquee was so packed that Sarah found herself saying 'Sorry' every five minutes, no matter who was bumping into whom. Her beautiful white Emma Hope shoes had turned yellow-green in the grass. She was amazed at how time had become distorted. The shoes alone represented hours, days and months of her life.

Sarah had made a list of possible marital shoes just one week after Richard had proposed – some of her friends had made her put down designer names like Jimmy Choo while Liz, who had just found out she was pregnant, made her hang around Selfridge's for so long that security began to think they were shoplifting.

I thought about shoe colours and heel heights and fabrics and pointy toes or non-pointy toes for months, Sarah realized. And now, here are my shoes. Grass-stained. Real. In just under five hours, the shoes that had obsessed her for so long had shrunk completely down to size.

'Phew,' she said to nobody in particular, but her mother lip-read her mouth, thought she was saying hello and came over.

'Hot, isn't it?' she said. 'When are you having the speeches?'

'No idea. Something about the band, then Richard's

mother wants to say something, then . . . Oh, I don't know. I'm feeling a bit drunk, actually. I'm not making sense. How are you feeling?'

'Fine,' her mother said.

'Look at our shoes,' Sarah mused. 'Yours were grey and now they're black and just look at what happened to the Emma Hopes.'

'I know. After all that trouble you went to. Poor Liz, you dragged her round town for months.'

'It's mad, isn't it?' Sarah said.

'Yes, I suppose so,' her mother replied, 'but my wedding was too.'

Moving away to get some water in the heat, Sarah's mother decided they had better not go into any more reasons why it might all be mad because she didn't want her daughter disappearing into a toilet that looked like Doctor Who's tardis again.

Alone at last, Sarah put her champagne glass down on the grass and looked at her shoes again. She'd thought vaguely about doing something practical, like dyeing them black for work, but she didn't even have a job to go to.

She thought about her old office in London and realized – to her joy – that she was truly, finally free of it all. No more freezing cold mornings. No more standing up on the train. No more Monday morning depression and boredom in front of a computer. No more months of being single and going home to an empty flat.

Keep on telling yourself how lucky you are, she thought. *Just keep on telling yourself.* But that wasn't the problem, and she knew it. Her head – the logical bit – knew that everything about the day was right. She had always wanted to get married, and now she was. She had known that Richard was decent and honest and true from the first moment she'd met him in London last June, and he was. She had found him sexy and kind and strong – and he still was. The life he had offered her in Compton was also what she had

55

fantasized about. A house, a garden, a beach and sun-shine.

I'm ticking off a list, she thought, miserably. Ticking off a list is something you do at work, not on your wedding day. She headed for the house.

Chapter Four

Richard's parents had a huge, three-storey house. It hadn't started out that way, but as Dr Gilby's practice took off, his wife had organized endless extensions. They'd both wanted Richard to become a doctor but he'd compromised by choosing animals.

Inside the house, Sarah stopped for a minute, leaning against the kitchen wall by the fan so she could feel the air on her face. Someone she didn't know kissed her again. She thought about her breath, even though she'd brushed her teeth three times after she'd been sick.

'I was just saying to my friend, that's a beautiful, beautiful dress,' said the woman who'd kissed her.

'I got it in Harrods,' Sarah lied, giving them a weak smile and hoping they couldn't see she was feeling drunk. Anything to shut them up.

How the hell was she going to get out of there? Women in flowery cotton dresses were everywhere, carrying giant cakes and yanking off sheets of foil.

She headed for her guest bedroom upstairs. Years ago, it had been Richard's bedroom and, although it was much smaller than Harry's old room, their parents had chosen this one for her for sentimental reasons.

Richard's mother had already put a present on the bed, and new towels and yet another bar of soap.

'Bless,' Sarah said aloud. It hadn't been a very nice day for Richard's mother.

She unwrapped the present, knowing she was about to hate it, but tearing the paper off anyway. Where the hell was her tiara?

Inside she found four shrunken heads, wearing tiny gingham hats. Two of them had little cigarettes, which she supposed made them men. The other two had curly hair, which on closer inspection she discovered was sheep's wool.

'Disgusting,' she slurred to nobody in particular.

'They're apple people,' someone said from the door-way.

It was Tom.

'Oh, hello,' she smiled and looked away.

'They peel the apples and cut in their faces. Then they soak them in lemon juice and dry them.'

'Oh, it's like a Tasmanian thing, is it? A local souvenir?' She found herself gabbling. 'I thought it wasn't the Apple Isle any more. Someone was telling me, in the pub the other night, that the whole apple industry had finished in Tasmania. It's a shame, isn't it?'

Tom smiled and said nothing, pushing the hair out of his eyes.

'Thank you for coming to my wedding,' she said stupidly.

And then, to her horror, she found herself sobbing.

Tom stayed in the doorway for a moment, not knowing what to do. Then he pulled the door behind him and sat down beside her on the bed.

'They are bad,' he said, not looking at her and turning the apple people over in his hands.

Sarah wiped her eyes with the back of her hand. What on earth did she look like?

'I don't know why I said thanks for coming,' she sniffed. 'You're the best man, you're supposed to be here.'

'It's OK.' Tom patted her hand.

How many times had she seen his hands in her dreams? How many times had she been lying in this bed in the past few weeks, wondering what it would be like to have him there too?

She pulled her hand away and rubbed her face, over and over, willing him to disappear.

'I'm sorry Annie couldn't come,' Tom said.

'Yes.' Sarah got up and found a box of tissues. 'I suppose she's busy,' she said.

'She's not that keen on coming into town sometimes,' Tom replied.

Sarah fought her desire to know more about Annie and failed. 'I've heard so much about Annie,' she said.

'She's a bit different from most of the people around here.'

'Oh no,' Sarah lied, 'I'd just heard that she was a great sculptor, everyone says that.'

'She is a great sculptor.'

'How much older is she exactly?' she said quickly.

Tom smiled. Sarah's mascara had come off under her eyes. They were black.

'Annie will be fifty-four in February and I'm thirty-two,' he explained.

'Nice, though?' Sarah said.

'Nice. And a bit moody.' Tom got up. 'I must go.'

No, don't, Sarah thought. *Don't, don't, don't.*

'Did you ever catch any fish after I saw you that day?' she said quickly.

'Not much,' he shrugged. 'Couple of flathead. They were too small. I threw them back in.'

'You're really a trout fisherman, though, aren't you?' she said, remembering their coffee shop conversation.

'Trout are harder, but they're more fun,' he said. 'You'll have to come out one day.'

The fact that he hadn't included Richard in the invitation made Sarah jump inside. 'I'm a bit tired and emotional,' she said, trying to explain her tears.

And you've had one too many, Tom thought, but that

wasn't a crime. He wondered if he'd better tell her that her mascara was all over her face.

'You know all the good places to swim, someone said.'

Tom smiled at her. 'Oh yes, and who said that?'

'Harry or someone,' Sarah said, though she now remembered it was Richard. 'You know all the little rivers and brooks and things.'

'We don't have brooks in Tasmania,' Tom said. 'Creeks, mostly. And waterholes. I could show you the waterhole at Lilly Creek. If you don't mind skinny-dippers.'

'Skinny-dippers, what are they?' asked Sarah, suspecting she knew.

'Lilly's so nice, people like to take their clothes off before they go in,' Tom said.

Sarah moved around on the bed. His sentence hung in the air, followed by a vivid picture in her head of Tom and herself naked at Lilly Creek – and there was nothing she could do to stop it. She blushed. Then she realized he could see her blushing and it got even worse.

Tom noticed and looked out of the window.

'Looks like we might have a band soon,' he said.

'Harry's done such a lot,' she answered.

Now that Sarah was embarrassed, Tom realized that him leaving suddenly would make things worse. He decided to stay.

'They put you in Richard's old room,' he said.

'Yes, and there's not a trace of him left in it,' Sarah said.

'His stuff's all in the attic now.'

'He told me he used to climb in through this window.'

'When we were out somewhere we shouldn't have been. Yes.' Tom smiled.

'How long have you known him?'

'Since we were six. We went up through the same

schools until HSC, then his parents sent him to Hobart and I stayed here.'

'And then what did you do?'

'Got a bit lost.'

Sarah hesitated. 'I got lost too, if it's any consolation.'

This was a white lie, of course. Sarah had taken a year off between college and her first job to go travelling around Europe, but it had been in a bus with one hundred other middle-class London students, and the most wayward thing she did the entire time she was away was float condoms in the communal chicken noodle soup.

'What happened to you?' Tom asked.

'Oh!' She shrugged. 'I think it happens to everyone.'

They sat for a while, side by side on the bed, Tom staring out of the window, Sarah staring at the top of Richard's old wardrobe. She wondered if he'd put stickers all over it when he was a teenager. Probably not. Her own wardrobe, back in her parents' house in London, was still plastered with the remains of Duran Duran and a Dymo-tape strip which read 'SARAH'S WARDROBE, KEEP OUT'.

'I'm thinking of studying horticulture,' Tom said, realizing that as he announced it to her, he was also announcing it to himself.

'Oh, soon?'

'Next year.'

'You like natural things, don't you?' Sarah said.

She was skilled at making people feel good about themselves, Tom noticed. Richard had told him that too. It was one of the reasons she'd done so well in her job, even if it was only insurance. And that was how they'd met, if he remembered correctly.

'Did you really do the insurance for that conference Richard was at?' Tom asked.

'What? Oh yes.' Sarah realized he was trying to steer the conversation back to her and Richard and she found herself feeling flustered. There was another uncomfortable pause and then Tom spoke again.

'I've looked after Annie's garden for long enough,' he said, trying to make it sound like a half joke. But when the words came out, he was surprised to hear it sounded more like an ultimatum.

'Annie doesn't do it, then?'

'She used to be more interested in the garden,' Tom remembered, pushing his hair out of his eyes. 'When I first moved in, it was amazing. Pumpkins, strawberries, asparagus. She never shopped. Didn't have to. Then she got these Americans interested in the horse sculptures and somehow there wasn't time for everything any more. So I kind of took over.'

'Could you get a horticulture degree, just like that?'

'I did my HSC.'

Tom sounded defensive for a moment and Sarah shrank back. She had no idea what an HSC was, but she supposed it meant that he wasn't the dumb country hick she'd just implied he was.

'We don't have that in England,' she said.

'You're lucky. Most boring two years of my life,' he replied.

'I suppose you were out fishing.'

'Having fun.'

'Did you have a girlfriend before Annie?' Sarah asked, pushing it.

'I had a girl who worked at the casino, who got me into trouble.'

Sarah knew a little bit about the casino story, from the bits and pieces Richard had passed onto her. It had started for Tom with a Hobart girl, who'd spent her weekends gambling and drinking. Pretty soon he was doing that too. He'd borrow Richard's car, or sometimes hitch down the highway, and spend whatever he'd made from his job in the local car yard on blackjack. And beer, of course. Without the beer, neither the girl from Hobart nor the lucky numbers would have made much sense.

'Do you ever think you'll get out of Compton?' Sarah asked.

'You make it sound like getting out of jail,' he said, smiling.

'Sorry. I mean, just travelling. Whatever.'

'Annie goes to America sometimes.'

And I wonder what that means, Sarah thought. Does Annie ever offer to pay or could Tom pay for himself? She wondered if she paid him anything for doing the garden. Richard was too nice to say so, but she had a feeling Annie was supporting Tom and had done for years. If I wasn't so obsessed, she thought, I might find something horrible about that arrangement. She allowed herself another, longer look at Tom.

He was golden, the way children sometimes are when they're on the beach in summer. But there was more to Tom than that. He just wasn't on the same planet as the rest of them. Perhaps that was it. Sarah's mind made a few illogical jumps into the future as the wine and champagne moved through her bloodstream. If Tom wanted to do horticulture, he could probably do it somewhere bigger, like Sydney or Melbourne. She could lend him the money to study then, when he was a horticulturist, or whatever it was he wanted to be, they could . . . She stopped herself.

'Tom, what will you be if you study horticulture?'

He gazed out of the window. 'Could be a landscape gardener.'

Someone knocked on the door and they both jumped slightly.

'Sarah?'

It was her father. Her mother had sent him up because in her opinion she'd done enough Sarah-nagging for one day.

'Just a minute.'

'Richard says speeches are on soon. See you down there,' he called.

They listened to him go, then Tom stood up and brushed down his uncle's suit.

'I was hoping they'd forget,' he said.

Not because he wants to stay here with me, it's because he hates making speeches, Sarah thought. But for one glorious moment, she allowed herself the luxury of imagining that was the real reason.

'Before you go,' she said casually.

He turned.

'Richard said I could have a dog.'

Tom looked blank.

'I mean, any dog I wanted. Any breed. Sort of as a wedding present on top of all the other presents.'

'That's good.'

'I'd quite like a blue heeler, one of the local dogs. Those cattle dogs, the puppies are so gorgeous.'

'They are.'

'Someone said Annie had purebreds.'

'She has three. Two bitches and a male.'

'I've found the mother dog. One of Richard's aunts has it.'

Tom knew the dog she was talking about.

'I was wondering,' Sarah faltered, 'do you think Annie would mind if I brought her over?'

Tom thought for a moment. He knew Merlin, Annie's dog, would oblige. But would Annie?

'I'll ask her,' he smiled.

'Thanks,' Sarah smiled back.

They looked at each other for a moment.

'I suppose I'll see you in there,' Tom said and left, closing the door behind him.

And then Sarah stood up, bent down to see if her tiara had fallen under the bed and went to the bathroom to re-do her face for the third time that day.

Chapter Five

When Richard and Sarah's father sat down at the bridal party table, it was the first real chance they'd had to talk to each other all day.

'Surviving so far?' Richard asked him.

'What about you?' her father replied.

'Oh, the local paper have been chasing me around, but I told them they'd be much better off with Sarah.'

Sarah's father glanced across at his daughter's empty place and noticed Tom's was empty as well. Where the hell were they? He looked quickly at Richard, but he didn't seem to have noticed anything. Something is bothering me, Sarah's father thought, and I don't know what it is. Then his wife came over, holding a glass of Riesling she had barely touched and he immediately forgot all about it.

Finally, Tom crept in from the back of the marquee and sat down.

'Sorry,' he said.

'I suppose Sarah's doing her face again,' Richard offered. 'It's so hot.'

'Something we don't have to worry about,' Sarah's father growled.

'Thanks for showing me the speech, Tom. I like it,' Richard told his best man.

'Thanks,' he mumbled.

Then, at last, Sarah made her entrance. She looked beautiful. Someone started to clap and then everyone joined in.

Tom glanced at Richard and smiled, then looked down at the floor because Richard was embarrassed and pleased all at the same time.

Up on stage with their drums and guitars, Harry and Pippin started clapping as well.

'Oh, I forgot,' Richard said, addressing everyone as Sarah sat down.

'What's that?' his mother called from the other end of the table.

'Harry's asked me if he can say something. I said yes. Just quickly, before everybody else starts.'

Harry looked to him for a signal and Richard gave it.

'My God, that suit,' Sarah whispered to Richard. Harry's brown suit had started sagging and his crotch was now swinging around somewhere between his knees and his thighs. He had the skinniest legs Sarah had ever seen.

Harry grabbed the microphone.

'Ladies, gentlemen, dogs, babies, children,' he started. Out of the corner of his eye, Richard could see his parents gripping each others' hands.

'I was there at Richard's first wedding. Anybody remember that?'

A few local voices at the back of the marquee piped up 'Yes', as if they were in the audience for Oprah Winfrey.

Richard stared at Harry, expressionless.

'Before I talk about that, though,' Harry continued, 'I'd just like to say – the English rose. Just look at her – the English rose!'

Sarah stared down at her green-white Emma Hope shoes.

'And Tom. That's his uncle's old funeral suit, but you wouldn't know it.'

More clapping.

'But what a lunatic, eh? Bronte – has she got kanga-roos loose in the top paddock or *what*!' To illustrate his point, he made the Gilby family kangaroo-paws gesture – but as nobody understood what he meant, the clap-ping stopped.

'You know, I saw Bronte,' he continued, 'that's Bronte, Richard's first wife, for those of you who weren't there, not so long ago. She came down to Compton to see Mickey. That's her old horse, once again, for those of you who weren't there. And I thought, Bronte, you fool. You fool, you fool. You had it all.'

Richard leaned across to Tom and whispered some-thing, while Sarah's mother looked as if she were personally taking on the embarrassment factor of every single person crammed into the garden.

'You're not on stage now, Harry, get off!' a man yelled from the side.

A pregnant woman, who had been sneaking along the back of the marquee trying to get to the toilet, stopped to listen. Then the drinks waiters started making too much noise stacking cans, to demonstrate how exactly they weren't eavesdropping – even though they clearly were.

'Bronte had it all with my brother, Richard,' Harry continued, 'and she gave it all away. Now she's living in Sydney. Sin City, if you've never been there.'

He paused and crossed his left leg tightly over his right leg as he wobbled around on the grass.

'Bronte Nicholson has the brains of a wombat!' he yelled. 'So here's to Richard's second wife!'

Then he smiled and bowed.

After a long silence, Richard got up and led him back to his seat.

'I didn't mean any harm,' Harry slurred. 'It's from the heart. Just being loyal, mate. Congratulations, mate. I love you.'

'You never mean any harm,' Richard said. 'Now *shut up*.'

After a long, embarrassed silence, people recovered enough to clap Tom when he stood up, blushing furiously at having to follow Harry. Then he read his poem out and, although Sarah remembered afterwards that it had been short and quiet and mostly to do with trees growing, she could never quite get all of it right in her head, mainly because she had been digging her nails into the sides of her hands the whole time he had been talking.

After that, Richard's mother walked forward to the microphone. In unison, two hundred people realized her hem had come down, but nobody commented.

'Thank you for coming everybody,' she said. 'We've had people from England and New Zealand and America and all over. We do appreciate it. I hope you're not too hot in here, but there wasn't enough room for you all in the house!'

People laughed at that. Not because she was funny, but because they wanted to be nice. Her hands were shaking, after all, and every time she moved her feet on the ground, she caught the thread of her hem a little more and pulled down another millimetre of chiffon from her floaty blue dress.

'I haven't got anything written down,' she said, 'though I must say what Tom said in his poem was beautiful.'

There were mutters of agreement and Pippin yelled 'Yeah!' from behind her drums.

'What I'd like to say is about Richard, my son, and how happy we are that he has found Sarah, and how pleased we are that she has decided to come here to live with us in Tasmania.'

More cheers.

'Now I think I should say something about Bronte.'

The waiters stopped, glasses stacked high under their chins.

'I wouldn't otherwise, but now Harry's gone and said what Harry's gone and said . . .' she smiled at her son loyally, '. . . so, I'd better do it. Richard married Bronte, as you all know, and it didn't work. They were very young and it was no-one's fault. Bronte is very happy now in Sydney and we'll leave it at that. This time, my husband and I both know that Richard has made the right decision. And I know he doesn't like me saying this, but from when he was a little boy, Richard always used to tell me about who he was going to marry when he grew up . . .

'Pamela Anderson!' someone yelled from the front row. Richard's mother ignored them.

'He told me, right from when he was little,' she continued, 'that she would be a beautiful lady, good and kind. And so she is.'

Shut up, Sarah thought, fighting back tears. *I knew you'd do this to me.*

'And the other thing about Richard I'll tell you, he did an operation on a mouse when he was six and he didn't sew an ear into its back either. He just saved its life, and that's the sort of man he is.'

Realizing she was slightly drunk and her hem was coming down, Richard's mother put the microphone down on the grass, starting a feedback squeal through Harry's speakers which lasted all through the first half of We've Got Blondie's Drumsticks' first song – a speeded-up version of 'In the Flesh'.

As Richard took her arm and whispered something she couldn't hear in her ear, Sarah could only stare straight ahead of her and thank God that Harry had been talked out of making a wedding video.

Chapter Six

When it was all over, Tom folded his uncle's jacket and tie in a plastic bag, secured it to the back of his bike and cycled home. He'd switched to a second-hand bicycle after losing his licence, and even though Annie had offered to buy him a better model, he'd grown quite fond of his black Malvern Star. Annie lived almost an hour's cycling distance out of town, up four hills and across two bridges, one of which was made up of oil drums and planks.

Tom didn't wear a watch, but he guessed from the sky that it must be approaching eight o'clock. He loved this time of year — daylight saving with everyone watching the cricket and the sharp smell of gum trees wherever you went. Everybody looked better in summer too, he thought. Sarah had been so pale, when she'd arrived two months ago, with dark circles under her eyes. Today she had been beautiful.

He cycled across the ridge of road where tarmac turned into orange dust and dirty quartz, where the council stopped paying for decent roads and nature took over. A kookaburra decided to laugh at him from the top of a tree. Tom took it seriously. Of course he was an idiot, thinking about Sarah.

He deliberately made his brain change the subject, shifting gears in his head as he shifted gears on his bike. He had enjoyed the wedding this afternoon, even though he didn't know how he felt about weddings in general. He and Annie had talked about getting married once. It had been a few months after he'd moved into her house. In those days, he was still getting drunk – just occasionally. He'd been at the pub and overheard two guys he knew from school discussing his relationship with her. He'd heard the words 'kept man' used, and a lot of laughter. And he'd lost his temper, threatened one of them, been thrown out and then bought a couple of bottles of Cascade at the bottle shop on the way home.

After walking the Malvern Star to Annie's with two empty beer bottles wedged under his armpit – even drunk, he could never throw anything into the bush – he had gone straight into the kitchen, found Annie up to her elbows in plaster of Paris, and said, 'What do you think about marriage?'

She had told him to take a cold shower and made him sleep on the couch. So that had been the end of it. He thought that might have been part of the reason she'd refused to go to Richard's wedding today. Weddings were a sensitive subject with her.

Sweating a little in the evening heat, Tom took the first hill. Thinking about all this now was putting him off his balance. In more ways than one.

Sarah had been in his mind on and off for weeks – ever since she'd turned up at Hobart Airport with her big London black coat under her arm and her pale face and dark eyes. There were two cars, and Harry and his parents had gone in one, while he, Richard and Sarah had taken the other.

Sitting in the back seat, he had stared at the back of her head all the way to Richard's house, and listened to her talking. The first thing he'd loved about her was the way she'd admired the bush. Not everyone from England did. The second thing he'd loved about her was her voice.

71

'Bugger!'

Tom's front wheel twisted and he nearly lost the bike. Just in time, he found his balance again. The thing about Sarah, he thought, was that she was Richard's property. He could never have her. Because of that, he wanted her more.

There, he thought, cycling up to the next hill. *You've admitted it.* Sitting next to Sarah today on Richard's old bedroom quilt, he had automatically pictured her lying under it. But the worst thing had been the sound of his own voice. Listening to himself talking to Sarah today, he had suddenly realized that she was inspiring plans and calling up dreams that he had never admitted to himself – or Annie. That, he told himself, was the dangerous part. The less he thought about it, the better.

Tom cycled on and took the third hill and the second bridge, then the blessed fourth hill. The mosquitoes were going for his arms as they always did when he left it this late to go home. Every so often, he cast his eyes down for snakes. Sometimes they got hit by cars going the other way and even a half-dead snake on the road was something he didn't want to run over.

Finally, he reached the top of Annie's long driveway. As usual, the lights were on in the kitchen. He loved that. It meant home to him. To get to her front door, you really had to try hard, though. She had deliberately constructed a driveway that was so twisted, so long and so hidden by banksia bushes and wattles that the only way you could really access the house at all was to leave your car on the side of the road and walk in. Annie's joke was that the skeletons of delivery men and postmen could be found all the way down her driveway.

Tom wheeled the Malvern Star down the gravel, collected his uncle's wedding jacket from the handlebars and propped the bike against the porch. He could hear

Percy Grainger on the stereo and smell pumpkin soup on the stove. He went in.

'Do you want a cup of tea?' Annie said, turning around at the sink.

He kissed her. 'Yeah. Thanks.'

She was wearing her work clothes – army pants covered in paint and glue, a white singlet of his, and no bra. He'd been noticing bras all day. Maybe women made more of an effort at weddings. Everywhere he'd looked there had been bows, frills, pinks, blues and padding underneath vast numbers of low-cut dresses.

'Everyone was dressed up,' he said, absent-mindedly thinking of Sarah's bra although that had not been one of those on display.

'Naturally.'

'It was nice,' he said. 'Harry played guitar.'

'The family let him?'

'But he said something about Bronte in the speech.'

'Ah, Bronte,' Annie said and smiled. She found a teapot and a tin of Earl Grey, and put two cups down on the table.

'It didn't go down too well,' Tom said.

'Well, the marriage didn't go down too well,' Annie replied. She knew instinctively that Tom was in the mood to talk and be sociable. Normally he went fishing on Saturdays. When he came home to her in the evenings, he was usually quieter than this. She preferred it.

'People asked after you,' he said.

'To be polite to you, Thomas,' she replied.

'Oh, I don't think that's fair.'

Two of the dogs came in, smelling frying bacon on the stove. She started talking to them. It drove him mad the way she did that. Long, rambling conversations with the dogs and two words for him.

'Pumpkin soup?' he asked, trying to cut in.

She ignored him and concentrated on making a fuss of the dogs instead.

73

'You know how I feel about the people in town and yet you still want to talk to me about them,' she addressed the labrador's head.

Tom sighed inside and pushed his hair out of his eyes. What could he say?

She made the tea in silence, turned the heat down on the stove again and gave the dogs the bacon rinds. He followed her into the living room. As usual, it was overflowing with her mess. If he ever got it together to study horticulture, he wondered where he could put his books.

'I had a good day,' she said, pouring his tea.

'Well, everyone had a good day then,' Tom said. He wasn't going to let her get away with it.

She turned and looked at him. 'You forget what some of those people are like.'

'There's nothing wrong with them, Annie.' He sighed. 'Here, let me rub your neck.'

'And there's nothing wrong with my neck!' she snapped, getting up. The dogs bounced off the couch after her.

One by one, she closed the wooden shutters on the windows. In the corner of the room was her sculpture of Elsie, her youngest horse. Automatically she started switching various lamps around the room on and off to see her work in different lights and shadows.

'I'm sorry,' she said, not looking at him. 'I wanted you to myself today, that's all.'

Satisfied with the light from two lamps, she went back to the couch.

'That wasn't a proper kiss before,' she said and kissed him.

They finished their tea.

'Sarah was asking me about Merlin,' he said.

'What did you say?'

'She was asking me about puppies.'

'Oh, that sort of question.'

'Richard says she can have a pup. She was thinking

74

maybe Merlin could be the sire. She wants a pure-bred.'

'She saw a blue heeler on a calendar in a souvenir shop at the airport,' Annie sniffed.

Tom smiled and shrugged. 'Sarah said she's willing to pay.'

'I'm sure she is, with all her English pounds. Don't insult me, Tom. I don't need the money. Not even for Merlin's dog food. Anyway, let's ask him, shall we?'

Annie looked across to the kitchen, where he was lying on the floor with the other dogs.

'Merlin!' she called. 'Do you want to become a gigolo?'

Hearing her voice go up, Merlin did his best doggy-smile, mouth open and ears up.

Tom forced himself to laugh. 'You're in the best mood tonight, aren't you.'

She didn't smile. 'Sex is on that girl Sarah's mind, isn't it,' she said.

'What does that mean?'

'I'm not an idiot. I've had Sarahs of all sorts in my life before.'

'And how do you make that out?' Tom asked.

'Two phone calls, two hang-ups. She thinks you're home on Sunday nights like most people, but she didn't know that's when you go fishing.'

Tom patted the couch, absent-mindedly inviting more dogs up. 'You didn't tell me that.'

'Since she got here, I've had calls on two Sunday nights in a row. Hanging up on me. Nobody calls and hangs up on me. Only a handful of people have the number, you know that. I suppose you gave her the number here?'

Tom swallowed. He had. 'You're mad, Annie,' he said. 'I don't think it's her at all. She's got no interest. She's just married Richard. Anyway. We should make an effort. She doesn't know anyone here.'

'I didn't know anyone either when I came here.'

'You came to Tasmania to escape from people, that's not the same thing.'

Annie smiled bleakly. He was beginning to hurt her these days – that was something new that she was only starting to notice.

'But anyway,' Tom went on. 'Phone calls on Sunday . . .' he shook his head. 'That's just mad,' he repeated.

'She goes walking up here early in the mornings sometimes, did you know?'

Tom paused. 'No, I didn't.'

'Why up here? Nobody comes up here except the people who live here. I suppose you gave her my address, that great day you spent together having coffee in town.'

'Oh, Annie,' Tom said. It was useless.

'She's not putting her dog anywhere near Merlin and I'm not having her anywhere near the house,' Annie declared.

She led him to bed. She always did.

It's funny, but I want you more tonight, Tom thought, closing the door and following her under the big, white mosquito net.

Chapter Seven

A fortnight later, Bronte Nicholson was at work when she received a piece of wedding cake from Richard's mother in the mail.

Bronte threw the cake against the wall, where it bounced off a very old Princess Diana calendar.

'Sorry, Diana,' Bronte said.

The package had arrived with all the rest of Bronte's mail at *Australian Woman* magazine. Also on her desk was an invitation to a pantyhose launch, a complaint letter about the magazine's astrologer and photos from women entering a makeover competition.

Bronte looked at one of the photos. 'This woman doesn't need a makeover, she needs to have her head surgically inserted in a bucket,' she said.

Her assistant, Laura, who knew what she was like on Monday mornings, smiled and stirred her coffee.

'Look at the letter this woman sent,' Bronte continued. 'Dear *Australian Woman*, I would like a makeover because I have enlarged pores on my nose and thread veins on my buttocks.'

Bronte screwed the letter into a ball and threw it at the bin, missing completely.

'Just kill yourself, darling,' she said. 'That's my advice to you.'

Laura passed her a mug of coffee.

'Thanks,' Bronte said, 'you're a goddess.'

'Are you upset about the wedding?' Laura asked. She knew all about Bronte's first marriage.

'Yes.' That was all Bronte could manage to say.

'Shall I burn some incense?' Laura asked.

'No, burn the wedding cake. Then I'll feel better. That incense you've got smells like men's loos anyway.'

The Chief Sub-Editor came in with a story on Gwyneth Paltrow.

'Can you have a quick look?' she asked Bronte and dashed out again.

Bronte spun around in her chair and scanned the page.

'Gwyneth Paltrow will not answer questions about Brad Pitt,' she sniffed. 'Well then, we'll just have to make it all up, won't we.'

Bronte was about to turn forty. That event and Richard's wedding both happening at the same time was a cruel fate. The fact that she knew Sarah was ten years younger than her wasn't helping her mood.

She opened another parcel on her desk and pulled out some free sample tampons, dangling them between her fingers.

'What are these exactly?' she asked Laura. 'Novelty ear plugs for cats?'

Then she read her invitation to the new pantyhose launch.

'Shocking stockings, the stockings with the shocking pink gusset,' she said, reading the press release. 'No, I think I'll be doing the washing-up that night.'

Laura wondered if her boss had even looked at all the yellow Post-It notes she'd stuck on her telephone. Bronte had been late for work this morning and Upstairs had been leaving messages for her since half past eight.

Upstairs was basically bad news. It was where the Editor, the Editor-in-Chief, the Publisher and the

Accounts Department lived. It was where people got attacked, and sacked.

'Did I tell you about the cake Richard and I had for my wedding?' Bronte sighed.

'No,' Laura said.

'It was beautiful. None of this crap marzipan stuff. We had profiteroles, with spun sugar and fresh cream. People raved about it.'

'*Croquenbouche*,' said Laura, who knew such things. Bronte opened another letter. It was addressed to their problem-page doctor.

'Any good?' Laura said.

'Oh no,' Bronte screwed up her face. 'This is absolutely disgusting. We can't answer this.'

'Show me!' Laura said.

'No, I can't. It's about frothy green discharges.'

Bronte screwed it up and threw it at the bin, missing again. 'You know what this magazine should be called?' she asked Laura.

'What?'

'*Australian Woman's Nether Regions*. Because that's all we bloody write about.'

The phone rang.

'Yes,' Bronte said, pushing her glasses up her nose. 'Mmm, mmm, mmm, mmm.'

Then she slammed the phone down. 'That woman is stuffed in the head.'

'Who?'

Laura knew it would be Cyclone Susan, the Editor. It was.

'We have to stick a free book on the front cover.'

'Why?'

'Because some other magazine is sticking a free book on *their* front cover.'

'Oh. What sort of book?'

'*The Wonderful World of Frothy Green Discharges*. I have no idea. She's going to ring me back in a minute and tell me.'

79

Bronte swung around in her chair, took her glasses off and rubbed her eyes.

When Cyclone Susan rang back, Bronte dropped onto the floor to take the call, kicked her trainers off and put her feet up on her swivel chair, pushing it one way, then the other.

'Mmm, mmm, mmm, mmm,' Bronte muttered. Then she ended the call, took the phone off the hook and flopped on the carpet.

'Oh, the stress, the stress,' she moaned to Laura. 'I am forty on Tuesday and Richard has married someone from London who does insurance for a living. And you know what Cyclone Susan told me this free book has to be about?'

'What?'

'Bananas. It's being sponsored by the Queensland Banana Corporation. What I want to know is, why can't they get Food to do it?'

'Food's off sick.'

'Well, what about Fashion then?'

'Fashion doesn't eat,' Laura said.

Bronte opened another problem-page letter.

'This poor woman,' she said, 'can only have sex if she imagines her husband is Darth Vadar. Well, good luck to her,' she sighed, making her third attempt to throw a letter in the bin.

When Bronte missed the bin, Laura picked the letter up along with the other paper balls on the carpet.

Then the Production Manager knocked on the door. She tried to pretend that she hadn't noticed Bronte lying on the floor.

'Can I show you this headline?' she asked her. 'It's for that story on sarongs.'

There's A Sarong In My Heart, Bronte read. 'Yes, that's quite brilliant.'

When the Production Manager had gone, Bronte groaned.

'Is there some rule about having a full-frontal

lobotomy when you get a job on this magazine?'

Finally, the Art Director arrived. Unlike the other staff members who had come into the office so far, he didn't look as if he could ignore the fact that Bronte was lying on the floor.

'Do you want me to lie down too?' he joked.

'You'll only whip yourself into a frenzy,' Bronte said. 'No, sit on the chair and talk to me.'

'We've come up with a name for the book,' he said.

'Oh don't tell me. *Fifty Things To Do With Bananas.*'

He rubbed his nose, looking embarrassed.

'Actually that's it. *Fifty Things To Do With Bananas.*'

When he had gone, Bronte got up off the floor and pushed her chair in front of the door.

'Nobody else gets in,' she warned Laura. 'And if they do, I can think of fifty more things to do with bananas and his bottom will be involved. Now the other thing is, I have to sack the astrologer today. The Great Gorgonzola or whatever he's called.'

'Gorzi? But he's really good!' Laura said.

'He's utter crap. We just got another letter about him. And if you ring up his horoscope line, it sounds like Donald Duck. Donald Duck, pissed out of his mind on Scotch. Quack, quack, quack. He can't talk. And he can't predict the future either. I'm getting rid of him.'

'Well, he's always right for me,' Laura insisted.

'Well, he said November would bring *me* fresh news of love and romance,' Bronte said, curling up her top lip.

'Oh, well.'

'He gave me five smiley faces for love and four big ticks for cash. I just got a massive Amex bill and my ex-husband has married some blonde tart from England he's only known for five seconds. You know what the Great Gorgonzola should have given me for November? Ten gloomy faces for depression and a picture of a bloody huge nuclear mushroom cloud for everything else.'

Laura decided to pin up the pantyhose invitation on Bronte's noticeboard.

'Can I take this down?' she asked, holding a card.

'What, take down the only Valentine's Day card I've had since the late fifteenth century?' Bronte said. She started doing deep-breathing exercises.

Laura decided she had better do something about the horoscope page if Bronte was serious about it and found the current edition of *Australian Woman*. The photo of Gorzi at the top of the stars column showed a smiling man with a moustache and rings around his head, which the illustrator had planned to look like the rings of Saturn. Instead, it made Gorzi look like someone in a cartoon who had been knocked out cold.

'He's got crossed eyes in that photo,' Bronte said, looking up from the floor. 'I never noticed that before. Tell me what it says for Sagittarius again? Something about bananas, perhaps?'

'Sagittarius,' Laura read aloud. ' "You will be on a giddy romantic high in November as amorous entertainments divert you and you reach a sizzling sexual peak." We've still got a few days to go, you know. Give him a chance.'

'No,' said Bronte. 'The Great Gorgonzola is a dead man.'

She picked up the phone. She'd been brave about Richard's wedding and her fortieth birthday so far, but the combination of the wedding cake, the letter, the deadlines and the coffee she'd been drinking was too much. Before she could even dial the astrologer's number, though, Bronte felt herself getting short of breath.

'This is going to sound really stupid, Laura, but I think I'm having a panic attack.'

She flopped back on the floor.

'Do you want me to ring him up then?' Laura asked.

'Can you? No, what am I saying, you're only twelve years old. You can't make these kinds of decisions!'

'I'm nineteen,' Laura said calmly.

'Nineteen, and you're already volunteering to sack people. God, your generation scares me. Is it because you grew up on Nintendo?'

But still, Bronte let her do it.

Laura smiled, crossed her legs and dialled Gorzi's number.

'Hello, is that Gordon?' she asked.

Bronte was amazed that Laura knew his real name.

A short and polite conversation followed. Then Laura put the phone down.

'Did it happen?' Bronte couldn't quite believe that she'd actually done it.

'Do you want me to start looking for someone new now?' Laura said, sounding casual.

Bronte looked at her. Such efficiency. Such professionalism. It made her shiver.

'You're going to be the bloody Editor one day,' Bronte sighed. 'And I will be back in Tasmania. Writing for the *Compton Gazette*.'

'Is that where you started?' Laura asked, flicking through the *Yellow Pages* under A for Astrologer.

'No, but it's where I'm going to end up.'

Laura rang a few names while Bronte tried to tackle the easiest Post-It notes stuck to her phone.

'Try to get an astrologer who's not cross-eyed this time,' she instructed from across the room. 'And tell the illustrator we don't need those stupid rings whizzing round their head.'

Laura nodded.

'And get someone who'll stop being so bloody chirpy about life when it's clearly such a sordid farce.'

Laura nodded again. She was dreaming about becoming the Features Editor of *Australian Woman*. If she got half as many freebies as Bronte, including the pantyhose launch invitations, she'd be happy.

'What about this?' she said, having got to P for Psychic. 'Bernard Bolton. He's a medium.'

'That's talking to dead people, isn't it?'

'I think so.'

'Well, that's something new. Oh damn.' She remembered something. '*New Idea* has got a medium. We can't do it.'

'He's very good looking in the ad.'

'Show me. That could make a difference.'

Laura picked up her phone while Bronte went outside the building for a cigarette.

When her boss returned, she was humming.

'Did you get on to him?' Bronte said.

'He did a reading for me on the phone,' Laura replied. She looked slightly stunned. 'He only told me a few things. But he was just amazing about David.'

Bronte didn't want to hear about David. She didn't want to hear about other, younger, more professional, more beautiful women's love lives. Not this morning, anyway.

'And what dead person was this Bernard man talking to at the time?'

'My guide. I didn't know I had a guide. He's an American Indian.'

'Oh, give me a break.'

'No, Bernard really knew all about me. And he told me about you.'

'What did he say?' Bronte swung around in her chair.

'He said that your ex-husband Richard's new wife was going to take him on a difficult journey.'

'That's *fantastic* news,' Bronte said.

Laura wondered at how someone else's misfortune could make her boss suddenly look so happy.

'Can you do me a favour?' Bronte asked, suddenly looking with interest at Bernard Bolton's advertisement.

But Laura already knew what it was.

Chapter Eight

Ten minutes later, an appointment had been made. As Bronte walked down George Street, swinging her briefcase, she thought about Sarah and Richard again. She knew thinking about them all the time was wrong, but it was like everything else in her life – if it was bad for her, she found it hard to resist. Thinking about Sarah and Richard was exactly like smoking fags while eating Sara Lee ice cream with a fork and using the lid of the container as an ashtray. It was also like buying Alannah Hill jackets when she didn't really need them. Sheer self-indulgence.

Shut up, Bronte, she told herself. Saying 'shut up' wasn't a positive affirmation, which everyone else on the magazine seemed to be so into these days. But it would have to do.

Shut up, shut up, shut up, Bronte!

She knew she was crumbling whenever she found herself thinking about Mickey these days, and at the moment she missed him badly. Richard had bought him for her when he was just one year old – and he'd arrived in his horsebox with a blue ribbon around his neck.

Bronte tried to go back to Compton to see Mickey whenever she could. It was the only contact with Richard she had any more. Or with any of them. Harry,

Annie, Tom – that had been her world once and now it had shrunk to the size of a Tic-Tac. She wondered if Annie and Tom were still together. Now that was a strange match. But she envied Annie sometimes – over fifty and living with one of the best-looking men in Compton. Then she reminded herself of how hopeless Tom was and immediately felt better.

Striding across the lights in her trainers and suit, she waved down a cab. When she got in, she wrinkled her nose at the lingering odour of other people's hamburgers and the unmistakeable smell of taxi driver BO. Was it the knobbly wooden seats that made them sweat more?

She got in and gave the address. Then she put her lipstick on with a brush and caught the taxi driver looking at her in the mirror.

'Don't even *pretend* this is erotic for you,' she warned. He gave her a blank look and drove on.

She let herself slide sideways onto the back seat and closed her eyes. She wondered if Sarah had met Mickey yet. Richard hadn't told her very much about Sarah so she didn't know if she rode or not. Hopefully not, Bronte thought. She felt very possessive about Mickey.

When Bronte was riding him out in the paddocks behind Richard's house, everything that was wrong with her life disappeared. Her job, her love life, her mortgage. And that was just the start, Bronte thought, gloomily. She hadn't seen Mickey for months. She'd nearly been tempted to go to the wedding just to take him out again, but in the end it hadn't been enough. *Of all the events this year I'd have died to avoid, Richard's wedding was one of them,* Bronte thought, feeling a wave of nerves just at the thought of it. She wondered if anyone had been convinced by her feeble excuse about work. Maybe Richard's parents had believed her. She doubted if Richard or Sarah had – or anyone else in Compton.

Sighing, she sat upright in the back of the cab and looked at Bernard Bolton's address. Ridiculous. Laura had written down the name of a fish and chip shop across town and he couldn't possibly live there. Or if he did, he obviously wasn't any good.

Bernard Bolton's flat was, as promised, above a fish and chip shop. And after she had paid the taxi driver – without tipping him – Bronte ordered two potato scallops with tomato sauce.

'And I might as well have a Mars Bar as well,' she said to the man behind the counter, getting her cigarette lighter out of her pocket so she could light up a Benson & Hedges as soon as she got out of the shop.

Cigarette in hand, she rang Bernard Bolton's doorbell. After a few minutes, a tall man with grey hair appeared. A Distinguished Grey, Bronte thought. After fifty, men could generally be sorted into two groups – Distinguished Greys and Tired Balds. Bernard Bolton was definitely a Distinguished Grey. In fact, he even looked a bit like Blake Carrington from *Dynasty*, Bronte decided. The readers would love him. They could call him Medium Rare, or the Happy Medium, or something. He'd get lots of fan mail.

'Hello,' Bronte said with her mouth full of Mars Bar, cigarette and tomato sauce.

'Did you know your horse was right behind you?' Bernard asked her. Then without missing a beat he added, 'Come on up.'

As she followed him up the stairs, Bronte looked behind her, then stopped herself.

'What horse?' she said, although part of her already knew.

'The white horse you had once. I'm having difficulty getting the name though,' Bernard said, wrinkling his nose. 'Something beginning with A?'

'Angel,' Bronte said. 'She was called something else when we first bought her, but I called her Angel.' She paused. 'I'm having a lot of trouble dealing with this information,' she managed to say, in a professional voice.

'Angel says she knew you'd end up working in magazines one day because you used to read them all the time in the stables.'

'What?'

'She says you used to keep them on top of a pile of hay bales.'

'Yes.' Bronte found she could hardly speak.

'And she says isn't it nice that the first story you ever wrote for a magazine was about horses.'

'Yes,' Bronte swallowed hard. It had been. But it had been published two years after Angel had died.

Bernard Bolton opened the door to his flat and waved Bronte inside. Like a lot of his clients when they first arrived, she was looking quite pale now.

He offered her an armchair and waited until she had relaxed again.

'Angel wants you to go down and see Mickey again too. Is that a man?' he said.

'Mickey is a horse too,' Bronte managed to reply. 'I got Mickey after Angel died.'

'Oh. Well, Mickey's off his feed. Your husband's been too busy to look after him because of the wedding. So you might want to go down there.'

Bernard Bolton went into his kitchen and put the kettle on.

'I'll make you some tea to wash down your fish and chips,' he said.

'Did Laura tell you all this about me?' she asked.

'No. Laura didn't tell me anything. You can ask her,' he said.

'Who's telling you all these things then?' Bronte called over the noise of the kettle boiling.

'Angel. Your horse is an excellent channel,' Bernard said. 'And by the way, Angel says please stop feeling guilty.'

'Angel?' Bronte whimpered as if she were really

there. Then she tried to finish speaking and couldn't. Instead, she found herself in tears.

'Sorry,' she sniffed when Bernard came back into the room with a box of tissues. 'I asked Richard to put her down, that's why she said to stop feeling guilty. And I do feel guilty – all the time.' She found herself gabbling.

'It's all right,' Bernard said. 'Angel is quite happy now.'

'We had to put her down, we had no choice, her leg was broken.'

'She is at peace,' Bernard continued.

'She's really here? You can see her in the room?'

'She's really here. And she keeps an eye on you. She likes to know how you're doing,' he smiled.

Still crying, Bronte thought back to the day of Angel's accident. It had been just a year after her wedding to Richard.

She could still only remember the vaguest details because they had given her so much brandy and valium to calm her down afterwards. It had been raining, though. She remembered that much. And after the fall, Angel had died in her arms with the rain beating down on the roof of the stables, with Richard by her side.

'What happened?' Bernard asked. 'Your horse is telling me something about a pink blanket too.'

'That was my blanket, off my bed. We wrapped her in it. I think we buried her in it,' Bronte sniffed.

'And Angel is showing me a fence.'

'She took a fence that was too steep. She threw me off and I cracked my ribs. She broke her leg . . .' and that was all Bronte could come up with before she had to blow her nose again. Shaking her head, she stumbled into the corridor and found the bathroom.

Once inside, she locked the door then turned around with a start, terrified that Angel might suddenly appear in front of her as some horrible, bloody apparition. It had been a terrible accident. Flipping the toilet seat down, she sat on it for a few minutes, yanking off more toilet paper from the roll on the wall and blowing her nose. She thought hard about what had just happened.

Bernard Bolton could not possibly have known any of the information he had just given her. So she had to believe him.

Bronte thought about it for a minute. No. It was all too mad. Firstly, Angel was dead. Secondly, she was a horse and she couldn't speak English. Thirdly, this strange man called Bernard Bolton seemed to know far too much about her and she didn't like it.

Shaking herself out of it, Bronte blew her nose again, threw her scrunched-up tissues into the toilet, flushed it and walked back out, determined to hold herself together.

'OK?' Bernard said to her.

'Fine,' Bronte replied. If she could get back into *Australian Woman* Features Editor mode, she thought, she might just have a chance of getting through this. 'Anyway,' she said, sitting upright in her chair, 'we need you to write a column of about one thousand words a month, just answering letters from the readers and getting in touch with their . . . dead people they know. Or . . . dead animals, I suppose.'

Her attempt to be professional failed and she found herself rubbing away tears again.

'I'm sorry,' she said. 'I'm not normally like this.'

'You're having a hard time,' Bernard reassured her.

'Yes, and it's not getting any better, let me tell you.'

'We can talk about the magazine column later, if you like,' Bernard said.

Bronte nodded.

She wanted to ask him why his office was above a fish and chip shop, but decided there must be some deeply cosmic reason and left it at that. Bernard Bolton had big, comfortable armchairs covered in green velvet and she felt herself sinking backwards into her chair.

'The spirit world tends to make contact for a reason,' Bernard said, looking straight at her.

'Even horses?' Bronte said.

'I've had messages from cats.'

'What?' Bronte exclaimed, but one look at Bernard's brilliant blue eyes and she knew he was serious. He had eyes the same colour as swimming pools, she thought. The *Yellow Pages* didn't do him justice.

'Angel says she has an important message for you,' Bernard continued.

'So Angel is actually talking to you at the moment?'

'Yes.'

'Can you see her?'

'She's over there by the mantelpiece,' Bernard explained, and wincing, Bronte slowly and carefully switched her gaze. But as she half expected, there was nothing there.

'It can be hard to see a spirit if you're not used to it,' Bernard said. 'They vibrate at a much faster rate. We vibrate at a very slow rate. Because their vibrations are so different, it's hard for them to manifest on the earth plane. This is taking Angel a lot of effort.'

'Well, it must have been hell for her climbing up all your stairs,' Bronte managed to joke.

Bernard smiled.

'Like us,' he said, 'animals communicate with telepathy. You understood that even when Angel was alive, she's saying.'

Bronte nodded. It was true. Before the accident, she and Angel had shared an incredible bond. Half the time, Bronte didn't even have to tell her what to do or where to go – Angel already knew from the moment that Bronte was in the saddle. The only day Angel had failed her had been the day of the accident.

'Angel says she remembers you holding her head when Richard gave her the shot. And she's showing me her saddle. It's in the dam.'

Shocked, Bronte swallowed her tears.

'I threw it in the dam after she died,' she said. 'Nobody knows that. I went out in the rain one night in my nightie and I chucked it in. I was drunk. I told Richard I had it sent to the tip.'

'Angel saw you do it. She was with you that night, you know.'

'Was she?' Despite everything, Bronte thought, she felt comforted by this.

'She says she always wanted you to buy her and that's why she guided you towards her. You bought her at a horse auction, she says.'

'Yes,' Bronte sniffed and rubbed another tear out of her eye. 'Angel was my wedding anniversary gift from Richard. And she's right, something made us go round the back of the auction and find her. She wasn't even supposed to be in the sale that day. But we made an offer on her and we got her.'

Bernard Bolton sat up in his chair. 'She's telling me that you don't believe in life after death.'

'Well, I don't.'

'Angel says you used to believe in heaven, though.'

'Well, I did. I mean, I got married in a Catholic church. I was brought up to believe in heaven and hell.'

'Angel says there is no hell. She says hell is only a mind construct.'

'Well, I'm glad there's no hell for horses,' Bronte said. 'They don't deserve it. Even if it is only a mind construct. And how come she knows how to say things like "mind construct" anyway?'

Bernard broke off, laughing.

'What?' Bronte insisted.

'I'm sorry,' he said. 'This is a very strange conversation.'

'*You* think this is a strange conversation!' Bronte said, shaking her head.

She picked up her mug of tea, but was too dazed to drink. Instead, she felt herself mindlessly stirring the spoon.

'Your ex-husband has married a woman who will take him on a difficult journey.'

'Yes, you said that to Laura.'

Bronte rubbed her face. She couldn't take much more of this. Suddenly, she longed for the office. It was mad and it was stressful, but at least it was normal.

'I might have to go now,' she said in a polite voice. 'Thank you for the reading.'

Bernard Bolton nodded. He really was quite good looking in a *Dynasty* kind of way, Bronte thought.

'Angel has come through to let you know that there is life and there is hope.'

'Well, yes,' Bronte said. 'I'll be in touch about the job.'

And after that, she really did have to leave.

As she walked down Bernard's stairs and out onto the street, she thought about it. What did Angel mean, hell was a mind construct? It sounded more like something Deepak Chopra might say. But what about all the other stuff – throwing the saddle in the dam and wrapping Angel in a pink blanket? Maybe Bernard had read her mind. But then again, why had he told her that Richard had just married a woman who would take him on a difficult journey? That wasn't mind-reading. If anything, Bronte thought moodily, Richard's new marriage to Sarah would probably be a great success. That was why it hurt so much.

She searched for a taxi in the street outside, and tried logically to work out everything she had just experienced, but it was all too confusing – she was getting a thudding headache.

You'll believe a horse can talk, she thought. It was all a bit like *Dumbo* – you'll believe an elephant can fly. If she wasn't careful, she would be locked up in the loony bin. She was going to have to be careful who she told about Angel.

She felt like crying again, but quickly stopped

herself and looked at her watch. Damn. She was going to be late back for work. Again.

She waved down a taxi and climbed in, looking quickly over her shoulder for a white horse, but the only thing she could see was the front window of the fish and chip shop.

Chapter Nine

Back at the office, Laura was sorting through photographs for the *Fifty Things To Do With Bananas* recipe booklet.

'Upstairs were wondering where you were,' she told Bronte casually. She was trying not to panic her, but the Editor, Cyclone Susan, had been furious when Bronte had failed to turn up for the editorial meeting.

'I'm sick,' Bronte said. 'Can you ring them up and tell them?'

'Well, I said that I thought you might be sick,' Laura answered.

'Thank you. Thank God.'

'You were lying down on the floor before you went out. So you sort of looked sick.'

'Yes, that's right. You're a genius.'

Laura began to make a pile of possible banana photographs and another for reject banana photographs. 'How was it with Bernard Bolton?' she asked Bronte, who had decided to lie down on the floor again. She was dying to know.

Her boss let out a huge sigh and shook her head. 'I'm in shock,' she said.

'Really?'

'He completely spooked me. The first thing he did was get in touch with my horse, Angel. The one who died. And he definitely said Richard and Sarah were going to have a crap marriage.'

'Wow!'

'Well, anyway,' Bronte corrected herself, 'he said that thing about the difficult journey again.'

Bronte decided she wasn't going to tell Laura the other bits about Angel. She might start crying again and she made it a rule never to cry at work unless she'd locked herself in the loo first.

'I think Bernard Bolton could be good,' she said. 'He's quite attractive, a bit like Blake Carrington from *Dynasty*. Not that I ever watched it, of course,' she added quickly.

'So he's got the job?' Laura asked.

Bronte nodded. 'Anyway, he lives above a fish and chip shop – that's got to be a good omen. But Laura, my horse, Angel, was actually there! Standing next to the mantelpiece!'

Laura smiled, but secretly wondered about Bronte. She knew about Angel – Bronte talked non-stop about her horses. But digesting the fact that Bronte was now receiving information about her ex-husband from a dead pony was too much, even for Laura, who after two years at *Australian Woman* thought she had seen it all.

'Now, can you do something for me?' Bronte said sweetly, rolling over onto her side on the floor. She was getting carpet fluff all over her jacket, Laura noticed.

'Can you please organize me a trip to Compton. I'll be going the weekend after next, so I'll be off Friday afternoon to get away – you don't know where I am if anyone asks – and can you get me back as late as you can on Sunday. Or if not, first thing Monday morning, which means I won't be in here until after lunch – and if anyone asks about that, you don't know where I am again. Thanks, darling.'

Laura spent a lot of her professional life not knowing where Bronte was, but she rang the travel agent anyway. Relaxing, Bronte let herself flop again. The thought of seeing Mickey was just too wonderful at the moment. Dirt tracks, green fields and the lovely way he always bolted over the paddock to see her at the fence, whenever she arrived – and rubbed his head against her hand . . .

If he was off his feed and Richard was too busy to notice, she felt she had to be there. The thought of Mickey suffering without her, in any way at all, was too much. She just had to go – and bugger Friday afternoon, she thought. She felt comforted to know that Angel cared about Mickey – it proved what she had always believed, that there was a kind of horsey solidarity in the animal world. She wondered if human ghosts were like that too, with people who were still alive. The only thing she knew about ghosts was that they wandered around with their heads under their arms with gigantic ruffs on.

Stretching out on the carpet, Bronte found herself thinking about the bush tracks around the back of Compton, where the gumnuts were thick on the ground. She took in a deep breath. She could almost smell the eucalyptus. The scent of gumnuts in your hand, especially when you squeezed them, was unlike anything else in the world. Suddenly Bronte frowned. Something very odd was happening. She could swear she had just smelled a horse.

She sniffed, opening an eye to see if Laura was looking, but her assistant was engrossed in her phone call to the travel agent. It was too weird, Bronte thought. There was definitely a warm, sweet, unmistakeably horsey smell just under her nose. Or was it just to the left of her?

Sitting up, Bronte looked around the room and felt herself beginning to panic. She sniffed two or three more times, each time expecting the smell to vanish, but it was as real and as strong as the inside of a stable. Except she wasn't in a stable. She was in a small airconditioned office with magazines all over the floor.

'Laura!'

Her assistant paused with the phone away from her ear. 'Could you hold on please?' she said to the travel agent.

'Is there a funny smell in here?' Bronte asked.

Laura thought about it. 'No. What do you mean?'

'Like a horse.'

'No, not really.' Laura sniffed experimentally, but all she could smell was her own Gucci Envy – a freebie from the Beauty Department – and Bronte's trainers, which tended to get whiffy in summer.

'No horse smell?' Bronte persisted. She was being overwhelmed by it now. And there was something else too – what was it?

'No, I can't smell anything,' Laura said and turned back to her phone call. Really, Bronte was becoming steadily more lulu every day that she worked for her.

Getting up off the floor, Bronte walked slowly around the room, sniffing the air. In one way, she wished it would go away because she was beginning to feel scared. But in another way, she wanted more of it – because it was Angel, unmistakeably Angel and, even though it had been years, it was one of the nicest, most familiar smells in the world.

She half listened as Laura went through the details of her frequent-flyer points on the phone.

'Angel?' she whispered, very softly. She looked around in front of her, then feeling slightly stupid, she checked behind her. Nothing. Just the usual towering bookshelves packed with old magazines and her noticeboard with its ancient Princess Diana calendar and Valentine's Day card pinned to the centre. She sniffed again, but there was nothing. She waited until Laura had got off the phone.

'It's completely gone now,' she said.

'Oh.'

'There really was a strong smell of horses in here.'

98

'Wow!' Laura said, trying hard to sound as if she believed Bronte, and failing.

The phone rang and Laura quickly picked it up to save herself. She didn't want to get into another crazy conversation with Bronte about horses – there had already been enough of those in her life at the office.

'It's for you,' she said, passing the receiver over to her boss. 'I think they want to have a meeting about *Fifty Things To Do With Bananas.*'

'Oh, for God's sake!' Bronte rolled her eyes and took over the telephone.

Meanwhile, Laura gave the air a quick sniff. She couldn't smell a thing. Just Bronte's cheesy trainers as usual. That was probably the horse smell.

'I'm allergic to bananas,' Bronte was saying on the telephone. 'I go into spasms if I'm forced to eat fresh fruit.'

Laura pointed dramatically to the ceiling, which was sign language for Upstairs, and then pointed to herself.

'Yes,' Bronte whispered to her, breaking away from her phone call, 'you have to come too.' Laura made a face. She hated meetings.

Bronte put the receiver down.

'The Test Kitchen have created something called Banana Cobbler and we all have to eat it,' she said. 'All the staff. Upstairs. Right now. So we might as well get this over and done with. At least we can amuse ourselves by watching all of Fashion run straight to the loo for a good old bulimia session as soon as the meeting's over.'

But Laura was already applying her lipgloss and squirting mint drops into her mouth, ready for her meeting with Upstairs.

'You're definitely more ambitious than me,' Bronte said to her in the lift. 'I can't even be bothered seeing if my skirt's on straight. Oh, I never asked. Was everything OK about my flight?'

'Down to Melbourne then onto Hobart on Friday at 3.30 p.m, then back on Sunday at 10 p.m.,' Laura said.

Bronte felt like doing a little dance around the lift in her trainers.

'Yay! Mickey!' she squealed, suddenly feeling fourteen instead of forty. Laura beamed. 'You got it on your frequent-flyer points, too,' she said.

'Aaargh! Too much!' Wildly happy, Bronte gave the air a tiny punch. 'You're the cat's pyjamas and the dog's dressing gown, Laura, can I just say that?'

When the lift doors opened and she saw the entire staff of *Australian Woman* in front of her, Bronte felt her mood plummet.

'Look, they're all here,' she whispered to Laura, out of the side of her mouth. 'And Cyclone Susan's got her padded shoulders on. Oh no!'

Obediently, Bronte and Laura followed the other staff into the boardroom.

Looking at the sea of black dresses and suits in front of her, Bronte sighed. 'The only person not wearing black in this room is her,' Bronte whispered to Laura, pointing to the Head of the Test Kitchen, who was wearing a white hairnet, a white cotton coat and a pair of white rubber gloves. She appeared to have put dozens of bowls of Banana Cobbler on the boardroom table.

'The windows are fogging up with all this Cobbler,' said Cyclone Susan. 'Can someone do something? Now, as this is going on the cover, I want everyone to try it. No ifs or buts. I don't want to know about your diets, just tell me if it's edible.'

Obediently, a few staff members sitting at the end of the table started eating.

'Mmmm,' said a woman in a black shirt and black skirt, carrying a black handbag. 'This is fab.'

'I'm worried the Cobbler won't photograph well,' said the Art Director. 'I mean, it's delicious,' he added nervously, 'it's just that I can see it starting to sag.'

'Just do what you always do then,' Cyclone Susan spat back. 'Squirt shaving cream on it and blow fag smoke out the back of the bowl.'

Bronte and Laura exchanged looks.

'It's revolting,' Bronte managed to say through a mouthful of squishy banana. 'It looks like something you scrape off nappies.'

She noticed Laura was eating hers around the edge of the bowl, scooping out all the sponge and avoiding the yellow slush in the middle. The smell was overwhelming – like every hospital kitchen she had ever walked past. She wrinkled her nose and turned away from the table.

'I'm going to open a window,' she said. But nobody was listening – they were all too busy making appreciative noises and watching Cyclone Susan's face.

It was incredibly hot in the boardroom, despite the airconditioning. Bronte tugged the strings on the blind at the end of the room and stood on tiptoe in her trainers, pulling it up as high as it would go. Outside, she could see two taxis cutting each other off on the corner and a mass of people trying to run across George Street ahead of the green light. *Ah, Sydney!* she thought, reminding herself that next Friday night she would be in a place where taxis did not exist and nobody even thought about jaywalking.

Looking down onto the street, she could see a police horse standing by itself without a rider. She felt sorry for it and wondered what had happened. Or was it a police horse? It seemed too small, somehow. Maybe someone had hired it from the stables at Centennial Park and it had got lost – but that didn't make sense either. Behind her, Bronte became vaguely aware of the Head of the Test Kitchen, talking to someone about the Banana Cobbler recipe. *Blah, blah, blah,* thought Bronte. *All this fuss about a bunch of bananas.*

And then, to her amazement, the horse flew away from the traffic lights. She watched in disbelief as it appeared to sprout wings and come closer and closer towards her.

'Angel!' she breathed. The long white nose, brown eyes and small white-grey ears were unmistakeable. Starting to half cry in shock and joy, she squeezed her nails into her hands to stop herself and pressed her face into the window to see better.

'Angel!' she mouthed through the glass, trying to reach her. But just as suddenly as she had flown across the street and up to the window, Angel disappeared. Suddenly yanking the window open, Bronte stuck her head out and looked frantically left, right and up into the sky – but all she could see was a traffic jam, and a crane and a few stray clouds.

Then she heard a voice in her ear. 'We'll be together again one day,' the voice said. With a start, Bronte turned her head. *What?* It had been a voice without volume or sound, and a voice without gender either – it was hard to say what it was, she thought, except that she had definitely heard it. She realized that her heart was thudding.

'Close the blinds, Bronte, the sun's far too hot.'

Turning around, she saw Cyclone Susan staring at her.

'I just thought it was a bit stuffy,' she managed to say, but she shut the window and pulled the blind down again.

'I might go outside,' she said to no-one in particular. 'I'm feeling a bit sick.'

'Bronte, we need your opinion on the back cover,' Cyclone Susan said.

'Sorry!' she managed and ran out, tripping over the shoelaces on her trainers.

Outside in the corridor, Bronte's heart was hammering. She punched the lift button to go down to the street and leaned against the wall until it arrived, feeling so flattened that she could hardly stand properly. It would be too unfair, she thought, if there were people in the lift when it came down – the last thing she needed was people crowding around her. But to her horror, when the doors opened, she could see it crammed with people from the floor above.

'Sorry – wrong button,' she stammered, looking and feeling like an idiot as the doors closed and the lift went away again.

She rubbed her face. Had she really seen Angel? Had she really heard the voice? And if so, was that *her*? And what about the wings?

'I should be locked up,' she said to herself, hoping that it would make her feel better – but it didn't. Something inside her knew the truth too well to believe that she was going mad or hallucinating. And after five years working on women's magazines, Bronte thought she knew the difference between fact and fantasy.

She went through the events in her head, one by one. She had seen a white horse standing by itself in the street. The white horse had grown wings. It had flown up towards her – and once she had seen its face, she had known without a doubt that it was Angel. Then Angel – and who else could it have been? – had spoken to her and told her that they would be together again one day.

I have to die if that's going to happen, Bronte thought. And she felt herself go cold as she saw the flash of a white tail disappear round the end of the corridor.

Chapter Ten

Sarah was cooking scrambled eggs when Richard told her about Bronte's visit.

'It's just for a few days,' he said, reading the paper and talking at the same time. 'She wants to see Mickey.'

'Where will she stay?' Sarah asked.

'At the pub. She always does. Don't worry,' he added with a smile.

'Oh, I'm not worried,' Sarah said, stirring the eggs and avoiding his eyes.

It would be better if she was worried, she decided. A few months before the wedding, she had felt sick at the thought of Bronte Nicholson. Now it was like hearing that Richard's aunty – or someone equally harmless – was coming to stay. She didn't feel remotely jealous.

Watching her turn the scrambled eggs over in the pan, Richard wondered if Sarah could be persuaded back to bed again. He was still getting used to the luxury of having her around all the time, instead of stealing her in London whenever he could. Something told him she was still feeling too married to behave like a lover – instead, since the wedding, she had been more interested in sleeping on her side of the bed, instead of sleeping with him. *Give it time*, he thought, brushing it off.

'Bronte said something funny,' Richard said suddenly.

'Did she?' Sarah stirred the eggs.

'She told me that she thought Mickey was off his food. Well, I just went down there now – and he was.'

'Do you think she's psychic?' Sarah managed to joke.

'Psycho, maybe,' Richard ventured.

'You never talk much about Bronte, do you?' Sarah said, putting the scrambled eggs down on the table.

Richard shrugged. 'It was a long time ago.'

In the six months they had known each other, Richard had never managed to tell her much about his first marriage, Sarah realized. At first it had been fine. All she really needed to know was that Richard had been young – just twenty – when he got married, and that Bronte had been five years older, and that they had tried for ten years, but it hadn't worked out.

Now she found herself feeling more curious. But there was no point in trying to interrogate Richard, she decided. He was far too much of a gentleman – and far too sensible – to feed her the details of a marriage that had gone bad.

They ate their scrambled eggs in silence, while Richard continued to read the *Compton Gazette*. Sarah couldn't believe the headlines. They all seemed to be about cows and new shopping centres. She missed the London papers. But if you wanted the *Telegraph* or the *Daily Mail*, you had to order them from Melbourne and they were always out of date when they arrived.

'So when does Bronte get here?' Sarah asked, working her way through the scrambled eggs. She wasn't used to cooking for two people and they were rubbery.

'She should be here in about a week,' Richard said. 'I thought we could have her over for dinner on Friday night.'

'Maybe we could ask some other people too,' Sarah said, thinking automatically of Tom.

'Oh, I don't know. It could be easier with just us,'

Richard said, pushing the newspaper away. 'Hey, did you see there's a new shopping centre opening up in Hobart?'

'Yes,' Sarah replied, clearing the plates away.

As she washed up, she realized she had just tried to get Tom back into her life again, even though it had been only a fortnight since she'd last seen him – at her own wedding. Turning on the hot tap, she tried – and failed – to feel jealous of Bronte for a moment, hoping that jealousy would help kick-start some kind of passion for Richard again. She was still far more hurt by the thought of Annie, though, if she was to be honest with herself. Furiously, Sarah scrubbed plates while she heard Richard go through the motions of getting ready for work, willing herself to feel the old, familiar sensation of missing him before he was even out of the door – but it was no good.

Stop forcing it, she thought. Perhaps if she just relaxed about Richard, it would all happen naturally. When he had gone, she went upstairs to the spare bedroom and pulled out a book from under the mattress. The title was embarrassing – it was an eighties paperback called *Relating and Mating* – but it was the only thing the local second-hand bookshop had to offer.

She tried to read the first chapter again – it was all about fear of intimacy and commitment. None of the examples of forty-something suburban Americans called Hank and Amy seemed to apply to her and Richard. She slid the book under the mattress again and went downstairs. If she had been looking for some deep psychological explanation for her obsession with Tom, it wasn't there.

There was nothing on the television – just ads for sheep drench. In London, she would be channel surfing with the luxury of cable. In Compton, there were just two channels – a trashy one with ads and a sensible one without. Not much choice, Sarah decided.

But then, she should be out in the open air – shouldn't she?

And you might run into Tom if you go for a walk, she thought, but stopped herself just in time. Clearing the clean plates away in the kitchen, she decided she had better do something constructive with her day or she would start going insane.

It had been months since she'd stopped work. And she was officially Mrs Richard Gilby with a new home, a new country, a new name and a new life. It was time to do something with herself, she decided. She rang up the second-hand bookshop where she had found the copy of *Relating and Mating*.

A woman answered.

'I was just wondering,' said Sarah, stumbling over her words, 'if you had – a job. A part-time job or something. Maybe.'

'No,' the woman said, 'not at the moment.'

'Can I give you my name and number in any case?' Sarah asked.

'I'll just get my pen,' was the reply and a lot of fumbling followed. 'It's Sarah Gilby.'

'Oh. You're the one who married Dick!'

'Ye-es,' Sarah said, wondering if the strange voice on the other end of the phone belonged to one of their many anonymous female wedding guests.

'Did you like the punchbowl?' the woman said.

'Oh yes,' Sarah lied. 'It was lovely.' What punchbowl? She could hardly remember it, they had received so many strange glass objects.

'Tell Richard that Beryl's got worms again.'

'Sure!' Sarah said brightly.

And then the woman put the phone down.

Mad, Sarah thought. But she had a feeling that life in Compton was always going to be like this.

In the meantime, she scanned the back of the *Compton Gazette* for other jobs The only thing she could see was an escort agency in Hobart looking for lovely ladies as dinner companions.

Sighing, she threw the paper down on the kitchen table and went back to the television, where they were still showing sheep-drench ads. She wondered if life had been like this for Bronte when she first married Richard and moved from Melbourne to Compton. Had Bronte coped with having two television channels, and one newspaper and one second-hand bookshop? The few things she knew about Bronte suggested otherwise. But maybe Bronte had been the perfect first wife at the beginning, she thought. Once again, Sarah waited for a reassuring stab of jealousy. But all she felt was curiosity.

Meanwhile, in Sydney, Bronte was fighting her curiosity about Sarah. She would be in Compton in a few days, she realized, and the less worked up she was about meeting Richard and his new wife, the better. But there was something about hearing that Sarah was blonde, English and thirty that brought out every insecurity Bronte had.

She wondered if Richard and Sarah had been bed-bound since their wedding day. It had certainly been like that the first time round – Richard had practically trapped her in the bedroom during their honeymoon. They had gone to Bali – a very eighties thing to do, Bronte realized, with a smile – and every time the maid had come to clean the room, Richard had yelled at her to go away.

She didn't find the memory painful. Bronte had resigned herself to the contradictions in her marriage years ago, long before the official divorce papers had come through. She and Richard had enjoyed some youthful – very youthful – passion. It had just taken a few years for both of them to realize they couldn't communicate.

Curling up on her couch with a cup of tea, Bronte

wondered idly if Richard had any plans to take Sarah somewhere glamorous. On the phone, he had told her that they would take their honeymoon later on, when Christmas and New Year were out of the way. If he took Sarah to Paris or Rome, Bronte thought, she would kill him.

She knew it was childish to resent Sarah. She had made Richard happy and he deserved it. He was a good person, even if their marriage had been hell. It had brought out the worst in both of them, there was no doubt about that. For a moment, Bronte remembered one Christmas Day, years ago, when Richard had stormed out and she had got stoned by herself on some of Harry's dope, and cried into the kitchen sink with the radio on so the neighbours couldn't hear her.

Getting rid of that memory, she thought about Harry for a minute. Richard had told her that he'd misbehaved at the wedding, but hadn't gone into details. Bronte wondered what he had done. One of the annoying things about Richard, she decided, was that he never told you anything. When they had been married, it had been like living in the Valley of Silence. Oh well, Bronte thought, she could always interrogate Sarah.

She ticked off the next two days in her head. Tomorrow at work, they would have the final meeting about the *Fifty Things To Do With Bananas* book. And then, the day after that, Cyclone Susan would be knocking on her door, asking for story ideas for the next issue. Bronte vaguely thought about suggesting a story on ghosts, then changed her mind. The less she thought about all that, the better. For a moment, she remembered the flash of Angel's white tail at the end of the corridor at work. No matter how much she had tried since then, she couldn't persuade herself that it had been a trick of the light or her imagination. All the more reason not to write about it, she decided. But still, when she finally slid sideways along the couch and drifted off to sleep, it was Angel's white face that Bronte saw last of all.

A few days later, she was on the way to the airport – and Mickey – with a small overnight bag.

The airport shop was full of things that Bronte couldn't use and didn't need, like inflatable neck pillows and furry koala backpacks. Still, with an hour to go before boarding, she managed to kill at least twenty minutes picking up Mars Bars and putting them back down again.

She realized she hadn't brought anything to read. Scanning the shelves, she saw the new Harry Potter, which she'd already finished, and endless books on the Internet. Bronte hated the Internet.

'Do you have anything on ghosts?' she asked the shop assistant, who was hovering.

'Ghosts . . .' the girl pondered. 'Er, we've got Stephen King.'

'No, like a *real* book on ghosts,' Bronte insisted, scanning the shelves.

The girl handed her a book with a picture of a rainbow on the cover. Why did everything New Age have to involve a huge great rainbow on the front? The title was dreadful – *Your Spirit, Your Soul, Your Self* – and the name of the author was even worse – Mungo Hyde-Winkler.

She flicked through Mungo Hyde-Winkler's book anyway. Chapter Four, the book read, 'Making Contact with the Other Side'. *Well I've already done that*, Bronte thought. Then she heard her boarding announcement.

'This'll do,' she quickly told the shop assistant and decided to take a Mars Bar as well.

Sitting back in her seat as they prepared for take-off, Bronte shoved her copy of *Your Spirit, Your Soul, Your Self* into the seat pocket, along with the free airline magazine and the plastic cards with pictures of people with curly hair sliding down inflatable rafts.

110

Bronte decided that the life-jacket demonstrations were ridiculous. Were you supposed to tie the whistle around your waist, or wait for a flight attendant to drop from the ceiling? And if they tell me one more time to stow my baggage securely in the overhead locker or under the seat in front of me, I'll throw it at them, she thought.

Laura had booked her a window seat, which Bronte was grateful for. Peering down over the wing, she could soon see Bass Strait below her. The change of plane in Melbourne had been uneventful. In the adjacent seat, a woman with garlic breath followed her gaze down into the water.

'Do you want my orange juice?' said the garlicky woman.

Bronte shook her head politely and smiled.

'I can't eat a thing,' the woman said. 'I'm too nervous we're going to crash.'

'Oh, planes never crash,' Bronte said breezily. 'Not in Australia.'

'Are you sure?' the garlicky woman said.

'Oh, yes,' Bronte reassured her, wishing she would either shut up or face the other way when she talked.

And then there was a huge bang as the plane dropped and Bronte was thrown upwards in her seat.

'Belt,' said the garlicky woman.

'What? What?' panicked Bronte.

'Put your belt on . . .'

But before the woman could say any more, Bronte had been thrown out of her seat again and this time she had to grab the seat pocket in front of her in order to steady herself. Suddenly the chief flight attendant was on the intercom.

'Ladies and gentlemen, as you can see, we are experiencing some minor turbulence and the seat-belt signs are . . .'

And then there was a huge bang and what sounded

like an entire trolley full of food and orange juice crashed to the floor.

Bronte quickly fastened her seat belt. The stench of garlic was now overwhelming – probably because the woman next to her was panting with fear.

'Don't worry,' she managed to say, although she was now beginning to feel very worried indeed. She couldn't even look out of the window – but she knew that the flight over Bass Strait went for miles and that dry land was at least another half an hour away.

They kept bumping and banging along and, to her horror, Bronte realized that someone – it sounded like a man – was sniffing in the seat behind her, as if he was half crying, half praying. *Bloody men*, she thought. *They're such cowards.*

In a flash, she thought about the possibility of dying. What would happen if it were to happen now – or in the next half hour? She wondered about her funeral. Which of the men in her life would turn up? Richard, of course. And possibly a few ex-boyfriends since then, she thought. Hopefully not that bloke with the lava lamp and the small feet, though. That would be a real let-down. She wondered if Cyclone Susan would make a nice speech at the funeral service. Probably not.

The garlicky woman was now crossing her arms tightly and staring straight ahead of her.

'Why doesn't someone tell us what's going on?' she muttered. *They're waiting until they can give us some good news*, Bronte thought. If it was bad news, then nobody was going to say anything. Vaguely, she remembered one of the air crew rambling on about an inflatable life raft. She wondered if it would be like *Titanic*, and then decided it would be far less romantic – not so much Leonardo and Kate as herself and a deranged woman with a mouth like an Italian restaurant.

She looked across the nervous woman into the far aisle. Some of the passengers there were clearly terrified now. It wasn't fair, Bronte thought. Someone should let them know what was going on.

'*Oh my God!*' yelped the man sitting behind her. Annoyed, Bronte twisted around in her seat, aware that she would probably be shouted down by a flight attendant, but fed up with the fuss he was making.

'Just calm down,' she told him. She was surprised to find that he was quite young with a beard and a flannelette checked shirt – a blokey type, she thought, not someone she would have picked as a wimp at all.

'*A horse!*' the man half whispered, staring at her. 'Did you see the horse?'

'What horse?' Bronte said sharply. But she already knew what he was talking about. Willing herself to behave normally, she reached over and patted him on the shoulder, turned around again and lowered herself gently back into her seat. She breathed in deeply. Where was Angel anyway? In the aisle? On the empty seat in front of her? Sitting cross-legged in the loo, having a fag? She tried to make herself laugh, and failed.

Of course he had seen a horse because it was Angel, and Angel had told her they would be together, and now she was going to die. Simple. Suddenly Bronte realized she was feeling sick. The fact that someone at the front of the plane was clearly heaving into a bag didn't make her feel any better.

'Ladies and gentlemen, if you'll please bear with us . . .'

But the speakers above their seats weren't working properly and all Bronte could hear after that was crackling.

'Excuse me,' she managed to say to the garlicky woman. Then she threw up, neatly, into a paper bag she could have developed her holiday snapshots in.

Afterwards, she was amazed to find herself folding the top of the bag over in an organized way and calmly shoving it behind the airline magazine in the front

113

pocket. For their entire married life, Richard had always told her she was neurotic. But look at me now, Bronte thought, placidly fanning herself with her copy of *Your Spirit, Your Soul, Your Self.* I should get a medal.

Then she lifted her head and realized something was different about the plane. It wasn't moving.

'Jesus, it's stopped!' she yelled at the garlicky woman. But she quickly realized she was wrong – it hadn't stopped at all. It had just stopped lurching from side to side and crashing up and down.

Soon, flight attendants – why weren't they allowed to call them air hostesses any more? – were handing out glasses of water and towels. Fat lot of good that would do, she thought, when half the plane was having hysterics. Some of the passengers were grabbing the arms of the attendants, others were trying to get out of their seats and were being lectured.

Wiping her mouth with the back of her sleeve, Bronte searched around the cabin for any sign of Angel. If she really had been there, she wasn't there now. Maybe the bearded man had just been hallucinating. Didn't a lack of oxygen do that? Maybe the air pressure in the cabin had dropped. *I really don't have a clue what I'm talking about here,* Bronte thought. But a pseudo-sensible rationalization was enough to keep her calm and that was all that mattered.

Finally she was allowed to get up and go to the toilet, where she hurriedly cleaned herself up with some toilet paper and a bottle of Eternity and swished water around her mouth. They would be landing in Hobart soon. She had to be ready. Although it was typical of her life that one of the most important first meetings she would ever go through – confronting her ex-husband's new wife – would be straight after the worst flight of her life.

At the baggage carousel in Hobart, she stopped watching the suitcases and bags circulate. It was making her feel worse. She half expected Angel to poke her head through the black rubber flap, where the luggage was coming out, and give a ghostly whinny.

'Stop being stupid,' she muttered out loud to herself. And then someone tapped her on the shoulder. She jumped. It was Richard.

'Sarah's got a bit of a headache,' he said, 'so it's just me. Have your bags come out yet?'

'I haven't looked,' Bronte explained. 'I'm feeling a bit sick to tell you the truth, I thought the plane was going to crash. Oh, hang on – there it is – the brown leather thing.'

Expertly, Richard stepped in front of a bewildered group of passengers, who were still recovering from their flight, and scooped the bag up by one handle. He was good at that sort of thing, Bronte thought. Gutting fish, carrying luggage, opening doors, booking restaurants – he really was the perfect husband. Except he hadn't been.

By now, five years after their divorce, Bronte was used to being physically attracted to Richard in the first few minutes that she saw him, letting it die down and then forgetting all about it. It was just part of life, she decided. Just because you gave up cigarettes didn't mean that people could light up in front of you without you lusting after one. Something occurred to her.

'Does Sarah smoke?' she asked as they made their way to Richard's Jeep. Richard had always lectured her about smoking when they were married.

'She used to smoke,' he said, 'but she's quite anti now.'

'Did you make her give up?' Bronte asked.

'I think someone else did,' he half smiled.

As they drove off to the house, Bronte persisted.

'What do you mean, someone else made her give up smoking? Who was it?'

He shrugged. 'Some other bloke. Some other bloke before me. Hey, you were right about Mickey. He's off his feed. Sarah was saying you must be psychic.'

'Was she? What else did she say about me?'

Richard swung the wheel of the Jeep round tightly as they cleared a corner.

'Now don't get thingy.'

'I'm not being thingy.'

'I can see you're being thingy.'

'Anyway, did I tell you about the flight?'

'No, what happened?'

And Bronte told him the full story – leaving out the part about Angel – but going into detail about the garlicky woman because she knew that it would make Richard laugh.

'And the bloke behind you was crying?' he said.

'Well, sort of snuffling.'

'Can't be a Tasmanian bloke then,' Richard declared, sticking his jaw out. Now it was Bronte's turn to laugh. Despite everything, she thought, they could still manage that. It wasn't bad, considering the pain they had gone through all those years ago.

She silently checked the usual Compton landmarks as they drove through the town. Nothing ever changed. They were still advertising twenty-dollar crayfish in the window of the newsagent's, and the faded red crepe-paper Santa, which always appeared on the front of the town hall in December, was back again.

'Tell me more about what Harry did at the wedding,' Bronte said suddenly.

'Nothing to tell,' Richard replied.

'Of course there is. What did he do that was so shocking?'

'He can tell you.'

'But I won't see him. Unless you ask him over.'

'It's just us for dinner,' Richard said hastily. 'I thought, the less fuss the better. Just casual. Sarah's made a quiche.'

'Great!' said Bronte heartily, thinking two things at once – how much she loathed quiche, and how amazed

116

she was that some women could still actually bake things. Instantly, a vision of a blonde, smiling Sarah wearing flowery oven gloves drifted in front of her. Bronte wondered if she'd enjoy reading *Australian Woman* as well. It was enough to make her feel sick again.

'Anyway,' Richard turned down his street, 'it's no drama. Just a chance to say hello, and then you can wander down and see Mickey. I had a look, by the way . . .' he changed gears as they went down hill, 'it's nothing serious, just a bit of colic.'

'That's good,' Bronte sighed. She took her glasses off and put them back in a leather case.

'Why are you doing that?' Richard said, noticing.

'Giving my eyes a rest,' she shrugged, but when she started to put her eye make-up on, Richard allowed himself a private smile out of the car window. He had forgotten how vain she was.

Inside the house, Sarah was in the bath. Richard had told her that nobody bothered with baths in Australia, but even though the shower was good – amazingly good, after years of London dribble – she still equated baths with relaxation and now, more than ever, she needed to unwind.

She had a vague idea of what Bronte might look like, and what Bronte might be like. She already knew that baking a quiche was a mistake. She should have just suggested they go out for dinner, but the nearest decent restaurant was in Hobart, and according to Richard, you had to book it seven days in advance.

A blurry photograph of Bronte riding Mickey was still in one of Richard's photo albums. The first thing Sarah had done when she arrived at Richard's house was go through all of his photographs, and the most recent picture of Bronte had shown her, sweaty and happy, with her glasses fogged up and her hair up in a ponytail, taking Mickey around one of the back paddocks. The difference between the twenty-five-year-old who had married Richard, and the forty-year-old today was incredible. In her mid twenties, Bronte had been skinny, shorter than Richard and tanned. Now she seemed to be paler, bigger and taller – at least according to the most recent photos. Perhaps it was just the camera, she thought. Her own wedding pictures – just back from the photographer this week – showed her looking much more blonde and much more pink than she was normally. And the dress had given her a waist like a wasp, she thought wryly.

In all Richard's albums, the photos of Tom were the most tempting, of course – even in the ancient black-and-white cricket and high school photos, he was still gorgeous, and still recognizably Tom. But Sarah had banned herself from going near the photo albums a few days before the wedding, and she still refused to let herself give into temptation.

The bath was beginning to go cold. Meanwhile, something was definitely burning in the kitchen. Leaping up, Sarah wrapped herself in a towel and ran down, just in time to meet Richard and Bronte coming the other way.

'Sorry,' she blurted out and shuffled back to the bathroom as quickly as she could without embarrassing herself – it was a very short towel, and it only just covered her thighs.

'Something's burning in here!' Richard yelled.

'I know!' she yelled back, 'it's the quiche. Can you fix it?' Bronte quickly sat down in one of the kitchen chairs, politely pretending to look at the *Compton Gazette*.

'Looks like it should have been turned down,' Richard muttered, switching the oven knob back to zero. Bronte put her glasses back on and saw that the glass in the oven door had turned black. In a way, it was all very reassuring, she thought. She was glad Sarah was as useless in the kitchen as she was. And she didn't like quiche anyway. The only thing that was bothering her now was the fact that Sarah had fantastic legs.

'We might have to go out and get something,' Richard offered. Then Sarah came back in a pink terry-towelling dressing gown that made her look even blonder. Like a lot of English people who came to Australia, Sarah was already in the throes of a super-tan. She almost looked Swedish, Bronte thought.

'I'm so sorry,' Sarah stumbled.

'Don't worry,' Bronte said, trying to be nice.

'Can we go somewhere, Richard?' Sarah asked. 'I think I've destroyed dinner.'

'Pub?' he suggested. 'We might as well. If you're staying there, Bronte, we can just get a counter, and then you've got your bag there already.'

'What's a counter again?' Sarah asked, mystified.

'Counter tea,' Bronte explained. 'It's basically five dollars ninety-five for a steak, a pineapple ring and about a kilo of chips.' She wondered if Sarah didn't eat. She looked as if she didn't eat.

'Or you can just have a salad,' she said kindly. 'The only thing is they put this plastic cheese in it. Triangles of plastic cheese.'

'You've destroyed the oven, honey,' Richard said to Sarah, rubbing her arm. Bronte quickly looked away. How dare he do coupley stuff in front of her? She had given him more credit than that, she thought, pushing her glasses up her nose.

Bending down to pick up an oven glove from the kitchen floor, Sarah came back up the other way and saw Bronte's face.

'Actually,' she said, 'Actually, my headache is still there, I think. So if you two just want to go . . .'

There was an embarrassing pause.

'You're really not well, are you?' Richard said

tenderly, rubbing her arm again. He had never thought of Bronte as an aphrodisiac, but seeing her in the kitchen standing next to Sarah just made him want Sarah even more. Especially in the pink dressing gown.

'Would that be all right with you?' Sarah said, quickly checking with Bronte.

'Sure.' Bronte nodded, then realized if she looked too enthusiastic that was just as bad as being put out.

Relieved, Sarah left the room and quickly went back to the bathroom, where she turned the key in the lock, took off her dressing gown and got back in the bath. *It's all too much*, she comforted herself as she slid back into the water, which was now just cold enough to feel like a swimming pool. The way Richard was acting with her in front of Bronte, the look on Bronte's face, the burned quiche, the fact that she'd just appeared half naked in a towel . . . no, she decided. It was better, and much safer, to just vanish in here and fake a headache.

Back in the Jeep again, Richard turned on the air-conditioning and moved dog blankets out of the way as Bronte climbed into the back seat and slumped sideways.

'Not you too?' he said, steering his way out of the drive.

'Well, I hate to say this, but she's not the only one with a headache.'

'What is it?' Richard said, shaking his head. 'Something must be going around.'

'It's called ex-wife meets new wife,' Bronte said.

'That's dramatizing it,' Richard objected.

'She didn't have a headache until I got there. I didn't have a headache until I saw her. You know, this stuff is stressful, Richard.'

'So that's why you didn't come to the wedding.'

'No, I was working!' Bronte lied, closing her eyes and massaging her forehead with one hand.

120

Richard made a noise that sounded like one of his dog patients, Bronte thought, and continued driving in silence until they got to the pub.

'Will I be in time to see Mickey before it gets dark?' Bronte pleaded as they sat down and looked at the blackboard menu. As she had predicted, it consisted of steak with a pineapple ring, cheese salad and – something new – spaghetti bolognaise.

'I think we'd better leave Mickey until tomorrow,' Richard said, deciding against the spaghetti. 'You've got all weekend with him anyway. I'm going to be out doing cattle and Sarah's running around.'

'Where is she running around?' Bronte asked nosily.

'Oh, for God's sake, Bronte, she's just been invited to a couple of barbecues!'

Richard's patience was wearing thin. It was easier, he decided, desexing feral cats than dealing with the weird and subtle world of female politics.

When the waitress came back, neither of them was talking. For a moment, Bronte felt herself transported back in time to 1993, the year that had gone down in history as The Very Bad Year – the year that had finally demolished their marriage. Apart from getting stoned, washing up and weeping, Bronte also remembered a record 28-day silence, when they had both communicated entirely by grunting.

'She seems nice,' Bronte said, trying hard.

'Yes, she is,' her ex-husband said politely. It was decent of Bronte to make the effort, he supposed. It can't have been too easy for her suddenly being introduced to Sarah half naked in a towel.

He hardly thought at all about Bronte these days, but in a towel he imagined she'd come off second best to Sarah. As Harry always said, ever since the divorce Bronte had developed Teletubby tendencies. Trying to turn his attention elsewhere, he looked up at the giant pub video screen.

'Pakistan have come back,' he said, raising his eyebrows.

'Oh God, don't start,' Bronte said. But the uneasiness between them had been broken and by the time the food arrived, she found herself gossiping, as usual, about the magazine while Richard listened, as usual, with half an ear.

'Oh, one thing I have to sort out,' he said, reaching for the salt.

'What's that?' Bronte said, chewing on a rare steak.

'I need to change my will. And for that matter, you should draw one up.'

'Why?' Bronte sat up with a start.

'Well, it's just common sense,' Richard said, surprised at her reaction. 'We never did clear it up after the' – he couldn't say the word 'divorce' – 'after the papers came through. And you don't want your worldly goods going to me any more than I expect you want Sarah to have Mickey. Or do you?'

'No, no,' Bronte shook her head quickly. 'And she doesn't ride anyway, does she?'

Richard shook his head.

'Well then.'

'Good,' he said. 'We can fix it up while you're here if you like. Or, you've got a solicitor in Sydney, haven't you?'

'Sure,' Bronte said, pushing the chips around her plate.

I never think about dying, she realized. *And now I've thought about it twice in one day.*

She looked at Richard for a moment, thought about telling him everything that had happened to her lately, and then changed her mind. He knew cricket and Jeeps and animals, she decided. But nothing else really made sense to him. And he didn't need to hear all her neuroses now that he had someone else's neuroses to look after. And she knew that about Sarah, even though she'd only had five minutes with her in a pink terry-towelling dressing gown. Sarah Kennedy was definitely a worrier, Bronte thought. In fact, in all the years that she had seen her various friends getting married, she had never seen anyone look so bothered by life, weeks after her own wedding.

Yawning at the cricket, which Richard was now totally engrossed by, she poured more tomato sauce on her chips. If Angel appears in front of me now, she decided, I'm going to ring Bernard Bolton up right this minute and tell him to get rid of her.

'Richard?' she interrupted him.

'Mmmm?'

'I don't want to think about making a will now. I'll do it another time. All right?'

'Yup, sure.' He wasn't listening.

'It's too morbid. I'm only forty, I'm not going to die yet.'

'Yup.'

He went back to watching the cricket.

'Everything in my life seems to be about death at the moment,' Bronte said, half talking to herself, half talking to him. 'I'd rather not think about it, that's all.'

But Pakistan's batsman was out, and her ex-husband was a million miles away.

Across town, the sun was setting. It was the mosquito hour, Sarah realized, as she slapped at her legs and ankles and kept walking up the road. She didn't expect Richard back for at least another hour. Just enough time for her to have a stroll, she thought. And if the stroll involved her wandering up Compton Pass near all the good trout streams, and if that meant a chance encounter with Tom, then who was she to argue with fate?

If there was only a small chance of seeing him, she had decided in the bath, then it couldn't be a sin. What was wrong about going for a walk if you had a headache? There was no guarantee that Tom would be waiting at the other end, and if she wanted to get some fresh air after all that smoke in the kitchen then she couldn't see Richard, or indeed God, having any objections.

Now that was an interesting thought. Sarah stopped, scratched a mosquito bite and stared up at a gum tree. If God wanted her and Tom to be together, then surely God would make Tom come out for a walk to the lake, right now? She thought about praying for it, then decided that really would be beyond the pale.

If she saw Tom coming round the corner now, with the sun behind him and his blond hair falling into his eyes, Sarah decided she would take it as a sign. She was so obsessed now, she decided she was almost at the stage where she could start mindlessly pulling petals of daisies and chanting 'He loves me, he loves me not.'

Closing her eyes, she put her hands on her hips and let herself breathe hard as she came to the top of the hill. Lilly Lake was below her now, full of trout as the mosquitoes drew all the fish to the surface. On the coffee shop day, that magical day when Tom had told her all about it, he'd told her how he liked to come down with his rod at sundown and try for all the biggest fish.

I feel like I'm fishing now, she thought. But sometimes, she knew, you could go out for hours and never get a bite. Weighing up her chances, and the time on her watch, she kept walking.

Chapter Eleven

Just after four o'clock the next morning, the rain came bucketing down. In his cabin at the back of his parents' garden, Harry woke to the sound of water gushing out of the downpipes and splashing onto the grass. He had been dreaming about Blondie – quite a good dream, with Debbie Harry in a black beret and a negligee – and he wasn't happy about the interruption.

'Curse the cabin,' he muttered, then squashed his pillow into a peanut-shape, shoved it under his head and tried to ignore the noise.

A few streets away, Richard was snoring into the mattress, holding Sarah to him as he always did. Wide awake, Sarah eased herself away from his arm and gently slid out of bed. The noise of the rain was incredible. Perhaps it was their roof, she thought. It was made out of iron – not like the roofs in London.

He had wanted to make love to her again tonight – and she hadn't. To date, she had successfully got away with it by making excuses about delayed jet lag, and the heat, and the size of the bed, but it didn't feel like any kind of achievement, Sarah thought miserably.

She put on her pink dressing-gown, which was still damp from the bath. It was so humid at the moment too, she thought. Everything stayed wet, or stuck to you. In the distance, she could hear thunder. She wondered if Tom had gone out fishing after all.

After an hour of solid walking the evening before, she had given up and gone home. When Richard had finally returned much later, she had been in bed pretending to be asleep.

Sleep seemed impossible now – the rain on the roof was too noisy and she had too much on her mind. Sighing, Sarah padded downstairs in her bare feet and put the kettle on. She wondered if Tom had woken up too, and if he was staring out of a window somewhere, thinking about her while she was staring out of a window thinking about him.

Across town, Bronte was screaming in her sleep at the end of a nightmare where she was being run down by a pack of white horses. When she woke up mid scream, she realized the windows were rattling with rain and the curtains were wide open. She was unbelievably thirsty.

'Too much beer,' she said aloud, trying to make herself feel normal. The bad dream was Richard's fault, she thought – he had been lining up the stubbies all night and now she had had a nightmare. Feeling her dry mouth, she wandered into the bathroom and found a glass. It was filthy – like most of the glasses at the pub.

She didn't mind staying at the Compton Arms though. It was familiar, and it was quiet – once everyone had gone home – and it was better than staying with Richard or his parents. Swishing hot tap water around the glass in an attempt to sterilize it, she then filled it with cold water. They were on tanks here and Compton rainwater was always sweet. In Sydney, Bronte thought, if you drank tap water you risked having your stomach pumped.

The horse nightmare was still bothering her and her pounding heart would not go away. *Think of something funny*, Bronte told herself, trying desperately to remember bits of old *Seinfeld* episodes – but she still felt rattled.

Yawning, she switched on the main light along with the light in the bathroom, and tried to shake herself out of it. The worst thing about bad dreams was the way she was always paralysed in them. If her arms and legs hadn't been frozen, then she could have run away and the white horses wouldn't have been kicking her to death.

Getting back into bed, she wished she'd bought a normal book at the airport, but she only had her copy of *Your Spirit, Your Soul, Your Self.* She looked at the jacket. Mungo Hyde-Winkler had big, frizzy hair like a young Michael Jackson. He also had a bad Hawaiian shirt on. Could she really read this?

As the thunder kept booming out across the Compton hills, she decided anything was better than lying awake listening to her thudding heart and watching the moths go around the lightbulb. Lying on her side, Bronte found Chapter Four – 'Making Contact with the Other Side':

There will be two occasions in your life when the spirit world makes a special effort to reach you, she read. At birth, and again, at death. When you make the choice to come back to earth as a new baby, with a new life, you are such a recent arrival from the spirit world that even when you are in diapers, your friends from spirit will be here to escort you into your new life.

If there was one word that annoyed Bronte, it was 'diapers'. And she couldn't forget that the author of these wise words had the most stupid name and possibly the worst hairdo in the world.

But she turned the page:

Prior to death, it is common to see, hear or experience spirits in other ways. Many old people who pass away in hospital are dismissed as crazy or senile when they report the presence of those who have died — for example, if Great Uncle Jim is seen standing by the bedside, the patient is often humoured, or even ignored. However, the truth is, Great Uncle Jim has merely announced his presence because he is there to collect his dying relative, and guide him onto his journey into the light. Sightings of spirits in this way are an assurance that death is coming, and should not be feared, but welcomed, as death will soon be the gateway to a new life.

Bronte sighed heavily. 'Thanks for nothing, Mungo,' she said gloomily, hurling the book on the floor.

She now felt even worse than she had before. Outside, the rain was bouncing off the ivy dangling outside her window. Even with all the lights on, she still felt rattled. She had heard that theory before — that the spirits of the dead gathered around the living when it was time for them to go. It had a horrible ring of truth about it and she wondered again about the terrifying plane trip yesterday and Richard's suggestion that she make a will. Most of all though, she wondered about the man sitting behind her on the plane, who claimed to have seen a horse standing in the aisle. No prizes for guessing which horse, Bronte thought.

Turning onto her right side, Bronte yanked her nightie round — as usual it had ridden up and she was now cutting off the circulation in her arm. Sleeping was out of the question, she decided.

She wondered how most women died at forty. Breast cancer, she supposed. Or car accidents. Or heart attacks. She pinched the fat on her stomach. She would probably be a prime candidate. She imagined dying of a heart attack during a *Fifty Things To Do With Bananas* meeting and sighed. It would be just her luck to have a trivial death.

The problem with dying, Bronte decided, was that it could happen at any time. She had no guarantees that it would not. The thought had never really occurred to her before. She had managed to reach forty without seriously thinking about death at all. But now it seemed like a reality, and seeing Angel again had brought it all home.

There was nothing safe about her life, Bronte decided. A bolt of lightning could come straight in through the window and strike her dead right now. The plane back to Sydney might crash after all. If she went out on Mickey tomorrow, who was to say that he might not bolt and throw her straight into a concrete wall?

She thought about Mickey for a moment, remembering his brown, friendly face. What would happen to him if she died? She had paid Richard one hundred dollars a month to contribute to his feed and stabling since the divorce. She supposed she would have to leave Richard something more, just to keep on looking after him. Angel had died young, but Mickey could live for years. Bronte made a quick calculation. Maybe if Richard cashed in her superannuation, she could afford it. Plus she'd have to get all her credit card bills paid off. Bronte thought about the new Alannah Hill skirt she had bought last week. It had sent her card over the limit. But what good would that do her, she thought miserably, if she were about to die? Unless they buried her in it, there was no point in Alannah Hill skirts or anything else in life, for that matter.

Staring at the moths as they circled the lightbulb, she willed them to bump into the globe so they could put themselves out of their misery. Better to fry now than to go through the torture of almost frying, she thought.

Someone had told her that if you made a will, you had to say if you wanted to be cremated or buried. She had already decided, years ago, that she would be cremated.

That way they could scatter her ashes over the back of the Compton Track, where she had spent so many years with Angel and Mickey – and in happier times, Richard.

She wondered if her parents would want some of the ashes to take back to their local church in Melbourne. Her parents weren't religious, though. Bronte made a face at the thought of her ashes ending up in a jar on the mantelpiece at home. Knowing her mother, she would probably drop them all over the kitchen floor and they'd end up being mopped with Ajax.

Bronte thought about Sarah riding Mickey and decided she couldn't stand it. Were you allowed to put nasty things in your will?, she wondered. She knew you were in Agatha Christie books. She would feel much better if the bit about giving Richard money to feed and stable Mickey was accompanied by another bit banning Sarah from having him too.

Sighing, Bronte sat up in bed and folded her arms. She was getting goose pimples now – either she was scaring herself or the rain was bringing the temperature down. Getting up, she found a two-bar electric heater in the back of the wardrobe, along with a condom left by a previous guest. She looked at the date on the condom – 'Use by 9.98'. Probably the last time she'd had sex, she realized. How sad to die now, with sex just a distant memory. And how sad to realize that it had been with a man with small feet and a lava lamp.

Even worse, she knew that he had meant so little to her – and she to him – that he wouldn't even be at her funeral. Staring at the ceiling, she tried to work out who would.

Richard, of course. That went without saying. And

her parents and her sister and all her nieces and nephews – though probably not her sister's ex-husband, who hated her because she'd always beat him at Monopoly. Richard's parents and Tom, Annie and Harry would come to her funeral, Bronte thought. For a moment, she wondered if Richard would bring Sarah. Or would his new wife offer to stay at home so that he, Richard, could mourn his first wife in private?

To her horror, Bronte realized she had a tear in her eye. Oh God, she was feeling sorry for herself now. She brushed it away, feeling pathetic.

The rain was still pounding the ivy outside the window. Scrambling in her bag for her diary, Bronte also found a Biro and sucked the end of it thoughtfully as she made an inventory of all her possessions. She might as well make an attempt at a will, she thought – while it was on her mind.

How much did she have in her bank account? Not enough to pay off her credit card, she realized. Then there was the mortgage and the fact that she hadn't paid her cable TV bill for two months.

'ASSETS', she wrote, determined to forget about these annoyances. Then she realized she couldn't think of anything except her microwave oven and her Esprit denim skirt. To Laura, she wrote next, copy of my 1998 *Let's Go Europe.* Well, she was always talking about going on holiday. She decided to throw in her aromatherapy burner as well. Laura went in for all that kind of smelly girlie stuff.

So far so good, Bronte thought. What next? There were annoying things in her flat like scratched Pretenders albums and shower curtains and director's chairs from Freedom Furniture that she was sure nobody would want.

It was important to make a will, she remembered, because if you didn't, the government got everything. She had a mental picture of John Howard sitting on

131

one of her director's chairs from Freedom Furniture listening to her Pretenders albums and decided she had better give all the small things to St Vincent de Paul. Or Harry – he was always shopping there so it amounted to the same thing. Perhaps she could give him the chairs. She certainly couldn't give him the 1998 *Let's Go Europe* – he never went anywhere.

While the thunder rolled and boomed across the back of Compton, Bronte continued to make her list. In a strange way, she realized, it was actually cheering her up. There was nothing quite like the feeling you got from knowing how pleased someone would be when they found out they'd got your Alessi kettle after you were dead. Equally, nothing could be more satisfying than leaving people *off* your will. Especially if they thought they might be *on*.

By the time the sun had come up, the rain had stopped – but Bronte was still writing.

Would it be enough, though? she wondered. Possessions and money were all very well, but if she were going to die, there were still some things she had to say to people.

And more to the point, Bronte realized, *how am I going to spend the time I've got left?*

Biting her lip at this new worry, she rolled over onto her left side. She was beginning to get pins and needles now and a headache as well. She got up and poured herself another glass of water from the bathroom tap. The three moths, which had been hanging around the lightbulb all night, were now dead on the floor.

Looking in the mirror, she decided she looked fifty, not forty. Staying up all night was something she couldn't afford to do any more. Bronte found herself looking for the bones of her skull, behind her eyes and cheeks. What sort of corpse would she make? She shivered and kicked the pins and needles out of her leg.

It was only when she switched off both the bathroom

light and the main light that she realized Angel had been there all the time, standing behind the bed.

'Oh, hello,' Bronte said. 'It's you.'

Then she screamed, kicked her glass of water over and ran out of the room.

Chapter Twelve

It was still raining a few weeks later at the opening of the seventy-seventh annual Compton Show. Standing at the front gates in the mud, Harry was disappointed to see a placard announcing that the medieval display and jousting had been cancelled.

'I suppose their armour got soggy,' Pippin said, twisting her woolly hat round on her head.

'It's pathetic,' declared Harry. 'Did a bit of rain stop Henry V from displaying and jousting? I don't think so.'

'I got a show programme,' Pippin said, waving it at him and hoping to cheer him up. But when Harry read through it, there was no mention of We've Got Blondie's Drumsticks And We're Going To Use Them, even though they were set to play at 4 p.m., after the Grand Parade.

'I find it hard to believe that they think "Novelty Door Stop Judging, Any Medium" is more interesting to people than live music,' Harry complained, stabbing a finger at the programme. 'But according to the dickhead who printed this, the novelty door stop judging is of great importance. In fact, they've written it in fancy letters.'

Pippin took the programme back.

'We're not in it anywhere,' she agreed, checking the

134

pages and making a sympathetic face. 'Oh look, there's a $25 cash prize for the best coathanger cover made by a senior citizen aged sixty-five and over.'

'That's more than I'm getting for the whole afternoon,' Harry sighed. 'Come on, let's set the gear up. I want to get it over and done with.'

Harry knew that all bands had to suffer on their way to the top – as Bon Scott had once sung, it was a long way to the shop if you wanted a sausage roll. He doubted that AC/DC had ever put up with this kind of indignity.

'Novelty Door Stop, Any Medium!' Harry whispered to himself, trying to absorb the full horror of it.

In the Poultry Pavilion, Witchy Wendy Wagner was looking at a prize-winning Khaki Campbell duck, wondering if it would be cruel to suddenly pluck a feather out of its bottom. Duck feathers – especially fresh ones – were ideal for money spells, according to the latest issue of *International Witch Quarterly*, and her bank balance had sunk below fifty dollars again.

The Poultry Pavilion stank, she decided. She didn't know how people could stand keeping chickens. The Rhode Island Reds were OK looking and some of the White Leghorns were pretty. But the noise and the smell were too much for her. She decided to wander over to the Photography Hall and see if any of her pictures had won a prize. She thought her self-portrait with red candles would at least get a Highly Commended. It had taken her hours to set the timer, light the candles and run back to the couch in time for the camera to capture the shot. A rosette would be nice after all that trouble, she thought. And a twenty-dollar runner's-up reward would be even better.

While Pippin set her drum kit up on the platform next to the Jams, Jellies and Preserves exhibition hall, Harry wandered over to the photography judging. It was about the most interesting thing at the show, he decided. The rest of it was just horrible – a tidal wave of pickled onions, shortbread and poncey little teenagers on ponies. Richard enjoyed the show, but only because it meant more business for him.

Staring at a wall of landscape photography, Witchy Wendy Wagner yawned.

Seeing her, Harry beat off a wave of longing – and a blushing attack – and went over.

'Hi,' he said, tossing his head, which he always did when he was nervous. 'Haven't seen you since the wedding.'

He wished he'd worn his brown suit with the orange ruffled shirt again. Instead he was wearing only his second-best band outfit – a black suit and skinny black tie, with white sandshoes.

'Did you see my photo?' Wendy asked.

'Which one?'

'Well, I entered three – me with my pentacle neck-lace, me with my crystals, and me with my red candles – but they only stuck up the pentacle one because in the others I haven't got my bra on.'

'Don't worry,' Harry said, trying to pretend he hadn't heard this last piece of trouser-torturing information. 'You think you've got problems – We've Got Blondie's Drumsticks And We're Going To Use Them aren't even in the bloody programme this year!' He tutted dramatically and tossed his head again.

Despite the heat, Wendy was wearing a low-cut purple velvet dress with criss-cross lacing down the front. She had also crimped her hair and dyed it red and plastered what smelled like patchouli oil over her neck. He supposed it was glamour on a budget. He knew how broke she always was because he had to check all her withdrawal slips.

She smiled at him.

'I'm really looking forward to seeing you play,' she said.

'Oh well – thanks,' Harry replied, trying to sound modest and failing.

'You know what I like best? Your original songs,' Wendy went on. 'I think you've got real talent.'

'Well, I think so too,' Harry said, getting it wrong.

'No – I mean, I think you've got real talent. In your photography. And your modelling too!'

This time he could not beat off his blushes and so he had to turn away, pretending he had suddenly seen something fascinating on the other side of the room.

'Seascapes!' he yelled unconvincingly, stalking off in the opposite direction and fighting his tight black pants, which were pulling the other way. 'I love seascapes! They're much better than landscapes!'

Smiling to herself, Wendy waved and went back to her self-portrait. It was typical of the old farmers who ran the Compton Show, she thought, not to hang up any of her nude shots.

Looking for Harry, Pippin rushed in through the back entrance, ignoring a sign which read 'DO NOT ENTER'.

'Harry!' she yelled, shouting across three walls of photographs.

'What?' he yelled back, coming over.

'They've cancelled it,' she said, panting. 'They just told me. They reckon we can't run the cables through the wet grass, someone's going to get electrocuted.'

Harry rolled his eyes and looked up at the ceiling. Then he looked down at his white sandshoes, which were rapidly turning grey in the muddy grass.

'How come the woodchopping hasn't been cancelled?' he said.

'Huh?' Pippin gave him a look.

'What's more dangerous – giving some neolithic, pea-brained, eighteenth-century convict throwback Tasmanian an axe in the pouring rain and telling him to stand on one leg and chop like a maniac, or running a cable on a bit of wet grass?'

'Well, I don't know,' said Pippin, noticing something

much more interesting on the other side of the room. 'Oh look, there's Wendy!'

Watching her go, Harry tutted. This should have been their final gig for the year – a grand finale. Now the band would go out with a whimper – unless a miracle happened and the bank asked them to play at its Christmas party. Harry had practised a special version of '(I'm Always Touched By Your) Presence Dear' for weeks. He had even learned to play the harmonica without getting itchy lips. And now, nothing. He swore aloud, shocking a toddler standing on the other side of the seascape exhibit.

'Do you mind?' said the toddler's mother angrily.

'No!' Harry muttered as she seized her child by the hand and took it away. 'No, I don't bloody mind at all, as a matter of fact.'

He was pissed off now, he decided. Seriously pissed off. And what about their fans? At least four people had come into the bank in the past fortnight, promising to turn up. Swearing again, he stuck his hands in his pockets and was on the verge of stalking out of the room when he saw Witchy Wendy Wagner standing very close to Pippin, who appeared to be fiddling with the criss-cross stitching on the front of Wendy's purple velvet dress.

'Greetings,' Harry said, marching across the room and interrupting them. He was already having a crap day, he decided. He wasn't going to make it worse by letting Pippin nab Wendy. He was sure that Witchy Wendy Wagner liked him. Certainly she was no Debbie Harry – if anything, the crimped hair and patchouli oil reminded him just a little too strongly of Stevie Nicks – but Wendy wanted him, he was sure of that. And now he really, really wanted her.

He had been celibate for so long that his common sense had now given way to his boxer shorts, which were on a private mission that had nothing to do with his brain.

138

'Pippin's been seeing a woman in Ulverstone,' he said meaningfully to Wendy, patting his drummer on the shoulder as if to congratulate her.

'No I haven't, Harry,' Pippin said, pulling away. 'I haven't been seeing anyone. In fact, I was just telling Wendy how lonely I've been since Nathan moved to the mainland.'

Nathan was one of Pippin's occasional male conquests. He had been famous in the Compton cricket team for having a face like a tea-tray.

'But I thought you told me you were *definitely* shagging that woman from Ulverstone?' Harry exclaimed in mock surprise.

'I don't shag,' Pippin said. 'You shag, your brother's horses shag, I . . . *make love.*'

Harry checked Wendy's face to see if she was as sickened by this last statement as he was, but instead, she was staring straight at Pippin as if she had never met anyone more fascinating in her life.

'The gig's been cancelled,' Harry told Wendy, hoping to distract her. 'Sorry – there's nothing I could do about it.' He looked hard at Pippin for a moment.

'Wendy said she was looking forward to hearing all my originals,' he said.

'And your drumming,' Wendy said quickly, noticing Pippin's face. 'Your drumming is just fantastic. It complements Harry's songs so well.'

Above their heads, the rain pelted down. Through the doors, Harry could see a crowd of people running in from the tea tent with sagging paper plates and soggy bits of carrot cake.

'I'll tell you what,' Wendy said suddenly. 'Why don't we just get out of here and go for a drive?'

Running her fingers through her crimped hair, she looked first at Harry, who was nodding enthusiastically at her, then at Pippin, who had fixed her with a deliberate smile.

'I've got lots of tapes in the car,' Wendy said. 'We

could go down to Lilly Creek or something.'

And take all our clothes off, Harry thought, filling in the rest of the sentence for her. It would have to be him or Pippin in the water, though. The three of them weren't going in together – he couldn't stand the thought of Pippin bobbing around in the water with her woolly hat on.

Together, the three of them left the photography exhibition. On the way, Pippin stopped at the Compton CWA stall to buy a plate of cakes and biscuits.

'I thought you had a sugar allergy,' Harry said, staring.

'Chocolate crackles, lamingtons and white christmas,' Pippin said, ignoring him. 'Yum, yum. You can't even buy this stuff any more – I'm making the most of it.'

'What about when your face swells up and you can't breathe any more?' Harry asked. But Pippin was gone, striding ahead of him in the rain with Witchy Wendy Wagner at her side.

Wendy's VW Beetle was parked next to a sign that read 'THIS WAY TO THE LIVE ENTERTAINMENT'. Harry supposed that this had meant him and Pippin, about ten minutes ago.

'It's such a shame they had to cancel everything,' Wendy said, with a sympathetic look at Harry. He melted, willing himself not to, but failing. It had been a very long time since any woman, apart from his mother, had been this nice to him. Wendy wasn't so scary after all, he decided. The witchcraft thing was probably just a hobby – like dressmaking.

'Love your V-Dub,' Pippin announced, patting the bonnet of Wendy's beaten-up car, which she appeared to have painted with a can of green house paint. 'And look at that!' Pippin exclaimed, peering through the windscreen at a huge green crystal on a blue cord, dangling from the rear-vision mirror. Harry noticed that Pippin wasn't actually doing anything about getting in the car. She was probably waiting for him to get in the back so that she could share the front with Wendy, he thought gloomily. The trouble with being a man, he decided, was that you couldn't force issues like car entry. So, with the rain splashing onto his back, he swung himself into the back seat, nearly braining himself on another crystal, which was dangling from Wendy's rear window.

He couldn't help thinking that all of Wendy's crystals and incantations – including the 'Threefold, threefold, threefold' she always did at the bank – were a waste of time. He had seen her bank balance last Friday and it had been about thirty dollars. Then again, perhaps Witchy Wendy Wagner just specialized in sex spells, he thought. If that was the case, she was certainly succeeding with Pippin, who couldn't stop staring at her. *And me*, he thought, feeling annoyed with himself. He knew he could kick the feeling if he tried – he was used to doing that after thirty years of living on the same planet as women. It was just that Witchy Wendy Wagner was still so very nearly in the bag, that to let Pippin win now would be like Winston Churchill surrendering to the Luftwaffe.

Only one of Wendy's windscreen wipers was working, but her tape deck – which seemed to be held together with sticky tape – made up for it. The speakers, Harry was surprised to see, were Sony. And the sound was incredibly rich and loud – much better than the tinny sound his parents got in their car.

'What's this?' Pippin said as an unfamiliar song hit her ears.

'Brecht,' Harry and Wendy said in unison. There was a pause as Wendy turned around in the driver's seat and stared at Harry, while he stared back, smiling.

'"The Bilbao Song" by Brecht,' Harry breathed. 'Blondie's first song the night they opened for The

Heartbreakers at Max's. Debbie wore a zebra-print dress.'

'When you were about three years old,' Pippin said sourly, hating the way that Harry and Wendy both knew the same song and she didn't. 'Anyway, what's the big whoop about Brecht?'

'I was six years old, not three, as a matter of fact,' Harry said. 'And if you don't know what the big whoop is, I'm not going to explain it to you.'

Apparently noticing nothing, Wendy turned back to the road again and hung tightly onto the steering wheel as a ute passed them on the road, spraying dirty orange water up against the windows.

'Let me show you something,' Harry said, addressing Wendy from the back seat.

'What's that?' she murmured, turning her head slightly.

Opening his black dinner jacket, Harry solemnly revealed a purple badge that read 'DEBBIE HARRY IN THE FLESH', stuck to his inside pocket.

'Wow,' Wendy breathed and turned around again.

'Do you like Courtney Love?' Pippin asked Wendy suddenly, fumbling for more cassette tapes and brushing her hand against her leg.

'Courtney Love is Pippin's answer to everything,' Harry said in a patronizing voice, but just as he was about to lead the conversation back to Blondie, Wendy let out a long, low moan.

'*Oh God*,' she whispered. 'Don't even *talk* to me about Courtney Love!'

Pippin ejected the tape with Brecht's 'Bilbao Song' on it, and immediately put on Hole instead.

'Eric Erlandson, Patty Schemel and Melissa Auf der Maur,' Pippin sighed. 'The greatest line-up Courtney Love ever had. Listen to this, Harry. You might learn something.'

Sitting in the back seat, Harry could see Wendy nodding vigorously in time to the music.

'If Courtney Love took a ten-year course in Being Boring she would still not scrape a pass,' Pippin said.

Dumbfounded, Harry stared at a field full of wet cows. Where the hell had she got that one from? One of his music magazines?

It was now raining so hard that Wendy's one windscreen wiper looked like it might snap with the strain. Outside, Harry could see more black clouds scooting behind them. It would be freezing in Lilly Creek, he decided. He wasn't going in. In fact, he might go home. Yes, that was it. He'd ask Wendy to drop him off.

Then, suddenly, she turned around in her seat and gave him the best smile he'd seen all day. 'Of course, Courtney Love isn't a patch on Debbie Harry,' she said sweetly. She had dimples, Harry suddenly noticed. He had been so distracted by her general witchiness, he hadn't seen them before.

'Wow, can I marry you?' he said quickly. Just for a second, though, he almost heard himself meaning it. On Harry's soulmate checklist, rating Debbie over Courtney was worth at least twelve hundred points.

'Harry says that to all the girls,' Pippin said grimly, turning up the volume on the Hole tape. 'You've got something on your cheek, Wendy. It looks like jam or something . . . Leaning over, she tenderly licked her finger and dabbed at Wendy's face. In the back, Harry wrinkled his nose in disgust. And *that* is something that *you* always do with all the girls, he thought – the old jam on the face trick – but of course he couldn't say anything because it wouldn't be gentlemanly.

Gazing at a field full of sodden sheep, Harry decided – not for the first time – that gentlemanliness needed to be stamped out. He was fed up with letting Pippin walk all over him, and he was fed up with opening doors for silly women with prams at the bank. Where had all this gentlemanliness started anyway? he wondered. It was probably the Scarlet Pimpernel's fault. Either that or Sir Walter Raleigh. He wished there was an equivalent for women – some pain-in-the-arse set of rules that meant they always had to take the bad seat in the car, or stand holding a door open, or give up their seat on the bus. Even if there was, Pippin wouldn't subscribe to it. That much, he knew. Harry stared at the back of her woolly hat with disgust.

Wendy's home-taping technique seemed to be quite erratic, Harry noticed. They had already heard half a Hole album and now, without warning, they were being launched into something that sounded strangely like a ukelele solo.

'Mmm, what's that?' purred Pippin. 'Sounds great!'

'Well it's me,' Witchy Wendy Wagner said, changing gears and sounding shyer than usual. 'It's me with my ukelele.'

Harry could now practically feel Cupid tearing his trousers off. It was just too much. She preferred Debbie Harry to Courtney Love, she knew about Brecht and she played the ukelele. He wanted to wind down the back window – rain or no rain – and scream with joy. Instead, he said, 'Wendy, did you know that David Bowie apparently wrote "Lust For Life" for Iggy Pop on a ukelele while he was watching TV in a German hotel room?'

'Wow,' said Pippin, despite herself. It was the kind of boring fact you could rely upon Harry to give you, but even she had to admit she was impressed.

'Wow,' said Wendy, swerving to avoid a pothole and peering over her one windscreen wiper.

Wow, thought Harry, leaning into the window, unable to take his eyes off the back of Wendy's head and feeling the cold glass against his face. He had changed his mind about Lilly Creek after all. But first, he had to get rid of Pippin.

'Oh,' Pippin said suddenly, turning round to look at Harry.

'What?' he said bluntly.

'I think I'm getting a reaction to the chocolate crackles.'

'Are you?' Harry said, suspiciously.

'Or maybe the white christmas,' Pippin said. 'Something I ate, anyway.'

'I told you your face would swell up if you had sugar,' Harry said unsympathetically.

'Do you want me to run you home?' Wendy offered, 'I don't mind.'

'Thanks,' Pippin sighed. 'Only, Harry . . .'

'What?' he said.

'You'll have to get the gear by yourself – but it's OK,' she added, seeing his face. 'You can borrow my ute and drive it all back from the showgrounds. I'll give you the keys. Here . . .' she threw her keyring, which had a skull on it, into Harry's lap. 'Wendy, do you think we could drop Harry back at the showgrounds?'

'Sure,' Wendy murmured, swinging the steering wheel around in the rain.

Sinking into the back seat, Harry pressed his face into the glass while Wendy put another tape on.

'This is a bootleg tape I got on the Internet,' she said, trying to cheer Harry up. She realized he had gone strangely quiet. 'Do you know it?'

Harry didn't. It sounded vaguely like Blondie singing 'Anarchy in the UK' with Joan Jett and what seemed to be Clem Burke singing 'I Wanna Be Your Dog'. Despite this, he couldn't get excited. The bootleg tape was just another reason to want Witchy Wendy Wagner, he decided. And now he couldn't have her because he was going back to the showgrounds and Pippin was being driven home.

'How's the allergy?' he called to Pippin from his slumped position in the back seat.

Pippin ran her hand down her throat speculatively. 'I'm not sure,' she said. 'I think the sooner Wendy can get me home the better.'

'Can't go swimming in Lilly Creek then,' Harry said

quickly, 'if your face is swelling up. Don't your ankles swell up as well? The last time you had chocolate crackles you had legs like Henry VIII.'

'Don't be such a bastard,' Pippin pouted.

A vision of Pippin and Witchy Wendy Wagner kissing at Lilly Creek and steaming up the Volkswagen windows swam before Harry's eyes. He could have kicked the floor in frustration, even though the rest of him wanted to listen to the rare treat of what sounded like Clem Burke singing 'I Wanna Be Your Dog'. *Damn* Pippin! The trouble was, her allergies were genuine. She always kept medication on the floor next to her drum pedals. It's just that she had selective allergies, Harry thought bitterly – it always seemed to directly relate to her love life. The man with the face like a tea-tray had also suffered from Pippin's selective allergies, if he remembered correctly.

'It must be terrible living with that,' Wendy said, sounding concerned as she reversed the car.

Terrible living with what? Harry thought moodily. Chronic bisexuality, bad drumming, crap taste in music or habitual lying?

There was no way around it, though. He couldn't argue with Pippin and if she wasn't going to drive their gear home, then it was down to him. Some passing pony club girl might trample all over his microphone.

'Sorry,' Pippin said, wheezing slightly above the noise of the rain.

'It's OK,' Wendy reassured her – and Harry caught her dimples again in the rear-view mirror.

'So we'll just drop you, is that OK?' Wendy asked, talking to Harry and looking at the road ahead.

'Yeah, sure, whatever,' he said. Then he cheered up, suddenly thinking of something.

'What about we catch up later, though,' he said to Wendy casually, 'after you've taken Pippin home?'

'Oh,' Wendy said, turning her head slightly. 'I'd really like to, Harry, but I can't. I've got ukelele practice.'

'Yes, Harry,' Pippin added. 'You can't keep her away from that. She might be trying to learn a Blondie song or something. Sheesh!'

She shook her head and put her hand on Wendy's knee. 'Do you realize that Harry hasn't listened to any music since 1980?' she sighed. 'And do you realize that he was only born in 1970?'

'What about the Blondie comeback album!' Harry yelled from the back. 'I bought that!'

But Pippin's head was close to Wendy's now and they were giggling, oblivious to Harry as the rain thundered onto the roof of the Volkswagen.

He knew a lost cause when he saw one. Whatever Pippin was whispering into Wendy's ear was obviously a lot more interesting than anything he had to say. Soon he would be stuck in a wet paddock at the showgrounds, dragging huge amplifiers into the back of a ute, with four thousand members of the Compton CWA getting in the way – and Pippin would be having her puffy chest massaged by Wendy in the front seat of the car. That was the way life was. That was the way it *always* was.

If you were any kind of man, Harry thought gloomily, you'd have some kind of macho James Bond solution for this terrible situation. But he didn't. And he couldn't see himself getting one in the next forty-five minutes. Admitting defeat, he closed his eyes and thought of Debbie Harry in a black beret singing 'Call Me' in French, as Wendy's one windscreen wiper pounded backwards and forwards.

Chapter Thirteen

There were many amazing things about Australia, Sarah thought, but nothing was more amazing than the fact that you could buy Yellow-Footed Rock-Wallaby chocolate bars, and for that matter, Eastern Barred Bandicoot chocolate bars. Cadbury's in England was nothing like this, she decided, throwing the wrappers in the bin.

Crossing the road in the centre of town, she headed into the second-hand bookshop. She knew the woman by now – and her dog, Beryl, who seemed to be suffering from either continual worms or glandular problems.

'Hello, Sarah,' the woman said as Beryl thumped her tail on the rug. 'Long time no see. How's Dick?'

'Richard's good,' Sarah said, meaningfully.

'Tell him Beryl's going to need her anal glands seen to soon,' the woman said cheerfully.

Sarah smiled to herself and started wandering up and down the aisles.

'Just browsing?' the woman asked.

'Yep,' Sarah replied, wishing she would go away. She was glad she hadn't ended up working here. It would have driven her mad.

The gardening shelves were crammed with books that had been stacked sideways and back to front. Pulling them out, one after the other, Sarah quickly realized that what she wanted wasn't here. She had imagined she might find some leatherbound volume of old botanical prints or some rare Tasmanian first-edition lithographs. Instead it all seemed to be rubbish about cactuses and bonsai.

Tom would not be impressed, she decided. And she wasn't going to give him some tatty book about fruit-fly on his birthday.

Wandering around the shelves, she passed the small section labelled 'SELF-HELP', where she had found *Relating and Mating*. She had since thrown it out, without Richard seeing.

The shop was a mess, she decided. Books on dogs seemed to be sticking out of every section on the shelves and old copies of the *Compton Gazette* lay in piles all over the floor.

Finally, Sarah found what she was looking for. 'FISH', someone had written in texta on the shelf and, for once, it was a true statement. Bending down, Sarah could see books on barramundi and Murray cod, and rainbow trout and John Dory. Once again, though, the leather-bound, gold-embossed antique she had in mind wasn't there. So much for her fantasies about finding a first edition of *The Compleat Angler*, she thought, stretching up and hearing her knees click.

And then she bit her lip hard as the back of a familiar blond head appeared at the end of the aisle.

'Tom?'

He took a step back and peered around the shelves. Then, when he saw her, he smiled. It's like seeing the sun again, Sarah thought. It seemed like years since they had been alone together. 'I was just getting your birthday present,' she said, so shocked to see him that she found herself blurting out the truth.

Tom raised his eyebrows. 'Really?'

'From Richard and me,' she lied automatically.

She stood still as Tom walked over to her side and stood behind her, inspecting the shelves.

'Well, I was just in here getting a birthday present for myself,' he smiled. Trying not to register how close he was to her, Sarah grabbed the book he was holding out. It was a poetry book, she realized.

He shrugged. 'I used to spend my money on whisky, now I spend it on poetry,' he replied.

For a minute, neither of them spoke. Sarah found herself staring mindlessly at a book called *The Elusive Snapper* while she fought off her desire to know more about him. Richard never told her anything about Tom – or anyone else, for that matter.

Suddenly Sarah realized that the woman behind the counter was eavesdropping and she gestured towards the doorway.

'Shall we get a coffee or something?' she said.

Tom breathed in sharply. 'I told Annie I'd get back,' he said.

'Just a quick coffee? Or I'll never know what to get you for your birthday,' Sarah said.

As they crossed the road, Sarah noticed he was wearing new boots – his beaten-up brown Hush Puppies had gone.

'Annie bought them,' Tom explained. 'Late Christmas present – they're Blundstones.'

Sarah tried not to let her heart sink too much at this information and pulled her hair forward. It was quite long now, and the sun had turned it blonder than ever.

'How is Annie?' she said automatically as Tom pulled out a chair for her in the cafe.

I know that he knows that I know that this is the place where we spent hours that day, Sarah thought.

'She's good,' he said, sitting down opposite her. 'And how are you?'

'Oh, fine,' Sarah said.

'You seem a bit – I dunno, bothered.'

'Oh no.'

Tom shrugged.

They ordered two coffees and Sarah crossed her legs,

150

wishing she was wearing something better than her old black pants from the last Jigsaw sale.

'I really do want to get you a nice birthday present,' she said at last. It was hard trying not to stare at him.

'I don't think Richard's remembered my birthday for years,' he said, half laughing. 'It must be your good influence.'

Sarah smiled and said nothing.

'The only thing I want for my birthday is an AA,' Tom said, taking his coffee from the waitress.

'AA?' Thinking he meant Alcoholics Anonymous, Sarah felt herself blushing.

'*Angler's Almanac*,' Tom explained.

'Oh.'

Sarah gazed out of the window, sipping her coffee. If Annie or Richard ran into them now, what then? But there was nothing going on here, she thought – nothing at all. And that was the whole problem.

She had planned Tom's birthday for weeks, ever since she had seen it scrawled in the back of one of Richard's old school yearbooks. In her daydreams, Tom was always at home in the garden when she arrived with his present – and Annie was always away – in America, or on the mainland.

'Where do I get *Angler's Almanac* from?' Sarah asked, and this time it was Tom's turn to be embarassed.

'Just at the newsagent's,' he shrugged. 'It's nothing much. You don't have to. I was just joking.'

'No, let's get it!' Sarah said, suddenly realizing that this meant she could stretch out her time with him even further.

Tom let it go and he stirred his coffee, making sure the froth went right down to the bottom. They never made coffee properly here – it was always better at home.

'I've been thinking about you,' he said suddenly, still staring at his cup.

Sarah breathed in and looked at him.

'Just wondering how you're getting on, how you're fitting in,' he added. Then he looked up at her and realized she was staring at him.

'Oh, it's fine, I'm fine,' she insisted. 'Compton takes a bit of getting used to after London, but you can leave your back door unlocked, I suppose, and I could never do that at home.'

This time, it was Tom's turn to stare. Her skin was incredible, he thought. On her wedding day it had been like looking at a photograph, not a real woman – and now it was golden, from the sun.

'And they play folk music in the supermarket and you get these amazing chocolate bars called bandicoots and possums and hairy-nosed wombats,' Sarah continued. 'At home you only get Fry's Turkish Delight,' she babbled on, 'and that's about as exciting as chocolate gets. Oh God, I just called it home, didn't I? I must be more homesick than I thought.'

'Are you homesick?' Tom asked, seriously.

'Oh yeah. A bit,' Sarah said, unable to look at him. Why, when Richard asked her this same question, did it fail to move her? Now she felt like telling Tom everything. It was like he could see into her soul, she thought.

'When Annie first came to Tasmania she was homesick,' Tom said kindly.

But Sarah did not want to know about Annie and she changed the subject. 'Let's go and find this *Angler's Almanac* then,' she said.

However, when Tom led her to the newsagent's to find it, Sarah was disappointed. The price sticker read $3.50 – not the priceless antiquarian volume she had imagined at all – and it only seemed to be like a glorified diary of good times to go fishing.

She tried to lean over Tom's shoulder as he flicked through the back of the book. He smelled of lemon, she decided – and bed.

'See, it's all about the moon,' he explained. 'That's what these charts show. When you see Moon Above or Moon Below, you know it's time to go fishing.'

Sarah nodded, smiling, and not listening to a word he was saying. Then Tom saw someone waving at him – it looked like yet another member of the Compton cricket team, Sarah decided.

'Back in a tick,' Tom said, handing her the little yellow book. Sarah sighed and looked at the drawings of fish in the middle. Eel was described as a 'worthwhile table offering' which, when she thought of the jellied eel she'd had in London once, made her feel sick.

Then she thought of something. Taking the book to the cash register, she also bought a pen and scribbled in the back.

When Tom returned, she also had a birthday card for him. 'There,' she said, handing it over. 'Don't open it until Wednesday.'

'Thanks,' Tom said. 'I don't deserve it.'

'Of course you do,' Sarah said. 'You're Tom. You deserve everything.'

Then they left the newsagent's and Tom found his car – which was actually Annie's car, Sarah realized, from the piles of sculpture magazines on the back seat. He probably didn't have a car, she thought. But this was yet another thing she could find reasons not to care about. It would have mattered to her in London, but it didn't matter here.

'I'll see you later,' Tom said, standing with one hand on the door handle.

'I'd love to catch up for dinner,' Sarah said.

'I never know if that means tea or lunch,' Tom replied.

'Whatever you like!' Sarah said, trying to sound lighthearted. But she knew, from long experience, that this moment was crucial. This was where things either stopped, stalled or started.

'I'll give you a call sometime,' Tom promised – and her heart shot through the side of her ribs, even though she knew his promise would come back to torture her later.

'Don't forget, you can't open anything until Wednesday!' Sarah called as he put the keys in the ignition.

Winding the window down, Tom waved and grinned.

'Thanks!' he yelled, then he drove away – as far as Sarah was concerned, to the other end of the world. Watching him go, she wondered if she had gone mad all over again, and then decided that even if she had, it was worth it, just to feel alive. Later that night, when Annie was in bed, Tom sat up watching TV with the brown paper bag from the newsagent's in his lap. Sarah was a funny girl, he thought. There was something so quaint and old-fashioned about being banned from seeing your birthday present before your birthday – even though he had already seen it, which made the whole thing even more odd. Without thinking, he ripped the paper bag open. There was a card in there too, marked to him in Sarah's beautiful, neat handwriting.

In the next room, he could hear the faint sounds of Annie's radio playing classical music. She was probably already asleep, he thought. He didn't like to think about her getting older, but she seemed to be going to bed earlier these days.

The card was probably the best thing Sarah had been able to come up with from the limited range at the Compton Newsagency. It showed a cat watching a goldfish in a bowl and had the usual loopy writing inside, wishing him all the best and many happy returns. If Annie saw it she would hate it immediately, Tom knew. He had already found her birthday card to him – a screenprinted design made by one of her artist friends on the mainland.

'To Tom,' Sarah's card read. 'With much love and

thanks for your friendship, which means so much. May all your dreams come true, Sarah.' She hadn't put Richard's name anywhere, Tom noticed.

Then he opened his *Angler's Almanac.* She had taken the price sticker off, which he also thought was funny as they'd both known how much it had cost. Sarah Kennedy was, he realized, a very odd girl. Then he noticed something else – she had put a circle around Sunday the 2nd, underlining the Moon Above time, 9.02 a.m. Next to it she had written 'Lilly Creek, north side' in Biro.

He wasn't sure if the note in the *Angler's Almanac* was there for him, or her, or both of them. He didn't think she'd have the courage to ring him to explain it.

Gazing out of the window at the town lights in the distance, Tom wondered if he should ring. But he already knew he would not. Sunday the 2nd was ages away – he'd think about it then. In the meantime, he should turn off the TV and go to Annie. But not yet, he thought, gazing through the window – not just yet.

What had she said to him today? That he deserved a birthday present for being Tom. That was it. Another funny Sarah thing to say – but a nice thing, and now he could not forget it.

Sarah had changed since he had first met her, he realized. Back then she had been nervous and shy and hardly ever taken off her big black London coat. Perhaps months of summer sun had melted her, he thought. He made room for Merlin, Annie's dog, as he jumped up onto the couch and continued to stare out of the window at the Compton town lights, pushing his hair out of his eyes and holding her card in his hand.

Chapter Fourteen

Bronte wasn't getting much sleep, and it showed. She was so tired at lunch that she tried to stick her ham sandwich into the slot at the ATM. Worse, she was now looking for Angel everywhere. At editorial meetings. In the bath. Even in the toilets at David Jones.

Trying to be logical about Angel's appearances was no help because there was nothing logical about a dead horse which could turn up on aeroplanes and in hotel bedrooms. Consequently, everywhere Bronte went, she feared Angel might go too. At any moment, Bronte realized she might see her sprouting wings and flying across a set of traffic lights. Or worse, hear Angel talking to her.

Bernard Bolton had been Bronte's last hope in sorting out Angel, and now he seemed to have disappeared. At first, Bronte thought he'd taken his phone off the hook, but then Telstra told her that his number had been disconnected. And when she went round to his flat, above the fish and chip shop, the piece of paper with his name on it had disappeared from under the doorbell.

She had stood there for fifteen minutes pressing the bell until she realized the curtains in his flat had also been taken down. In the end, she'd comforted herself with more fish and chips, Mars Bars and cigarettes.

After that, Bronte had told Laura to re-hire the Great Gorgonzola, and forget all about Bernard Bolton.

'Gorzi said he predicted you'd give him his old job back,' Laura told her. 'He said it was in his horoscope.'

'Bloody Gorzi,' Bronte muttered.

Fifty Things To Do With Bananas was now printed and ready to be stuck on the front cover of *Australian Woman*. Bronte managed to force herself to look up one recipe – for banana-stuffed fish – and then hurled it on the floor.

'I'm going out,' she said to Laura. It was nearly lunchtime – if you could stretch ten to twelve as early lunch – so she felt she could brush off any guilt.

Bronte had no idea where she was going, but she had a vague idea that she needed to be somewhere where she could look at the water, and think. Striding down George Street, she reached Circular Quay, then turned right and walked around the Opera House in the direction of the Botanical Gardens.

She sometimes forgot she was living in Sydney. Then occasionally she would turn a corner and bump into the Harbour Bridge and the Opera House at the same time, and she would instantly remember.

All the bankers and lawyers also seemed to have taken early lunchbreaks and hundreds of them were jogging. Bronte couldn't believe some of the lard-like objects that were shuffling towards her. By the law of averages, she thought, if fifty men passed her now, at least one of those should be someone she could vaguely imagine falling in love with. Instead, she found herself dodging huge, sweating, red-faced men with bald heads and corporate-event T-shirts. Now and then, someone who looked like Yasser Arafat would wheeze past her and smile, otherwise – nothing.

Bronte kept walking. She wondered what all the beast-like corporate males thought of her, wandering around the Domain in her suit and trainers looking like she hadn't slept for a month. They probably thought she was just another person who'd gone mad, she realized – and they were right.

She had more or less accepted that she was going to die now. She could see no other reason why Angel kept turning up – except to take her away. More than that, Bronte had a strong, intuitive feeling that she would not be around for her forty-first birthday. She had always pictured dying as some far-off event, possibly caused by the occasional Benson & Hedges, or too much fish and chips, or bad genes. She had also pictured dying as something which might possibly happen when she was over seventy. Now she felt fated to go a lot sooner than that. It wasn't something she could tell her friends about, either. Instead, Bronte was keeping it to herself. And now she had bought a do-it-yourself will kit from the newsagent's, so it was all official.

The thing that bothered her most about dying was not the fact that she would miss the twenty-first century, she realized. It was the fact that she had led such a boring life. All she had managed to achieve after forty years seemed to be one divorce, a few trips overseas and a booklet on bananas. If she were going to die – and Bronte almost felt resigned to it now – she didn't have much time left to organize a life worth living.

Striding past the Art Gallery, she wondered what life after death would be like. She was looking forward to riding Angel again, but she was not looking forward to seeing her grandmother, who had stopped talking to her after she'd divorced Richard. Her grandmother's favourite TV show had been *Sale Of The Century*. If her grandmother was in heaven, then no doubt *Sale Of The Century* was too because that was her idea of bliss. Not much of an after-life, Bronte thought gloomily, with the TV blaring, her grandmother giving her dirty looks and people playing endless rounds of Who Am I?

She climbed up the steps of the Botanical Gardens, past the statues of Winter and Spring and into

Elizabeth Street. And then she saw it – a large brass plaque announcing 'DR VALERIE TAN, PSYCHOLOGIST'.

It was exactly what she had been looking for, she thought, except she hadn't realized it until now. Suddenly she felt herself relax. Why hadn't she thought of it before? A shrink was exactly what she needed.

Bronte wandered through the sliding doors of Dr Valerie Tan's building and found the lift. There were eighteen floors, most of which contained other counsellors, psychologists and psychiatrists and the occasional podiatrist, but Bronte decided that Dr Valerie Tan was the woman for her. With a name like that, how could she not be?

Dr Tan's office was on the fifth floor. The carpet was beige, the abstract oil painting above the reception desk was beige and the secretary was wearing a beige jumper that looked like cashmere. Bronte felt soothed. Even the goldfish in the bowl on the desk was dark brown – it was all very chocolatey and comforting. She sank back against a pile of caramel-coloured suede cushions in a huge brown armchair and closed her eyes.

'Do you have an appointment?' the secretary asked politely. And Bronte was just about to ask for the first available vacancy when Dr Valerie Tan herself appeared, waving off a worried-looking man with glasses who was on his way out of the waiting room.

'Come in, come in,' she said to Bronte, looking at her appointment book. 'I had a cancellation so I can fit you in.' And suddenly, Bronte found herself being welcomed into Dr Tan's office, which was also beige – with one elegant Chinese screen in each corner and a porcelain stork on the desk. The stork was guarding a bowl of Minties, but Bronte didn't feel brave enough to take one without asking.

'I didn't actually mean to see a psychiatrist,' Bronte

159

blurted out. 'I just went for a walk and then I saw your sign on the street. I'm not even sure I need a psychiatrist, it's just that my dead horse keeps following me around. Also, my dead horse is talking to me. Which she never did when she was alive. Obviously. And I think I'm going to die. So I just wanted to know, am I going mad? Am I going to have a nervous breakdown?'

'First of all,' said Dr Tan, 'I am not a psychiatrist. I am a psychologist.'

'Whoops, sorry,' said Bronte. She never could remember the difference, except she knew one of them would give you Prozac and Valium and the other one wouldn't. She thought Dr Valerie Tan was one of the ones who probably wouldn't.

'Now, tell me about the horse,' Dr Tan said, crossing her legs, which Bronte noticed were a slightly darker shade of beige than the chairs.

It was a relief to talk honestly at last and Bronte found herself confessing everything, from her first visit to Bernard Bolton to the terrible night at the pub in Compton, when Angel had been hiding behind the bed and she had sat up until dawn making her will.

'Why do you think you're going to die?' Dr Tan asked gently.

'Because Angel said we would be together soon. She told me during a meeting about bananas. And I read this book and it said that spirits came to collect you when you were due to die. And she's been hanging around *all the time.* And Richard wanted me to make a new will, which was a bit weird, and then the plane nearly crashed and killed us all on the way to Tasmania. It's like someone's trying to tell me something,' she added, looking desperately at Dr Tan. 'And the other thing is, give me a guarantee that I'm *not* going to die soon. You can't, nobody can. And honestly, it just feels like I am. Sometime this year – I don't know when. But I'm just going to die, I can feel it coming.'

'Is Richard your husband?' Dr Tan asked.

'Ex-husband. He just got married again.'

'*Right*,' said the doctor, in a voice that made Bronte think she might have given the doctor some important information.

She was surprised that Dr Tan hadn't asked her to lie on a couch yet – but looking around the room, Bronte could only see comfortable armchairs and Chinese wall scrolls to match the screens.

'Do you want me to just keep talking?' Bronte said nervously. She had noticed that Dr Tan wasn't taking any notes.

'Yes, please talk as much as you like,' she said.

'Angel was the horse I lost my baby on,' Bronte said, taking a deep breath.

'You had a miscarriage?' Dr Tan asked.

'Yes. She threw me off. I woke up that night and I had my period, except it was worse than my period. There was just blood everywhere.'

'When was this?'

'About a year after we were married.'

'And what happened to Angel?'

'Richard put her down. He's a vet. She broke her leg. He had to,' Bronte said.

'Tell me more about the baby,' Dr Tan said, sitting back in her chair.

'Well, we tried for ages after we got married, and nothing happened. Then I remember we had something really gooey for breakfast – it was porridge – and I felt sick all of a sudden. And I kept on feeling sick, every day. Then I got one of those kits from the chemist, and then Richard bought me another one, just in case I'd stuffed up the first one. Then we both went to the doctor and it was all confirmed. If it was a boy it was going to be Angus, and if it was a girl it was going to be Miranda.'

'And you were riding Angel when you were pregnant?'

'Yes. Well, nobody told me not to. And I thought it would be OK because it was so early. Well, I didn't even think, to be honest. I actually think I woke up one day and forgot I was pregnant at all. So I just got dressed and got Angel ready and we went off on the back of the Compton Track together, the way we always did. And then Angel fell and her leg went underneath her and I landed on my side and cracked one of my ribs. I thought the baby would be OK. Then I was just doubled up with cramp and Richard's parents had to take me to hospital, and I knew it wasn't OK.'

'Tell me about when Richard put Angel down,' Dr Tan probed gently.

'Well, she was a bit wobbly, she kind of gave a whimper, then she went. I was holding her. It was raining. Then a few weeks later, I got up one night in my pyjamas, and I got her saddle, and I chucked it in the dam. I was so upset. I think I went a bit mad. I was sort of trying to bury her. We never did have a funeral for her.'

'Did you have a funeral for the baby?' Dr Tan asked. Bronte shook her head.

'And did you and Richard try to have another baby?' Dr Tan asked.

Bronte shook her head again. She couldn't speak. Then she felt her bottom lip wobbling.

'Have you got any tissues?' she asked meekly, half expecting to see Dr Tan produce a beige box to match her office, but when they appeared from her office drawer, they were pink.

She blew her nose, hard, then waited for her to speak, but instead Dr Tan seemed to be more interested in staring out of the window at the harbour. Then she turned around suddenly and clapped her hands together.

'I want you to tell me the ten things you are most scared of,' she said.

'Big hairy spiders and my tax return,' Bronte began, thinking that it was some kind of trick.

'No, the ten things you are most scared of now – very specifically,' Dr Tan said.

'Um. Everything?'

'Everything.'

Too easy, Bronte thought. But the hard thing was telling a stranger. Still, there was something about Dr Tan's gaze, and her warm, beige armchairs, and the sun shining through the window, and the sweet smell of Minties, that made her relax.

'OK. Ten things that scare me, specifically. One, when I die I'll meet my grandmother watching *Sale Of The Century*. Two, when I die I'll see my dead baby. Three, Richard and Sarah will have beautiful children and be very happy. Four, I haven't done anything with my life and I'm going to die. Five, I've left my assistant Laura a copy of the 1998 *Let's Go Europe* in my will, and she's going to hate me. Six, if I get cremated my mother will drop my ashes all over the kitchen floor and they'll end up in the vacuum cleaner. Seven, I'll lose my job if they find out I'm seeing dead horses everywhere. Eight, I'll lose my job anyway because I'm always taking time off – like now. Nine – I haven't got a nine.'

Dr Tan nodded, smiling faintly.

'*Let's Go Europe* 1998 is a little out of date,' she said.

'Ten, I suppose I'm scared of seeing Angel in the toilets at David Jones. I mean, I've seen her everywhere else, why not there?'

Dr Tan looked at her watch.

'I'm afraid I have another appointment soon,' she said, 'but this has been very interesting, Bronte. I'd like you to see me early next week. Is that possible?'

Bronte nodded and wondered if she should call her Valerie. It only seemed fair to be on first-name terms now that she had told her all her secrets.

'Grieving can take years,' Dr Tan said, looking at her

thoughtfully. 'And a marriage ending is a kind of death. Along with a horse, or a child.'

Bronte realized she had never really used the word 'child' when she'd thought of her miscarried baby.

'I suppose it was a child,' she said slowly.

'You lost a lot.'

Bronte nodded, trying to hold herself together.

'I can help you through the stages, if you want,' Dr Tan said. 'I can keep pointing you ahead.'

'But I'll do the stages?'

She nodded. 'Of course. You have to grieve in your own way and I think that's what this might be about.'

Then it was clear the session was over. Smiling, Dr Tan let Bronte go out ahead of her and then vanished into the lift.

Bronte paid with her credit card, feeling slightly dazed, and made another appointment with the beige secretary, who was feeding the brown fish in the bowl, and took the lift down to the ground floor. The sun was still shining and Bronte decided she would walk back the way she'd come, even though it would make her even later. Maybe if she walked faster, she could manage to be back by two, she thought.

Hurrying past the statues of Winter and Spring in the Botanical Gardens, she realized that two of her top ten fears were all about work — and both of them contradicted each other. You couldn't be scared of losing your job *and* of dying without doing anything with your life. Something had to give in that equation, Bronte thought, averting her eyes as a huge rhinoceros of a man thundered past in satin shorts and a Citibank T-shirt.

When she thought about her life, it made her feel very small. Everything she produced for *Australian Woman* was so trivial. It was almost as if everyone who created the magazine, and everyone who bought it, thought that life was going to go on forever.

Consequently, they thought there was time to do things like cut radishes into flower shapes, and read all about Emma Thompson's love life, and do crossword puzzles, and find out if they could save half a percentage on their mortgages. It was such a *waste*, Bronte thought. If she were going to die, it was certainly the wrong thing to be doing with her life.

She stared as a woman jogged past her, pushing a pram at the same time. It was hard to believe that there was a baby inside it because the woman was pounding the pavement so hard, but Bronte could just make out a small pink face peering out of a white rug.

She hadn't thought about her dead baby for years. That had all been very strange, Bronte decided – one minute she was talking about Angel, which was actually what she'd come to discuss – and the next minute she was telling Dr Tan about the day Angus – or had it been Miranda? – had died. She wished the doctor had taken notes – she had serious doubts she was going to be able to remember everything.

Bronte let her mind go back to the miscarriage. Richard had wanted her to try again, but she had been terrified of losing another baby. It had also seemed wrong, somehow, to want another chance. Even though everyone had told her not to blame herself, of course she had – and she was right. No sane woman would have been riding during her pregnancy.

Bronte swerved to avoid a group of men in Gay and Lesbian Mardi Gras singlets, heading for the swimming pool. She wished so many joggers wouldn't make that stupid whistling sound as they breathed out. She also wished that the rhinoceros man in the Citibank T-shirt would run a bit faster. She could see him in the distance and, any minute now, she was going to have to squeeze past him.

Men, men everywhere and none of them are for me, she thought. She wasn't entirely sure if she knew which man was, any more. And that was another fear she could tell Dr Valerie Tan, she thought, heading for Circular Quay. She seemed to have spent her thirties being scared of always being single. Now she was worried that she was going to spend her forties not even caring.

Bronte decided her life would have been much easier if she'd stayed married to Richard. They might not have had any more children, but they would have had horses. She could have run a stables with him eventually, or invested in racing. She could have even ended up as a racing writer, if she'd tried hard enough.

Even now, people still asked her why her marriage had ended. Bronte had two automatic answers: one, they had been too young, and two, they'd had communication problems.

The truth was different, though, Bronte knew. It was just that there had been too much death for two people to bear.

Richard had stopped talking about the dead baby, even when she'd wanted to, and then he'd just stopped talking altogether. The subject was still closed between them. She wondered how much he'd told his new wife about what had happened. To this day, they had never had a discussion about Angel dying either.

Bronte stepped out across the gutter to avoid the rhinoceros man, who was now just ahead of her, and was nearly run over by the jogging woman with the baby in the pram coming the other way. Sydney was becoming impossible, she decided. You couldn't even go for a walk around the harbour without people waving their lifestyles in your face.

If she were going to die, Bronte decided, she didn't want to do it in Sydney. The place wasn't set up for death, it was far too healthy. She should go out in Paris, she decided, like Jim Morrison. Except not in a bath – she didn't want to be all wrinkly when they found her. A nice four-poster bed with velvet curtains would suit her fine, Bronte thought. Then they could pack her in a coffin – real oak, not wood veneer – and fly her back to Australia on Qantas. God knows she had enough frequent-flyer points.

Chapter Fifteen

Every time the phone rang, Sarah thought it was going to be Tom – but it never was. She had not really expected him to call her about fishing at Lilly Creek on Sunday, but it did not stop her hoping. As Sunday came closer, even Richard noticed something was wrong with her.

'Something's up,' he asked one morning. 'What is it?' Sarah could only tell him what she always told him. She was homesick. After four months it had finally hit her. She still wasn't sleeping properly in their new bed – and maybe they should get another one. She was still adjusting to the weather – everything was back to front in Australia. She was still adjusting to married life – she had, after all, not had a husband until she was thirty.

Patiently Richard learned to get used to back mass-ages in bed and learned to roll over and read when Sarah did. When they did make love, it felt as good, as natural and as right as it had in London, he knew – but it also felt *married*. Perhaps that was the problem.

Sarah knew it was ridiculous to hide her copy of *Angler's Almanac* like a guilty secret, but it was there, nevertheless, under her side of the mattress, like a diary or a love letter. After she had given one to Tom as a present, she had gone back to the newsagent's and bought her own copy. She was embarassed at her own desperation, but the funny little yellow book of fishing dates and times seemed like her only possible connection to him.

Every so often, she took it out and looked at it. Despite its unromantic references to eels and freshwater cod, it was about as close as she could get to actually being with Tom. One morning, after she and Richard had made love, she had even pulled the *Angler's Almanac* out from under the mattress as soon as he had gone back to sleep and spent hours gazing at it, hating herself for being so weak.

And now the day had come – Sunday, the Moon Above day. Sarah was so nervous that she woke up while it was still dark. She listened while Richard made sleeping sounds, wondering when she could allow herself to sneak off.

Staring into the darkness of their bedroom, she willed Tom to be at the river. She had still not seen him since his birthday. Sometimes Richard mentioned Tom on the phone, but only in connection with their cricket team. Still, even that was enough to make her heart jump-start.

The sentence in *Angler's Almanac* was like a mantra in her head – Sunday the 2nd, 9.02 a.m., Moon Above. Squinting at the alarm clock on Richard's side of the bed, Sarah could now see it was just after ten past five. All her life she had woken up too early for things – she never got it quite right.

Sighing, she rolled over onto her side, gently moving Richard's arm out of the way. If she let herself go back to sleep, she could still be up by eight, and then she'd have plenty of time to walk up to Lilly Creek. There was no point in getting up now, so she might as well give in.

Taking a deep breath, Sarah closed her eyes and forced herself to keep them shut until she finally fell asleep.

When she woke, she could hear the sound of a lawn-mower outside, and the curtains were open, letting in brilliant Sunday morning sunshine. Then she realized that Richard's side of the bed was empty and it was quarter past ten. *Quarter past bloody ten!* Sarah realized.

She could have cried. Was the clock wrong? But she knew it was right. She had just blown it, that was all. She thought of Tom, walking along the riverbank and looking for her, and felt total despair. Maybe he had gone back home by now – she would have to ring him. Even if Annie picked up the phone, she had no choice. The idea of Tom searching for her this morning and going home alone was the worst kind of torture, and Sarah couldn't stand it.

Padding downstairs to the phone in the kitchen, she noticed a note on the table from Richard. He had gone to the surgery to find some files, he wrote, and hadn't wanted to wake her. Sarah breathed out. At least she could make her call in private.

As she dialled Tom and Annie's number – which she knew at least as well as her own – she winced, waiting for a voice at the other end. If it was Tom it would be terrible and wonderful, all at the same time. If it was Annie, it would just be terrible. And if nobody answered, Sarah thought, she would just go off and throw herself in the lake right now. She felt sick. Then someone answered, 'Hello?'

It was Annie.

'Oh hi. It's Sarah here.'

She realized she could actually hear her own heart thumping inside her ears.

'Yes?' Annie's voice was as cold as she could possibly make it.

'Um,' Sarah said, thinking quickly. 'Um, it's about the dog.'

'Yes?'

'It's just that I asked Tom one day if I could come

170

round and try for some pups with your dog.'

'I know,' Annie said abruptly. 'I'll have to think about it.'

'Oh – thanks,' Sarah stumbled.

She wondered if she dare ask if Tom was there, then overheard someone – it had to be him – talking in the background. 'Tom's here now,' said Annie. 'I think you'd better speak to him.' And then suddenly he was there, on the other end of the line.

'I was going to go to the creek this morning,' Sarah said quickly. 'But I slept in.'

There was a long pause. She could almost hear Tom trying to think of something to say.

'I've been in the garden all morning,' he said.

'Oh.'

So he hadn't gone. Part of her was relieved, and part of her wanted to quietly die because, despite all her wishing and hoping, he clearly hadn't cared enough to turn up.

'I was just saying to Annie about your dog,' Sarah said. 'I was wondering if I could bring over Richard's aunt's dog and try for a puppy.'

'I'll see if I can talk her into it,' Tom said.

Sarah realized she must have left the room after all.

'Is Annie there?' she checked.

'No, she just went out to the shed,' he said.

Sarah was feeling like part of some bizarre MI5 conversation and she spoke quickly.

'So you didn't go out fishing this morning,' she tried to joke. 'Even though it was the perfect time in the *Angler's Almanac*.'

'Annie asked me to get the mowing done,' he said. 'So I got up and did it first thing, before the rain started.'

'Oh.'

'Shall I let you know about Merlin?' he asked.

'Yes, that would be great,' Sarah said, remembering the dog's name.

She was trying to sound casual, even though every single part of her was screaming with questions for Tom. Hadn't he seen the note she'd made in the back of the *Almanac*? Had he seen it, but decided to ignore it because he couldn't be bothered? Had he seen it and wanted to go, but been stopped by Annie? Was he lying about being in the garden this morning and had he really gone to the river, then turned around and come back when she'd failed to appear?

Miserably, Sarah pushed the side of the phone harder and harder into her head, willing herself to focus.

'I might give you a call,' Tom said. 'I'll see how it goes about Merlin.'

'Yes,' Sarah replied, trying to keep a fake smile in her voice and trying to sound as casual as he did. 'See how it goes.'

'Bye,' he said, putting the phone down.

Feeling numb, Sarah went through the motions of putting the kettle on and then realized they didn't have any milk. It was amazing. She was home all day and had nothing to do except go to the supermarket and randomly apply for jobs, and she couldn't stock the fridge properly.

At that moment, Sarah decided she hated herself. It would be so easy, she thought, if Richard was right. But Richard was wrong. And the reason she knew Richard was wrong, was because Tom was so right. *And he needs me*, Sarah consoled herself. *I can help him.*

It had been going around in her head for so long now that she felt sure she had almost worn grooves in her brain. Taking a cup of black tea outside into the garden, she dropped down on the grass under the big gum tree at the side of the house.

She was still in her pyjamas and dressing gown, but didn't care if anybody saw her. She needed to think – she had to think. And because every room in her house

172

was filled with Richard, it was the wrong place to try to sort out Tom.

She had to see him. If Annie wouldn't let her bring the dog over, then she would have to think of something else. For a moment, Sarah tried to work out how she really felt about Annie. She realized that she didn't care one way or another, and it surprised her. Annie was just Annie. A minor part of the landscape in comparison to the real picture, which was Tom.

Hearing his voice had been wonderful. If she tried, she could almost recapture some of the things he'd said and the way he'd said them. Sarah felt herself clinging on again. It was like trying to catch air.

Then she heard the phone ring. It was probably Richard, she thought, but she scrambled up anyway and raced to the back door in her pyjamas, her bare feet catching the grass as she went.

'Hello?' she panted, snatching the receiver before the phone switched over to the answering machine.

'It's Tom.'

'Oh!'

'I've just had a talk to Annie about Merlin and your dog.'

'Right.' Sarah tried to sound in control and failed.

'She says it's OK.'

Sarah tried to take this information in and then realized what it meant.

'But that's fantastic,' she said.

'Maybe bring your dog round next Tuesday morning.'

'Will you be there?' Sarah said quickly.

'Sure,' Tom said evenly. He was giving nothing away, Sarah realized.

'So next Tuesday. About ten or something?' she asked hopefully.

'Sure,' Tom said again. 'Anyway, I'd better get back to it in the garden. Just thought I'd let you know.'

'Thank you,' Sarah said, gratefully, trying to keep the

love and longing out of her voice, and heard him put the phone down.

She wondered about the conversation that must have just taken place between Tom and Annie, trying to imagine what Annie must have said, and then gave up. All that really mattered was that in a few days from now, she would see Tom. Annie could look after Merlin and the other dog, and whatever it was they had to do to produce a puppy, and she could sit with Tom and talk. And this time, Sarah realized, she would have to get some answers.

She had to know how Tom felt – she couldn't go on like this for another day, another week, another month. And more importantly, she thought, she couldn't do it to Richard. Then she heard him pulling up in his Jeep, and saw him getting out of the car with a box of files. He worked so hard, she thought – a lot harder than she ever had in London.

'Hi,' he kissed her. 'You slept in a long time.'

'About ten hours,' she said, trying to smile. Her stomach was churning like a washing machine.

'Richard, do you still want to have that puppy?'

He looked at her. He had forgotten about it, mainly because she had.

'Sure, if you want to.'

'Annie said I could breed your aunt's dog with her dog.'

'Merlin.'

'Yes, Merlin. Only if it's OK though,' Sarah added quickly.

'Of course it's OK,' Richard smiled. 'And if we get a full litter it won't be a problem getting rid of the other pups. It's hard to find purebreds round here.'

'What's the other dog called?' Sarah asked politely, feeling she should at least make some attempt to seem interested.

'Fifi,' Richard grinned.

'More like a poodle's name,' Sarah said.

'When does Annie want to do this?' he asked.

'Tuesday morning.'

Sarah realized she was almost holding her breath.

'I'll be at work,' he said. 'But I'll get Fifi in the morning if you like, and drop you off.'

'Thanks,' Sarah said gratefully. She watched Richard as he started to unpack his office files on the kitchen table. The nicer he was, the more she felt angry with herself. And the more she felt angry with herself, the more she desperately craved Tom to make everything seem better. It was like the worst kind of merry-go-round.

'I'm glad you want to get a dog,' he said suddenly, looking up at her.

'Well, they're so gorgeous,' she said quickly. 'Those Australian cattle dogs, they're just beautiful.'

'We've got animals in common anyway,' he said absent-mindedly, thumbing through a cashbook. Staring hard, Sarah wondered if he had realized the full meaning of what he had just said, but Richard was already lost in rows of facts and figures.

The quicker Tuesday came, the better, she decided. One way or another, she had to find a way out of this.

When Fifi finally arrived in the back of Richard's Jeep a few days later, the first thing she did was leave a yellow puddle on the back seat.

'Yuck,' Sarah said, but Richard was used to cleaning up after animals and already had a bottle of ammonia ready. By the time the Jeep was at the end of the drive, Fifi was already drooling long strings of saliva over Sarah's leg.

'I hope your puppy doesn't do that,' Sarah said, but Fifi wasn't listening – she was too interested in trying to stick her nose up the leg of Sarah's jeans.

'Are all blue heelers like this?' Sarah asked.

'No,' Richard smiled faintly. 'Just this one.'

When they pulled up in Annie's driveway, Tom came over, wearing a crumpled white shirt covered in grass stains and a pair of jeans with such a long rip in them that it was all Sarah could do not to stare.

'Hey!' Richard yelled as Fifi tried to push her way out of the car door first.

Tom watched as Fifi flashed past him, trailing her lead on the ground.

'Looking for Merlin already,' he shrugged, pushing his hair out of his eyes. 'Well that's a good sign.'

'I can't stay long,' Richard said. 'I'm just off to work. How's Annie?'

'Good,' Tom shrugged, and Sarah noticed that he was trying not to look at her, keeping his gaze steadily focused on Richard instead.

She got out of the car.

'Are you sure you can look after Fifi?' Richard checked.

Sarah nodded.

'Call me when you're ready,' he yelled as he tried to reverse up the driveway, then started laughing as he saw Fifi racing back round the other side of the house with one of Annie's shoes in her mouth.

'I'd love to stay and watch,' he shouted through the open car window, 'but I've got to go and see a man about a cow.'

Tom waved him off, while Sarah tried to grab Fifi's lead and failed. Then, at last, Richard had gone. Despite herself, Sarah sighed with relief, then instantly felt guilty.

'Let's go and find Annie,' Tom said, grabbing Fifi by the collar as she tried to take the shoe on another lap of the house. 'Lucky Annie never wears those shoes anyway.'

Fifi was drooling all over Tom's jeans, and as he bent down to rub them, Sarah caught sight of his skin through the ripped denim. He was still brown, she realized. His tan never seemed to fade, whatever the weather.

'Fifi and Merlin are going to have an interesting time,' Tom smiled.

Sarah loved it when he smiled. It didn't happen often, but when it did, it felt like someone was giving her a free gift.

'I hope Annie's OK about this,' she said politely, but Tom didn't reply. He was miles away, she realized. She was almost getting used to the way his blue eyes would suddenly switch focus under his long, blond fringe.

Meanwhile, Fifi had discovered something else – Annie's goats wandering over the far paddocks of the house on the north side of the garden. Whimpering with excitement, she strained against Tom's hand, trying desperately to escape.

Finally they found Annie with Merlin – standing in the doorway of her shed.

'This is Fifi,' Sarah explained, watching in embarrassment as Tom let her go, and she raced straight over and stuck her nose in Merlin's bottom.

'Well, at least she's enthusiastic,' Tom smiled, but Annie wasn't smiling back, Sarah noticed.

'Thanks for doing this,' she said, trying to catch Annie's eye, but she seemed determined not to look at anything except the two dogs.

'Are you sure this one's a purebred?' she addressed Sarah, still without looking at her.

'Richard said she had papers,' Sarah explained.

'Papers!' Annie rolled her eyes. Fifi's head had now practically disappeared up Merlin's tail.

'D'you want a cup of tea?' Tom asked Sarah vaguely, but before she could say anything, there was a loud yelping sound from Merlin and she realized Fifi must have bitten him. Annie shook her head. 'Are you going to supervise this, or shall I?' she addressed Sarah again, still not looking at her. 'Because,' she added, 'I get the feeling that you don't know the first thing about dogs.'

177

Then there was another yelp from Merlin as Fifi swung around and nipped him on the ear. 'Come on,' Annie said sharply, dragging Merlin and Fifi along by their collars.

'Oh, Annie!' Tom said softly, trying to turn it into a joke – but it was clear to Sarah that Annie was furious. She bit her lip as she watched Annie drag the animals away.

'Do you want some tea?' Tom mumbled. 'That's what I was trying to ask you before Fifi lost the plot.'

'Bloody Fifi,' Sarah made a face. 'I feel terrible. It's so embarrassing.'

'I think she might be part rat,' Tom smiled. 'Are you sure about those pedigree papers?'

They walked past rows of vegetable beds and herbs – Tom really did have green fingers, Sarah thought. It was nothing like their garden at home, or even any other garden she had seen. There was cabbage and lavender and pumpkin and mint. There was asparagus and rhubarb and lettuce and thyme.

'Did you grow all this?' she said, amazed. He nodded, feeling a wave of pride as he looked around him.

'Come in,' he said, as they finally reached the back door of the house.

Stepping in, Sarah could immediately smell chalk, but it turned out to be buckets of plaster, piled up against the side of the kitchen table.

'So how are things?' Sarah asked, trying not to stare at Tom's tanned legs through the holes in his ripped jeans.

'Good,' Tom said. 'It's a shame Richard couldn't stay. I haven't seem him much lately.'

'Well, he's working so hard,' Sarah shrugged. 'I hardly see him myself. Before we got married, he told me he really loved his job. But I didn't realize how *much* he loved his job.'

Tom smiled politely.

'It's a problem actually,' she heard herself saying. 'He spends so much time with things that don't speak – they only bark and miaow – he forgets how to speak to me when he comes home.'

Tom looked at her for a moment, then tried to concentrate on making the tea.

'You should get a nice puppy from today anyway,' he said.

'Oh yeah,' Sarah agreed, absent-mindedly looking around the house.

'Do you want herbal tea or normal tea?' Tom asked.

'Actually, I was just wondering if I could use your loo,' Sarah replied.

'Sure. It's that door on the right, by the stereo.'

As she picked her way over piles of sculpture magazines and old newspapers, Sarah eventually found the bathroom. An old black-and-white postcard of Picasso was wedged under one corner of the mirror above the sink, and the shower rail was bending under the weight of what looked like all of Annie's wet clothes. A pair of red men's bathers – they must be Tom's – were slung on one of the bath taps.

Feeling slightly stupid, Sarah picked them up and felt them – they were sopping wet, but they were something that belonged to him. For a moment, she even contemplated stealing them, just to have something of Tom's she could finally call her own. *I must be really losing it*, she told herself, staring in the mirror.

When she went back to the kitchen, he had made them tea and found a half-empty packet of biscuits.

'I hope Fifi's going to behave herself,' Sarah sighed.

'Oh, she'll be fine,' Tom said kindly. 'She's just trying to show Merlin who's boss.'

Sarah smiled and caught his eye for a moment.

'I thought you might have gone out fishing this morning,' she said. 'But I'm glad you didn't – because then I would have missed you.'

'I thought about it,' Tom said evenly.

'Did you?' Sarah's heart shot through the side of her ribs.

'The garden had to come first,' he replied.

Which in a way, Sarah decided, meant that Annie had to come first. Perhaps that's what he was trying to tell her. More than anything else, she felt she had to stay calm and remain standing. It was hard, when every instinct she had was to buckle at the knees, grab Tom and never let him go, but she had to hang onto her mug of tea, her biscuit and her common sense. *Calm down*, she lectured herself.

'I saw a painting of someone who looked like you the other day,' Tom said suddenly, watching Sarah as she gripped her mug of tea.

'Did you?'

'Well, it was a painting of a mermaid. But she did look like you.'

'Oh my God!' she laughed.

'Must have been the association. Fish and you. You and fish. I was thinking about them together after you bought me the *Angler's Almanac*, and then I saw this painting in a book – and it was just like you. You with a fish's tail, anyway.'

Sarah swallowed. 'What else do you think about me, Tom?'

Flustered, he smiled and shook his head.

'*Do* you think about me?' she persisted. Now that she had started, it was easier than she'd expected. And something inside her knew that on no account could she let this moment go. She had had enough of waiting and wondering.

'What do you expect me to say?' he said at last. Then, very calmly, Sarah found herself putting her tea down on the table, walking over to Tom and kissing him. Up close, he smelled of bed and lemons, just as he always did – but there was something else too. Shampoo, and sweat, and mint.

'God!' Tom pushed her away. 'Sarah!'

'I think I'm in love with you,' Sarah whispered, hanging onto his hands, unable to let him go.

Tom stared.

'I mean, I know I'm in love with you. I can't cover it up any more.'

And then, to his horror, Tom heard the dogs barking at the side of the house with Annie shouting after them.

'Fifi! Merlin!' she yelled. She sounded furious.

Leaving Sarah standing in the kitchen, Tom raced out to see Fifi covered in blood and feathers and Merlin whimpering and running around in circles behind her.

'What happened?' he breathed. He felt utterly in shock after Sarah's kiss.

'This little madam,' Annie yelled, 'just tried to take the head off one of the chickens!' In reply, Fifi yawned and lifted her leg against a drainpipe at the side of the house, releasing a stream of yellow wee.

'What about Merlin?' Tom asked quickly.

'Merlin's on strike.' Annie said. 'And I don't blame him. Whose idea was this? It's just a disaster.'

Annie jumped as Fifi raced towards her, drooling long strings of saliva and smiling a doggy smile.

'Oh Fifi,' Tom sighed, patting the dog, which immediately tried to bite his hand.

Sarah came out of the kitchen.

'I'm sorry, Annie,' she said, finding Fifi's lead and trying to fasten it onto her collar without being drooled on.

'Chicken-killer!' Annie hissed at Fifi, who was unrepentant.

'We'll go,' Sarah said quickly. She couldn't bear to look at Tom. 'I'll go. Come on, Fifi. We'll just walk it. It's not far.'

There were white feathers stuck to Fifi's mouth, her ears and her tail. She looked like she'd been in a pillow fight, Sarah thought. Grabbing the lead, she turned the dog around and headed up Annie's driveway.

Her heart was hammering and she could feel a lump rising in her throat. For no reason, she thought of her old flat in Battersea. Everything's wrong, she thought, as she pulled Fifi along on the lead. Wrong, wrong, wrong.

She walked blindly away from the house and up the road, staring at the ground as feathers blew off Fifi's coat and long strings of doggy saliva kept hitting the legs of her jeans. She could still taste Tom and smell him. It was almost like a drug, she realized. Perhaps that's what she had turned into – Cupid's version of a drug addict. *But he kissed me back*, she suddenly realized, with a small stab of excitement.

She kept walking faster, breathing hard as she took the first hill on the rise. At least Fifi seemed to be enjoying herself, she realized. It had probably been her idea of the perfect day – attacking chickens, biting humans, urinating on everything she could see and sexually molesting a fellow dog.

Walking ahead, she kept pulling Fifi behind her until they came to the top of the last hill before the start of the road to town. Exhausted and still rattling with nerves, Sarah found a large piece of slate to sit on and pushed down Fifi's back so she was forced to sit too.

She had no idea what to do next. She could neither think, nor feel, in straight lines. Everything had gone pear-shaped, Sarah decided, and all she could manage at the moment was to sit down.

Methodically, she started picking the feathers out of Fifi's coat. When she heard a car, she instinctively ducked her head down and hoped she wouldn't be seen. People in Compton had a habit of offering you a lift, whether you wanted one or not, and she was in no mood to be around other people.

'Sarah!' Tom called, winding the car window down.

'Oh,' she said blankly. 'It's you.' Then he parked the car and came over, while Fifi barked endlessly.

'Well,' he said, sitting down on the ground next to Sarah, and ruffling Fifi's ears.

'I'm sorry,' Sarah said, shrugging. 'I'm – oh, I don't know what I am. Insane, probably. I'm just sorry.'

'It's OK,' Tom said automatically. Her mascara was all over her face. Sarah was the only woman he knew who managed to do that.

'I'm sorry about the dog, I'm sorry about me,' she said. 'But I'm glad I said it, I don't regret it. I love you. I've been in love with you since before the wedding. In fact, I nearly didn't get married because of you. I love you, I love you, I love you, Tom.'

Tom kept smoothing down Fifi's coat, while Sarah continued to absent-mindedly pick out feathers from her tail.

'I don't know what to say,' he said at last.

'I know you don't.'

'I was your best man.'

'I know you were.'

'Does Richard know any of this?'

Sarah shook her head. 'I told you, he doesn't talk. I mean, we don't talk. It's a mistake. We got engaged too fast and – oh, I don't know. It's more about you, if you must know. I met him first, and then I just . . . I just met you. And I tried so hard, Tom. But these feelings won't go away.'

He shook his head. 'I was at school with Richard,' he said. 'I've known him for years.'

'Yes,' Sarah said simply.

'This is terrible for him. It's the worst thing for him.'

'I know it is.'

Tom looked at her. 'Are you really sure about this?'

Exasperated, Sarah stared up at the top of the gum tree overhead, with her eyes full of stinging tears.

'I've thought about this every minute, and every hour, and every day since I got to this country,' she

183

said, realizing how croaky she sounded. Fifi thumped her tail on the ground and kept on drooling more streams of saliva.

'With or without you, Tom, I'm going to have to leave Richard. Or who knows, maybe he'll leave me. Whatever we had in England, well – it wasn't the real thing.'

'Like "Heart of Glass",' Tom said slowly, remembering Harry's odd choice of music on her wedding day.

'Yes. What an omen that song turned out to be,' she smiled. 'But there have been omens all the way along if I think about it. When you sent him that poem in London – even before I ever saw you, or met you. The poem you wrote did something to me.'

'Did it?'

Sarah nodded. 'Probably because part of you was in it. Anyway,' she sighed, 'I've made a mistake. Richard's made a mistake. If I think about it that way it doesn't hurt so much. But Tom, I have to know how you feel. I mean, have I imagined it? Am I wrong, do you not care at all?'

Staring hard at the ground, Tom felt Sarah's hand take his. Her hands were so small, he realized. Almost like little paws.

'It's a shock,' he managed to say at last.

'Is it?' Sarah replied.

He nodded. 'I have to have time to think about this, and take it in.'

'And you're not attracted to me? You don't have any feelings about me?' She realized she was sounding pathetic now, but her dignity had disappeared about an hour ago.

He shook his head. 'No, you're wrong. I do care about you. I mean – OK, on your wedding day . . .'

'On my wedding day,' Sarah prompted him hopefully.

'I thought about it then. What it would be like to be with you.'

184

He reached for Sarah's other hand and held it tightly, trying to help her.

'Why do I think there's going to be some horrible "but" after this?' Sarah pleaded.

He smiled. 'You have to realize Richard is one of my best friends,' he said. 'I don't think you know what he's done for me.'

'I know what he's done for you.'

'Even talking like this now, I just feel like a criminal.'

'It's not a crime to love somebody,' Sarah sighed, finding another feather in Fifi's coat. 'The crime is faking it. Or staying there because of the money. Or because you're too frightened to leave. Do you actually love Annie?'

Despite himself, Tom shook his head. In a moment, he realized, she had finally forced the truth out of him. And then, when Fifi had finally settled down on the ground, with her head on her paws, he reached properly for Sarah and kissed her until even she thought they would have to give up.

'You want what I want,' she said at last.

Tom sighed. 'I don't know what I want,' he said. 'I've never felt this amount of guilt before.'

'Because you know it's right,' Sarah said. 'It's not easy, but it's right.'

Inside she could almost feel her heart rocketing up past her throat, then out through the top of her head. This morning, Tom had felt miles away from her. Now, he almost seemed like part of her. It was all she had asked for, and now she had got it. She was certain of it – and now she understood why people talked about dying of happiness.

Chapter Sixteen

It was unusual for Richard to be the only vet on call at the surgery. On weekdays, he normally had help from at least two other vets in nearby towns, but today everyone was busy with cattle inoculation. By 10 a.m., he already had two house calls – one for a sheep with lambing problems, and one for a cat with snakebite – and with a colicky horse to treat in the afternoon as well, he was beginning to panic.

In desperation, he rang his father. It wasn't the first time he'd asked Dr Gilby to switch his talents from humans to animals, but it turned out that his father had gone to a Lions Club function in Melbourne.

'Damn,' Richard said to his mother, when she picked up the phone. 'I forgot about that.'

'Don't you remember? They've got this fundraising conference.'

'Sorry, I do think he said something now. But I've got two house calls and I'm going to need a hand with the sheep – the girl who rang up said she thought it was having twins.'

'Well, I'll do it then,' Mrs Gilby said suddenly.

Richard paused and thought about it. She'd oohed and aahed over kittens in his surgery before, but his mother had never had to deal with sheep, or hold down a cat with snakebite.

'Do you think you could help me?' he said, feeling unsure.

'Of course I can. Just tell me what to do and I'll do it. Sarah's not around to help?'

'I'm not sure where Sarah is,' Richard explained. 'I just rang home now and she was out. She might have gone for a walk or something.'

Her new daughter-in-law always seemed to be going for walks, Mrs Gilby decided, but she didn't say anything.

'So will you come?' Richard asked, giving her a chance to change her mind.

'I'd love to,' his mother said quickly. 'I'm not going to sit here listening to Margaret Throsby talk to David Suzuki all morning.'

'I'll be there in a minute then,' Richard said, putting the phone down and feeling strangely relieved. If nothing else, his mother could help navigate while he drove.

When Richard arrived at his parents' house, his mother was dressed in her housepainting clothes, an old tweed coat of his father's and a pair of gardening gloves.

'I don't want to get bitten,' she explained as she climbed into the front seat of Richard's Jeep. 'What happened to the cat?'

'They found it under the house, crouching down on its stomach,' Richard explained. 'Its left eye is shot – the pupil's the size of a five-cent piece apparently. And it's got a tick in its back as well, so it's got poison going both ways. The snake got into the bloodstream and the tick's just about paralysed the rest of it.'

'Poor thing,' his mother tutted, and turned the map sideways as she tried to find the address.

'The sheep's in difficult labour, so it's hard to choose,' Richard sighed. 'But the cat can hang on for a while yet, so I think we'll take a look at the lambs first.'

They drove past all the usual familiar Compton

187

landmarks – the Disappearing House, an old building which seemed to vanish as you glanced back at it, driving past the hill, and Hedge Road – a long stretch of roadside hedge which had been trimmed into the shape of kangaroos, and even the occasional bear.

'So how's Sarah?' Mrs Gilby asked carefully.

'Good,' Richard said, avoiding a pothole. It was the polite answer his mother had expected to hear, and she'd got it.

'And Tom?'

'I saw him the other day. He's good.'

'I was very proud of him at the wedding,' his mother said. She still liked to talk about it, Richard realized, as if it had been yesterday.

'Why proud?'

'He didn't touch a drop,' his mother explained. 'And when you think of how he was a couple of years ago . . .'

'Bugger!' Richard swore as a wallaby appeared from nowhere and hopped in front of the car.

'Goodbye wallaby,' his mother said cheerfully as the animal bounced back into the bush.

Eventually they came to a small footbridge over an unmarked creek. According to the instructions Richard had been given on the phone, this was the last land-mark before the farm.

'And there it is,' his mother said, pointing in her gardening gloves. 'Abbotsville. Must be a big property, look at all those sheep they've got lined up over there. I wonder which one's got the lambs?'

Parking the Jeep next to the barn, Richard got out and was immediately greeted by a young girl in dungarees.

'Hello, I'm Linda,' she said. 'I rang about our sheep. I'm off sick with a cold. I've got the day off school. The sheep's got a lamb sticking out of her.'

She looked about nine years old, Mrs Gilby thought.

'Mum and Dad not here?' she asked, but Linda's bottom lip immediately started wobbling.

'Mum's gone,' she said.

'That's OK,' Richard said quickly, patting her on the shoulder and getting the picture. It had been a while since he'd visited Abbotsville, but the last time he had been here, he remembered, her parents hadn't been getting on.

'Your dad's up the top working, is he?'

'Yes,' Linda said, her wobbling lip returning to normal.

'Well, we can sort this out together, then,' Richard said, introducing his mother.

'The sheep's right at the top of the hill,' Linda said. 'I call her Samba. And I tried to get her into the shed but she wouldn't go. She's not going to die, is she?'

'Let's just have a look,' Richard said carefully. 'I don't think so, no.'

Together, Richard, his mother and Linda walked steadily over a chain of paddocks, pulling the fence wires apart each time and squeezing through.

'Lucky I gave up smoking years ago,' Mrs Gilby said, panting slightly. She noticed how much calmer Linda seemed now that Richard had taken over. He reassured people, she realized. He didn't even have to say very much – it was just his presence and the way he was so sure about everything.

Finally, they found the sheep. As Linda had promised, it had a lamb sticking out of one end – or rather, two spindly lamb's legs.

'Oh dear,' Mrs Gilby said.

Linda's lower lip wobbled again.

Kneeling, Richard got to work. Samba was making a lot of noise and was clearly in pain, and he cursed himself for not getting out to the farm sooner.

'I didn't know how to pull the lamb out,' Linda said nervously.

'That's OK,' Richard said, struggling to keep his footing in the mud.

'You hold her head, Linda,' he said, 'and you just

189

hold her backside, Mum, make sure poor old Samba doesn't struggle too much. I think the other lamb's behind this one.'

Gently, he felt for the first lamb.

'I'm sorry,' he said quietly to Linda. For a farmer's daughter, she seemed unusually sensitive to animals and he didn't want to upset her too much.

'It's dead?' she said at last.

Nodding, he gently eased the first lamb out. It was tiny and still slippery – with its eyes closed.

'Oh, poor thing,' his mother said. 'It's still got its little umbilical cord.'

Grimacing, Richard felt behind it, to see if there was any chance that the second lamb might be alive – but he doubted it. For Linda's sake, he hoped otherwise, but within seconds, another dead lamb followed the first.

'She's an old sheep,' he said, seeing Linda's face. 'I think Samba might just be too old to be a mother. I'm sorry, Linda.'

Digging his boots into the grass to stop himself sliding, he pulled out the second body and with it, something that Mrs Gilby thought must be the placenta – whatever it was, it was bloody and messy and she couldn't look.

'Oh, poor Samba,' Linda said, rubbing the sheep's neck.

'Listen to her baaing like that,' Mrs Gilby said. 'She knows.'

'She'll be OK,' Richard said. 'Trust me, they forget things.'

He dragged one dead lamb under the tree, while his mother nobly dragged the other one across the grass in her gardening gloves.

'I should have rung you earlier,' Linda said, blowing her nose, 'but I didn't know it was happening. I only found out by accident – I could hear her baaing and making this crying noise, so I went over to see

190

what was wrong, and then I realized. I wish Mum was here!'

'It's really common, Linda,' Richard said kindly. 'I see it all the time. An old ewe, and twins – it's not a combination that works a lot of the time.'

'What are we going to do with them?' Linda said, unable to look at the small white bodies under the tree.

'I'll bury them if you like,' Richard said gently. 'Come on. You go back to the house and sit down for a bit. You did everything you could. Mum and I will sort out the rest.'

As they walked down the hill to the farmhouse, Mrs Gilby caught her son's arm.

'I don't think I can dig a hole for them,' she said.

'No, I'll do that,' Richard said quickly. 'I mean, I wasn't asking you to. You just talk to Linda for a bit. She's more upset than she's letting on. Maybe her dad will turn up for lunch.'

He patted his mother on the shoulder and then turned around and headed for the shed, where he was sure he'd find a spade. He felt sorry for Linda, with her brave face and her dungarees. Witnessing a stillborn delivery wasn't something you'd really want a nine-year-old girl to go through, even if he had seen it a million times before.

His mother was a natural, he thought – even if she was squeamish. If she hadn't spent her life raising him and Harry, and looking after her father, she might have done something in medicine. At one point she had been working as her husband's medical receptionist, but then Harry had been born and life – predictably – had gone haywire.

Finding the spade in the shed, Richard headed back up the hill, feeling the wind against his face as he trudged over old rabbit burrows and cow pats. It was quite true that the sheep would forget – he hadn't been fobbing Linda off. Without warning, Angel came to mind. Quickly, Richard brushed the memory away. He

191

hadn't thought about her for years and he wasn't about to start now.

In the kitchen, Mrs Gilby took over and put the kettle on, while Linda found some homemade Anzac biscuits in a tin in the pantry.

'He was amazing,' Linda said, 'the way he just got them out. He didn't hurt her at all, he was so quick and gentle.'

'He's a very good vet,' Mrs Gilby said proudly. 'Even if he is my son.'

'He got married, didn't he?'

'Yes, he did.'

'I know someone at school whose sister went.'

'Oh, who was that?' Mrs Gilby asked, immediately interested, and soon she and Linda were indulging in a favourite Compton pastime, tracing the half degree of separation that existed between men, women, cats, dogs and horses in the town.

When Richard had buried both the lambs and cleared away the mess, it was well after lunchtime. Heading down the hill, he peered around the door of the farmhouse to see his mother and Linda absorbed in conversation about Posh Spice and David Beckham.

'Do you think they've got the same hairdresser?' he heard his mother asking.

Feeling happier about leaving Linda now, he waved from the doorway.

'Come on,' he said to his mother. 'We've got a couple of fang marks to get out of a cat.' Linda looked a little less pale now, he thought, even though she had hardly touched any of the biscuits on her plate.

Smiling, his mother followed him into the Jeep, and wound the window down so she could wave goodbye to the girl.

'Say hello to your dad for me,' Richard yelled through the window – then he wound his window up and they were off.

'You know if you hadn't ended up with animals you would have been good with people,' his mother said thoughtfully as they drove towards the next destination – a house in Richmond, about twenty kilometres away.

'I could never have been a doctor,' Richard said. 'Apparently I can't communicate.'

'Oh?' his mother said innocently. 'Who told you that?'

'Various women in my life,' Richard grinned, accelerating up to the speed limit.

Shaking her head, his mother returned to the map. 'Well, I hope the cat's all right now,' she said. 'I don't think I could stand more sadness.'

When they arrived, though, the cat was very much alive.

'Come in,' said a woman, opening the door. 'I'm Maureen and this is Mishka.'

'Hello, Mishka,' Richard said, spotting the animal cowering on the carpet.

Lying on his stomach, Richard pulled the cat out from under the couch. It was black with green eyes and a snub nose.

'Come on, puss,' he said, wriggling forward on his stomach and trying not to handle it too roughly as he slid it out.

The cat's fur was flat, Mrs Gilby saw, and one of its eyes really was almost black too.

'Like a five-cent piece as you described it,' Richard said to Maureen, inspecting the pupil of its left eye, which was almost completely shot. He looked at her worried face. 'I came as fast as I could,' he explained, 'but as I said on the phone, with this kind of snakebite you can generally hang on for a bit – nothing's going to happen to Mishka in a hurry.'

Maureen bit her lip.

'I got the tick out,' she said. 'I had to do it with my nail-varnish remover and my tweezers, I didn't have anything else. But is that what's making him breathe like that?'

'The rattling sound?' Richard asked.

Craning forward, both Maureen and his mother listened to Mishka giving a low, gasping rattle.

'It's just Mishka's system starting to slow down, but we can fix that,' Richard said. 'What's probably happened is, Mishka's got the tick, started to stagger around, and that's when your snake got him,' Richard told Maureen. I see a lot of it. The tick weakens the cat, then the snake strikes. Mishka's going to be fine. Don't worry.'

'I don't know where the snakebite is, though,' Maureen explained. 'He's got such dark fur, I can't tell where it went in.'

'Here,' Richard automatically pointed to the inside of Mishka's mouth. 'See those two tiny marks? Looks like the snake bit him right on the inside of his mouth. I don't suppose you saw what kind of snake it was?'

Maureen shook her head.

'Snakes,' Mrs Gilby tutted. 'They're worse than politicians.'

'I'm going to do something for Mishka now,' Richard explained, reaching for his bag, 'and then I'd like to get him back to the surgery. He needs to go on a drip apart from anything else.'

'A drip?' Maureen said, looking worried.

'Just overnight,' Richard said again.

'Will it be expensive?' she asked.

Looking around her, Richard's mother realized the house was definitely a poor house – she'd been so busy making sympathetic faces at Mishka, she hadn't realized, but it looked as if Maureen couldn't even afford a TV or stereo.

'I won't charge you for coming out,' Richard said quickly. 'It was on my way.'

Maureen smiled gratefully.

'Just so long as he's alive afterwards,' she said.

Richard stroked the cat's head as it crouched low on the floor and wheezed. 'He'll be stronger than ever,' he promised, 'and next time he'll have more resistance to the venom. It'll help him fight back.'

Finding a cardboard box, Richard and his mother gently lifted Mishka inside and then carefully slid the box onto the back seat of the Jeep.

'Mum'll sit here with Mishka,' Richard said, 'and we'll be back to the surgery in no time. Ring me tonight and I'll let you know how he's getting on.'

'I'm so grateful,' Maureen smiled. Mrs Gilby noticed how relieved she looked – even more so since Richard had offered to lower his bill.

'No problem,' Richard smiled back, turning the key in the ignition.

As they drove back to the surgery, Mrs Gilby held onto Mishka's cardboard box to stop it from sliding around on the seat, while Richard drove up against the speed limit again.

'It would have been nice if Tom could have helped you today,' she said thoughtfully. Privately, she thought Sarah could have helped too, but something told her not to ask questions.

'Oh,' Richard brushed this off. 'Tom's got Annie to look after.'

'Annie doesn't need looking after,' his mother said sternly. She was still annoyed that she hadn't turned up to the wedding.

'Tom's got the garden, anyway,' Richard said. 'And half the time when I ring up, there's no answer.'

'He should get an answering machine,' Mrs Gilby said. 'Or she should. Anyway, it's antiquated not to.'

'Can you see Tom with an answering machine?' Richard said, sighing. 'He can hardly manage to get a stamp on a telephone bill.'

'So good looking,' his mother sighed. 'But looks are nothing if you're not a hard worker. The two of you were so close, weren't you?'

Richard shrugged, trying to concentrate on the road in case any more wallabies bounced out of the bushes. 'You were neck and neck for the science prize. Him with plants, you with animals. And then look what happened.'

'Mum, he's happy now,' Richard insisted.

'Well, I wonder sometimes,' his mother sighed, stroking Mishka's head. 'And then there's Harry. What am I going to do about Harry?'

Richard swore as he hit another pothole. He wasn't sure where all the Compton Council rates went, but it certainly wasn't on the roads. It was like driving on the moon.

'Harry's talented,' he said. 'You don't have to worry about Harry.'

'Well, I know he's talented,' his mother replied, 'but what at? He's going to be a cook with too many trades and spoil his own broth.'

'I think you're mixing your metaphors,' Richard said patiently.

'You know what I mean,' she said. 'He's got the music, then there's the bank, then he says he wants to be a painter, or an actor. It changes all the time. I can't keep up. Thank God I know where I stand with you, Richard, or I don't know where I'd be.'

Despite himself, Richard smiled.

'Now, Mishka,' his mother told the cat, 'I think you should give up snakes for Lent. Are you listening?'

But the cat was asleep, dazed by the rhythm of the car and the injection Richard had given it at the house.

'Here comes the rain,' Richard said suddenly, narrowing his eyes as the first splashes of an afternoon shower hit the windscreen. Switching on the wipers, he watched them flick backwards and forwards, enjoying the mindlessness of their left–right motion – and the sweet silence in the back seat as his mother appeared to be dozing off, along with the cat.

The rain was so hard that Richard couldn't have

seen Tom if he'd tried, but even so, as he took the Jeep over the first of several hills back to town, Tom was just a few metres away on the other side of a wall of trees.

Tom's excuse to Annie was that he'd decided to go out fishing – rain like this often brought the big trout he wanted to the surface. In reality though, Tom had decided that he just needed time alone to think. Stuffing his *Angler's Almanac* deeper into the pocket of an old cord blazer of Annie's, he kicked his way along the side of Lilly Creek, letting his socks get drenched as the occasional leech landed on his boots. It was just an *Angler's Almanac*, he knew – just a little yellow paper book from the newsagent's. It had Sarah's handwriting in it, though, and Sarah's love, and that was the difference. Blinking as the rain started dripping from his eyebrows down into the corners of his eyes, Tom walked on with his hands in the pocket of Annie's blazer, deep in thought.

Chapter Seventeen

When Bronte went to work on Monday morning, she knew something was wrong. Instead of talking about *Ally McBeal* by the photocopier, the sub-editors were at their desks, typing furiously and not talking. The radio, which was normally switched to Triple J, had been turned off. And the presence of Cyclone Susan was felt, but not seen, as people rushed around in silence, giving each other meaningful looks. Even the normal cappuccino run seemed to have been cancelled.

'There's been a problem,' Laura explained at last, when Bronte finally sat down at her desk.

'Don't tell me, someone in the Fashion Department developed cellulite over the weekend.'

'Worse than that.'

'Someone got a clue wrong in the crossword?'

'Nobody wants the bananas book,' Laura sighed. 'Upstairs are furious. Susan's ropeable. The readers are actually ripping the bananas book off the front cover and giving it back to the newsagent and complaining. And the one person who did buy it, made the Banana Cobbler and now his whole family's got food poisoning.'

'Ha ha!' Bronte whooped.

'We all got yelled at about an hour ago,' Laura explained.

'I was stuck in traffic,' Bronte said quickly, making excuses.

'You're in trouble too,' Laura said nervously.

'Me? Why?'

'That story you bought from America about Cher and Hugh Grant having a buttock transplant wasn't true.'

'Well, of course it wasn't true. But it was bloody funny, though.'

'Some bloke rang up and he's going to sue us. For ten million dollars.'

'Oh well, we'd better start shifting some of those banana books. Sorry Laura, but I just don't care. You know what I mean? I don't care.'

Laura gave her a look.

'We're all going to die one day,' Bronte said. 'Everyone – Susan, you, me, Cher, Hugh Grant, the Fashion Department, the man who made the Banana Cobbler.'

'Well, he might die sooner than we think,' Laura said, smiling nervously.

'We'll all be dead, in the ground,' Bronte said firmly. 'And if you think I'm going to spend my last moments on this earth worrying about bloody *Australian Woman*, then you've got it all wrong.'

'Right,' sighed Laura.

'And I'll tell you something else,' Bronte said.

'What?'

'I've got an appointment with a shrink this afternoon, and I never felt more sane in my whole life.'

At 12.30 p.m., Bronte set off to see Dr Valerie Tan, relieved to be out of the office. The staff had been skulking around as if the end of the world had just started, and she was fed up with hearing everyone whisper into their phones. Working for *Australian Woman* was like labouring on a chicken farm, she decided. Everyone pecked everyone else and eventually someone got pecked to death, usually a secretary. Cyclone Susan had the biggest beak, of course, but even she had some other corporate rooster at the top to deal with. They really were like a pack of demented chickens on a battery farm, Bronte thought.

Crossing the Domain, she swerved to avoid a pack of other corporate roosters, who looked like they pecked people to death for a living. They were all red in the face and shuffling forward in designer trainers. Bronte decided they looked like the sort of men who actually ordered battery-operated nose hair-trimmers from magazines on aeroplanes. Not one of them could be bothered to grunt a hello, she noticed. This was what life had come to – women seeing shrinks and men turning into Nike-wearing automotons. She caught one of them looking surreptitiously at her bottom and made a face at him.

'You're not in a lap-dance restaurant now,' she said, but her voice was lost in the wind.

When she finally arrived at Dr Valerie Tan's clinic, she found her psychologist eating Minties from the glass bowl on her desk.

'Hi,' she said with her mouth full, waving Bronte into one of the beige armchairs and offering her the bowl. 'How are you?'

'Well, I haven't seen Angel since I was last here,' Bronte explained, 'so that's good.'

'I've been talking to one of my colleagues about that,' Dr Tan replied. 'To set your mind at rest, you should know that there is no clinical evidence for apparitions. There never has been, and there probably never will be.'

'Nobody's ever photographed a ghost?' Bronte asked.

'No. They've photographed people dressed up in white sheets,' Dr Tan waved her hand dismissively, 'but even in the most exhaustive parapsychological research, there has never been any hard evidence for the existence of a ghost, a spirit, an entity – or anything else.'

Bronte sat back in her chair and relaxed.

'Of course, I'm not saying that you didn't see something,' Dr Tan said.

'Right.'

'But it is unlikely to be what you think it is. In fact, I believe that your apparition problem is also linked to your fear of death.'

'I suppose that's got a name, hasn't it,' Bronte said. 'Grimreaperphobia or something.'

Dr Tan smiled and crossed her legs. 'It does have a name, but what I believe you are suffering from is more complex than that.'

'Mmmm,' Bronte agreed, letting a Mintie slide around her mouth.

'You see, I believe you may not have come to terms with your miscarriage. You think you have forgotten it, and in many ways so you have – it is filed away in your subconscious. I would guess you sometimes dream about the baby because of this – indirect dreams, or direct dreams.'

'I do,' Bronte shivered, remembering a recurring dream about a dead baby at the bottom of a dam.

'Your subconscious has been doing you a favour by processing the event,' Dr Tan explained. 'It has made life safe for you by allowing you to forget. But you have actually not forgotten at all. It has taken a new event – your former husband marrying for the second time – to trigger an awakening.'

'I see,' Bronte said, although she didn't entirely.

'It's possible the death of your horse, and the death of your baby, may be one and the same thing for you.'

'And that's why I keep seeing Angel?'

'Perhaps,' Dr Tan said. 'It is like a waking dream for you. Things are moving to the surface of your conscious mind at last.'

'Hmmm,' Bronte nodded.

'Fear of imminent death may be linked to unresolved guilt.'

'You mean I think I deserve to die?'

'On some level, perhaps.'

Bronte took another Mintie. She didn't think she deserved to die at all – she could think of a handful of people, including Cyclone Susan, and the man with the small feet and the lava lamp, who probably did – but she wouldn't have put herself on the list.

'Sleep deprivation too,' Dr Tan said. 'That's not helping your condition. Your parasympathetic nervous system may be in collusion with your subconscious in creating your current problems.'

Bronte nodded, not understanding a word.

'The main thing is,' Dr Tan said at last, 'you are not seeing a ghost, and you are not going mad, as you fear. And you are very unlikely to die in the short term. Not that I wish to play God,' the doctor gave a faint laugh, 'but statistically, a woman of your age in this country, in your condition, stands more chance of getting run over by a bus than – er, dying.'

'I don't think you mean that,' Bronte said, smiling at last as Dr Tan looked embarrassed. 'But, anyway, I've got more chance of getting married again, basically. Are you married, Dr Tan?'

'I am,' she admitted. 'In fact, my husband works not far from here. He goes jogging over there,' she pointed to the Domain, where Bronte had just been, 'every lunch hour.'

Bronte smiled. Poor Dr Tan. She might know how to say things like 'parasympathetic nervous system' and 'unresolved guilt', but she was still married to a corporate jogger. Maybe it was the man who looked like a rhinoceros. Hopefully it wasn't the man she had just shouted at.

'That's a huge relief,' Bronte said. 'I mean, not that you're married, that you're telling me nothing's wrong.'

'Well, something is wrong,' Dr Tan said. 'But we can fix it. It may take time, but you will be able to deal with all that has happened in your life – after repressing it for a very long time, it would seem.'

'No more ghosts?'

'No more ghosts,' Dr Tan promised, smiling. 'Would you like some coffee to wash down the Minties?'

As Bronte got into the lift and pushed the ground floor button, she breathed out a long sigh of relief. Apart from the fact that the inside of her mouth tasted like she had just swallowed a tube of toothpaste, she was actually feeling better. She trusted Dr Valerie Tan. And if she said she wasn't about to die, she could go along with that. It all made sense, when she thought about it – Angel and the baby. They had happened too close together and she'd never got over it, and now Richard had married again and it was all coming back.

Stepping out onto the pavement, Bronte looked for a taxi to take her back to the office, deciding to treat herself – but after ten minutes of trucks, courier bicycles and speeding cars, she realized she would have to walk instead. Hopefully the corporate joggers would have gone back to work by now so she wouldn't have to face any more sweaty men thundering past her.

Bronte stepped out onto the kerb. And then, without warning, she felt something shove into her, coming from the left-hand side of the road. She turned her head and saw a flash of white, and a flash of wings. And then she fell, knees first, onto the pavement as someone on the other side of the road began screaming, and a battered Holden braked hard to a halt in front of her, just inches away.

The woman who had screamed rushed over, waving the traffic out of the way, while the driver slowly pulled his vehicle over to the side of the road, forcing the honking queue of cars behind to pile up in zig-zag lines behind him.

'Are you OK?' the woman panted, looking up into Bronte's face. She was very short.

Bronte nodded automatically, then realized her knees were killing her and looked down and saw blood. The gravel on the road had also taken off the top layer of skin from her fingers.

Suddenly she realized someone vaguely familiar was standing in front of her. With a jolt, she realized it was Bernard Bolton.

'I am so sorry,' he gasped. He looked terrible.

'She's lucky,' the woman said, staring at him and guiding Bronte by the elbow to the side of the road. As soon as she reached the soft grass of the Domain, Bronte flopped down. She was quite trembly, she realized – and her knees felt like marshmallow.

'Thanks so much,' Bronte said to the short woman, who had put all her shopping bags down on the pavement to help, while Bernard Bolton hovered, looking pale and worried.

It was only after she had got her breath back, and taken in the vehicle parked at the side of the road, that Bronte realized it must be his car that had nearly hit her.

'Will you be OK?' the short woman with the shopping bags asked and Bronte nodded.

'Thanks,' she said, as the woman walked off, leaving her with Bernard.

Wincing, Bronte stretched her legs out in front of her on the grass. She would probably have giant bruises tomorrow, she realized.

'I saw Angel push you out of the way,' Bernard said, also trying to get his breath back.

Bronte nodded. 'You saw her too?'

'I saw her,' he repeated. 'I didn't have time to do anything. I'm so sorry, Bronte. I thought I could avoid it, but I couldn't.'

'What do you mean?' Bronte stared at him. Bernard's face had lost so much colour that the bags under his eyes actually looked blue, she thought.

'I was told this would happen, I was warned about

it. And I thought I could avoid it,' he said again.

'Bernard, start again. Do you mean you could have run me over?'

'Worse,' he said.

'You could have killed me?'

He nodded.

Bronte shook her head. Her knees were stinging and she wished she'd thought of asking the short woman with the shopping bags to get help, but it was too late now. She'd gone.

'I'll get a doctor,' Bernard offered.

'It might be a good idea,' Bronte said, falling over her words. 'I think I'm in shock. I feel a bit funny.'

He nodded. 'You're not the only one,' he said.

'You could have hit me,' Bronte said, taking it all in.

'Angel pushed you away,' he said.

'So she really is here,' Bronte said, wonderingly, and then burst into tears while Bernard found a handkerchief.

He let her cry for a while, patting her shoulder, while Bronte heaved out wave after wave of sobs.

'No, don't stop,' he insisted, when she paused for breath and realized, to her embarrassment, that people on the pavement were staring. 'Let it all out, it's the best way.'

'It's all too much,' she managed to say. 'I can't cope with it.'

'I know,' Bernard said, kindly. 'I know.'

'Can we go somewhere else?' she said at last. 'Somewhere private?'

'My club,' Bernard said. 'How about that? It's just around the corner.'

Seeing that Bronte was in no condition to make decisions, he helped her up and steered her carefully across the traffic lights. Glancing back at his car, he could see he would have to risk a ticket, but there were other, more important things to take care of.

'What sort of club is it?' Bronte managed to ask as

she half walked, half stumbled with stinging knees in the direction of Park Street.

'Just a normal club,' he said.

'Not some sort of witches' coven?' she insisted.

'They serve roast dinners and I know for a fact witches don't like roast dinners,' he said, smiling. 'They've also got a first-aid room. And they've got medicinal brandy at the bar.'

They kept walking and eventually arrived at the club, a solid-looking building off Hyde Park with stained-glass doors and shiny oak floors and – Bronte was pleased to see – it was well equipped with bottles of Scotch as well as brandy. While she stretched her sore legs out across two armchairs, Bernard found her cotton wool, Dettol and Band-Aids from the club's first-aid room.

'You knew this was going to happen, didn't you?' she said at last.

'I thought I was helping you by leaving,' he said, handing her a wad of cotton wool.

'You really did a bunk, didn't you?'

'I had to. But I should have known, you cannot escape your fate.'

'Except I did. Angel did it for me.'

'Angel was the one who told me I might end up killing you,' Bernard sighed, reaching for his glass of Scotch.

'She actually said that?'

'I couldn't tell you. What could I say? But she made it very clear. The only thing was, I wasn't sure *how* it was going to happen.'

'You thought you might attack me with a set of steak knives or something, I suppose.'

Bernard managed to laugh.

'I just knew it was too dangerous to stay. So I packed up the flat and now I'm living in Queensland.'

'Oh, my God! You didn't have to do that.'

'Well, I didn't as it turns out,' he shrugged. 'I only

came back here for a day to see a client and I seem to have met my fate anyway. It was a close call – one minute the road was clear and the next minute, there you were in front of me.'

Bronte winced as she dabbed at the scratches on the heel of each hand. She could already feel the bruises forming down each shin and she was sure she'd have a huge, purple bruise on her left side as well.

'I've been seeing a shrink,' she told Bernard as the waiter bought them cubes of cheese. 'I had this impending fear of death and I kept seeing Angel all the time. She said it was my parasympathetic nervous system and my subconscious mind.'

Bernard smiled faintly.

'I saw Angel too,' he said. 'So maybe it's *my* subconscious mind.'

'Angel went to all that trouble to warn both of us,' Bronte mused, 'and then when that didn't work, she just flew in and pushed me out of the way. I wonder if that nice woman with the shopping bags saw her too?'

Bernard shrugged. 'That's three of us with a problem then,' he said. 'Better tell your shrink.'

'Oh, I'm not going back,' Bronte said, patting down the Band-Aids on her legs. 'I don't have to now. I know Angel exists.'

'And you know you've escaped your own death,' Bernard replied.

'Oh, I'm not scared of dying any more,' Bronte said. 'But I was right all along. I knew I could feel it coming, and it was coming today. Now I just feel happy. In fact . . .' she broke off, catching the waiter's eye, 'I feel *happy*. My God, I've forgotten what it feels like, you know?' Motioning to the waiter, she asked for champagne. 'And French, not Australian,' she added.

A few minutes later, when a bottle of Möet had been wheeled out in a silver bucket, she watched as Bernard clapped his hands together, solemnly, five times in a row. His eyes were shut and he looked very determined about something, Bronte thought.

'What are you doing, or is there a mosquito in here?' she asked.

He smiled. 'I'm farewelling your horse,' he said. 'She's gone to the light.'

'Well, that's funny,' Bronte said, 'because I'm sure I just felt a gust of wind go past me. And the door's closed in here.'

'She's gone,' Bernard said at last. 'She had a job to do and now she's gone. But she did say goodbye.'

'Well, that's nice,' Bronte said, feeling sad and relieved at the same time.

'She did say one thing before she left, though,' Bernard offered.

'Oh?'

'Something about bananas,' Bernard said, looking confused.

'Oh, I know what that's all about,' Bronte said happily, pouring herself and Bernard another glass of Möet. 'No, she's absolutely right about that one.'

By the time Bronte finally left the club and Bernard had gone back to his car, the afternoon sun was starting to fade. This time Bronte had no problem finding a cab and she was back at the office just before 5 p.m.

'I've had a lot of messages from Upstairs,' Laura said nervously when Bronte finally strode into the office. 'My God, what happened to your legs?'

'I had some of that instant lunchtime liposuction,' Bronte slurred. She was feeling slightly drunk. 'They sucked my knees out and inserted them where my boobs normally go. What do Upstairs want?'

'Well, actually,' Laura said, 'I think it's serious. They want you to go up there.'

'Good,' Bronte said. 'I will.'

Smiling broadly, she marched back out of the door

and headed for the fire escape stairs – it was always faster than catching the lift and she could never stand the smell in there, anyway.

Finally reaching the top floor, she stood at the top of the stairs to catch her breath and then smoothed down the Band-Aids on her knees and headed for Cyclone Susan's office. At the sight of Bronte, the editor's secretary froze.

'She's busy,' she said.

'No she's not,' Bronte replied. 'She's just ringing up Clinique trying to get free moisturiser. I know what busy means.'

'Bronte!' the secretary pleaded, but it was no use. She had already turned the door handle and was walking into the office.

'Excuse me,' Cyclone Susan muttered into the phone, seeing her Features Editor in the doorway. She placed the receiver carefully on top of the desk and stared hard at Bronte and then at her knees and finally at her trainers, which were speckled with what looked like blood.

'Hello,' Bronte said cheerfully.

'What,' said Cyclone Susan slowly, 'is wrong with you?'

'I heard someone got poisoned by the Banana Cobbler,' Bronte said.

'Bronte, what are you doing here?'

Bronte shrugged, feeling like a fifteen-year-old in front of the headmistress.

'I think you'd better go,' Susan said in a steady voice, but Bronte could see that she was twisting her ankle underneath her on the carpet below the desk.

'I'm not going anywhere because I've come here to resign,' Bronte replied.

'Your employment has already been terminated,' Susan said quickly. 'It was organized this morning with management.'

'Bullshit,' Bronte said cheerfully.

'I'm going to call security,' Susan said, cutting off her other phone call.

'Don't worry, I'm going,' Bronte replied. 'Going to a place where the women are women, not battery hens. Going to somewhere where Goldie Hawn without her make-up on isn't a piece of news. Going to a more meaningful existence, Susan.'

I wish I wasn't forty, Bronte thought, *because it's the only thing stopping me from blowing a raspberry and sticking up two fingers.*

And then she closed the door behind her and ran down the fire escape stairs to pack up her office.

Chapter Eighteen

The mosquitoes were unbelievable. Swearing, Tom slapped one of them between his hands, at the same moment that he was being stung by another one on his ankle. He already had three itchy lumps on his arm and wished he'd rubbed some of Annie's tea-tree oil on before leaving home.

Where were all the frogs when you needed them? he thought. Lilly Creek had once been full of them, but these days the insect population seemed to have taken over. It had been months since Tom had come here. He could see by the piles of black logs and ash that people had been lighting campfires over the summer and there was even a pair of soggy pink pants hanging off a tree branch – how long had they been there?

As the mosquitoes continued to bite, he decided that he probably deserved every one of them. It was a minor punishment for what he was doing to Richard, but it was better than no punishment at all.

Looking around him, he wondered what Sarah had been expecting. It had been her idea to come to the creek – if it had been left up to him, Tom would have suggested meeting in some anonymous cafe in Hobart. She had insisted, though, and he had given in. To be safe, they had decided on Wednesday afternoon –

when Richard would be seeing his patients and Annie would be visiting friends. At least they would be alone, Tom decided, looking around him. He shifted position on the old tree trunk by the side of the creek. Now that the afternoons were so cool, hardly anybody wanted to come here. He longed to go in, though.

The water was so clear that he could peer over the creek and see all the orange and white quartz stones lying on the bottom, right in the middle of the deepest pool. Part of him wished he was just here fishing today – it would be far more peaceful and his heart would not be thumping quite so hard, especially when he thought about Richard. But another part of him could only wish Sarah would hurry up.

Ever since she had suggested this Wednesday afternoon meeting, he had found it difficult to get through thirty minutes of any day without automatically thinking of her. If he treated his feelings for her as some kind of passing madness, he decided, it made it better. But the best thing of all was not to think about any of it too much. *Just let it go*, Tom decided. *Fall into it, see what happens*.

Then suddenly she was there. Looking up, he saw her pushing her way between the bushes. She was covered in leaves and smiling.

'Hi,' she said, panting. 'I found you.'

'You have found me,' Tom said, shyly.

She was wearing a long, white lacy dress he had never seen before. For a second, it reminded him of her wedding dress.

'Can I sit on here too?' she asked, looking at the tree trunk. Tom moved out of the way to make room for her and then she was next to him, and so close that he could see a ladybird in her blonde hair.

'Let me get this,' he said, carefully making a balcony out of his finger so that the ladybird could be lifted to safety on the ground.

'In books they're always red, but they're really

212

orange,' Sarah said quickly. She was nervous, Tom realized. He could hear it in her voice.

'Oh my God,' she said suddenly, pushing her face into her hands. 'My God, we're here!'

Tom smiled and pulled her towards him. Instantly and instinctively, her head went onto his shoulder.

'Are you OK?' he asked, gazing at the orange and white stones at the bottom of the creek.

Suddenly looking up at him, Sarah kissed him. Immediately, he kissed her neck, her shoulder and her lips again, and for a few minutes it seemed like they were in the creek already, swimming, almost under the water.

'Off the log,' Tom suggested, pulling her up by the hand.

'Yes, off the log,' she agreed.

'Your shoes are going to get dirty,' Tom said, looking at her white sandshoes as she stumbled after him on the muddy banks, hanging onto his hand.

'Wrong shoes, I know,' she said, and then neither of them spoke as Tom pulled her through the bushes and onto a narrow trail passing between the gum trees. Each time they came across a spider's web, Tom yanked it down for her, but always on the opposite side to the spider so it had a fair chance of escape.

They are so like each other, Sarah realized, thinking of Richard's similar concern for spiders and ladybirds and beetles – and then she deliberately lost the thought, pushing it away.

'Almost there,' Tom said, turning slightly and smiling at her. At the same moment, the trees suddenly became shorter so that the afternoon sunlight could break through. For a moment, Sarah allowed herself a shot of sheer bliss. She had thought about this, and hoped for this, and longed for this. And now it was here. It was real and it was happening.

Finally, Tom found what he was looking for. Stopping to catch his breath, he pointed at a small, dark, deserted pool of water that was almost entirely enclosed by trees.

'Only a few people know about this,' he said at last.

'Totally private,' Sarah said wonderingly.

'Lilly Falls and Lilly Creek both feed this place. You can't fish in it – but you can swim in it.'

'Skinny-dip in it,' Sarah said. 'Do you remember that day when we were sitting on my bed and you told me about Lilly Creek and the skinny-dippers?'

Tom smiled.

'I wanted you so much then,' she said.

'You were blushing,' he remembered.

Yanking his shirt off his shoulders, Tom hung it on a low-hanging tree branch, then pulled off his T-shirt underneath.

'Oh, OK,' Sarah smiled and reaching behind her back, she felt her way up the back of her zip with her fingers.

'Allow me,' Tom said and tugging carefully, he pulled the zip straight down from the back of her neck to the bottom of her spine.

'No pants,' he said, approvingly.

'No pants,' Sarah said. 'After all – I knew we were only going to have to take them off.'

'I'd just like you to lean against this tree though,' Tom said, pushing his fringe out of his eyes with one hand and propelling her with the other free hand.

'Why?'

There was really no why, though, Sarah decided. Nor was there a what, or a when, or even a how. There was just Tom now and she did not want him to stop kissing her. She could feel mosquitoes feeding on her and sharp bits of bark digging into her back, but feeling Tom touching her at last was an anaesthetic against everything.

Finally he pulled himself away.

'Eaten alive,' he said, half smiling, slapping a mosquito on his bare shoulder. 'We should go swimming now.'

Everything about him seemed new, Sarah realized. His face seemed new because he looked so happy, but also because she was gazing at him in a different light from the one she was used to – this was shady, dark green, late afternoon light. His face also now had a neck – and shoulders and a chest below it, and that was new too. The chest had small scars and stray blond hairs and the neck was warmer than she had ever realized. And the smell – the Tom smell she had craved, all lemons and sweat and garden mint – was all around her now.

'I wish I could bottle you,' she said, feeling drunk with love.

'Let's get in,' he said, grinning and nodding his head at the water.

Sarah loved the fact that Tom looked so happy now. She had never, ever, seen him this happy, she realized.

Pulling off his boots and then his thick woollen socks, and finally his jeans and leather belt, Tom left them on the bank of the creek and, without looking at her, dived straight in.

'Oh my God,' Sarah breathed to herself, watching him go.

And then he bolted up from the water almost on the far bank, shaking his head back to get rid of the shock of the cold.

'Come on!' he yelled.

Unclipping her bra, Sarah waggled her hips until her unzipped dress fell down and caught at her knees. Then she carefully pulled it off and folded it, placing it neatly next to Tom's pile of jeans, socks and boots on the grass and hung her bra on the tree next to his shirt. Next, she took off her watch and – last of all – her wedding ring.

Watching her, Tom hated the fact that he could not take his eyes off her, but there was no point in trying to pretend he was anything less than hypnotized. He was used to Annie's body after all these years, and Sarah was something else. He smiled at the white London skin she had managed to keep all these months, making strange animal stripes with her newly acquired Australian tan.

'Come in, come in,' he waved her into the water and then swam freestyle towards the bank. Realizing he would pull her in if she didn't dive in first, Sarah suddenly pushed her hands together automatically – and as she hit the water, she realized that was something only schoolgirls did, and she was thirty years old.

She was determined not to gasp and splutter when she came up and, by breathing hard through her nose and keeping her lips pressed together, she managed to get away with it.

'Lovely dive,' Tom said, trying not to laugh and swimming around in front of her.

'Shallow dive,' Sarah said. 'I'm amazed I can still do that.'

With his hair wet and off his face, he looked new to her yet again. Two new Toms in one afternoon, she thought.

'I am so in love with you,' she said, reaching out to put one arm around his neck.

Shaking drops out of his eyes, Tom pulled her to him. 'And I am so grateful to you,' he whispered in her ear. He felt as if his life was beginning again, somehow, and until now he hadn't even realized he'd been half dead.

Trying to kiss and lose themselves in each other, without also losing their balance in the water, they swam around each other and then together, until the sound of another whining mosquito in Tom's ear made him suddenly duck his head under.

'Come on,' he said, swimming away from Sarah and towards the furthest bank. 'Let's get away from these insects.'

Admiringly, Sarah realized that he actually had muscles in his arms that were put there by nature and

216

hard work. Watching Tom's strong brown back and shoulders moving through the water, she almost felt like getting on her knees and thanking God for him, except God had nothing to do with it, as she knew very well.

Letting herself gaze at him without feeling self-conscious about it, she wonderingly watched him lift himself out of the water and onto the bank, and for a moment, remembered picking up his wet red bathers from Annie's bathroom and almost holding them up to her face.

Following his lead, she swam over, found the same shallow patch of the creek bed and the same large slab of slate and, with Tom's help, she lifted herself up and out of the water.

Sarah looked so young, Tom realized. Or maybe Annie just looked so old. Annoyed with himself for comparing the two, he slapped both Annie and the mosquitoes away with one wet hand.

'I know a tree-house,' he said, taking her in his arms.

'Do you?' Sarah nuzzled into him.

'It's a tree-house that's been here for a very long time.'

'Is it?'

'You know, I could do without clothes,' he said, smiling at her. 'Why do we need them?'

'Imagine getting on the Tube without them,' Sarah said.

'You're in Tasmania now, Sarah,' Tom said, kissing her again. Now that they were both out of the creek, they were warming each other up. She felt unbelievably soft and almost hot in his arms.

Holding her close, Tom walked with Sarah for a few minutes and then stopped at an ancient gum tree, looking up at a tree-house slightly above their heads.

'Oh,' said Sarah, thankfully, 'it's only just off the ground.' She was trying not to feel like a Londoner who had just gone native – and embarrassed – but the fact that she would not have to climb, ape-like and naked, up some fifty-foot Australian tree was a relief. Someone had cleverly built in quite a large tree-house over a series of planks nailed into two forking branches and then hung a rope ladder with three rungs to climb up.

Tom went up first and in a second he was inside the tree-house, smiling down at her.

'That's it,' he said, as Sarah climbed up. 'Just hold onto the ropes on both sides.'

Crawling forward through the doorway, Sarah couldn't help laughing.

'My primate past,' she giggled. 'I remember now.'

'And the best thing is,' Tom announced, 'there are no mossies up here.'

Bending down to get inside, Sarah was amazed to see a lantern, some blankets and even a half-burned candle.

'Isn't it someone else's?' she said quickly.

Tom shook his head.

'They just left it for us to enjoy,' he said, finding a box of matches on the tree-house floor and lighting the candle. It was beginning to get dark outside.

'I love dusk,' he said. 'All the cicadas are out.'

Sarah shook out the blankets and spread them on the tree-house floor.

'No pillow,' said Tom, lying down and pulling her towards him. 'Can I use you?'

Feeling his wet hair against her skin as he sank onto her, Sarah marvelled again at the fact that it was all really happening and nothing seemed to be stopping it. Even more incredibly, she realized, it was all happening with Tom in a way that even she could not have dreamed or begged for. Tom in a tree-house with a candle on the floor – it was something he had delivered to her, rather than something she had imagined for herself – and that was what made it all the more amazing.

Silently moving with each other on top of the blankets, they shifted left, then right to avoid knocking over the candle, until Tom slid it out of the way into the doorway of the tree-house with one arm. They were incredibly slippery together, Tom realized – all water and sweat and wet kisses.

'And nobody's here?' Sarah gasped, after what seemed like hours as he finally pulled her to him.

Tom bit her shoulder in reply, on top of the three mosquito bites she had already gathered, and then to prove there was nobody there, just when she thought he was the quietest, strangest man she had ever loved, he shouted her name so loudly that she thought the tree-house roof might fall down.

'Oh lord,' she said eventually, when it was all over. 'My watch. My watch is on the ground.' And her wedding ring too, she remembered, pushing the thought away.

Sleepily, Tom pushed the hair out of his eyes – it was still wet, he realized. The swim had seemed like hours ago.

'I never wear a watch,' he said.

'What time do you think it is?' Sarah tried again.

He yawned and kissed the top of her head.

'Do I taste of creek water?' she asked.

'No. And it's time for us to go back to our real houses now,' Tom replied.

Sarah felt her heart drop down to the bottom of the ground.

'No,' she said. 'I want to live up here.'

'Candle's nearly gone out,' Tom said. Sticking his head out of the tree-house entrance, he could see Venus shining brightly and a few other stars.

'Can we come here again?' Sarah asked, longing for him to say yes. But Tom was already on the first rung of the rope ladder.

'Never again,' he shook his head.

'What?' Sarah crawled forward on all-fours to look

219

at him as he swung his way down.

'Never. It's like a poem,' he shook his head again, 'it's a one-off.'

Just as long as you and I aren't one-offs too, Sarah caught herself thinking. But he had yelled her name through the trees and up to the stars and somehow she didn't think it would be.

Chapter Nineteen

It was well after nine o'clock when Annie finally heard Tom coming in.

'Shhh!' she said to the dogs, who'd started barking as soon as they heard his bicycle wheels turn on the gravel.

Settling back, down on the couch again, she tried to concentrate on her book, and ignore the fact that he was so late. They had fought about this before – him disappearing and her waiting up – and she didn't want to start another argument. Instead, Annie thought, she had done a fairly good job of trying to consciously enjoy herself without Tom. She had lit candles and poured some oil into her aromatherapy burner and put on her favourite music. She had dug out an old copy of *Wuthering Heights*, which she had forgotten well enough to go back to. And now he was here – and that was the end of it. She would finish her chapter, turn down the music and welcome him back as if nothing had happened. Even if it killed her.

'Hello,' Tom said quietly, standing at the doorway.

'Merlin not with you?' Annie asked sleepily from the couch.

'I thought he was here,' Tom said, looking around. 'Why? Has he wandered?'

'I haven't seen him since this afternoon,' Annie said.

'I just thought he'd gone with you – wherever it was you went.'

'Fishing,' Tom said quickly.

'Aaah.'

Annie turned back to her *TV Guide*.

'Merlin will turn up,' Tom said.

'I expect he will,' Annie replied, scanning her magazine.

'Anything on?' Tom asked, quickly going to the bedroom to change out of his clothes.

'A film,' Annie said, holding the *TV Guide* up to the candle light. 'Something Italian about a love triangle.'

In the bedroom, Tom stopped halfway through pulling off a damp sock.

'Why don't we get a video?' he called through the doorway. Annie made a face. 'No thanks,' she said. 'All that way to drive into town and anyway, it'll be closing.'

'What about we play cards, then?' Tom suggested.

Annie sighed. 'We haven't played cards since you first moved in. I'm surprised you can remember how to do it.'

Shaking her head, she lifted herself off the couch and padded barefoot into the kitchen to put the kettle on. Watching her go, Tom was struck by her light, quick movements. Sarah was slower and softer, somehow. Like a girl in a dream. Annie was like a bird.

'So where were you anyway?' Annie said, deliberately trying to sound casual as she filled the kettle.

'Trout,' Tom said, walking into the kitchen and rubbing his face. He hoped he was getting away with it.

'Ah, trout,' Annie said, finding the teabags.

Then she turned as she heard a car coming down the driveway, sending its headlights through the kitchen windows. Immediately, the dogs went flying out through the back door to meet it, falling over themselves at the excitement of an unexpected arrival.

'Dogs! Dogs!' Annie yelled, trying to stop them.

Following them, Tom pushed his way through the back door, feeling his heart hammering inside his chest. Surely Sarah couldn't be here now? As he walked out onto the driveway, he shielded his eyes with his hand, trying to make out the car and the driver through the glaring headlights. Abruptly, the lights went off. And then Tom could see it – not Sarah's car, thank God, but a dark red ute with a frantically yapping Merlin in the back.

'G'day,' someone said, winding down the window.

Squinting into the darkness, Tom could now see it was Andrew, one of their neighbours from the end of the road. Even if he couldn't see Andrew's face clearly in the dark, he could see his cap – it was an old tartan baseball cap and he never took it off.

Suddenly, with one leap, Merlin cleared the side of the ute and then he was down on the ground with the other dogs, who were frantically pushing each other out of the way in order to get to him. Hearing footsteps behind him on the gravel, Tom turned and saw Annie, also squinting into the darkness.

'My porch light's blown, sorry,' she said, waving at the ute. 'Is that you, Andrew?'

'I'm just bringing the dog back,' Andrew said. 'I figured you'd lost him, Tom.'

'Lost? When?' Tom said quickly.

'Well, I saw him following you out to Lilly Creek . . .' Andrew started.

'Shit,' Tom said, then realized his mistake as he caught sight of Annie's face.

'Anyway, he's come back with me now,' Andrew finished. 'Did you have a good swim?'

'Great,' Tom muttered, staring at Merlin as he disappeared under a tidal wave of other dogs.

'I didn't want to intrude,' Andrew smiled, looking at Tom, then at Annie. 'I could hear you were having fun in there, splashing about.'

And then, with Tom silently cursing his back,

Andrew pushed his tartan cap back on his head, swung back into the front seat of his ute and started the engine. As he reversed up the long, gravel driveway, Annie put her hands on her hips, gazing up at the night sky, waiting for him to disappear. And then, when he had finally gone, she sighed – a hard, heavy sigh that made Tom feel as if the end of the world were coming.

'Well, who were you there with?' she said simply, turning her back on him and walking into the house.

Letting her go, Tom walked over to Merlin, who was still surrounded by the other dogs. Bending down beside him, he put his hand under his hard, leather collar and scratched his neck as he always did.

'Why didn't you let me know you were there?' Tom hissed. Grinning happily, Merlin yawned at him, gave a half squeal, half groan and then ran off into the house after Annie.

Sighing, Tom stood up again and let him go. It wasn't unusual for Merlin to follow him up the road – he had done it a couple of times before. Tom was furious that he hadn't caught him, though. And he was even angrier that Andrew had been hanging around in his ute near the creek, obviously hearing every splash – and more – that he and Sarah had been making. Of course, Andrew had assumed that the other person he could hear was Annie, but that didn't really make things much easier for Tom.

Venus was still out overhead, looking sharp and white in the dark night sky. It was exactly the same star that he had been staring at with Sarah from the tree-house hours before, but now Tom was finding it hard to believe that it had even happened. He remembered yelling her name and felt himself blushing horribly in the dark. Thank God, Andrew seemed to have missed that bit.

Turning on his heel in the gravel, Tom shoved his hands into his pockets and went back inside. Annie was back on the couch again, reading *Wuthering*

Heights in a determined way – but she had turned the music off.

'Andrew thought it was you and me up at Lilly Creek,' Annie said, looking up at him at last. 'But it wasn't you and me because I was in town. So I'm asking you again, who were you with?'

Tom thought quickly of a few convenient lies. He could say that Andrew had been imagining things and that nobody else apart from him had been up there. He could also say he'd been swimming with Harry – not Richard, though – that would make life even more complicated than it already was. In the end, though, Tom took his hands out of his pockets, blew out one of Annie's candles and decided there was only one thing he could say.

'I have to go, Annie.'

'Go where?' Slowly and deliberately, she put her book down.

Tom had always found it hard to find the right words when there was something important to say. On paper, he could turn things into poetry, but that was no good to him now. Struggling to say what he really meant, he found himself trying to speak, failing, and then giving up. Hating himself for it, he sat down at the table opposite Annie and put his head in his hands.

'If you want to go as in *go*,' she forced an attempt at a laugh, 'then just say it. Don't muck around, Tom.'

'I want to leave,' he said.

'You want to leave. Well – good.'

Quickly, she reached over to pick up the candle that was still propped up next to her on top of a pile of art magazines. Bending her arm back as far as it would go, she threw it at the wall behind Tom's head, where it bounced, then rolled onto the floorboards. Silently, they watched it roll backwards and forwards until it came to a stop.

'Well, look at that,' Annie said. 'The flame's still there. The flame hasn't gone out.'

Tom knew something else was coming and he sat quietly, waiting for her to finish.

'You wanted to marry me once,' she said.

Staring at her, Tom felt the beginnings of a painful stretch in his throat. The lump, he decided, felt as big as a nectarine.

'Is this a passing thing?' she tried again. 'It often is – it passes. It's like an illness.'

He shook his head. 'Annie, it's over,' he sighed.

'Over? But what does that mean exactly?'

'Can we be both be honest about this?' he asked, staring at her. Then he cringed as he realized it was the worst thing he could have said.

'Honesty is your special subject, then? Creeping around at Lilly Creek in the middle of the afternoon?'

Getting up from his seat at the table, Tom picked up the candle where she had thrown it on the floor, blew out the flame and put it on top of Annie's old piano. When he had first moved in, their first kiss had been at that piano.

'Have you been unfaithful to me?'

'Oh, for God's sake, Annie!'

'Well, have you?'

'Be honest enough to admit it's gone wrong with us, will you?' Tom shook his head angrily.

'Why has it gone wrong? Where?'

'This is not a life. It was something that made sense when we were younger.'

'*Not a life!* Well, what sort of life would you have without me?' Annie shot back.

'And that's what I'm sick of!' Tom found himself shouting. 'It's always the same thing. I'm not going to last without you. I can't have a decent life without you. Do you realize how much less of a man that makes me feel?'

'Who's been talking to you?' she said, swinging herself up on the couch so that she was sitting up straight and facing him. 'Has Harry been in your ear? Or

226

Richard? Someone's got at you, I can hear it in your voice. Has Sarah been talking to you?'

'And somehow,' Tom said quickly, 'I can't ever make up my own mind without being influenced by someone – at least according to you.'

'Stop it!' Annie yelled.

'It's over!' he yelled back. 'My own decision, my own independent decision.'

'You and independence,' Annie said wearily, throwing her copy of *Wuthering Heights* down on the rug. 'What a combination.'

'You don't respect me,' Tom insisted. 'So why must we be together?'

'There's no *must* in it,' Annie said quietly. 'It's down to love, that's all. And I can see now that you don't love me any more.'

Tom knew that if he could stay angry with Annie, it would give him the strength to go. He forced himself to think of every single time he'd wanted to walk out and never had.

'We used to talk about this at the meetings,' he said.

'Oh, Alcoholics Anonymous,' Annie sniffed. 'Those meetings.' She had hated Tom going to AA.

'At the meetings, they used to say that the person you take on at the beginning is not the person you have at the end,' he insisted. 'And that's what has happened to us.'

'Rationalize, rationalize.'

'I'm going, Annie. That's it. I'm going.'

As he pulled piles of T-shirts, socks and shorts from the chest of drawers in their bedroom, Tom felt like punching himself in the throat just to stop the pain. She would be all right, he told himself. She had rich artist friends in Melbourne, in Sydney, in New York – everywhere in the world. And they were people far more like herself – the same age, the same outlook on life – in the end, she would thank him for leaving her.

Stopping for a moment, Tom pulled the bedroom curtains back and stared up at the night sky. Venus was still there, shining bright and hard overhead. Automatically, he knew that Sarah would be looking up at it too, from her own bedroom window in Richard's house on the other side of town. Thinking of her made it easier to keep going, he realized. Remembering her funny, clumsy, schoolgirl dive into the creek this afternoon – and her warm, wet skin in the tree-house – he pulled more clothes out of the wardrobe and threw them onto the bed.

At Sarah's house on the other side of town, though, it was Richard – not her – who was staring at Venus.

'Incredible night,' Richard said, getting into bed beside his wife. She hadn't closed the curtains yet and he could see a huge spray of stars through the windows.

'In London,' Sarah said quickly, 'you can hardly see any stars because of all the buildings. You just see satellites sometimes. It's like that Billy Bragg song about wishing on shooting stars, then finding out that they're really space hardware and wondering if you should be wishing on them at all.'

'Billy who?'

Sarah sighed and rolled onto her left side, facing away from Richard. She wished he'd just go to sleep tonight, but he wanted to talk. At any other time in the past few months, she would have loved it – but it had to be tonight, just hours after she'd been with Tom.

By the time she'd driven back from Lilly Creek, soon after half past nine, Richard was only just leaving a farm where he'd been treating a family of pups. She'd wanted to jump straight in the shower and then put some calamine lotion on her mosquito bites, but he had beaten her to it and got to the bathroom first. Scratching a bite on her ankle now, Sarah realized she had to have a shower or she wouldn't sleep at all.

'I'm just going to the bathroom,' she said.

'Wash all those dead leeches and things out of your hair,' he said. 'Good idea. I can't believe you went bushwalking without a hat.'

Squeezing his hand, Sarah swung out of bed – she was still in her dressing gown – and headed for the bathroom. *That's your husband*, she told herself. *Your nice husband who loves you, who you have just betrayed.*

Inside, she bolted the door and then found a bottle of Listerine. She never used the stuff – though Richard seemed to live on it. But now she found herself gargling glass after glass. Running the shower, she pulled off her dressing gown and glanced at her white dress and bra, still soaking in a bucket of bleach on the bathroom floor. Somehow, she thought, if she could just make it into the shower and wash off the smell of Tom – and this afternoon – she could hang on to her sanity.

Turning on the hot tap full-blast, she followed it with as much cold water as she could stand, then swivelled the shower head around until the water ran like needles on her back.

'Dreadful,' she spluttered, letting the water fall in her face. 'Dreadful mistake.' Grabbing the shampoo, she squeezed a huge blob of blue gel into her hand and then foamed her hair as hard as she could, digging into her ears with her fingers and letting the shampoo stream down both sides of her face. She felt sick. Not sick enough to throw up, but sick enough to feel like trying. It reminded her of getting married and being in the portaloo again.

She found the loofah, which she had carefully packed and brought all the way from London, and scrubbed at her shins, her knees, and then her feet. Scratching mosquito bites was wickedly addictive, she knew, and they would bleed if she didn't stop, but she felt like scrubbing every inch of this afternoon away.

How could she have been so stupid? Almost panting with panic now, Sarah started scrubbing her back. Her heart was beginning to bang hard inside her chest and she didn't know how to stop it. All she knew was, the more she paid attention to it, the faster and harder it seemed to bang.

Then suddenly she thought of something. Liz. Dear, intelligent, normal and reassuring Liz of Flat 12, 48 Turnpike Road, London. The voice of reason. Pregnant, sensible, Liz, who had been going out with Dave for eight years, been married for two more and had never had a problem.

Quickly brushing herself down with the last of the hot water, Sarah pushed her hand against her heart to make it slow down and then frantically turned off the taps. Why hadn't she thought of it before? Liz, more than anyone else, would know what to do. And if there was anyone in the world Sarah could trust, it was her. It would be almost lunchtime in London. If she rang her at home, she was bound to get her.

Almost crying with relief, Sarah found two towels – one for her hair, one for her body – and quickly stepped out of the bathroom, padding her way downstairs and dripping all over the carpet.

She knew exactly what Liz would say, but she still needed to hear it. She needed to know that Richard was her husband and that Tom was a mistake, and that her husband was the one who mattered. More than anything else, she needed to hear that she was being a stupid cow. And Liz was probably the only person in the world who could tell her.

Dragging a chair over to the telephone downstairs, Sarah kept her towel up with her hand and tried not to notice all the wet footprints soaking into the carpet. As she thought, she had made the mosquito bites on her foot bleed. She knew Liz's number off by heart, but it was still a struggle to remember all the country codes before it. And Richard had just changed their phone company, which made it harder. Where was the phone book?

And then, without warning, the phone rang. Sarah's heart, which had been banging steadily until now, suddenly thudded forward.

'Hello?' she snatched up the receiver.

'It's Tom.'

'Oh my God.'

'I'm really glad you picked up the phone.'

Dripping in her towel, Sarah sat down on the chair. 'Are you at home?' she whispered.

'Phone box,' he said quickly.

'I can't talk . . .'

'I know you can't talk. I wasn't going to ring. But then I saw Venus and I thought of you. I've left Annie.'

'What?' Sarah felt her heart rocket sideways again.

'It's OK. It was time. I'm staying with friends. Look . . .'

'Where are you?'

'I'll call again. I have to go. I just wanted to talk to you before I went to sleep. That's all.'

'Oh Tom . . .'

'Today was so fantastic, Sarah.'

'Tom . . .'

'I just wanted to thank you. That's all.'

And then he was gone. Pushing her hand through her wet hair, Sarah remembered Tom biting her on the shoulder in the tree-house and, with another sick thud of her heart, she checked to see if he had left a bruise there. He had – but it was tiny and red and, if Richard noticed, she could always pass it off as another insect bite.

'Venus,' she whispered, getting up to look out of the window. As he had promised, the star was brightly overhead. Holding her towel up with one hand, she felt the small bruise on her shoulder with the other. If she

231

bent her head down at the right angle, she could almost kiss it.

'Tom,' she whispered into the glass, leaving a foggy patch. She could still hear his voice in her head. 'Tom. What am I going to do?'

Chapter Twenty

At 5 p.m., Harry left the bank, put on his Walkman, turned Blondie up to ten and headed straight for the pub.

Tonight, he decided, he was going to prop up the bar and drown his sorrows. It was something he had never done before, but he was almost thirty and, he decided, it was time to try.

'Propping and drowning,' he said to his reflection in the mirror above the toilet at work. 'Smart plan.'

He had been in agony over Witchy Wendy Wagner for weeks. And seeing her in the bank this morning had just about broken him – especially as she had been wearing the purple velvet dress that showed the lace on top of her bra.

Humphrey Bogart drank alone, John Wayne drank alone and James Bond drank alone, Harry decided – so why shouldn't he? It seemed like the manly thing to do, under the circumstances. Perhaps if he tried really hard, he'd finally get hair on his nipples as well.

'G'day Harry,' the barman said, recognizing him as he walked into the pub. 'Are you early, or is she late?'

'There is no she,' Harry said gloomily, pulling his Walkman headphones off and sitting on a bar stool. 'If there was a she, I wouldn't be here.'

'Cascade?' the barman asked.

'Scotch on the rocks,' Harry replied, deciding that this was the only sort of drink to have if you were going to drown sorrows and prop up bars.

'That's a lady's drink,' the barman grinned, but he got it anyway.

'And give me another Scotch after that, and make it a double,' Harry said, wishing he could curl his lip – but he had never been much good at that. He couldn't raise his eyebrows either, or roll his tongue, or bend his thumb back.

'Let me know when you want to get onto the hard stuff,' Don said, with his back to him.

'A little less ice and a little more Scotch and I'll be a happy man,' Harry said, folding his arms up on the bar.

'So who's broken your heart then?' Don said, giving in. Harry obviously wanted to talk.

'A little lady who should know better,' Harry muttered into the bottom of his glass.

'My wife got *Casablanca* out on video the other week,' the barman mused, rinsing out some glasses. 'Top film. I can't think why, Harry, but something in here's reminding me of it.'

'I'll come clean,' Harry said at last, giving up on trying to curl his lip and talk like Humphrey Bogart. 'I'm in love with Wendy Wagner.'

'The witch?'

'How do you know?'

'She comes in here and gets kahlua and milk and says "Threefold, threefold, threefold" so that I'll give her more kahlua.'

'My God!' Harry was amazed. 'That's exactly what she does at the bank!'

'Anyway, so Wendy's got the hots for Pippin and you're out in the cold. Is that it?'

Shocked, Harry felt his right elbow go shooting off the bar. 'You speak the truth!' he exclaimed, grabbing the second Scotch as Don rested it in front of him.

'They were in here,' the barman admitted. 'All over each other like a rash. I nearly had to chuck them out.'

'Lesbians,' Harry said unhappily, feeling his heart sink down past his knees at this horrible piece of news. 'It's unnatural. It's against evolution.'

'If there were lesbian dinosaurs, we wouldn't be here today,' Don agreed.

'The thing that gets me is, Pippin's not even a lesbian – she's a have-it-both-ways sexual 7-11!' Harry yelled.

'Another Scotch?' the barman offered, getting it without waiting for his reply.

'Mike it a treble,' Harry said.

'A threefold,' Don countered. But Harry didn't seem to get the joke.

Sighing, Harry lifted his elbows up from the bar and carefully arranged them on the stickiest bits of the blue Foster's beer towel to prevent them from sliding off again. It was embarrassing trying to drown your sorrows and prop up a bar when you couldn't even keep your elbows on it.

'If you want my advice,' Don said, putting down another drink, 'you should be asking a woman about the situation.'

Harry nodded heavily.

'Not because women know more – they don't,' Don said. 'But this situation with Pippin and Wendy is like secret women's business. Men like us can have no insight when life becomes this strange.'

Please to be included as a man, Harry cheered up a little.

'The thing is, I know Wendy still wants me!' he said.

'I'm sure she does,' Don said. 'You can get her a cheap mortgage at the bank.'

'No, she wants me because she has recognized a soulmate,' Harry insisted. 'Another Scotch please. We knew the same Brecht song! She plays the ukelele!'

'Avoid women who like it both ways and play the

ukelele,' Don muttered as he reached for the Johnnie Walker yet again.

'Pippin doesn't want Wendy. She's just toying with her affections to get back at me,' Harry sighed.

'Like I said,' the barman countered, 'ask a woman about it. Why don't you write to one of those agony aunts?'

'What, like the problem pages in *Dolly*?'

'Well, *Dolly* might be a bit young. But you know – all those women's magazines are full of them. My wife loves them.'

'Don, you're married,' Harry said suddenly 'And you've been married for years. Thus, I think you know what you're talking about.'

'Mate, of course I know what I'm talking about,' Don said, watching Harry's elbows slide off the top of the bar again. 'And I'll tell you something. Helen, my wife, also writes to those agony aunts on a regular basis.'

'Does she?'

'Think of it as a cheap shrink,' Don shrugged, 'and it's been very good for our marriage.'

'Really?'

'Oh, yes,' Don shrugged again. But he clearly wasn't going to reveal anything more.

'Do you think your wife would give me her magazines?' Harry asked.

'No,' Don said.

'Well, I'll just have to go and buy them, then,' Harry slurred. He was beginning to feel pleasantly warm at the front of his head now and he could now smell Scotch all around him.

'Don't go and buy them, get them from your brother,' Don suggested.

'Richard reads women's magazines?' Harry said, shocked at this new piece of inside information.

'In the waiting room,' Don explained patiently. 'At the surgery. He's got all of them there. We took Henry in for his fleas the other week and he had stacks of them.'

'Sarah must buy them,' Harry said, suddenly cheering up. 'Don, you have incredible insight into life. Agony aunts! That's it! No, really mate,' he repeated, slurring, 'that's just incredible insight. Did you know that you had that?'

'Yes,' Don said, stacking glasses.

Harry quickly finished his drink. 'I'm going to see Richard right now!' he insisted. 'Going to solve all my problems!'

'You do that,' Don smiled, watching him trip over a chair on the way out.

As Harry arrived at the surgery, Richard was pulling down the blinds and checking the burglar alarms. It had been a long day and he was tired and ready to go home.

'I need to borrow some magazines from your waiting room,' Harry said as soon as his brother opened the door.

'You can't,' Richard said firmly. 'I need them here.' He sniffed for a moment. 'Have you been drinking?'

'Drowning my sorrows and propping up the bar,' Harry said, falling over his words. 'I just need to solve my problems. I need to get a woman's perspective on life. Write to a problem page. An agony aunt.'

'What?'

'Witchy Wendy Wagner and Pippin are embarking on an Alice B. Toklas and Gertrude Stein odyssey into unnatural activities in Compton,' Harry said. 'And I'm in the middle of it.'

'Say that again?' Richard sighed. His father always said that when he was drunk, Harry made about as much sense as Bill and Ben the Flowerpot Men. Richard had to agree.

'I need to write to a problem page. Get a woman's perspective,' Harry repeated.

'And if I give you the magazines, will you go?'

Harry nodded.

'OK then,' Richard gave in. 'Take whatever you want. Just bring them back, that's all.'

Gleefully, Harry scooped up as many magazines as he could fit under his arm, and then rolled up two more and crammed them into the pocket of his jacket.

'Thanks, mate,' he said.

'Don't call me mate,' Richard replied, walking behind him so that he'd leave the surgery faster.

'Do you know Don who works in the pub?' Harry asked.

'Yes. Did he tell you to do this?'

'Don has insight,' Harry said.

'Does he?'

'Don said if there were lesbian dinosaurs, we wouldn't be here today.'

'Did he?' Trying to stand back from Harry's drunken breath, Richard switched off the last of the lights in the hall, found his coat, and opened the door, letting his brother go out ahead of him.

'Can I have a lift back to Mum and Dad's?' Harry asked, waving a copy of *Cosmopolitan* at him.

'I think you'd better walk home,' Richard said kindly. 'And have some water on the way.'

Making a face, Harry held on tightly to his pile of magazines and headed off in the opposite direction, trying to follow the lines in the pavement just in case Richard was watching him in his rear-view mirror as he drove off.

The best thing about being pissed, he decided, was the incredible speed at which he could walk home. It normally took ages to get back to the cabin in his parents' garden. Tonight, it seemed like a mere quantum leap – although a quantum leap which involved his legs rubbing together in his corduroy jeans as he walked.

Singing old Blondie songs as he went, Harry beat time on his leg with a rolled-up copy of *Woman's Own*.

He felt drunk enough to consider taking a leak behind his father's lemon tree, next to the mailbox, which meant he must be very drunk indeed. That, and a raging desire to write love letters to Debbie Harry, were usually Harry's personal barometers of excess alcohol consumption.

Then suddenly he seemed to be home – it appeared to have taken him about three minutes. Skipping the temptation of the lemon tree, Harry ran straight to his cabin, flung the magazines down on his bed and leaped into the toilet. The cabin had originally started life as his parents' garden shed and the bathroom had been added on in the eighties, which accounted for the pinkness of everything inside it.

'I think I'll write to Debbie again,' Harry told his reflection in the mirror above the sink. Finding paper and a pen, he rolled himself onto his bed, stared at the Blondie poster on his ceiling for inspiration and patiently wrote his address at the top of the page. Debbie had never replied yet, but there was always a first time. And, as his mother always said, if you threw enough mud at a wall, some of it would stick. Not that he wanted to think of his letters as mud, of course.

Dear Ms Harry, *he wrote in his best running writing.* I have recently been reading about a new social trend in your country called Beyond Toyboy. I would like to offer you something that takes you beyond, Beyond Toyboy. My name is Harry Gilby, I am 29 years old, I have no diseases and my side-burns have often been compared to a young Nick Cave (PS: He is an Australian musician, you might not have heard of him). I have a reduced mortgage rate from the bank if I ever want it, and some extremely valuable collectors' item Blondie bootlegs. Although I'm not sure how you feel about bootlegs. Please feel free to phone me any time as I have put my number on the top of the page, BUT remember the time difference in Tasmania!!! Also, if my mother answers, please hang up and try again later.

It's lonely in my cabin, Debbie, and I long for you tonight. I believe we have a lot in common. Like you, I am a musician. Like you, I know what it is to be one of the unmarried. I feel in my heart that New York is my city, although Destiny has cruelly placed me in Compton. We have low air pollution and cheap butter, though, and you would be very welcome here. You might even want to join my band. It's called *We've Got Blondie's Drumsticks And We're Going To Use Them.*

Cherishing you in love and admiration (but not in a Mark Chapman John Lennon way)

Harry Gilby

PS: There may be a personnel change in the band by the time you get here.

Smiling in satisfaction, Harry re-read his letter, folded it inside the envelope and then sealed it with a kiss, sniffing it quickly afterwards to check it didn't smell of Scotch. He imagined Debbie opening it in the privacy of her bedroom, her lips slightly parted in surprise, her eyes softening in delighted anticipation as she realized that this time, he had also included his home phone number. Harry hoped to God she would work out the time difference – it was really worrying him now. If Debbie rang in the middle of the night, his father would have a fit and probably shout at her.

'Now, Stage Two,' Harry announced to himself, grabbing a pile of magazines. Flicking through them, he could see a variety of caring agony aunts to write to – although they all seemed to be called 'Advice Columnists' or 'Professional Counsellors'. He liked the look of one called Mary O'Flanagan, even though he suspected she'd made up her name. She had a nice smile and round cheeks, like a hamster.

'I'll start with you, Mary,' he told her picture, finding a new piece of paper and thoughtfully chewing on the end of his pen.

Dear Miss/Ms/Mrs O'Flanagan, *he wrote*, or can I call you Mary?

My name is Harry Gilby (please don't print this as I will lose my job) and I am in the middle of a heterosexual-bisexual-lesbian love triangle. If you picture a piece of Toblerone, then I am the pointy bit at the top. A few weeks ago, I realized that there was a deep mutual attraction between myself and a woman who lives locally. For years I had assumed she was a raving lunatic, but it turns out she is my sexual soulmate. At the same time, another woman, who I have loose professional associations with, has embarked upon an affair with her, or at least embarked upon being all over her like a rash in the pub. What do you suggest I do?

Faint heart never won fair lady, but this is not the 1800s Mary, it's the '00s. Is it possible to convert a suspected lesbian or bisexual to round-the-clock heterosexuality? What about a bisexual? What tell-tale signs should I look for to confirm sex has taken place between them? How do you tell the difference between a bisexual and a lesbian? What do lesbians have that men haven't got? Should I break up the band?

Yours sincerely,

H. G., Tasmania

PS: I am almost thirty years old and I have only had two girlfriends who lasted more than a fortnight – is this normal?

PPS: I will also be writing to the other agony aunts Dana Gray, Randy Steinbergen, Harriet Hugo, Fenella Dunleavy and Tracey Cox about this problem. I hope you don't mind. My father always says, get a second opinion and my mother always says, if you throw enough mud at a wall, some of it might stick.

'There,' Harry said, sitting back on his bed. He felt very smug – two letters in one night wasn't bad at all, especially under the influence of alcohol. He decided he'd leave his letter to Mary O'Flanagan out, so that he could copy it to all the other agony aunts later. He'd post Debbie's letter first thing, though – he didn't want to make her wait.

The only magazine Harry didn't want to write to was *Australian Woman* – mainly because Bronte worked there. Harry didn't trust her an inch. He was sure his letter would be recognized, even if he had printed everything in block letters. The first thing Bronte would do, would be to ring his mother up about it – or Richard.

Lying back on his bed, Harry closed his eyes and remembered the last time he had seen Bronte. It had probably been a year ago, on one of her flying visits to see Mickey. She had gone through a rich hippy phase for a while, and he was sure he'd seen her riding around in a purple beaded skirt. Or was it a weird orange shawl and furry orange clogs? Frowning, Harry tried to work it out, gave up and then fell asleep with the lights still on, rolling sideways on top of his Biro. When he woke up at 4 a.m., fully clothed and dying of thirst, he was horrified to discover that he had been dreaming about Bronte.

'She was wearing red suspenders too,' he told his bathroom mirror. 'Oh my God!'

Worse, he realized it had been the kind of sleepy, warm, wonderful, erotic three-part epic that he normally couldn't wait to go back to.

'Not with bloody Bronte though,' he told the mirror again as he filled a glass with water. Blaming his tight trousers and his full bladder, he tried to put her out of his mind. Still, as he finally fell asleep again just before the sun was coming up, it was Bronte in her red suspenders that Harry thought of last. And at 8 a.m., when his parents were banging on his window, he was still dreaming of her, riding across the paddocks on Mickey with her hair flowing behind her like Lady Godiva.

Chapter Twenty-one

Sarah had never taken much interest in Mickey, so when Richard saw her out in the paddock with him, he felt something approaching warmth – even though it was cold outside and getting dark.

Putting on his gumboots and coat, he decided to walk down and join her. She had never asked to ride Mickey and he had never forced it, but maybe now was the moment. Bronte wouldn't mind, he decided. And she couldn't hang onto sole use of her horse forever. For a start, because she was now his wife, Sarah owned half the paddock he was in – and half the stable too.

He hadn't really viewed his marriage to Sarah like that before, Richard realized. But the fact that they were both equal owners of his property made him feel better about life, somehow. Perhaps given the way things were between them these days, he just found it reassuring. Then he dismissed the thought.

Digging his hands into his coat pockets, Richard walked faster across the back garden until he reached the fence. It was amazing how Sarah's blonde hair stood out, even when the light was fading. He preferred it loose rather than up in a ponytail, but even when her hair was scrunched on top of her head as it was now, it seemed almost luminous.

Facing the other way, Sarah could neither see nor

hear Richard. Instead, she was gazing at the mountains. She was still amazed at the difference in colour between Tasmania and England. Nothing came close to the blue of the mountains here, she thought – and even the sun seemed to be a different kind of pink when it slid behind the hills.

Idly, she wondered if Venus would appear tonight. It had almost become a secret signal for her and Tom now. Thanks to him, she had been forced to become an expert on the Southern Hemisphere night sky. If she did see Venus, she decided, she would permit herself one phone call to him – even if she had to make it from a phone box. It had only been a few days since she had seen Tom, but every hour away from him was killing her.

Twisting her ponytail around in her fingers, Sarah allowed herself the luxury of remembering their last afternoon together. All the people in Tom's new house in Hobart had been out so they had gone to his room up in the attic, pinned a blanket over the window and shared a bottle of wine. Tom had found some incense – she could still remember the smell, sticking to his body. They had played Ravel as well, then laughed at themselves for being so tacky.

Hugging the memory to herself, Sarah pulled down the arms of her suede jacket so that they were covering her fingers. People had told her that Tasmania would eventually get cold, once the summer had gone, but she'd never believed them. They were right, though – her fingers were starting to freeze.

Then, just as she was making up her mind to call Tom whether Venus appeared or not, she saw Richard. Delighted, Mickey gave a whinny and started to canter towards him.

'Hey!' Richard called, walking towards her.

'Hey!' Sarah called back, trying to force a smile into her voice.

She walked up to meet him, trying to shut Tom out

245

of her mind. The call would have to wait, she realized – and now Richard was here, she wouldn't allow herself one more thought about him until bedtime.

'Making friends with Mickey?' Richard smiled.

He looked tired, Sarah thought. She supposed he had just finished work – it must be getting late.

'Oh, Mickey's all right,' she shrugged.

'Want me to book you some lessons?' Richard asked.

'Not really,' Sarah shook her head.

'Are you sure?' he asked again.

'No, really. Look, you did ask me this ages ago and I said no, and it's still the same answer. I'm fine. Mickey's fine. We can . . . co-exist.'

For a minute, Richard said nothing. Then at last he took her hand.

'Cold hands,' he observed. 'Maybe we should go inside. Let me warm you up.'

'I think I just want to go for a walk actually,' she said.

'I love it when you say "actually",' Richard smiled.

'Oh, Harry's hilarious joke about me,' Sarah said. 'The English girl who says "actually" actually.'

'Fine!' Richard said briefly, feeling her irritation. 'OK! I get it!'

'Well, good,' Sarah said, 'because I just want to be by myself. Mickey just happened to be here too.'

'Is that how you feel about me?' Richard asked suddenly.

'Don't be stupid.'

'You just want to be by yourself, and I just happen to be here too?'

Tutting, Sarah walked away, pulling her sleeves down over her hands again.

'Mickey and I are both part of your life now,' Richard insisted.

'Mickey was part of Bronte's life!' Sarah said suddenly, shocked at the way her irritation had just leaped into anger. 'And stop going on at me!'

For a moment, neither of them said anything.

Turning from her, Richard walked slowly towards Mickey, holding out his hand to stroke his head.

'I don't know what's wrong with me, I'm sorry,' Sarah said quickly.

'You don't sound sorry,' Richard said, with his hand on Mickey's mane.

'The thing is – oh, I don't know what the thing is,' she sighed.

'Are you regretting our marriage?'

'What?' Sarah felt as if someone had just punched her.

'I said, are you regretting our marriage?'

'No. Oh, for God's sake!'

Concentrating on stroking Mickey's face, Richard found himself unable to even look at Sarah. All he had to do was pick up everything from her voice, he realized – and it hurt.

'I bought a king-size bed and I don't think we've done much except sleep on it,' he said. 'So it isn't the bed that's the problem any longer.'

Sarah stared miserably at the ground, unable to speak.

'You had jet lag, the weather was too hot, you weren't used to such a small bed. Now it's almost winter and you have the biggest bed in the whole of Tasmania for all I know.'

'Please,' she said. 'Just don't go on at me.'

'But I never do go on, and maybe I should.'

'Richard, please just give me a break.'

'You know what someone told me the other day? You were buying some marriage guidance book.'

'What?'

'Some marriage guidance book. Well, I never saw it. Were you hiding it? When did you buy it? Right after we got married, or did you wait?'

The woman in the second-hand bookshop, Sarah realized – remembering that her dog, Beryl, was always in at Richard's surgery. Blushing in the dark, she remembered her secondhand copy of *Relating and Mating*, and how she'd wrapped it in two plastic bags to disguise it before throwing it in the bin.

'Is it a crime to read a book?' she asked, suddenly feeling angry. 'I hate this town, Richard! It's so small. I can't cross the road without someone putting it in the paper.'

'And now you hate the town as well. Right.'

'Oh . . .' Sarah bit her lip. 'No I don't hate it, I'm sorry, it's just that – oh, I don't know what I'm on about. Can we just talk about this later?'

Leaving Mickey, Richard walked over to her and pushed the hair out of her eyes. 'We have to talk now,' he said gently. 'Because there's a problem.'

By now it was so dark that Sarah couldn't tell what was going on in his eyes, but she knew Richard's voice well enough to realize he was serious.

'The problem,' she said, 'is me.'

'I'm here,' he said, sighing and taking her hand. 'I'm here to help you. We always said that it would be this way for us, remember? If one of us went near the rocks, the other one would be the light.'

'I'm not near any rocks, really I'm not,' Sarah said, and hearing herself say it immediately made her feel better.

'You're not alone. I'm here with you. We can sort this out,' he said patiently. 'Not in a way that makes you feel like I'm having a go at you. I'm sorry if that's how I sounded now.'

'Well, you have a right,' she admitted, twisting her hands.

'But I don't,' Richard insisted. 'Whatever is going on with you is my problem as well. That's always how I saw us together. So – whatever it takes.'

'Oh my God,' Sarah sighed, taking his hand as well, so they were both locked together. She remembered the promise they had made once, in England, about being each other's light. And now Richard was delivering it to her. *Faithful deliverer*, she thought, hating herself for hurting him.

'Sarah?' he asked quietly.

'Sorry. I just – I just need a minute.'

Swallowing hard, she took her hands away from his and folded her arms tightly in her suede jacket, staring out to the mountains. There would be no stars tonight and no Venus, she realized – as if she had ever expected it to be there.

'I did have a strange feeling a few weeks ago,' Richard said at last.

'What strange feeling?'

He shrugged. 'Like you had met someone. I mean really, it got that bad.'

'Did it?' Horrified, Sarah felt her heart beginning to pound and pulled her sleeves down again to distract herself.

'If you ever did meet someone, you'd tell me – wouldn't you?' he said.

'What do you mean?'

Richard looked at her suddenly, and realized it had become so dark now that he had to guess where her eyes were – or if they were looking at him.

'Oh, I don't know,' he said quickly. 'This is a stupid conversation. A non-conversation.'

Annoyed with himself, he dug his hands in his pockets against the cold and walked slowly over to her side. *Tell him*, Sarah suddenly thought in a panic. *It's now or never. Be fair to him. Tell him the truth. It's not your fault. You just fell in love with his best man, that's all.*

'You think this is all you. Well, it's probably just as much me,' Richard said softly, taking her hand again.

'Let's go back,' Sarah heard herself saying.

'Yes, it's too cold to stay out here,' he agreed.

Slowly, they started walking towards the house with Mickey following at a distance. It was always so hard to find the first words for anything, Sarah realized.

And the more you tried to invent the magic phrase or the miracle sentence, the more it didn't happen. Perhaps she should just speak straight from the heart, that was it. Silently she kept on walking, with her heart thudding, waiting for some part of her to leap up and speak – but it was more than she could manage.

It had been a long time since she'd ticked off a Richard list in her head, but she decided to do it now. At one point she'd stopped, just because the very exercise of dividing her marriage into pros and cons was already an admission of failure. Now, she thought hurriedly, if she could cram something together in her head, perhaps she could convince herself.

She started where she always started with Richard – with the day he'd helped her measure a window by holding one end of the tape while she held the other. She'd been struggling with a clipboard and a briefcase stuffed full of insurance papers and nobody else in the conference room had even bothered looking at her, never mind helping her. Typically, Richard had been there in a second, just helping, quietly, and just as prepared to vanish again once he'd finished. *That* was Richard, Sarah thought. Then suddenly she remembered something else which never came up on her mental lists – a day in Canterbury when a woman had tried to sell them a bunch of white heather and Richard had ended up buying the whole tray for her.

'I wish I could go back,' Sarah said suddenly. 'Back to where I was before with you in London, when I first met you. Back to that time when I couldn't believe my bloody luck.'

Richard gave an embarassed laugh, but felt himself – unbelievably – warming up again. *From the heart out*, he thought, *and straight through the lining of my coat.*

'Any other woman in the world would think I was insane,' Sarah said. 'Any other woman would take one look at you and wonder if I'd just lost my mind, the way I've been behaving lately.'

'Silly,' Richard said, squeezing her hand, but for the first time in weeks he felt hope again.

'You are a light for me, and you do guide me,' she said simply. 'And I'll tell you something else, you're much too good for me.'

Turning to kiss him, she let Richard kiss her back, squeezing her so tightly in his arms that she almost could feel the buttons on his coat digging into her ribs.

'I don't deserve you,' Sarah said, meaning every word.

Arm in arm, they walked back to the house. She could never tell him about Tom, Sarah realized. And at that moment, she also realized that her self-loathing, her longing for Tom and her love for Richard were all pretty much equal. She wished she had the bravery to stay or go, but instead she realized that she was stuck in the middle. Maybe next month, she told herself *Maybe in July, then I'll know what to do.*

Chapter Twenty-two

Sometimes, Harry thought, life stopped being an endless shower of rat excrement and actually delivered the goods. Smiling to himself, he looked again at the phone message stuck to the cabin door.

'WENDY WAGNER RANG CONFIRMING SATURDAY NIGHT', it said, in his father's handwriting. Even more excitingly, under that it said: 'TV SHOW RANG – PLEASE CALL BACK'. Harry wished his father had been more forthcoming with information but at the same time, it was all he needed to know.

Punching the air, he yelled a victorious 'Yessssss!' and then, for good measure, kicked the cabin door with his Doc Martens and followed it with 'Wooohooo!' Asking Wendy Wagner for a date had been a fifty–fifty gamble, he decided. And he would never have bothered if Mary O'Flanagan with the hamster cheeks hadn't answered his problem page letter and told him to do it. But a call back from Channel Nine was even more incredible, Harry thought. What's more, they wanted him to ring them again – *again!* He couldn't believe it.

Everyone in Tasmania seemed to be auditioning for *Hot Debut*, the new Channel Nine talent show. Since the ad had appeared on TV the previous week, Harry had heard that dozens of people were applying – from his cousin in Ulverstone, who played the bugle, to the woman at the Compton post office, who was famous for being able to quack like a duck. And now it seemed they had chosen him – or rather they had chosen We've Got Blondie's Drumsticks And We're Going To Use Them.

The bank manager at work had gone mad when he found out Harry had been using the office photocopier to run off pictures of himself and Pippin for the entry form – but it had all been worth it, Harry thought smugly. And now all he had to do was tell Pippin. Because she disapproved of television, he had kept their entry into *Hot Debut* a secret until now. But he couldn't wait to ring her with the good news. And, he thought, he might even let her know that he was going out with Wendy on Saturday night as well. Just to let her know the score, Harry decided.

First of all, though, he had to ring the *Hot Debut* people at Channel Nine in Melbourne. Smiling to himself, Harry walked into the cabin, kicked a pile of women's magazines out of the way and found his telephone, buried under a pile of pyjamas. He knew the number off by heart and with any luck, he thought, they'd put him straight through this time. After they'd started showing all the TV ads for *Hot Debut*, the lines had been constantly engaged.

'Hello, Flip,' a female voice said on the other end, after the long-distance beeps had stopped.

'Flip?' Harry said stupidly.

'Yes, Flip. This is Flip from *Hot Debut*.'

'Ah, Flip. We haven't spoken before. I'm Harry Gilby.'

'OK.'

'OK!' Harry agreed. Then there was an awkward silence.

'Flip, are you still there?' he asked, tentatively. It sounded like she'd gone off to make herself a cup of coffee.

'Yes. Who are you, Harry? Why are you ringing me?'

'Well, apparently my band has been asked to appear on *Hot Debut*,' Harry said, irritated that Flip didn't know who he was. 'We've Got Blondie's Drumsticks And We're Going To Use Them. From Compton.'

'Oh, right,' Flip said, sounding as if light was dawning. 'Yes, we want you in Hobart on Sunday. You'll be on at 10 a.m. – come with your own clothes, we'll fix make-up. Sorry it's short notice.'

'No worries,' Harry said, suddenly feeling intensely worried.

'It's all on at the town hall. You know where that is?'

'Yes,' Harry said, springing to attention. He hadn't been there since 1976, since his parents had taken him to see Sooty and Sweep on their world tour, but he knew where it was.

'Good,' said Flip.

'Er – good. Will you be there?' Harry asked.

'Yes,' Flip said quickly. 'Listen, I've got to go. Bye!' And she put the phone down.

Perhaps it came of having a stupidly short name like Flip, Harry thought, putting his phone down, but she seemed to speak faster than most human beings – and mostly in words of one syllable. He decided he was frightened of her already and he hadn't even met her yet. Trying to picture Flip, Harry had a mental picture of someone like Bronte – but younger.

It was amazing, Harry thought, how all the people with the glamorous jobs – like Bronte and Flip – seemed to have stupid names. Did the stupid name come before the glamorous job, he wondered, or did everyone change their names to something more glamorous once they got into TV or magazines? It was like the chicken-and-egg law of being groovy and successful. But he couldn't do much with a name like Harry Gilby, he thought.

Sting had been lucky – all he had managed to do was wear a striped jumper that made him look like a bumblebee – and everyone had stopped calling him Gordon Sumner and started calling him Sting instead. Poor old Gordon hadn't even had to think about it – the name had been chosen for him, by destiny, Harry decided. He was nearly thirty and people were still calling him Harry for some strange reason. Sometimes they even called him worse things than that.

Suddenly, the phone rang. Harry pounced on it straight away – it was Witchy Wendy Wagner.

'Wendy!' he almost yelled. 'I'm going to be on TV!'

'Wow,' she said placidly. 'Is that the *Hot Debut* thing? Did you send off for it? I saw the ad again last night.'

'Yes,' said Harry, slightly annoyed that she seemed to know all about it. 'Anyway, me and Pippin have got to go to the town hall on Sunday morning.'

'Oh, right,' Wendy said.

She didn't sound very enthusiastic, Harry thought.

'What's the matter?' he said quickly.

'I don't think Pippin knows about it,' Wendy replied.

'No, I'm going to ring her now,' Harry explained. 'God, she's going to die when she finds out!'

Wendy breathed in sharply. 'The only thing is, Pippin might not like it,' she said quickly. 'Are you sure this is a good idea?'

'Why? What? Of course it's a good idea!'

'It's just that I know something,' Wendy said, faltering.

'What?'

'Er – she doesn't think it's a good idea. This talent contest on the TV. She was at my place when the ad came on and then we were talking about it in the pub. The thing is, she hates it.'

'Yes, but she might not hate it when she finds out we're *on* it,' Harry persisted.

'No, really. She – um. She hates TV. She hates commercial TV especially. She thinks music should be live and for the people. And she doesn't think creative

255

people like musicians should compete with each other. She thinks it's wrong.'

'Oh, give me a break,' Harry said. 'We'll only be competing against a woman impersonating a duck and a man with a bugle. Did she really say all that to you?'

'Yes. In the pub last night.'

Harry suddenly had a mental image of Pippin and Wendy all over each other like a rash again, with Don the barman making disapproving faces in the background – not to mention comments about lesbian dinosaurs.

'So you've been seeing Pippin, then?' he asked.

'Yeah, sure.'

'Right.'

Now, Harry realized, he didn't have a clue what to say. If only Mary O'Flanagan with the kind smile and hamster cheeks was here to advise him, he thought. But she was far away in an office somewhere, answering everybody else's problems.

'So anyway,' he said, 'I thought we might go out to dinner on Saturday night.'

'Oh,' Wendy said awkwardly. 'I think I might have to take a raincheck.'

If there was one word in the English language Harry hated, it was 'raincheck'.

'Something come up?' he said suspiciously.

'Yes.'

'What, so it came up between the time my dad took a phone message from you saying you were confirming, and now. Right. I get it.'

'Sorry,' Wendy mumbled. 'Anyway, I might give you a call.'

'Sure,' Harry said, putting the phone down, knowing that she wouldn't. Suddenly, he thought, he could feel the rat excrement raining down on his head again.

Furiously he picked up the receiver and dialled Pippin.

'I'm in the bath,' she moaned. 'Can you call back?'

Pippin was the only person he knew who had a phone extension cord that stretched all the way from the kitchen to the bathroom. He knew exactly what she would be wearing too – a scungy old shower cap with bows on the front of it to keep in all the Body Shop henna she ploughed through her hair.

'I can't call you back,' Harry sighed, 'I've got too much to do. Channel Nine want us to go to Hobart Town Hall on Sunday morning and do a gig for this *Hot Debut* show.'

'What?'

'Like I said, Channel Nine want us to do a set at the town hall. For this show.'

'And here you are trying to make it sound all casual and normal, like an ordinary part of life, so I won't get too upset. Yeah, well bad luck, Harry – you'll be doing it by yourself,' Pippin said, abruptly.

'What?'

'You never asked me. How could you go ahead and send them a tape without asking me? I hate *Hot Debut*. I hate Channel Nine. In fact, I don't even own a television set!'

'Do you realize how many thousands of people have been trying to get onto that show?' Harry shouted. 'This is the only Tasmanian audition!'

'Big whoop,' Pippin answered, making splashing sounds in the bath.

'This is our only chance for success!'

'Oh, bull,' Pippin said. 'Anyway, I can't talk about this now. I've got my henna on.'

'If we win *Hot Debut* we get a trip to LA and a recording contract,' Harry said flatly. 'And I don't care if you haven't got a TV set.'

'You're a sell-out,' Pippin said, making more splashing noises in the bath. 'You're just selling us out.'

'Oh, right. Just because I want us to get somewhere.'

'I don't want to be on a poxy TV show with poxy ads

in the middle with some poxy bunch of judges holding up numbers,' Pippin complained.

'Well, piss off then,' Harry said, losing it at last.

'I already did,' Pippin said, trying to stop herself from throwing the phone into the bathwater. 'I quit the band. Finito. We just have different value systems, Harry,' she said sweetly. 'I'll put the drumsticks in the post.'

Slamming the receiver down first, Harry paced up and down in the cabin, mindlessly folding up his pyjamas until he felt able to think normally. In the space of five minutes, he appeared to have lost his new potential girlfriend, his band and the chance of being on national TV. Swearing, he picked up his pyjamas by one leg and slammed them against a mosquito which was buzzing around the window.

'Die, bastard!' he yelled, hitting his pyjamas against the window again and again, even after the mosquito had been flattened.

Almost on the verge of tears, he reminded himself that Robert Smith and The Cure had once sung *Boys Don't Cry*, and that as he had grown up singing that song all the way through school, he had better stick to it. This was the worst minute in the worst hour of his entire life, he decided. Picking up the phone, he dialled Richard at the surgery. He would know what to do, he thought. Richard always did.

'Hello?' his brother said quickly. By the sound of his voice, he was working, Harry thought.

'It's me. I'm in deep shit,' Harry said. 'Are you busy?'

'Not too bad,' Richard replied. He could hear the strain in Harry's voice.

'Pippin's left the band. And we're playing on that show, when they come to Hobart.'

'The TV talent thing – congratulations – Dad told me.'

'But it's on Sunday. What am I going to do?'

'Talk her back into the band?' Richard suggested,

trying to concentrate on the dog he was working on at the same time that he was trying to listen to Harry.

'I can't do it. The band's over. And anyway, she hates the idea of being on TV – that's why she quit. She didn't want me to enter us in the contest.'

'Is there anyone else who can play the drums for you?' Richard asked, holding the dog down.

'Not at this short notice. And another thing. Bloody Witchy Wendy Wagner's stood me up for Saturday night. And I think she's having it off with Pippin.'

'Aaah,' said Richard, who was now finding it almost impossible to concentrate on Harry and the dog at the same time.

'I don't want to give in,' Harry said.

'No,' Richard said firmly. 'No, you shouldn't give in.'

This terrier was a trial, he thought, and he'd never get its stitches out properly if it kept wriggling. But his brother sounded terrible.

'I've got the afternoon off,' Harry said. 'You don't feel like going to the pub, do you?'

'I can have a coffee,' Richard said cautiously. 'I'll just finish with this temperamental canine first. I'll meet you outside the post office if you like, we can go from there.'

'Twenty minutes?' Harry said hopefully.

'No worries,' Richard replied, putting the phone down.

Harry's crises were part of life, Richard decided, and part of being in the Gilby family involved putting up with them. It always surprised him when Harry turned to him because their lives were so different – but then again, there was nobody else. None of Harry's girl-friends had stuck around long enough to give him any support and, in any case, they had been getting younger and younger in recent years and could barely look after their own lives, let alone his brother's.

Reading between the lines, Richard could see that

Wendy and Pippin were creating a sense of togetherness by ganging up on Harry. It was sad, he thought, that the two of them had so little in common that they could only find his brother to talk about – and victimize – as a kind of mutual bond. Harry shouldn't have gone behind Pippin's back to enter the talent show, he knew that. But part of him also knew that Harry had done it hoping that Pippin would be pleased. He had meant well, Richard decided – usually his brother did. Because of that, he felt he should do something, no matter how small. Besides, he'd never liked Pippin.

Richard decided to make a phone call. He had once been at university with a boy called Neville Scruby, who had enjoyed several claims to fame – an asymmetrical haircut like the lead singer of Human League, a pierced nipple, the worst exam results in the history of the Veterinary School and an outrageously expensive, loud drum machine. It was the drum machine that Richard was thinking of now.

Finding Neville's number in his diary, he rang – and for Harry's sake, crossed his fingers.

In a way, he was glad that it hadn't worked out with Wendy. He'd never really taken it seriously, anyway – one day, he knew, Harry would grow up and when he did, the right woman would appear. Bronte had always said that about his younger brother, and he thought it was true. Once Harry finally sorted himself out, Richard thought, he'd probably be happier than any of them.

In the meantime, though, the TV show was a more urgent issue. It would make him late, he realized, but he had to solve the Pippin problem first. He didn't know much about music, but he vaguely remembered Neville entertaining them all at parties with his guitar and his drum machine. And if he could do it, he thought, Harry could do it.

'You're late,' Harry said, moodily, when Richard finally arrived at the post office, half an hour later.

'With good reason,' Richard replied, waving a hand at the coffee shop across the road. 'Why don't we go in there?' he suggested. 'The flat whites are a bit too flat at the other place.'

'One day,' Harry moaned, 'when I finally get out of Compton, I'll be able to choose from more than two coffee shops at once. And I won't know what to do with myself.'

Smiling, Richard found them a table at the window. The waitress knew him – he had once desexed her cat – so the menus appeared almost instantly with bread rolls and butter while they waited.

'There are so many women around,' Richard said, looking pointedly at the waitress. 'So many incredible looking women, Harry. Don't dwell too much on Wendy.'

'Oh, I'm over it already,' Harry said, airily waving a hand. 'She clearly had other fish to fry. Other, *female* fish.'

'Anyway,' Richard said casually, 'I've found a drum machine – if you want it.'

'What? Where?' Harry said.

'This bloke called Neville Scruby who I know from uni's got one. In his garage. He said he'd lend it to you.'

'A drum machine!' Harry said, wonderingly. It was one of the worst ideas he had ever heard – drum machines were so eighties. At the same time, though, he felt the beginnings of something that resembled faint, mad hope.

'Do you want Neville's number?' Richard asked, ordering coffee.

'A drum machine!' Harry said again.

'You know what they are.'

'Yeah, yeah,' Harry waved him away impatiently. 'But the weird thing is, Richard, it could just work. In fact, it's such a bad idea it might even have a certain vibe.'

'Well, good,' Richard said.

'I mean, yeah! Brilliant!' Excitedly, Harry thumped his hand on the table.

'You didn't sign anything that said the band had to be a duet, did you?' Richard asked.

'No. They just got a cassette tape. I mean, they got photos of me and Pippin. But I'll just say Pippin's sick. Anyway. It was practically a one-man effort, that band. All she did was go "Thwack, thwack, thwack" on her snare drum.'

'Well, I thought you could do it on your own.'

'I'll just say she got sick because all the henna leaked into her brain from under her shower cap,' Harry nodded with satisfaction. 'That's brilliant!' he repeated, staring wonderingly at his brother. 'Me and a drum machine! Except – oh bugger.'

'Oh no,' Richard said, suddenly understanding the problem.

'We've Got Blondie's Drumsticks And We're Going To Use Them – what am I going to do about the name?'

'Does it matter?' Richard shrugged.

'Well, no. But how am I going to use the sticks if I don't have a drummer? That is, assuming Pippin mails them back to me. She said she would,' Harry said sadly.

'I suppose if you don't have a drummer, you could always change the name of the band,' Richard mused.

'My Brother Got Me Neville Scruby's Old Drum Machine From University And I'm Going To Use It,' Harry pondered. 'Alas, no.'

'Hmmm,' Richard agreed, drinking his coffee.

'Oh, I don't care,' Harry said at last. 'I'll just beat myself over the head with the drumsticks when I'm on stage. That's *using* them, isn't it? So that means I can still keep the name. It's just that there won't be any "We" in it any more. The "We" is over, Richard. It's going to be "*I've* Got Blondie's Drumsticks and *I'm* Going To Use Them".'

'Yes,' his brother said, hastily drinking his coffee to stop himself laughing.

'What?' Harry challenged him.

'Nothing.' Richard shook his head. But it was no good. Suddenly, he snorted into his coffee and was helpless with laughter.

'Oh, piss off,' Harry said, annoyed.

'I'm sorry!' Richard said, gasping.

'Yeah, really funny. You always know how to make me feel like my life is a joke, d'you know that?'

'Oh, Lord,' Richard sighed, swallowing hard and suddenly becoming serious. 'Harry, it's not like that.'

'Yes it is. I come to you with a genuine problem, a definite problem and it's just this big piece of free entertainment for you.'

'Harry!' Richard looked behind him and realized the waitress was now eavesdropping.

'If you want to help, great. Otherwise, don't bother,' Harry complained, stirring his coffee at twice the normal speed.

'Well, can I say something?' Richard offered.

'Yeah, what?'

'Don't be so bloody over-sensitive. That's all. You've asked me to help and I have helped.' Richard sighed. 'I'm sorry if I laughed. I don't know. I'm tired. You know how it gets when you're tired.'

Looking up at his brother, Harry shrugged, and gave in. 'Oh, it's fine,' he said suddenly. 'I'm tired too. I'm just so conscious that you have this life, I suppose – this proper, normal life and I've just got all this – crap, I suppose. Like worrying about the name of my band . . .'

'Spare me the drivelling insecurity,' Richard snapped. From long experience, he knew it was the only way to get Harry out of the mood he was currently in. For a moment, neither of them spoke. And then, finally, Harry managed to smile.

'Yes,' he croaked. 'You're right. That's me, all right.

Two scoops of drivel with extra added insecurity.' Sighing, Richard ordered two more coffees. He had seen Harry go into a slump once before, years ago, with another crisis, another band and another woman. He didn't think he could go through it again and he knew his parents certainly couldn't. If Harry was being de-railed, then he needed to be sorted out as fast as possible.

'If life were a soap opera,' Harry began.

'Yes?' Richard followed it up.

'Well, if it were some bad soap opera, this is where I'd put my hand on your shoulder and say "Gee, thanks." You know. But I'm not going to do that.'

'Of course not.'

'Well, good,' Harry said, leaving a tip for the waitress. 'Just so long as you know.'

On Saturday night, Harry went to bed early with all his clothes carefully laid out and ironed for the audition the next day. He had decided to put his Doc Martens on top of Neville Scruby's drum machine, which Richard had delivered as promised from Neville's garage in Hobart.

In addition to the Doc Martens, Harry had also decided to wear tight blue shark-skin pants, a leopard-skin shirt that his mother had given up on, a long raincoat and a single earring in his left ear.

'Post-modern, post-eighties irony,' he muttered to himself, smelling the leopard-skin shirt to make sure all traces of his mother's perfume had vanished. 'It'll go with the drum machine. *They'll* get it.'

Everyone at the bank had wanted to take him out and get him drunk the night before, but Harry had refused – partly because he didn't want to have blood-shot eyes on television, but also because he knew that he would probably run into Pippin and Wendy at the pub – and even though he'd told Richard he was over it all, it still caused him pain whenever he thought about it.

He already knew exactly what he was going to play on *Hot Debut*. All the acts were only allowed two songs each so it had been difficult but Harry had decided to do his own version of Blondie's 'Rapture' – mainly to make the most of Neville's drum machine – and a new song he had written about Wendy a few weeks before, just in case she turned up to watch him, even though he knew she wouldn't.

Even though part of him hated her, he still couldn't give up on her yet. As soon as she realized that Pippin spent her life wearing a scungy shower cap and dyeing her hair, he thought, Wendy might change her mind about everything. Besides, without the band Pippin had lost any trace of glamour in her life. What did she have to offer Wendy now?

On Sunday morning, Harry woke early – just ahead of his father, who decided to bang on the cabin door at 7 a.m. with a tray of toast, jam and strong black coffee.

'We anticipated a hangover,' his father explained. 'Hence the coffee.'

'No, I got an early night,' Harry yawned. 'Trying to be professional about it.'

Reeling at this information – he had never heard of Harry trying to be professional before – Mr Gilby put the tea-tray down carefully on Harry's floor.

'Thanks, Dad,' Harry said.

'Your mother still wants to come and watch you at the town hall,' his father said, 'I did say I'd ask again. The answer's still no?'

'Sorry,' Harry shrugged. 'But you can watch it on TV when it comes out.'

'As long as it's not on at the same time as the *Two Fat Ladies* repeat,' his father warned, closing the door. 'I don't miss that for anyone.'

The rest of the morning passed in a blur. When Harry was nervous about something, he always found himself checking everything two, three or even four times. After he had plugged in and unplugged the drum machine twice, and rolled deodorant under his arms three times, and checked the glove box five times for the first-aid kit in case of any accidental maiming on the way to Hobart – he almost felt ready to go back to bed.

Finally, though, at twenty minutes to ten, after the drive from Compton, he found himself strolling into the Hobart Town Hall with his guitar case in one hand and bits of Neville's drum machine in the other.

'Flip?' he said nervously to a likely-looking woman with short blonde hair, a mobile phone and a clipboard.

'Yes, I'm Flip,' the woman said.

'I'm Harry Gilby. From We've Got Blondie's Drumsticks And We're Going To Use Them. Except there's been a slight change . . .'

'You should be in make-up right now,' Flip said quickly, pointing to a small, screened-off section of the hall.

'Can I get a cup of tea first?' Harry asked, noticing that she had one in her hand.

'No,' Flip said. 'Just go into make-up. Sorry. I've got musicians up the yin-yang at the moment. I don't know what to do with them all.'

Walking over to see the make-up girl, Harry realized that one of the acts was already on the stage in front of three cameras and a lot of bright spotlights. It seemed to be a six-year-old girl with fake Heidi plaits, an accordion and a small ferret on a lead, from what he could make out. She was singing 'The Lonely Goatherd' song from *The Sound Of Music*, and the ferret – wearing a tiny gingham headscarf – seemed to be swaying around in front of a tiny cardboard accordion.

Shaking his head, Harry decided he could look no longer. At the side of the stage, someone had pinned up a long sheet of butcher's paper, with the names of all the acts written in thick black texta. Harry already knew some of them – Satan's Underpants, the notorious heavy-metal band from Mole Creek, played in Compton sometimes. With a groan, he saw that The Intercontinental Playboys were also on the bill. If they were playing, he decided, then everyone else might as well go home now. There were five of them for a start – and they all had gold lamé suits and cravats.

'Are you We've Got Blondie's Drumsticks And We're Going To Use Them?' the Channel Nine make-up girl asked, coming up to him.

'Yes,' Harry said. He couldn't be bothered explaining. 'Sit down,' the girl said, pinning what seemed to be a dinner napkin under his chin and sponging thick pancake foundation over his nose. 'Just put your raincoat over the back of the chair.'

'I'll keep it on, thanks,' Harry managed to say through a half-closed mouth. 'It's an ironic eighties thing.'

'What?' said the make-up girl, who Harry realized had probably been born in 1980.

'There were two of us and now there's only me. And I've got a drum machine instead of my drummer. So don't worry about her. But that's why it's an ironic eighties thing. Because of the drum machine.'

'Oh well,' the make-up girl said, not listening.

'Please, no powder,' Harry said, noticing that she was approaching him sideways with a large powder puff.

'You sure?'

'I'd rather sweat if it's all the same to you.'

'Everyone else has had powder this morning,' the girl pouted.

'Yes, but did Chris Stein and Clem Burke ever use powder puffs on their climb to the top?' Harry asked. 'I don't think so!'

'Clem who?' the girl asked.

Getting up before the make-up girl could do any

more damage, Harry stepped carefully around the side of the screens and lights around the portable make-up table and then, to his horror, tripped over the bottom of his raincoat, skidding forwards.

Gathering up the bottom of his raincoat, Harry sighed and walked away. He felt like a complete dickhead. Everything he was wearing was wrong. And the make-up girl had put so much orange foundation all over his face that he now looked like a dried apricot.

'Harry!' Flip shouted from the other side of the hall. Cringing, Harry realized that his moment must have come. It was now or never – and Neville Scruby's drum machine was waiting.

'Over there!' Flip pointed at a man with a baseball cap and a headset on. 'Go and see the floor manager!'

The man in the cap waved and was then immediately distracted by the ferret girl's parents, who had turned up with what appeared to be her ten identical sisters and brothers. At the back of the town hall, the woman from the post office, who sounded like a duck, was warming up with low, confident quacking noises.

Then someone tapped him on the shoulder. It was the floor manager with the baseball cap and the headset.

'You're on,' he said flatly.

Harry shook his head. 'Can't,' he mumbled.

'You don't want to?'

Suddenly feeling precisely six years old, Harry shook his head again. At this moment, he thought, he would give anything to have half of Richard's or his father's courage.

Instead, he just wanted to be lifted up by some friendly, passing alien and sucked safely into a spaceship leaving Flip, the floor manager, the girl with the ferret, the woman who sounded like a duck and the entire mess behind him. He felt like he needed to go to the loo – urgently. But also, he realized, he felt like he wanted to die.

'Fine,' the floor manager shrugged his shoulders at him. 'We'll just call in the next one. Hey, Flip! Can you get The Intercontinental Playboys over here?'

Realizing he had already been waved away, in the space of a second, Harry sunk into his raincoat and his mother's leopard-skin shirt. He seemed to have made so little impression on people anyway that no-one was even bothering to stare, even if he was being ironically eighties. Flip was making another call on her mobile phone. The cameramen were just standing around, looking like they wanted a cigarette. And all the other acts traipsing into the hall hardly noticed him at all.

Picking up the drum machine and his guitar, Harry lifted his chin up – it was still itching from all the make-up – and walked slowly and carefully towards the fire exit doors, praying that he could lift the bar on them and get out. If he had to walk all the way back again to the front, he thought, he'd just die.

Luckily though, someone had already lifted the bar – and holding the hem of his raincoat up, Harry managed to get himself, Neville Scruby's drum machine and everything else out of the door without falling off the fire escape and breaking his arm.

Standing there for a minute with his chin itching, Harry wondered if some giant Monty Python foot was about to appear from a cloud and slam down on his head, squashing him into the ground. It seemed to be the way life was going at the moment, he thought. And nobody would miss him. Putting down the drum machine for a second so he could scratch his chin, he caught the first drops of what looked like rain moving in from the west.

'Here love died between me and the music industry,' he announced sadly to a couple of wet pigeons. Then he wrapped Neville's drum machine in his raincoat so it wouldn't get soaked and stumbled in the direction of his car.

Chapter Twenty-three

Bronte had never realized the lotus position could be so painful. Uncrossing her legs, she waggled them out in front of her as her right ankle seized up with pins and needles. In front of her on the rug was a picture of a Tibetan Buddhist monk with his eyes half closed, and his hands gently clasped with both thumbs touching. Try as she might, Bronte couldn't even get the thumbs right.

'Bugger!' she said, unspiritually, as the pins and needles took over her left leg as well. After half an hour of trying to meditate, she felt even more confused about life than ever – and all she had realized while sitting cross-legged was how bad her circulation was. Did everyone in Tibet have to get up off the temple floor every ten minutes to jiggle their legs around for pins and needles? she wondered. The Buddha might have found enlightenment under the Bodhi tree, Bronte thought, but she had more chance of finding enlightenment by going down to the shops and buying a packet of fags.

Hinduism was no good either. She quite liked the little statue of Ganesh, the elephant god of wisdom, that she had bought from the markets. She had even propped him up on her dressing table, clearing a special space for him among the bottles of Body Shop peppermint foot lotion, and the packs of vitamins and boxes of tissues. Ganesh, however, did not seem to be supplying any of the answers. She might as well have a statue of Babar up there, Bronte decided.

Shaking her legs out again, Bronte decided to banish her pins and needles by walking down to the park and back, getting some cigarettes on the way. All the deep breathing she had been doing during meditation had given her an incredible craving for a packet of Benson & Hedges.

She was still getting used to not working. Every so often, on a weekday, she would look at her watch and panic at the time. This would then be followed by a blissful moment of relief as she remembered that she didn't have to be anywhere any more. Increasingly, this would be followed by a lurch of anxiety as Bronte also realized that she didn't have much money any more, either – but she was learning to ignore it. The Buddhist monks got by on a pair of thongs, a sarong and a bowl of rice, as far as she could see – and they were happy. Why not her? And she was one up on them already as she had at least four pairs of thongs, and an Alannah Hill party dress.

Setting off for the park, Bronte took her favourite old duffle coat – a relic of her life in Compton – and shoved her purse and keys in her pocket. To her satisfaction, she discovered she had left half a packet of chewing gum in there. Popping the last two squares of gum in her mouth, she started chewing as she walked. With any luck, it might put her off buying the cigarettes. It seemed stupid to have escaped death in a car accident, then to buy packets with 'WARNING – SMOKING KILLS' stuck on the packet.

Crossing the road, she passed one of her neighbours. 'Having the day off?' the man asked cheerfully.

Bronte shook her head. 'All my days are off now,' she called, waving her hand.

The local park was a good place to go, if you could

271

avoid the endless piles of dog crap in the long grass. It wasn't quite the same as the freedom of riding Mickey around the bush behind Compton, but it was the best she could come up with today.

Ahead of her, a Catholic priest was carrying two white plastic bags full of groceries. He must be a young one, Bronte thought, judging by the back of his head. He almost had Richard's haircut – short, clipped brown hair, cut in a slightly wavy line above his collar. She decided it was sad when men became priests in their twenties – unless, of course, they'd tried everything that sex, drugs and rock'n'roll could offer up until the age of nineteen. That way, Bronte thought, priesthood might come as a bit of a relief – almost like a long holiday on a health farm.

Despite the fact that she had forced Richard to get married in a Catholic church, Bronte decided she had never been very religious. She had been christened and baptized a Catholic, but she had never quite managed to cope with the life-size statues of Jesus and Mary.

Suddenly the priest's shopping bag broke. Biting her lip, Bronte watched several cans of baked beans go rolling into the gutter and what looked like a bag of frozen peas land in a puddle. Immediately she caught up with him and started bending down, picking up the cans.

'Thank you,' he smiled, looking embarrassed.

'There's another one under here,' Bronte said, suddenly spotting a fugitive can of baked beans rolling underneath a patch of bushes.

'Thanks,' the priest said again. 'I think if I put everything in one bag I can just about make it back.'

'Do you live near here?' asked Bronte, making conversation now that they were walking at the same speed.

'I live a few streets away, but I'm actually at St James',' he nodded, motioning towards a small church on the corner of the park. Bronte was amazed that she had never noticed it before. She supposed churches were like bus stops, or give way signs, or lampposts – unless you actually went to them, they were just part of the background of life.

The priest was really very good looking. He had dark blue eyes with almost-black lashes and eyebrows, and the kind of mouth that you wanted to watch all day – no matter what he was actually saying. He had amazingly clear skin, too, she thought. Perhaps it was a happy side effect of being so holy.

'I used to be a Catholic,' she said suddenly, without thinking.

'Used to be?' he smiled. 'Sometimes we think, once a Catholic, always a Catholic.'

'Well, I did confession once, anyway,' she said.

'Ah, yes, I get a lot of that,' the priest smiled again. '"Dear Father it has been quite a few decades since my last confession . . ."'

Catching his smile, Bronte found herself being outrageously attracted to him again, and then quickly stopped herself. This was the height of unspirituality, she thought. It was bad enough not being able to meditate without craving a packet of fags. Lusting after a Catholic priest was even worse.

'I'm Father Ballard,' the priest said, not noticing that Bronte was now staring fiercely at the pavement in embarrassment.

'I'm Bronte Nicholson,' she said politely, still trying not to look at him in case she had impure thoughts again.

'And have you been into our church?' he asked. 'You should at least have a look. It's quite old – at least 1870.'

'I haven't,' Bronte smiled. 'Too busy.' Then she realized she was lying to a priest and looked at her feet again.

'You know, people have a lot of trouble talking to me,' Father Ballard said.

273

'Perhaps it's because they have to keep calling you Father, Father,' Bronte said. 'I mean, you're only young.'

'Twenty-eight,' Father Ballard explained. 'And actually my real name is Nick.'

He was just a bit younger than Harry, Bronte realized with a start.

'Nick, can I ask you a question?' she said suddenly.

'Sure.'

'Why do none of the religions – I mean, absolutely none of them – agree on anything?'

'That's a hard one,' he said, now holding the shopping bag in both arms.

'Who's right about heaven, for example? And hell? And you know, where's the proof?'

'Right,' Father Ballard said, thinking hard. The cans of baked beans – he had bought far too many – were now digging into his arms through the shopping bag.

'And what are we here for? How do I know what I'm here for?' Bronte persisted.

'I'll tell you what,' the priest said, 'this is really a two-cups-of-tea conversation. How would you like to come in for a bit, then maybe we could talk more about this? And I'll put the kettle on. I've got a service at six, but otherwise we've got some time.'

If he had been a normal man and not a priest, Bronte thought that this offer would have made her day. Instead she had a horrible feeling that he felt he had found a lost lamb in the flock and all he wanted to do was grab a long pole with a hook on the end and drag her back in again. Then again, she'd had worse offers. She might even be prepared to baa at him if he'd just let her gaze into his long-lashed, deep blue eyes.

'OK then,' she said, 'you're on.'

Following Father Ballard through the front doors of the church and past rows of wooden pews, Bronte realized that, for the first time in her life, she was about to be allowed past the red velvet curtains at the back.

'Through the curtains,' she whispered, despite herself. 'Wow!'

'It's not too much of a mystery,' Nick admitted. 'In fact, what we've got here is really my little office and a few more – for the other priests – and then it's just the church hall, where we have the Christmas parties and so on.'

Bronte wondered what Nick – she couldn't possibly keep calling him Father – would be like at a party. A dismal vision of orange cordial and asparagus sandwiches, with people playing ping-pong, floated in front of her. It was such a shame, she thought, that God had kidnapped Nick Ballard in his prime.

'Nick,' she said, following him into his office, 'do you really, really, really believe in it all? I mean, it's a job, isn't it? Like any other job. There must be things you don't agree with.'

'But I do believe,' he said simply, giving her a long, honest, blue-eyed look and offering her an armchair. When he sat down in the other one, she could almost see his ankles. She could understand now why in Victorian England that had been considered erotic.

'Some strange things have been happening to me lately,' she said. 'And I've been looking for answers.'

'Ah.'

'First of all I thought I was going to die. Then my horse came back from the dead and started talking to me, and then I was stopped from being run over by a car – by the same horse. Anyway, now I have all these things to sort out.'

'Such as?' Father Ballard asked.

'Such as . . . Well, are you ready?'

'I'm ready,' the priest said, though Bronte didn't think he was.

'Well then,' she said, taking a deep breath. 'How did Jesus move the rock? How did he?'

'Mmmm,' said Father Ballard.

'Is it the same thing as my horse pushing me out of

275

the way on the road? And what was I saved for anyway? I don't do anyone much good.'

'I'm not sure about that,' the priest smiled.

'Where is heaven? Where is hell? Are there elephants up there?'

'Excuse me?' the priest said.

'Is Ganesh the elephant up there? And Buddha? Why are the Catholics right and not the Indians? Anyway. The other thing was, if you go to hell, can you come back afterwards in your next life? And more to the point, will I go to hell? What about Angel, I know she's called Angel but is she in heaven? And is there a separate horse heaven and human heaven because I can't imagine my grandmother being happy frolicking around in a field eating hay.'

'No,' Father Ballard said.

'And what about all the other fifty million horses who've died since the beginning of time? Where are they all? How do they *fit*?'

'A-ha!' Nick Ballard said, leaning forward and getting ready to speak, but Bronte was already onto the next thing.

Lifting one leg under her on the chair, she gave a long sigh. 'I mean, Father, I just don't have a clue about why I've been spared. I quit my job because I hated it, that was the first thing I did, but since then I've just been wandering around. It's not like I've got a purpose or anything. I'm just – waffling around. I mean, why me? So I've just been asking myself a lot of questions.'

'Searching,' Nick suggested.

'Yes, searching. I mean, the Buddhists say this is just one of about a hundred lives I've got, but what proof do they have?'

Nick smiled.

'I mean, have I been revolving around since the time of the Romans, and why don't I remember any of it? I mean, I can't even speak Italian. I don't even like lasagna. And then there's Ganesh. But he's been on my dressing table for a full fortnight waving his trunk at me and I'm still none the wiser. I don't know, maybe he only helps Hindus.' She sighed. 'I don't know, Father, maybe the communists have got it right – it's all just opium for the masses.'

Biting her lip, Bronte wondered if she had offended him, but instead Father Ballard looked as if he were going to fall off his chair with excitement. *I am a lost sheep*, she thought, resignedly, *and I'm probably the best lost sheep he's had all month.*

'Mormons, Moslems, Jews, Jehovah's Witnesses, Spiritualists,' Bronte recited. 'Hare Krishnas, Theosophists, that thing Madonna's into . . .'

'The Kabbalah,' the priest helpfully supplied.

'The Baha'i, the Protestants, the Anglicans, Zoroastrianism . . .'

'Zoroastrianism,' Nick raised his eyebrows. 'You *have* been searching.'

'If you ask me, it's basically down to this – too many revelations,' Bronte sighed. 'And that's the only revelation I've had about it.'

'You think so?' the priest said.

'I mean, *everyone*'s had a revelation,' Bronte said, sounding exasperated. '*Everyone!* They have them under trees, they have them on mountain tops – and they're always different, every time. Nobody agrees. You can eat pork, you can't eat pork. Women can be priests, they can't be priests. What I want to know is, who's right? Enough of the revelating, what about the facts?'

'Can I ask what do you do?' Nick asked suddenly. 'Or what you did before you resigned?'

'I worked on a magazine,' Bronte said, realizing that she was instantly giving herself away.

For a minute, neither of them spoke – Bronte stared mindlessly at the cross on the wall above the mantelpiece, while the priest gazed steadily into the fireplace.

'You know how I said this was a two-cups-of-tea conversation?' he said at last.

Bronte nodded.

'It's actually a whole year's worth of tea,' he smiled.

'Maybe a lifetime's supply of tea,' Bronte said, giving in.

'You're very welcome to come back,' Father Ballard said. 'But I'm aware that I have people to see in about quarter of an hour. Would you like to come back to-morrow? Or maybe you'd like to see one of the senior priests in the parish?'

'I see,' Bronte smiled, 'Bringing in the big guns.'

'Just one of those questions would occupy us for a whole afternoon,' Father Ballard said, getting up from his chair.

Following his lead, Bronte also stood up, then took his hand and shook it.

'Thanks, anyway,' she said as he showed her out past the curtains and past the pews through the front of the church.

Before she left – and she knew she wouldn't come back – Bronte allowed herself one last, luxurious look at his face and tried to imagine what life would be like if he was a normal man as opposed to a priest, and he had been on the way back to his flat rather than a Catholic church. Then she pushed the thought aside and walked outside, leaving Father Ballard to stand in the doorway holding up his hand in a half wave as she went.

If nothing else, she thought, he had managed to get rid of her cigarette craving so maybe there had been an act of God after all. Walking back to the park, she wondered if all the women in his congregation had secret crushes on Father Nick Ballard. Probably not, she reprimanded herself – everybody else round here was probably a hundred times more spiritual than her. She had always been a shameless, shallow heathen – she'd even picked the church she'd married in on the grounds that it had nice stained-glass windows.

Then something struck her. Father Nick Ballard was the first man she had fancied in over a year.

'Amazing!' Bronte said out loud, making a woman walking past turn round.

Checking over the last twelve months in her mind, she realized that she was not mistaken. In all that time, she hadn't registered even one molecule of attraction for anyone – and now six giant atoms had hit her over the head all at once.

Perhaps God would forgive her for being so sacrilegious if He knew what had just happened. It wasn't so much a feeling of lust that had come back, Bronte thought, as a sudden lust for life as well – she had forgotten how much the two were connected. And wasn't that supposed to be what God was on about anyway? Creating life, then making it worth living?

Bronte knew she would forget Nick Ballard tomorrow. In the meantime, she would stop driving herself mad by sitting cross-legged on the carpet holding her thumbs and talking to small plastic elephants. Perhaps the meaning of life was that it was what it was, she thought, and you just had to put up with it, and if you were lucky, enjoy it now and then – not counting unspeakable cravings for priests ten years younger than you. Maybe Angel had saved her life for no other reason than to show her that, she thought. But the most interesting thing of all was that she had completely forgotten what it was like to have a crush on someone. It had been so long that the part of her brain that normally made it all happen had probably frozen. Thanks to Nick – although she was ashamed of it – something had woken up again. *But the only question is*, Bronte thought, *what do I do with it? And where do I send it?*

Chapter Twenty-four

Tom never felt comfortable in the Compton Arms. He had passed out too many times in the toilets, for a start, and the rows of bottles above the bar just reminded him of all the months he had lost in his life and all the times he couldn't remember. Worst of all, though, the bottles also reminded him that occasionally he still couldn't trust himself. *One drink's never enough*, Tom thought.

He couldn't change the will of the Compton cricket team, though, and on the first Wednesday of the month, all the players traditionally met in the back bar. Sometimes they talked about cricket rosters and the treasurer's report, but usually they just got drunk, played pool and bet on the races at Flemington.

When Richard arrived, Tom was carefully sipping an orange juice and trying to make it last.

Richard nodded at him and pulled a bar stool over to the table where Tom had propped himself up with the paper.

'Are we the first ones?' he asked.

Tom nodded back and put the paper aside.

'You got the bus in?' Richard asked.

'A bus from Hobart and then I biked it. I had to fight to get my bike on the bus, though.'

'And it's OK in the new place?'

Tom smiled and shrugged. 'Better than living with Annie. But I've forgotten what it's like to live with more than one person at a time. You have to wait for the bathroom.'

'Well,' Richard offered, 'if it's any consolation, when you live with Sarah, it's the equivalent of having three people in the bathroom. She takes longer in there than Bronte ever did, and I thought Bronte had the world record.'

Concentrating hard on his drink so he wouldn't have to look Richard in the eye, Tom pushed himself to think of a subject other than Sarah.

'Harry's not having much fun,' he said at last.

'Yes, it's terrible,' Richard agreed. 'You heard about the TV show?'

Tom made a face into his drink. 'And Pippin.'

'I did my best,' Richard said, looking up at him. 'I got him a drum machine.'

'He told me.'

'I don't think he appreciated it.'

'No, he did. He did,' Tom insisted. 'It's just that Harry's got a funny way of showing it. Anyway, it wasn't your fault that he pulled out.'

'No.'

'It's just a confidence thing with him. You know how it is. Well . . .' he shrugged, 'he's your brother, you know about it.'

Waving to some members of the team who had just arrived, Richard looked at his watch.

'Everyone's early today,' he noticed. 'We've got at least half an hour before it starts.'

'Do you want another drink?' Tom asked. Richard shook his head. Looking at his friend now, he wondered how he'd been coping since leaving Annie.

'Do you think you made the right decision – moving out?' he asked him.

Tom nodded. 'Annie wasn't happy either,' he shrugged. 'She just wouldn't admit it.'

'Right,' Richard agreed.

'I miss the garden, that's about all,' Tom said.

'And any action in Hobart?'

Blushing, Tom looked away. He hated the fact that he was over thirty and Richard could still make him blush.

'I can't believe you haven't worked your charm on someone yet,' Richard said.

'Well, you know,' Tom said helplessly.

'I think single life is going to be good for you,' Richard said. 'Finding someone more your own vintage. Or younger.'

'I don't want to go as young as Harry, though,' Tom mumbled, trying to divert the attention away from himself.

'Oh no, not the twenty-one-year-olds,' Richard grinned, agreeing with him. 'Maybe you just need someone more Sarah's age.'

Swallowing hard, Tom downed the last of his juice and tried desperately to stop a second blush taking over his face. If he thought about missing the garden, he might just manage it.

'Just going to the men's,' he said, swinging off his bar stool. Turning his attention to the giant pub video screen, Richard watched the boxing for a few minutes until Tom returned. He felt like ordering some food, but the thought of the pub's spaghetti bolognaise was putting him off. Maybe they'd all switch to the local Chinese after the meeting. Or maybe Sarah might feel like cooking something later.

'Sarah won't let me watch the boxing,' Richard observed, when Tom sat down again. 'We have this steady diet of English television at home instead. It's like she never left London sometimes, except everything's two years out of date.'

'If I moved anywhere, I'd miss the TV,' Tom said quietly.

'Oh, it's more than that,' Richard sighed, letting his

attention wander back to the boxing. 'It's more than feeling homesick.'

Saying nothing, Tom also looked up at the boxing, wishing that at least one of the boxers would knock the other one out, just so Richard would be distracted.

'Sarah's a good example of what happens to women when they first get married,' Richard sighed, looking back at Tom again.

'Really?'

'There's this change of rules. It happened with Bronte, too. Though not this fast. One minute they're like this with you . . .' Richard held his hand close to him '. . . and then they're over here somewhere.' He moved his hand away. 'Sarah's been hard to live with, Tom, and it's only now we've been married this long that I can say it to you.'

'Getting used to things,' Tom ventured.

'Well, there's getting used to things, and then there's arguing.'

'Right,' Tom nodded, trying to stay in control.

'We never really argued before we were married,' Richard said. 'And now it's slamming doors time. It's a terrible thing,' he shook his head at Tom, 'but even the fights are about the only time I even feel we're an honest-to-God couple. Even when we're doing that, at least it's proof that we're somehow *together*.'

Feeling his heart start to pound, Tom kept gazing steadily at the boxers on the giant video screen, who were now dancing around the centre of the ring.

'She won't explain anything to me and so I can't help,' Richard admitted. 'God knows I've tried.'

'Bad,' Tom agreed, trying desperately to keep his voice level.

'Very bad, to the point where I basically thought she was – I don't know.'

Willing himself to stay calm, Tom kept nodding, as casually as he knew how, and staring at the TV screen.

'I thought maybe she was seeing someone else,' Richard said at last, putting his beer down on the table. 'It got that bad, Tom. Anyway. Enough of the truth drug.' He indicated his drink.

A commotion at the back of the pub distracted him for a minute and he looked away, suddenly recognizing Harry, who was swinging a pool cue like a microphone and pretending to sing into it, entertaining the rest of the cricket team.

'Harry!' he yelled across the bar.

Waving, Harry put his pool cue down and came over, holding a can of beer in each hand. His brother, Richard noticed, was wearing something he had never seen before – pinstriped pants, from the bottom half of a suit, with a pair of neon green underpants pulled above the belt loop.

'Yeah, yeah,' Harry said, noticing Richard looking him up and down. 'You can see my daks. Big deal. It's a look. Better to have a look than no look at all,' he told Tom, who was wearing jeans and a jumper with holes in the elbows.

'We were just talking about that TV show,' Tom said. 'Sorry to hear about it.'

'Not as sorry as the Australian television viewing public when they see a six-year-old with fake plaits and a ferret with a headscarf singing "The Lonely Goatherd",' Harry sighed, chug-a-lugging his beer back in his mouth.

'What's all that about?' Richard asked.

'Oh, ferret girl won the heat. The heat I piked out of,' Harry said airily. 'By the way, was everything OK with the drum machine?'

'Neville didn't say anything.'

'Good,' Harry nodded. 'Not that it ever got to see its moment of glory. But I was worried that the practise run in the cabin might have destroyed it.' Making snare drum sounds with his tongue, Harry drummed the tabletop with his hands, while Tom and Richard turned back to the TV. Instead of boxing, they were now watching sumo wrestling.

'The height of entertainment,' Harry observed. 'Two fat Japanese wankers in women's underwear. What can I get you boys to drink?'

'Nothing, thanks,' Tom said, shaking his head.

'Slow it down,' Richard cautioned. 'We've got a meeting to get through.'

'Just asking,' Harry said, picking up his second can and waving it at them. 'And by the way, you'll both be pleased to hear that Pippin and Wendy are now an item.'

'Really?' Tom asked. He thought Harry was putting a brave face on things, but he could also see, by the bags under his eyes, that he hadn't been sleeping.

'Yes, they're walking down the street holding hands and everything,' Harry sighed. 'I mean, do you do that, Richard? Do you and Sarah walk down the street holding hands?'

Embarrassed for Richard, after everything he had just said, Tom stared at his boots while Harry kept talking.

'Holding hands is a bit of a statement, I agree,' Richard said, smiling.

'Yeah, well, watch out, because Pippin and Wendy are making statements all over town from what I hear,' Harry warned. 'And personally I wouldn't want children or animals watching.'

'Pippin wasn't that great,' Tom said, sympathetically. 'You could get another drummer.'

'Nah,' Harry waved this idea aside. 'Music's over.'

'Really?' Tom asked.

'I've had it,' Harry said, sticking his jaw out. 'Love died between me and the music industry at the Hobart Town Hall. I knew it as soon as I walked out of there. And I'll tell you something else.'

'What?' Richard asked.

'Debbie Harry's over too.'

Staring hard, Richard tried to work out if his brother was serious or not.

'You can't give up Debbie,' Tom said at last. 'Debbie's part of your life.'

'No she isn't,' Harry said quickly.' I'm sick of getting letters back from New York saying, "Not known at this address". Anyway. I'm turning thirty soon. Things are changing.'

'What do you mean, things are changing?' Richard asked.

'Things,' Harry said mysteriously, opening his second can of beer.

'Is this something you found out on a problems page?' Richard asked. Tom smiled to himself. He had heard all about Harry's one-man mission to write to every agony aunt in the country.

'Actually, that's one of the things,' Harry told his brother. 'One of the changing things.'

'Right.'

'I've decided I'm going to become a problems-page writer,' he declared, tilting his beer can back into his mouth.

'Seriously?' Tom asked, despite himself. But Harry looked extremely serious.

'I'll keep the job on for a few weeks at the bank until I get myself established,' Harry explained to Tom, deliberately not looking at Richard. 'Then I'll just do it full time. I'll have to take a pay cut, of course. And I can forget about the cheap mortgage. But then, I never wanted one anyway. When I buy a house,' he vowed, 'I'm going to pay cash. I'm saving it all up in a trunk under my bed. Screw the bank.'

'Problems pages, Richard said slowly. 'As in, problems pages in newspapers and women's magazines.'

'Yes,' Harry nodded. 'I think it's time they let a man get in there. Especially someone like me. Someone . . .' he paused, 'someone who's lived a bit.'

'And you think you're qualified?' Richard said sharply.

'Well, that's typical,' Harry sighed, putting his beer can down. 'You know, that's exactly what I expected from you, Richard. You're such a . . .' he groped for the words, 'such a paper head! Am I qualified? Well, who cares? The hamster woman probably isn't qualified either.'

'Who', asked Richard patiently, 'is the hamster woman?'

'Mary O'Flanagan. She's got cheeks like a hamster. She's the one who wrote to me and told me to ask Witchy Wendy Wagner on a date.'

'Well, she's certainly not qualified then,' Richard said. 'But surely you need a psychology degree – or *something*.'

'And tell me, what does it take to understand the mysterious and unfathomable depths of the human heart? A certificate in a frame?' Harry asked.

'Oh, for God's sake,' Richard said.

'What? What?'

'Well,' Richard sat up on his bar stool, 'I mean, Harry, is this *really* serious?'

'Bloody serious,' Harry said, folding his arms on the table. 'I already handed in my notice at the bank.'

'What?' his brother yelled.

Look, I wrote to a lot of problems pages. And you know what? They're useless. Most of them. I could have solved my own problems better than half those women on the magazines. Every month, millions of people all over the world are being led astray by the worst kind of ill-informed advice! It's a scandal! Think how many relationships have suffered, how many men have been driven to suicide!'

'Harry . . .' Richard tried to interrupt him.

I think I've got what it takes to do one of those pages,' Harry insisted. 'And I don't care if you don't believe in me, Richard. I believe in myself Except . . .'

287

'What?' Richard asked.

'I just need to ask one favour,' Harry said.

'One favour,' Richard countered. 'It's never just one, though, is it?'

'Hey,' Tom interrupted. He hated it when the brothers got to this stage. And increasingly, he didn't think he could be around Richard. What he was hearing about his marriage to Sarah was beginning to make him feel sick. He realized that suddenly everything had become much too real. It had been a mistake coming to the pub, Tom decided. He should have stayed at home – the other people in the house had been cooking curry, and at least he could have chopped some onions and done something useful.

'Don't fight,' Tom said suddenly, looking at Richard and Harry simultaneously. 'Not you two.'

'It's not fighting,' Harry shrugged, staring blankly at the sumo wrestlers on the video screen. 'It's just, Richard needs to realize something about me.'

'And you need to grow up,' Richard replied.

'Exactly what I *am* doing,' Harry said.

'So what's the favour then?' Richard asked. 'How am I going to have to put myself out for you this time?'

'Well, I'm sure this is really going to kill you, Richard, but anyway . . .' Harry began.

'What?'

'I need Bronte's home phone number.'

Nodding, Richard rolled his eyes, sighed and looked at Tom for sympathy, but his friend was frowning, miles away.

'Bronte, I might have known,' Richard said. 'And you think she'll get you a job?'

'Of course not,' Harry replied, 'I just thought she might know someone.'

'Well, you know she's quit the magazine business?'

'Wow.' Harry hadn't known.

'She quit ages ago. So I don't know.'

'Well, just give me her number anyway,' Harry

persisted. 'Come on. She can only hang up on me.'

Sighing, Richard found a pen, ripped off part of the newspaper and handed Bronte's number over. Tom, he noticed, seemed to be sinking further and further down on his bar stool.

'And will you do something else for me?' Harry pleaded.

Richard nodded. He was expecting to be asked for money at any moment and he was already calculating how much he could afford to lend his brother.

'I need someone to read what I've written,' Harry went on, noticing the look of relief on Richard's face as he realized it wasn't about money. 'I've made up some fake problems, then I've written my answers. Like a sample of what I can do. I just thought you could look over them.'

'Sure,' Richard nodded politely. *Too* politely, Harry thought. Suddenly he pushed his drink away.

'You know, you never acknowledge that I might have something to offer the world,' Harry complained.

'That's not true,' Richard hit back.

'You never thought I'd make it in music – and hey, I didn't. You never thought I'd get married – and hey, I haven't. Tom, would you agree that I've become a self-fulfilling prophecy of everything my brother expected me to fail at?'

'Stop it,' Tom protested.

'Well, psychologists would have a field day with my life. Funnily enough, every doubt he ever had about me, I've managed to manifest.'

'He doesn't doubt you!' Finally, Tom was driven to shouting. 'He doesn't, so just shut up about it!'

Slamming his glass back on the table, he shoved the bar stool aside and walked out of the pub.

He knew neither of them would come after him, but just in case, Tom crossed the road against the on-coming traffic and deliberately zig-zagged away from the pub across a children's playground and then up a quiet street full of old weatherboard houses. Finally he found an empty block of land where he could sink down against a wall and think. He felt closer to tears than he had for years. He still hadn't cried since he'd left Annie, Tom thought, and that was probably part of it.

Even worse, though, was the feeling that Richard had just woken him up from some kind of dream. With a start, Tom realized he and Sarah had now been seeing each other for three months. The only thing that felt bigger than his guilt at the moment seemed to be his craving for alcohol.

'My old friend,' he told a passing stray cat, 'a full bottle of Scotch.'

He knew he wouldn't do it, and couldn't do it – but the bottle shop was only a few streets away.

'Come here, cat,' he said to the animal, a black, scrawny mongrel with a thin tail – but it hopped away as soon as he reached out for it. It couldn't get much worse than this, Tom thought. He was being seriously tempted by alcohol for the first time in over a year. He was living in a house with people he hardly knew. And he was still, occasionally, cheating on the one person in his life who had asked him to be best man at his wedding. And, he realized, Sarah was no closer to leaving Richard – and despite everything, she was still married to him.

He had seen an ad in the paper for casual gardeners, working with National Parks and Wildlife. The pay was so low he'd still have to stay in a share house, but, the time had come to make some decisions. Getting up from the wall, he vowed he'd ring up about it the following day.

Chapter Twenty-five

Two weeks later, Sarah was also making decisions. And picking up the phone, she did something she realized she should have done at the beginning.

'Liz,' she said, hearing the beeps as her call was picked up in London. 'It's Sarah. Can you talk?'

'Sure,' Liz said. 'Josh has just gone down, so you're in luck.'

Liz's baby, Josh – Sarah's godchild – was turning out to be more co-operative than anyone had expected.

'I've got something to tell you,' Sarah said. 'It might be a shock.'

Liz paused, wondering if her friend had also become pregnant – but something told her that was the last thing she should expect.

'I've been having an affair,' Sarah said, hearing herself use the word for the first time. It was like that other word – *adultery* – which had also come into her head lately.

'Oh,' Liz said.

'With Tom. Richard's best man.'

'Yes, I know. Tom. The best man. The blond guy. The one who wrote the poem.'

'I'm losing it, Liz.'

'Yes. Have you told anyone else? Have you told Richard?'

'I'll never tell him. No, you're the only one.'

'And is it serious? How long has it been going on for?'

'I don't know if it's serious,' Sarah sighed. 'I just don't know any more. It's been going on for months.'

Sinking down in her armchair, she stared mindlessly at the bright winter sun bouncing off the gum trees in the garden. In a few weeks, it would be Richard's birthday. In a few months, it would be their first wedding anniversary. In the background, she could hear the theme music for the BBC news, filtering through the telephone from London to Australia.

'God, the news,' Sarah sighed. 'I never thought I'd miss the news.'

'What does Tom want?' Liz pressed her.

'He doesn't know. I mean, we've tried to break it off, but it's too hard. It's on, and then it's off, and then it all starts again.'

'What about Richard?'

'I can't leave him. I couldn't do it to him.'

Checking her baby in his pram, Liz raised her eyebrows at her husband, who was watching the television, and motioned for him to turn the sound down.

'I can't sleep, I can't do anything,' Sarah continued, whispering.

'So when did you last see Tom?' Liz said.

'Only last week. I wasn't going to call him. I thought if I stopped first then maybe it would make it easier for him. But then he called. And then he was at a party Richard and I went to, and just seeing each other was too much.'

'Right.'

'We had a huge fight at the party. We were outside in the garden, just by ourselves. He wants me to think about leaving Richard – or, at least, he wants to know if Richard's going to leave me. But it's all too soon, Liz.'

'At the same time, it's just going on and on,' Liz observed. 'And where have you been meeting Tom?'

'At his place, when his flatmates are out,' Sarah confessed, feeling ashamed as she heard herself telling Liz. 'You know, when I talk to you now, and it's all out in the cold light of day, it's almost like it's someone else.'

'Yes, but it's you. And Tom left that woman too – Annie. I remember you telling me that.'

'Yes, he left her.'

'So he's free.'

'Yes, but I'm not. In a way, I wish he *weren't* free, it would just make it easier for both of us to stop now. Instead, I feel like the decision is mine.'

'Well, it is,' Liz said bluntly. 'And you say it's been going on for months. Well – you're going to have to decide.'

'Tom drives me mad,' Sarah said simply. 'I wish you could see him then you'd understand. He's so easy to love. He's such an amazing man. And he needs me. We've both needed each other.'

'But you still love Richard?'

'Yes. But in a different way. I still care about him. That's why I can't leave.'

'Well, you know what I'm going to say,' Liz said, gazing fondly at Josh in his pram.

'Yeah,' Sarah said, 'I know.'

'Are you happy with yourself or your life?'

'I hate myself.'

'Well then,' Liz said. 'And what's Tom doing with his life?'

'He's got a new job with National Parks and Wildlife as a gardener,' Sarah said. 'There's a woman there he might be interested in. I don't know, he mentions her sometimes and I can just tell – *you* know. And then I think, I have no right to complain.'

'That's right,' Liz said. 'You don't.'

'How did I get into this?' Sarah sighed. 'It's been like

293

a dream or something. It's all been so weird and unreal.'

'Well, I hate to sound like your mother,' Liz said, 'but the reason you got into it doesn't matter. And even if it has been like a dream, there comes a point when you have to say no to one, yes to another, or no to both of them. Anything else is just crap, Sarah, and I hate to be like this, but in a way, you probably rang me just to hear it.'

'Yep,' Sarah said, close to tears.

'Most of all I care that you hate yourself,' Liz said. 'If it's got to that stage, then you don't need advice from me.'

'Tom was planting a camellia tree the other day,' Sarah said, 'for the spring. He said he was planting it for me because no matter what happened to us, he always wanted to remember me.'

'Yeah, well,' Liz said, trying to be tough with her oldest friend. 'Tell him to plant it for someone else. You know, once upon a time we used to talk about women who cheated on their husbands, and women who moved in on other people's relationships.'

'Yes,' Sarah said, feeling herself shrink.

'We used to hate those kinds of women, Sarah. And now you're telling me that's what you've done?'

'I know.'

'Because it's not just Richard, it's Annie as well. Look what you've done to her.'

'Liz, please, Sarah said. 'I think I have to go now.' Stuffing a scrunched-up tissue in her eyes to stop the tears before they could come, she put the phone down and gazed out of the window at the night sky.

A few days later, Tom was watching Perdita, one of the other gardeners, watering the same camellia tree. National Parks and Wildlife had given them all regulation khaki overalls and Perdita was almost swimming in hers, she was so tiny. For some reason, though, Tom found he couldn't stop looking at her.

'Want a hand?' he asked, coming over. He was enjoying his new job, partly because they were replanting a dead patch of parkland with new shrubs, and partly because it had delivered him into a life that seemed more real – and a lot more normal.

'I'm going to go to the pub for lunch,' Perdita said, straightening up. She was wearing plaits today, Tom noticed – from a distance she looked like a tiny American Indian.

'Well, the pub sounds good,' Tom said, watching her as she gathered a pile of woodchips around the camellia tree with her gardening gloves.

'The tree's dying,' Perdita observed.

'Yeah. Dying even before it's had a chance to grow,' Tom said, measuring his words. It wasn't really surprising, he thought. It was, after all, the camellia he had planted for Sarah.

Looking at Perdita, Tom decided that at least some of Richard's advice might be paying off. Perdita was thirty-four, almost his age, for a change. And from the little he knew about her, he had gathered that she was single. Instantly, Tom felt a stab of guilt about Sarah, but then tried to push it away. Sarah wasn't his, he decided. And he wasn't hers. She belonged to Richard and he belonged to nobody any more.

'Maybe the others want to come to the pub too,' Perdita said, pushing one plait behind her ear and looking back at the team of gardeners now working at the bottom of the hill.

'I'll ask,' Tom said, hoping that they wouldn't. If he could get Sarah out of his head for just two hours, he reasoned, he might be able to let someone like Perdita in. And the weird thing was, he realized, even Annie would probably like her.

Tom had no idea where this gardening job would take him, but for now, he was content to live in the present. Anyway, there was no point in worrying about the future where Sarah was concerned, he decided. One day at a time made more sense to him. And if the days added up to a different direction, he'd just go with it. Now that Annie had gone from his life, he was finally learning to swim, he realized.

Chapter Twenty-six

'Happy birthday!' Harry yelled, shoving a gift into Richard's hands. 'Happy spring!'

'Is this for last year, or are you actually on time for this year?' Richard asked.

'It's a two-in-one present,' his brother replied. 'I haven't forgotten.'

Unwrapping it, Richard found himself looking at a pair of second-hand salt and pepper shakers in the shape of cows. Harry had even left the price stickers on from the op shop.

'Just what you always wanted, I know,' said Harry.

'So the cow on the left is for last year's birthday . . .'

'Yeah. And the cow on the right brings you up to date for this year, so we're even. The salt and pepper comes out of their udders,' Harry explained. 'I found it quite astounding when the woman at the Red Cross shop showed me.'

'Mmm,' Richard smiled. 'Yes. Great, Harry. Thanks.' The two brothers were alone in the kitchen, surrounded by Richard's birthday cake, piles of tuna sandwiches and an Esky filled with beer and ice.

'Am I the first here?' Harry asked.

'Yes,' Richard said. 'I'm not expecting Sarah back from the supermarket for another half an hour. She's bringing chicken, which means we can try out your salt and pepper udders, I suppose.'

'By the way,' Harry said suddenly, 'I've got some good news.'

Richard looked at him as Harry pulled out a pile of paper with a rubber band around it.

'I've finished my very first problems page,' Harry said happily. 'Thanks for all the suggestions, by the way. I got Tom to help me as well. It's a lot better now. More realistic.'

'Right,' Richard agreed. He had almost forgotten about Harry's idea of becoming a male agony aunt. Harry had come up with so many mad ideas over the years that it was hard to take them all seriously.

'The difficult bit was making the problems up in the first place,' Harry explained. 'But anyway, it's done now. I thought I'd bring it so you could see the finished article. I've decided to send it to *Cosmopolitan* first, see what they think.'

'Right,' Richard repeated, taking the sheaf of paper from Harry. 'And did Bronte say she'd help you?' Richard asked.

'Oh yeah,' Harry said, picking at a tuna sandwich from the plate on the table.

'She did?' Richard was surprised.

'Well, she said she'd think about it,' Harry admitted. 'But I'll give her another call to remind her. I think she's one of those two-call people.'

'Maybe three calls,' Richard joked back.

'Right. Hey,' Harry said suddenly, 'any news on Tom's new woman? Is she coming to the party?'

Richard shrugged. 'Perdita. The gardener. I don't know if she's quite reached new woman status yet. It's only been a few weeks. But I left the invitation open. Maybe he'll bring her, I don't know. He's not saying much about her. You know what he's like.'

After this, a knock on the door announced the arrival of Dr and Mrs Gilby carrying two crayfish in a plastic bag with Max, the dog, following behind.

'This is our present,' his mother said, kissing Richard. 'Happy birthday. Are we early?'

'Doesn't matter,' Harry said, picking another tuna sandwich from the plate and throwing it to Max. 'It just means we get the food faster. Though I have to say, canned tuna sandwiches on your birthday, Richard! What *can* Sarah be thinking of?'

'Tch,' his father said, giving Harry a look. 'Stop whingeing.'

'Don't worry, she's picking up some chips from the supermarket too, Richard consoled his brother. 'Corn chips. Refried beans. All your kind of food.'

Walking to the stereo, Harry decided he'd take charge of the music. Sometimes, Richard's CD collection surprised him and he discovered a band or singer, that he'd always shuddered at, could convert him. He had come across certain interesting songs from Barbra Streisand that way, he mused. There was no point in expecting to find any really decent music, though – the likelihood of Richard owning the latest Supergrass album was nil. Instead he thought he might make a discovery – perhaps, after all, track four, side two of the *Titanic* soundtrack really was worth listening to.

Flicking through the CDs, Harry noted everyone he'd ever wanted to decapitate with a machete – Celine Dion, Elton John, Mariah Carey, Harry Connick Jr – as well as some heavily scratched singles left over from Richard's schoolboy record collection.

'The Knack,' Harry yelled across the room. 'Richard, what about putting The Knack on?'

'What?' his brother yelled back, frowning. Harry decided to put the single on anyway and started absent-mindedly pelvic thrusting to the opening chords of 'My Sharona' until his father gave him a disapproving look.

'He told me love had died between him and the music industry at the Hobart Town Hall,' Richard confided in his mother, watching Harry thrust his pelvis in and out and singing along with the music.

'Well, that sounds like the kind of thing your brother would say,' his mother agreed.

'Look at him, though.' Richard shook his head as Harry pranced around on the carpet with an imaginary microphone. 'He can't help himself.'

Then a hand on his shoulder made Richard turn round and suddenly he saw Tom – with the shortest hair he'd seen for years.

'Happy birthday,' Tom said, handing over an unwrapped bottle of Tasmanian red wine.

'Thanks,' Richard smiled, putting the bottle on the table. He loved Pipers Brook, and Tom had even managed to find a vintage year.

'We're all early,' Mrs Gilby said, passing Tom a tuna sandwich from the plate and trying to stop Max from jumping up. 'Sarah's at the supermarket. She's getting some more food. Oh!' she noticed Tom's new short haircut. 'I like that. They've gone up the back of your head with the clippers for a change.'

'Refried beans!' Harry yelled across the room, waving at Tom. 'We're waiting for refried beans! Real food!'

Joining him at the stereo, Tom knelt down and started flicking through the cardboard box full of Richard's old singles.

'Can't go past "My Sharona",' Harry declared, taking the needle off the record and putting it back to the start again.

'What about this?' Tom threw Harry another single in a faded, red paper sleeve.

'Oh my God,' Harry breathed. '"Video Killed the Radio Star"– I was a mere child.'

'I remember Richard getting off at the school disco with someone when this was on,' Tom laughed.

'That sounds like him,' Harry agreed. Nobody else except my brother would try to pash someone during that song.'

'I thought you'd had it with music,' Tom said, challenging him.

Harry shook his head. 'Well, I have. Professionally.'

'Ah, professionally.'

'So anyway, mate, enough about me,' Harry said, pushing the box of singles away. 'What's happening with this woman with the plaits?'

'Perdita,' Tom grinned, looking at the carpet.

'Yes, her. Perdita in the overalls.'

'Nothing's happening.'

'Yeah, right.'

'She's a friend.'

'A friend who has been at your place at least twice when I've rung.'

'I think you'll find it's always been at a decent hour,' Tom shrugged.

'Well, anyway. Good to hear you're making progress,' Harry said. 'I'm not bitter about it. As a celibate man, I can still share in your joy.'

Standing up again, he took 'My Sharona' off the turntable and put Buggles on.

'Oi, Richard!' he yelled across the room. 'Bring back any memories?'

'Calm down!' yelled Richard back, raising an eyebrow at his mother.

'I think it's because he's left the bank,' his mother explained. 'He's having some sort of hormonal reaction at the moment.'

Pulling the Jeep up in the driveway a few minutes later, Sarah frowned as she heard thumping sounds coming from inside the house. What was going on? One look through the windows, though, and she had an immediate explanation – Harry, jumping up and down in front of the stereo, with his arms held rigidly by his side, accompanied by Max the golden retriever, also jumping up and down.

'Oh God,' she muttered, getting a box full of roast chicken out of the boot. There were days when she could take Harry, and days when she couldn't, she decided. Today was not a Harry day.

As she carried the box of chicken into the kitchen, she was pleased to see that Richard's parents had donated some crayfish as well. She was also pleased that she could recognize the difference between lobster and crayfish at last – she was almost qualifying as a Tasmanian, she thought.

Forcing herself to concentrate on the food, she tried not to look too hard for Tom, but it was useless – within seconds of walking into the kitchen, she had found him, standing next to Harry by the stereo. And, she realized, he had cut his hair. For some reason, it immediately depressed her.

'I'll start cutting up the chicken if you want,' Richard said, kissing her on the cheek. 'You go and talk to Mum and Dad. Nobody else is here yet.'

'Oh, thanks,' Sarah said, still trying not to look at Tom.

'You look lovely,' Mrs Gilby said, admiring Sarah's pink gingham shirt and white jeans.

'Spring weather's here at last,' Dr Gilby noted – but Sarah was miles away.

Look at me, she transmitted to Tom, but it had no effect. Instead his back was almost deliberately turned as he and Harry kept on fiddling with the controls on the stereo. Tom must have heard her pull up in the car, Sarah thought, but he hadn't made any effort to come over and talk to her.

'That music,' Mrs Gilby sighed, 'I remember that song. What were they called? The Biggles? The Buggers?'

'The Buggles,' Sarah said, remembering the song from the days when she and her schoolfriends used to watch *Top Of The Pops*. 'I might just go over and say hi to Harry.'

Smiling, Dr and Mrs Gilby let her go.

'So gorgeous,' Mrs Gilby said, 'I used to have a gingham shirt just like it.'

'Greetings,' Harry said as Sarah came over. 'We're just doing the Richard jukebox here. I have to say, it's all downhill in his record collection after the age of fifteen.'

Sarah smiled. 'Hello,' she said to both of them, but looking at Tom. His floppy blond fringe had almost disappeared with his new short haircut.

'Any preferences for music?' Harry asked.

'Well, I should say Blondie if you're here, Harry,' Sarah said, trying hard.

'No, no,' Harry said quickly. 'Blondie and me are finished.'

'That's a shame,' Sarah replied, not really listening and trying to catch Tom's eye.

The haircut made him seem harder and older somehow and, she realized – feeling herself weaken – sexier.

'I got too many letters from New York marked "Debbie Harry not known at this address",' Harry explained.' Anyway, it's about time I found myself a real live woman. As in – someone who lives in the same hemisphere.'

'And what about you, Tom?' Sarah asked, staring hard at him as Harry went back to the stereo. 'Are you looking for someone in the same hemisphere?'

For a few seconds, neither of them spoke. Then suddenly Harry jumped up with a record in his hand, yelling 'LEE REMICK!' at the top of his voice.

'What?' Tom said blankly.

'Richard's got a picture sleeve of "Lee Remick". I can't believe it, he never told me!' Harry panted, excitedly.

'What?' Sarah repeated.

'"Lee Remick" by The Go-Betweens!' Harry said, brandishing the record at them. 'I've got to tell him. It's a collector's item!'

'Means nothing to me,' Sarah shrugged, watching Harry race to the kitchen to find his brother.

There was a pause, then both of them tried to speak at once.

'You're ignoring me,' Sarah said.

'No,' Tom denied it.

'Really. You can hardly look at me. What is it?'

'Nothing,' Tom shrugged. 'Anyway, we can't talk now.' Trying to push his fringe back out of habit – even though it wasn't there any more – he moved back a step. 'Just going to the loo,' he said.

'Well,' Sarah replied, watching him walk away, 'you know where it is.'

In the kitchen, Harry found himself being grilled by his parents.

'Richard told us Tom might have a new girlfriend,' Mrs Gilby said. 'Has he told you anything?'

'Ask him yourself,' Harry shrugged.

'And what's this about you wanting to do a problems page?' Dr Gilby asked.

'Just a thing I'm experimenting with,' Harry said. 'What is this, the Gestapo in the kitchen?'

Before he could say anything else, though, he was interrupted by Richard motioning for him to go into the hall.

'Hang on,' Harry muttered, 'I'm wanted.'

'Outside,' Richard said bluntly, holding Harry's bundle of problems pages in his hand.

'What do you mean?'

'Just get outside for a minute, I need to talk to you.' Wincing slightly, Harry pushed his way out of the back door and into the garden with Richard close behind.

'These aren't made up,' Richard said, slipping the rubber band off Harry's collection of problems and answers.

'No, they are,' Harry said, trying to defend himself. Richard looked furious.

'This is about me and Sarah and you know it,' Richard challenged him, pointing his finger to the first page.

'Oh, look, nobody's going to know,' Harry said quickly. 'It's all anonymous.'

'Dear Harry,' Richard read straight from the page, *'I have only been married for six months and already I am being driven to buy self-help relationship books. Have I made a mistake by rushing into marriage? My husband is very good at communicating with animals, but he cannot communicate with people. For weeks, I used the size of our bed as an excuse not to sleep with him. His first marriage ended in divorce. I am frightened the same thing will happen to me, what should I do?'*

'Yes, but read the reply,' Harry insisted. 'It's a really good reply, don't you think?'

'That's not the point,' Richard said, staring hard at his brother as Max rushed out into the garden.

'Look I don't know why you're upset. Nobody's going to know it's you. Not that it is you, of course.'

'Oh, right.'

'It's sort of a composite of you and – lots of people I know.'

'Oh bullshit, Harry.'

'And it's only a sample, honestly,' Harry pleaded. 'I mean, the magazines probably won't use that. I'll be getting real letters to reply to soon.' Smugly, Harry folded his arms.

'If you're lucky,' Richard shot back.

'Thanks,' Harry said, hurt. 'As usual, thanks.'

'What the hell were you doing talking to Sarah behind my back?' Richard challenged him.

'What?'

'Well' I've hardly been giving you the inside story on our marriage. Have I? So you must have got it from her.'

Uncomfortably, Harry felt himself beginning to squirm in his suit.

'My private life is private,' Richard said. 'And I can't believe Sarah trusted you.'

'But she never said anything to me!' Harry said desperately.

'Well, how did you find out, then. What have you been doing, spying on us?'

'Look, calm down. It's just – I don't know. The woman in the bookshop isn't exactly discreet. I can't remember who told me about you and Sarah.'

'Someone did! Christ, Harry, that was personal stuff.'

Harry shrugged. 'I don't know. Maybe someone on the cricket team told me – it's no big deal. Maybe Tom, I can't remember.'

'Well, was it Tom? And anyway,' Richard challenged him, 'how would Tom know about my marriage? I mean, Harry, has this been free entertainment for the whole town? Am I just waking up?'

'Well, it might have been Tom who told me,' Harry admitted. 'But you'll have to ask him.'

'And why were you and Tom discussing my marriage?'

Harry shrugged. 'I dunno. I think we were talking one day and I said it looked perfect. I caught a look from Tom that suggested he might know otherwise. He didn't want to tell me anything but I sort of interrogated him and Tom finally said that things aren't always as they appear.'

'How could Tom know so much personal detail about my marriage' Richard said furiously.

'Calm down!' Harry yelled as Max danced around his feet. 'God, Richard, everyone has problems. It's no drama. Nobody cares. Anyway, I don't know why you have to keep so many secrets in your life.'

'Oh, right,' Richard said, feeling his anger rise. 'So now I'm secretive. As well as only being able to talk to animals.' Obligingly, Max thumped his tail on the ground as he saw Richard look at him.

'I didn't say you were secretive,' Harry protested. 'You just said it yourself.'

Shaking his head, Richard stared his brother down.

'Well, according to your problems page – I can't communicate In fact, my own wife is frightened we'll get a divorce. *God*, Harry!'

Rolling over, Max asked for his stomach to be rubbed and Harry found himself obliging, grateful for some kind of distraction.

'It's not a crime to have stuff going on in your marriage,' he said at last. 'And you did rush into it, you know you did.'

'I don't have problems in my marriage,' Richard shot back.

'Yeah, you do.'

'How?'

'We can all see it,' Harry said as gently as he knew how. 'You don't have to be a genius to work it all out.'

'What do you mean, you *all* see it? Is this some kind of club you've all got? You, Tom, half the Compton cricket team? I mean, who else gets together with you and discusses my love life? Tell me, Harry, has Sarah been talking to Tom about me? I mean, something must have been going on.'

'I don't know!' Harry tried to defend himself 'God, Richard, just chill!'

Neither of them spoke for a few minutes, then Richard felt himself returning to the letter again.

'Is that what you think about me?' Richard asked. 'That I can only communicate with animals?' He was, he realized, now feeling hurt beyond belief.

Shrugging, Harry scratched his chin – he hadn't shaved and it was beginning to itch – and stared out over the tops of the trees.

'Well, thanks for your loyalty,' Richard said quietly, rolling the sheaf of paper back up inside the rubber band and throwing it at his brother. Silently, Harry watched him go back into the house, then put his face in his hands.

'Max,' he groaned to the dog. 'Max, Max, what's going on?'

Upstairs in the bedroom, Sarah sat on the bed for a moment and gazed at her fingernails. She hadn't bitten her nails since she was a teenager, but the habit seemed to have come back lately. She supposed she should go back downstairs and greet the guests, who were now arriving in groups. The last thing she felt like doing was playing hostess to all of Richard's cricket friends.

Turning as she heard a noise by the door, she saw Tom looking for her.

'Quickly,' she said.

Closing the door behind him, Tom came in – but instead of moving towards her, he stood carefully by the door, at a distance.

'I have to talk to you,' he said quietly.

'Not while everyone's here,' Sarah said.

'It can't wait,' Tom replied, taking a deep breath. 'Sarah, I've met someone.'

'I know,' she said, watching his face. 'I heard.'

'It's got to be over between us now. It's got to be finished. That's all I have to say.

'I still care about you,' she said sadly, but Tom was already shaking his head.

'I don't want to make this too long,' he said. 'I just decided – it may as well be now, while we're both here.'

'You can't wait for me any more,' Sarah sighed, staring out of the window.

'I've probably waited for six months, if you want to count,' he insisted, his hand on the door. 'At the beginning, I thought it was the start of something. You seemed so sure about your marriage being a mistake. And I believed you. But I can't do – this.'

'Don't go,' Sarah said, trying to stop him.

'What else do we have to say?'

'I don't know if I can take it not seeing you any more,' she said.

'But you love Richard and you're his wife. If you didn't really love him you would have left him a long

308

time ago. I don't know. He deserves to be loved.'

There was a pause, then Sarah spoke first.

'We talked about going to Melbourne once and finding a little house together, do you remember?' she said, her eyes fixed on his hand still resting on the door handle.

'We also talked about me going to college and a whole lot of other things that haven't happened. Look, I'm back in the real world now, partly thanks to you.'

'Well, I'm glad I did something for you,' she said, squeezing her hands tightly together and trying to stay in control.

'You woke me up and got me out of that life with Annie. And now, I've got another life – not a half life, though, a proper life.'

'With this woman.'

'I have to go. You have to go back down there. Richard will wonder where you are.'

'Are you really in love with this woman you work with?' she pleaded, watching him turn in the doorway.

'It's just over, Sarah,' Tom said quietly, desperate not to hurt her any more, as he closed the door behind him.

Back inside the kitchen, Harry heaved a sigh of relief as he saw Richard being led away by his friends from the cricket team. His brother would soon forget what had happened, he reasoned. He felt bad about criticizing him to his face, but at the same time, he also felt he had got something off his chest. Things hadn't been right between them for weeks.

'Harry!' his father suddenly interrupted his thoughts.

'What?'

'Where are these problems pages you've been writing?'

'Oh no,' Harry stalled him. 'Not for public consumption yet.'

'So are you going to send them off, or what?'

'I thought I'd try a few places,' Harry shrugged.

'And then you'll go back to the bank,' his father said hopefully.

'No, Dad. I'm never going back to the bank,' Harry said.

'Well, anyway, if you're going to help people with their problems . . .' his father began.

'Yeah, what?'

'You'll want to get that tuna off your chin.'

Putting a hand up to his face, Harry realized his father was right and that he had managed to smear both oil and small bits of fish around his mouth and under his nose.

'Back in a minute,' he said, heading for the bathroom. Checking his lapels, he realized he'd also managed to drop fish all over his third-best suit – a mid-seventies tartan number with red piping on the cuffs.

Tutting as he realized someone had beaten him to it, Harry jiggled around outside the bathroom door waiting for the tap to stop running. He stank of tuna now and he was dying to wash it off.

'Just me,' Sarah said, emerging. Her eyes were red, Harry noticed. 'Have you seen Richard?' she asked.

'Back down there,' Harry jerked his thumb, 'having his back slapped by the boys.'

'Thanks,' she muttered, running off

Harry hadn't meant it literally, she realized, but when she found her husband, he really was being slapped on the back by a few people she vaguely remembered from last summer's cricket season. *A lifetime ago*, she thought, thinking of January and February.

Catching her eye, Richard made a face which suggested he wanted to talk to her. Smoothing her hands on her jeans, Sarah tried to think herself into a normal frame of mind, despite Tom, and went over.

'Sarah!' said one of the back-slappers. 'Long time no see!'

'Actually Richard, can you help me in the kitchen?' she asked.

'It's the actually girl,' someone from the cricket team said. 'She actually says "actually", you know?'

Ignoring them, but smiling politely, Richard pushed past his friends and took Sarah by the arm.

'I've just got a question for you,' he said quietly, steering her into the corner.

'Mmm?' Sarah looked at him, trying not to register that her heart was slamming into her ribs.

'It's about Harry. He seems to think our marriage is in trouble.'

'Oh.'

'He's been talking to Tom. And he seems to know all about the fact that you went and bought yourself a self-help book. And other stuff – personal stuff. Arguments we've had.'

'Oh, for God's sake,' Sarah rolled her eyes.

'And a few other things. Like, I can only communicate with animals. Did you tell Tom that as well?'

'What? God, Richard. What is this?'

'So thanks for the vote of confidence, Sarah. Who else apart from Tom have you made your personal confidant lately?'

Looking desperately around the party, Sarah realized that every face she saw was smiling or laughing, and she had to look away again.

'Richard, do we have to?' she protested.

'Have to what? Talk about the fact that I'm last on the list of people you want to talk to in your life?'

'Richard, stop.'

'Are you frightened we're going to divorce?'

'No!'

'Is the fact that I've been divorced a problem for you? Because it wasn't when I first met you. But, hey, that's in Harry's masterpiece as well.'

'I can't talk about this,' Sarah said, staring hard at the

carpet. 'I don't know what Harry's done, and in any case, I just can't talk.'

'But you never can talk,' Richard said, angrily. 'And that's pretty ironic, isn't it? Given that I'm the one who can't communicate?'

'Please. It's a party.'

'Did you tell Tom about the bed?'

'No,' Sarah swallowed hard.

'Have you been crying on his shoulder?'

Shaking her head miserably, Sarah kept her head steadily turned to the wall so that nobody in the room could see her face. 'I have to go,' she mumbled. Pushing past him, she raced outside and found the car, still with the doors unlocked, in the driveway.

'Sarah, wait!' Richard called, watching his wife get into the seat of the Jeep. Getting in beside her, he waited until she was ready to speak again.

'Perfect birthday party for everyone, seeing us have an argument in front of them,' he muttered, watching her face. He was aware that his guests were staring from the house.

'Well, I think people need to know you're not perfect,' Sarah said, feeling her anger rise.

'Meaning?' Richard shot back.

'You're like – oh, I don't know what you're like. Most people in this town seem to think you're a local hero or something.'

'Give me a break.'

'You make it hard for him – for Harry. And I think you make it hard for Tom. You always have. You don't show them anything of yourself. You never screw up. You're – this perfect man they have to put up with.'

'Right,' Richard folded his arms, trying to keep his anger in. 'So that's your theory.'

'They struggle in their lives – like we all do. But they never see you struggling. I mean, I struggle too, you know. And there you are, this kind of person who's just

312

– out there, beyond our reach. You've never done anything wrong, Richard, not once.'

'I got divorced.'

'And you don't talk about that either. How much do I know about you and Bronte? About *this* much . . .' Sarah indicated with her fingers.

'Oh, for God's sake,' Richard sighed, closing his eyes. Through the kitchen window, he could see the guests inside the house trying not to stare at the scene in the Jeep, and failing.

'What goes on inside you? Nobody ever knows, Richard, not even me, and I've been with you for almost a year.'

'What do you mean?'

'Oh, look,' Sarah gave up, rubbing her face with her hands. 'We can't do this now. We can't do this here.'

'Well, let's go somewhere else then. Let's go to the surgery and talk about it.'

'What?'

'Start the car.' Richard felt himself almost shaking with anger. 'Just drive.'

Uncomfortably aware of the audience they now had watching them from inside the house, Sarah put the keys in the ignition and started the engine.

Neither of them spoke as she drove the short distance to Richard's clinic. Silently, Richard got out of the Jeep first, and then waiting for her to follow, he unlocked the back door, which led straight into his office. Only when he had closed the door behind Sarah did he finally feel able to speak.

'It's our wedding anniversary in a couple of months,' he said quietly.

Sarah nodded.

'Bronte and I didn't do anything after the first year,' he remembered. 'So I wanted it to be different for us. I was even thinking I could surprise you and we could go away somewhere.'

'Why does everything we do, or don't do, have to be

313

there because it's so different to what you and Bronte did?' Sarah shot back.

'You see,' Richard said furiously, 'when I talk about Bronte, suddenly – wham. I can't talk about her. And then you complain that I don't communicate, that I never tell you anything about my life.'

'That's not what I meant,' Sarah said, digging her hands in the pockets of her jeans. The surgery smelled like a hospital, she thought, but there was still a faint doggy smell in the room too.

'Well, what is this all about?' he asked.

'You've said exactly one thing to me about having the miscarriage with her!' Sarah shouted back. 'One thing! You said . . .' she groped for the exact words he had used, back in London, when they had first met, 'you said it was sad. I mean, Richard, is that all you have to say? It was *sad*?'

'But what's that got to do with us now?' he replied, staring at her.

'Only that I'm married to you. And you're supposed to be part of me. Except you're not. And I'm sick of being with a saint.'

'What?'

'You never get it wrong, you never stuff up, you never commit any sins, you never fall apart, you never let a single thing show, do you? In fact, I'm not even sure if you really need me at all!' Sarah shot back.

After that, neither of them spoke – and Sarah suddenly became aware of the barking in the next room, where some of Richard's overnight patients stayed.

'So did you choose to open up to Tom instead?' Richard said at last.

'No! That's got nothing to do with anything,' Sarah snapped.

Sighing, Richard started mindlessly moving empty jars around on his desk. He would be back in here tomorrow, he realized – talking to the animals, just like the husband in the letter Harry had invented.

'When Bronte lost the baby,' he said at last, 'we both lost Angel at the same time. And normally, when you destroy a horse, it hurts you – they're such beautiful animals after all – but anyway, you deal with it. That's what you're trained to do. And you know in your heart you're *right* not to feel anything. Once you begin to do that with one animal, you end up doing it for all of them – and then you can't do your job and help any of them.'

Sarah nodded.

'Part of the routine is holding the horse – propping it a certain way and supporting it,' Richard said, hearing the words come out in a rush. 'Instead, I had Angel in my arms. Almost like a human being – which she was to me. To Bronte, she was family too. You know, we lost a baby and a member of our family all on the same day.'

Staring at him, Sarah nodded slowly.

'It screwed me up for months,' Richard said quietly. 'I wouldn't go near any horse jobs. I passed them all on.'

'I'm sorry,' Sarah said, swallowing hard.

'You think I'm a local hero or whatever and I don't suffer, but you're nowhere near the truth,' Richard said. Now, he realized, he was close to tears. Instantly he felt like a six-year-old boy and ashamed of himself, all at once.

'I need you,' he managed to tell Sarah at last. 'When I met you, it was like a miracle – the right woman – at the right time. You seemed heaven-sent to me. I mean, what do you think life was like for me before I met you, Sarah?'

As he stood in the corner of the room, Sarah realized how utterly alone he looked.

'It bothers me if people think I'm some sort of saint,' he said. 'It shouldn't because it's rubbish, but it does. But it also bothers me that Harry is right.'

'How?' Sarah said.

'I spend too much time in here,' Richard said, sighing and looking around the clinic. 'I spend too much time with animals. Basically, I feel alone.'

'But you're not alone.'

'No,' he shook his head at her. 'I am. It's like I've created it. I don't know.'

'You're not alone,' Sarah said slowly, 'because you're married to me. Come here . . .' She went over to him.

'Sarah, you can talk about that local hero bullshit all you like, but it's wrong,' Richard said.

She had never seen him cry, Sarah realized, in all the time they had been married. And now he was wiping at his eyes with the back of his hand.

'Richard, I love you with all my heart and I will never leave you,' she said simply, taking him in her arms.

'I've lost you,' Richard said into her shoulder. 'I can feel it's over – I felt it weeks ago.'

'Found me,' she said quickly, holding him to her. 'Found me, found me, found me,' she said, kissing him, unable to let him go.

Chapter Twenty-seven

Six weeks later, Tasmania was experiencing a three-day heatwave.

'I tell you what, Harry,' his father said to him, knocking on the door of the cabin one hot Friday morning, 'those polyester shirts you're wearing have got to go.'

'Why's that?' Harry said, yawning and taking a pile of letters from his father's hand.

'Put it this way. It's not the weather for them. And I can smell you from here.'

'Oh,' said Harry. 'You mean, I'm fragrant, but not in a good way?'

'One way of putting it,' his father shrugged, shuffling back to the house in his slippers.

Harry had always hated summer weather and even though it was the end of October, the temperature was already over thirty. His arms were too puny for T-shirts and shorts were out of the question. Instead, Harry thought, if he just sprayed an extra layer of CK One on top of his shirt, over his armpits, he might get away with the polyester shirts. He was particularly fond of the one he was wearing today – it had little egg-timers all over it.

Deliberately he tried not to get too excited about the envelopes, which had the names of newspapers and magazines printed on the front. He could see one from the *Age* newspaper, and another one from *Elle*, along with a predictable pile of bills. So far he had counted eight rejection letters for his problems page. If he left these new letters until last, he decided, it would make the rejections matter less. It was time, he thought, to become casual about it all. And if, by a miracle, someone was finally interested, it would be a pleasant surprise.

'No, a pleasant shock,' Harry told the cat, which had just stuck its head around the door. 'That's what it would be.'

Sitting on the end of his bed, Harry opened a frightening final notice bill for his credit card and a letter from his favourite second-hand record shop in Sydney, demanding a final payment of one hundred dollars:

Dear Mr Gilby,
Sadly we can no longer continue to ignore your debt of $100, dating from last June, for the following items:
Blondie – Blondie, *Plastic Letters* – Blondie, *Parallel Lines* – Blondie, *Eat To The Beat* – Blondie, *Def, Dumb and Blonde* – Deborah Harry.
Yours sincerely, Egg Records.
P.S. How's the band going?

Sighing, Harry opened the letters from *Elle* and the *Age*. It was uncanny how many magazines and newspapers longed to keep his name on file, he thought. According to all his rejection letters, his problems pages were now being treasured in ten separate filing cabinets around the country.

Shoving the letters in a chest of drawers, Harry wondered if he could bring himself to ring Bronte again. It had been weeks since she'd promised to help him and he hadn't heard anything from her. If he didn't get a problems-page column soon, he thought, he might have to go back to the bank and the thought of that was enough to reduce his body temperature, even if he was sweating in a polyester shirt.

Picking up the phone, he found her number scrawled in the margin of his diary. To his embarrassment, he realized he had also been doodling a pair of women's lips next to her name, along with what appeared to be a pair of red suspenders.

'Yes?' Bronte said sleepily, picking up the phone in her flat in Sydney. It was Friday morning, but it felt like Sunday and she had allowed herself to sleep in.

'It's Harry,' he said. 'Did I wake you up?'

'Didn't get to bed until three,' she yawned, finding a scrunched-up tissue in her dressing-gown pocket and blowing her nose.

'Wow, wild night,' Harry suggested, nervously.

'No,' Bronte said. 'Wild nights are what happens when you're 20. When you're 40, if you go to bed at 3 a.m. it just means you were watching a Harrison Ford video and drinking too much coffee.'

'Anyway,' Harry said, stretching out on his bed with the phone, 'this is an embarrassing call for me to have to make, but I'm now officially a desperate man.'

'Really?' Bronte answered, settling into her armchair.

'Nobody wants my problems-page idea,' he said, beating away a fly as it did laps around the pillow.

'Send it to me,' Bronte said, yawning again.

'It's just a sample,' Harry said quickly, 'and I already got rid of one of the problems I made up. I had to. Richard thought it was about him.'

'Oh no, keep that one,' Bronte laughed. 'Get it out of the bin and fax it to me now.'

Her voice sounded different these days, Harry realized, listening to her laugh. She seemed to have slowed down, somehow – or become more relaxed.

'Richard told me you'd resigned from your job,' Harry said.

'And Richard told me *you'd* resigned from *your* job,' she countered

'Yeah, well, I'm just starting to get the credit card bills,' Harry sighed, sitting up on the bed against the pillows. 'I'm not sure it was such a great idea.'

'Nah, of course it was a great idea,' Bronte replied. She was starting to wake up now. 'Follow your bliss, Harry.'

'Is that what you're doing?' Harry was curious about Bronte's decision to leave her career behind.

'Put it this way. I just realized life was too short,' she said quickly. It was far too early in the morning to tell her ex-husband's brother all about the past six months, she decided. And she hadn't even told Richard what had been going on yet.

'You know, I used to worry about dying all the time,' Harry mused, chasing the fly away from his bed. 'Every day of my teens I used to think I was going to die.'

'Interesting,' Bronte replied, giving nothing away – but feeling as if he had just read her mind.

'I wish I'd made more of it now. I mean, I wish I'd used all those days when I thought I was going to die as a motivation to do something more with my life,' Harry confessed.

'Like what?' Now, Bronte was curious.

'Oh, you know. Driving across America or something. God. I haven't even been to Queensland, what am I saying?' Harry sighed.

'I drove across America once,' Bronte remembered. 'With a couple of girlfriends. You know, it's not all Jack Kerouac, Jack Daniels and wild sex, Harry. Don't believe the hype.'

'Well,' Harry admitted, 'that makes me feel better. Maybe I didn't miss anything after all.'

Wriggling in her armchair, Bronte decided to take off her dressing-gown. The temperature was beginning to climb in Sydney and she hadn't switched the air-conditioning on yet.

'You split the band up,' Bronte said. 'Richard told me that as well.'

'Yeah, the drummer went off with this – oh, I don't know,' Harry sighed. He was still trying to forget Wendy and Pippin.

'So no love in your life at the moment?' Bronte asked, tactfully.

'I can't even get the cat to sleep with me,' Harry said, watching the animal stick both its legs over its head like a roast turkey.

'Look, I just had a crush on a priest,' Bronte said, laughing. 'It doesn't get any better than that.'

'That's cool. I fell in love with a witch,' Harry confessed. Somehow, telling Bronte now, it didn't seem so bad.

For a moment, neither of them said anything – and then Harry spoke first.

'This is a weird conversation,' he said. 'I mean, it's a good conversation – but it's weird.'

'I was just thinking that,' Bronte agreed. 'I mean, how long since I saw you?'

'The last time I saw you, you were riding Mickey and you were wearing orange furry clogs,' Harry remembered.

'Oh no,' Bronte shuddered, 'not the clogs.'

'The Rich Hippy look. No, it suits you.'

'Two things I'm not – rich and hippy.'

'Well, what are you these days?' Harry asked, amazed that he could talk to Bronte on the phone like this.

'I'm an ageing tart,' Bronte said, 'running out of money fast.'

'Shut up about yourself already,' Harry said, putting on a joke American accent. 'God, Bronte, where's the ageing bit coming from?'

'But I am, I'm falling apart,' Bronte insisted. 'I've got grey hairs, I don't fit into any of those clothes made out of pantyhose that everyone's wearing.'

'Well, you can always dye your hair,' Harry suggested, seriously. 'And I probably shouldn't be admitting this, but . . .'

'Go on,' Bronte suggested, sensing something interesting was coming.

'I had one killer of a dream about you a few months ago.'

'Really? What?' Despite herself, Bronte found herself squirming in her nightie.

'If it's going to make you feel any better, you were looking quite lush.'

'Lush?'

'Look, I'm going to shut up now,' Harry said. But he could tell by her voice that he had just cheered her up.

'Lush? What do you mean, lush?'

'Lady Godiva,' he mumbled, feeling mown down by embarrassment. 'You were riding Mickey and you looked like Lady Godiva.'

'And you're not just saying this so I can help your career in the media?' Bronte laughed again.

'No, really,' Harry shook his head uncomfortably. 'It's the truth.'

'This *is* a weird conversation,' Bronte repeated after a few seconds.

'You're telling me,' Harry replied, conscious of the fact that his STD phone bill was also creeping up.

'But a good conversation,' she insisted. The last person she would ever have imagined who could make her morning was Harry Gilby – but it seemed to be happening.

'So anyway,' Harry kept going, 'are you coming down for the big anniversary party?'

'Wow. Richard and Sarah,' Bronte was jolted back to reality. 'Has it been a year already?'

'It's Sarah's idea,' Harry explained. 'They had some kind of fight on his birthday so she wants to do some big party thing for him to make up for it.'

'What, they had a fight on his birthday?' Bronte

322

asked – she had avoided that invitation as well.

'Yeah,' Harry sighed. 'Anyway, it's all fine now. I mean, they were all over each other last night. It was enough to put you off your dinner.'

'Too much information,' Bronte said quickly.

'Yeah, sorry, I forget you were married to him. But hey – how's this, Sarah's asked me to be the DJ at the anniversary party!'

'Well, that's good,' Bronte said.

Harry shrugged to himself 'I don't know, though. Love died between me and the music industry at the Hobart Town Hall,' he admitted. 'Even if I am just playing tapes all night, I've still got my reservations.'

'Oh,' Bronte sympathized.

'Something to do with a girl and a ferret in a headscarf. You don't want to know.'

'Never mind,' Bronte said diplomatically.

For a second, she wondered if she could get Harry to tell her anything else about Richard and Sarah's fight at his birthday party, but then she decided that would be pushing it. Besides, she thought, if she was curious, it was only out of habit these days. For some reason, Richard and his new wife had ceased to obsess her.

'Well, I'd like to go to their anniversary party,' she said. 'But then I didn't turn up to the wedding, so I'm not sure.'

'No,' Harry agreed, flushing slightly as he remembered his terrible, drunken speech about Bronte at the reception. Thank God she hadn't found out about it, he thought.

'Do you think I'd be invited?' Bronte said tentatively. 'I mean, I'm surprising myself by the fact that I even want to go, but . . .'

'Of course you should go,' Harry said kindly. 'You've had time to get over them getting married and all that now.'

'Yes,' Bronte agreed.

'I don't see why you wouldn't be invited,' Harry

323

continued. 'Anyway, you usually come down to see Mickey around this time of year, don't you?'

'I suppose,' Bronte said, thinking about it.

'Well, then,' Harry said at last. 'Come to the party.'

'I suppose if I flew down I could talk to you about your problems-page idea,' Bronte mused.

'Don't go out of your way,' Harry said, feeling embarrassed. 'But,' he admitted a few moments later, 'it would really help. If you wouldn't mind.'

'Done,' Bronte said, immediately.

'Done?' Harry had forgotten the way she could make decisions in five seconds flat – it was something he had always envied.

'I'll call Richard about the party,' she warned, 'just in case, but if I'm invited, then you'll definitely see me there.'

'Well, if you do fly down . . .'

'Yes?'

'Maybe, I don't know. Maybe we should have a drink or something.'

Cringing inside his polyester shirt, Harry realized what his father had meant about the sweating.

'I'd like that,' Bronte said smoothly, sensing his nervousness on the other end of the line.

'Dye the grey hairs before you come down though,' Harry said, preparing to hang up.

'Well, I might just grow my hair,' Bronte shot back, 'it's not *quite* Lady Godiva length yet.'

Putting the phone down, she blew her nose again and then, with a mixture of horror and excitement, realized she had just been flirting with Harry Gilby at ten o'clock in the morning.

'Lord,' she said to her mirror reflection as she brushed her teeth and rubbed in her cleanser. It was bizarre, she thought, how long they had been on the line for. And what had he said about her? *Lush.*

If she was a cynical human being – which she probably had been six months ago – she might have interpreted his flirting with her as an attempt to get her to help his magazine ambitions. But, Bronte decided, that wasn't Harry's way. It never had been. So she might just have to believe him when he said he wanted to meet her for a drink. And he had practically invited her down there, she realized with a start.

Plugging in the kettle to make some tea in the cabin, Harry was also trying to take in the phone conversation they had just had. He had never told anybody about his fear of dying in his teens, he realized. It had been a terrible, private secret until now. But something about her voice had made him want to tell her everything.

'Plus I think I just asked her out for a drink,' he told the cat as the kettle started to whistle. Purring, the cat changed position and curled up on his pillow. *Bronte Nicholson*, Harry thought. The woman who had made him wear a kilt to her wedding. The woman who had divorced his brother, and gone to Sydney and become such a success that she had terrified him ever since – and, if he was going to be honest, made him deeply envious.

There had definitely been something happening in the lust department while he was talking to her just now, and he wasn't sure if he should feel worried by it, or excited. It was the second time it had happened in the past six months.

'Hot weather,' he said to the cat, who was purring like a drill. 'I blame the hot weather.' Then he made his tea and went back to bed.

Chapter Twenty-eight

On the morning of Sarah and Richard's anniversary party, the temperature had already hit thirty degrees, with a predicted high of thirty-eight for Hobart. Hearing this on the radio, Harry immediately panicked about what to wear. If Hobart was going to hit thirty-eight, Compton would be even hotter and that meant forcing himself into a T-shirt, which had never been his favourite item of clothing.

His parents had threatened to take a camera to the party and he didn't want to be photographed for posterity looking like a stick insect – but suits and long-sleeved shirts were out of the question. His log cabin already felt like a Swedish sauna, Harry thought – all that was missing were a few naked people called Sven beating each other with birch twigs.

Shampooing his hair in the shower, Harry started singing one of his all-time favourite Blondie songs – 'Dreaming' – without even realizing he was doing it. It felt strange to be singing again, he realized, even if it was behind a plastic shower curtain. He had to admit that it felt good, though. Nevertheless, he didn't intend to play any Blondie CDs at the party tonight. That phase of his life was over, he told himself.

His feelings about music would never be the same again, Harry decided, rinsing off the last of the shampoo and sliding a bar of Imperial Leather soap under each armpit. Even if Pippin had posted Blondie's drumsticks back to him in the end, there was still no way that he could ever consider being part of a band again, or fantasizing about playing to an audience of fifty thousand people all waving their arms at him like barley in the wind.

Still, there was something to be said for singing in the shower, just like every other human being, Harry thought, getting to his favourite part of 'Dreaming' which involved Debbie singing about having a cup of tea.

As he got out of the shower and wrapped a towel around his waist, he heard a pair of heels clicking up the path to the log cabin. His mother, he remembered, had wanted him to help her blow up balloons for the party.

'I'm not ready,' he yelled through the bathroom door. With any luck she'd change her mind and disappear again. Blowing up four packets of foul-tasting balloons was more than his lungs could stand, he decided. They didn't seem to realize he had a chest like a weasel.

'Harry?' a voice called through the cabin entrance – and then, with a start, he realized it was Bronte.

'Are you in there?' she called again, stepping inside the cabin.

'No!' he yelled, panicking. 'I thought you weren't coming until tonight.'

'I decided to get an early flight in the end,' she explained. 'And I've been ringing your parents' number for you all morning but no-one's answering. And I can't find Sarah and Richard either, so I thought I'd come and harass you. You don't mind, do you?'

Shrinking with embarrassment, Harry realized that he only had a towel for coverage.

'Can you wait outside?' he shouted, hitching the towel even further up his waist.

'Sure,' Bronte agreed, stepping back out into the garden again.

What he hadn't realized, she thought, smirking to herself, was that he was perfectly visible through the top of the bathroom window anyway. Harry had always been skinny, she remembered – even in a kilt at her wedding to Richard, when he was still at school. His lankiness suited him though, she thought, gazing at the sparrows in the garden as they gathered around the tap. The idea of Harry having muscles or even a suntan, seemed all wrong. He was a black suit and dark glasses kind of boy and he always would be.

'I bought a case of Möet for the party,' Bronte addressed him through the door of the cabin while she let him get dressed. 'It's probably going to destroy what's left of my credit card. But I thought they wouldn't have any decent champagne at the bottle shop.'

'You're right there,' Harry interrupted. 'It would be cause for national celebration if you even found Fanta at the Compton bottle shop. You know, their idea of Tequila is a bottle of beer with a dead mouse in it.'

'So, anyway, that's my present to Richard and Sarah – the Möet,' Bronte explained. 'I lashed out this morning and got a dozen bottles at the airport.'

'Good on you,' Harry said nervously, dressing in a hurry.

If he put on his polyester shirt with the boomerangs on it first, and then changed into his other polyester shirt with the horseshoes on it in a few hours time, he might just get through the heatwave without massive sweat rings under his arms, he thought. One thing was certain, though. There was no way he was going to face Bronte now in a T-shirt that made him look like a small flying thing with six legs.

'I've had a generous offer,' Bronte yelled through the doorway. 'Sarah said I could borrow their house to get ready in – they're going out for the day.'

'Wow, first she invites you to the party and next she lets you take over the house,' Harry observed.

'Yeah, it was amazing,' Bronte explained. 'She just rang up after you called me – I didn't even have to bother Richard. But I'm going to stay in the pub overnight,' Bronte explained, squinting in the sun. 'I don't want to sleep on their couch – that's going too far.'

'Well, it's less distance to walk home afterwards if you stay at the pub,' Harry observed. 'In fact, you could probably crawl up the stairs on your hands and knees if you wanted to.'

'Whose idea was it to have the party at the pub anyway?' Bronte said, still shouting through the door.

'Mine,' Harry replied. 'My new best friend, Don the barman, said he'd give us the back room for nothing.'

Finally, he emerged, blinking in the sunlight, in tight black pants, his favourite Converse sneakers and a red polyester shirt with a boomerang print.

'My God,' he said, shielding his eyes against the sun, 'someone turn that weather off.'

'It's so typical that Tasmania gets a heatwave and it's raining in Sydney,' Bronte tutted, waving a bottle of Möet for emphasis. 'You should have seen it when I left this morning.'

'So you've cracked into the champagne already,' Harry noticed, staring at the bottle.

'Well, I thought you might like to have a glass while we discuss your future career as an agony aunt,' Bronte shrugged. 'And anyway – there's nothing else to do in this godforsaken town today except drink.'

'I know,' Harry said. 'Everyone's gone to the beach today. A population of three thousand people, and two thousand nine hundred and ninety-four of them are probably roasting themselves on a piece of sand somewhere.'

'Well, that's where Sarah and Richard have gone,' Bronte nodded. 'They left me a note.'

'And Mum and Dad are at the pub doing the balloons,' Harry sighed. 'I'm supposed to be helping.

It's like, they think I'm in possession of a respiratory tract or something.'

'Oh no,' Bronte said quickly, 'don't do the balloons, Harry. It could endanger your health and I'm telling you that as a lifelong smoker. Let's just sit under here instead,' Bronte indicated an aged gum tree in the corner of the garden.

She was wearing an old green skirt and a short-sleeved white cotton shirt with coffee stains down the front, and Adidas sandshoes, Harry realized. Strangely, though, she was also wearing red fishnet stockings.

'I've got half dressed,' she explained, catching him looking at her. 'The stockings are for tonight, but the rest of it is what I flew up in. I sort of tried a few things, and then I lost interest – and then I thought, I'll just leave the underneath bit on and do the rest later.'

'Well, red fishnet stockings and Adidas,' Harry mused. 'You might get away with it.'

'Or maybe,' Bronte said mischievously, 'I should just go naked tonight, let my hair out and turn up on Mickey.'

Cringing, Harry put his hand over his eyes. 'I wish you'd just forget about the Lady Godiva thing,' he said.

'Too late,' she smiled, popping the Möet cork neatly into a patch of grass. 'You've told me now. But don't worry, Harry, your older woman complex is safe with me.'

'What older woman complex?' Harry said, watching her drink champagne straight from the bottle.

'You know what I mean,' Bronte smiled, wiping her lips with the back of her hand and passing him the Möet.

'Well, I've given up on Debbie Harry if that's what you mean,' he said, swigging the bottle.

'How could I possibly have meant anything else?' Bronte said, wide-eyed and teasing him. She was beginning to enjoy herself, she realized – and she

330

was also beginning to enjoy the fact that Harry couldn't stop staring at her legs.

'You're wearing red suspenders as well,' he said at last. Her green skirt had ridden halfway up her thighs.

'Well, how on earth am I supposed to keep the fishnet stockings up without them?' she pouted, taking the bottle of Möet back.

'That was in my dream,' Harry said, feeling himself start to sweat.

'The Lady Godiva dream?' Bronte interrupted.

'No, no,' Harry shook his head and staring down at the grass feeling overwhelmed with embarrassment. 'Another dream.'

'Well, clearly it wouldn't be historically accurate if it had been the Lady Godiva dream because we all know they didn't have suspenders in those days, let alone fishnets – and anyway, she didn't even have those on according to impartial peasant observers,' Bronte announced, taking another swig from the bottle. She loved the feel of warm, fizzy, French champagne. It reminded her of barbecues and summer – and love, she thought hazily. *Probably love.*

'So anyway,' she started, unwilling to let Harry escape. 'You're now confessing you've had a second dream about me?'

'I think I must be psychic,' Harry muttered. 'Red suspenders. I mean, I'm shocked. You've actually got them. You're actually wearing them.'

'Well, I'm impressed,' Bronte said slyly, putting the Möet back down on the grass. 'Not so much by your psychic powers – but Harry, it's not every day some bloke has *two* dreams about me,' she smiled.

For a moment, neither of them spoke, watching the sparrows hop around under the puddle beneath the garden tap and feeling the heat burn through their clothes.

'This is weird,' Harry said, rubbing his face.

'Why?'

331

'I mean, I hardly know you.'

'Right.'

'But I've also known you for half my life.'

Bronte nodded. 'I know,' she sighed. 'I've thought about it too.'

Lying back on the grass, Bronte shrugged off her left sandshoe with her right foot and then switched legs, shaking out her feet in the red fishnet stockings.

'I wouldn't be surprised if you were being psychic about my suspenders,' she sighed. 'A lot of strange things have been happening to me this year. There was a bloke called Bernard Bolton who lived above a fish and chip shop who seemed to have an uncanny insight into my life as well.'

'Who's he?' Harry said quickly.

'Oh, just this man who talks to dead people,' she explained. 'And dead horses.'

'So was that your boyfriend then?' Harry prompted her.

'Oh, God no,' she said. 'He was just this man who nearly ran me over and killed me.'

Giving in, Harry also flopped down on the grass. He wasn't going to take his shoes off, though, he decided. He had holes in his socks.

'Well, who was the priest then?' he asked. He knew he was giving himself away, but he had to know more about Bronte's love life.

She shook her head. 'Just a priest whose shopping bag exploded – and nothing happened,' she sighed. 'But I have to confess, I was smitten for about ten minutes. Until I realized he wasn't going to explain the meaning of life to me.'

'And why did you want to know that?' Harry asked, watching an ant on a blade of grass.

'You know how you were saying that you wished you'd taken a road trip across America when you thought you were going to die?' Bronte said suddenly.

Harry nodded.

'I mean, your secret's safe with me Harry,' she reassured him, 'but something like that just happened to me.'

'How?' Harry turned on his side, squinting at the bottle of Möet to see if there was any more champagne left – but Bronte appeared to have drunk the last of it.

'Well, first of all I kept seeing Angel,' she explained, and every time I did, she was trying to warn me that I was going to die. And then Bernard Bolton, the man who talks to dead people, nearly ran me over – except Angel pushed me out of the way at the last minute. And then, when I realized I wasn't going to die after all, I decided to quit my job and go looking for the meaning of life. Are you following?'

'Not really,' Harry admitted, propping his chin up on his hand. 'But I get the point. And I can see about the Angel thing.'

'Can you?'

'I believe in all that stuff,' he shrugged.

'Oh, that's right,' Bronte sighed. 'You had it off with a witch.'

'No,' Harry corrected her. 'Pippin did. My drummer. I was just the pointy bit at the top of the Toblerone Triangle of Love.'

'Now I'm the one who's not following,' Bronte said, putting her hand over her eyes to shield the sun. 'But weirdly enough, I also know what you mean.'

'It's nice when someone knows what you mean and you know what someone else means,' Harry said, feeling himself becoming sleepy in the heat. 'Even if you're both talking bollocks.'

'Yes,' Bronte said, smiling with her eyes closed as she lay on the grass. 'I know what you mean – about knowing what the other person means.'

She was beginning to feel drowsy and warm and slightly drunk and she wondered if she could drop off under the tree without ending up with a bad case of sunburn, and criss-cross shaped lines on her legs where her fishnet stockings had been.

'So are you still feeling old?' Harry asked, looking over at her.

'Only my hair,' Bronte sighed. 'I was thinking about it on the plane. I need to do something about the grey.'

'How about blonde?' Harry said, looking at her eyes. 'I think you'd look good as a blonde.'

'Do you?' she asked, sitting up on the grass.

'I've got some dye in the bathroom,' he offered. 'If you want it, you can have it.'

'What, you mean I just squirt some bottle on my head?' she said, frowning.

'It's easy,' Harry sat up and looked at her. 'I've done it before. You just need to know Italian.'

'What?'

'Well it's a cheap job-lot. A dollar a box. From Salamanca Markets. Italian hair dye. The instructions are all like – lasagna, lasagna, lasagna. Anyway . . .'

'Italian blonde hair dye is probably very sexy,' Bronte mused, feeling the champagne hit her bloodstream. 'Like that woman in *La Dolce Vita*.'

'Oh *yeah*,' Harry said, forgetting himself for a moment as he remembered the voluptuous Anita Ekberg in the film.

'And you're telling me this is completely safe?' Bronte insisted.

'Well, I did it on Pippin once,' Harry muttered.

'Fair enough,' Bronte shrugged. 'Let's do it.'

There she was again, Harry realized – making five-second decisions.

'You know, I really admire that about you,' he said, watching as she got up in her stockinged feet.

'What's that?'

'You're so fast about everything. You make up your mind – and you just do it.'

'Well, *grazie, grazie*,' Bronte said, in the worst Italian accent Harry had ever heard.

334

'You'll look great as a blonde,' Harry said, looking at her. 'Trust me.'

'Weirdly enough,' Bronte said, following him back into the log cabin, 'I'm beginning to.'

Across town, Tom was wheeling his bike downhill towards Lilly Creek. It was too far to the beach and he couldn't think of anywhere else he wanted to be today, except in fresh-running water. He had caught the bus in at 9 a.m. – there were only two bus services a day to Compton – and now he had all day to kill until the party – *if I end up going*, he told himself.

Richard had rung and invited him and he'd even managed to have a fairly normal conversation with Sarah on the phone afterwards, but he couldn't pretend that he felt comfortable about going now that he had actually arrived in Compton. He hadn't even found them a present yet, he realized, sighing.

Although nobody had yet explained to him exactly what had happened at Richard's birthday party, Tom had a feeling that when Richard had stormed off with Sarah, it had all had something to do with him. Harry wouldn't talk about it, though – and he could hardly ring up Richard or Sarah and ask – so instead, Tom had tried to push it out of his mind. Last night had been his third consecutive bout of insomnia, though.

To make himself feel better, he tried to concentrate on the bush around him. He missed Compton. Working on the new park gardens was peaceful – and with Perdita around to talk to, it was more than just a boring job – but there was nothing like a proper gully to walk through, he decided – or a proper creek to go swimming in.

Idly, Tom wondered if Sarah ever came back here. Probably not, he thought. For him, today's swim would be a kind of exorcism, he thought.

Hearing an animal rush through the bush behind

335

him, he turned and listened. Perhaps the heat was bringing all the wallabies out early in the day. Instead, though, he saw himself being followed by a small, stocky familiar-looking dog.

'Merlin!' he said, overjoyed to see him again.

'Hello,' Annie called, walking up the track behind the dog.

'Hi,' Tom said, catching his breath.

And then, a few paces behind her, he saw a tall, grey-haired man with a rucksack, walking steadily up the track with a bottle of water in his hand.

'This is a friend of mine,' Annie indicated the man. 'I'm showing him round.'

'Hi,' the grey-haired man said in an American accent. 'I'm Alec.'

Introducing himself in return, Tom shook his hand.

'Want some water?' Alec offered the bottle. Taking it gratefully, Tom took a swig and then handed it on to Annie.

'They're saying it could get as high as forty degrees,' Annie said, watching Merlin dance around the base of a gum tree in search of rabbits.

Tom shook his head. 'Too hot for me,' he agreed. Judging by their wet hair, he realized Annie and Alec were returning from a swim in the creek.

'We found the most incredible tree-house back there,' Alec waved a hand behind him.

'Yes,' Tom agreed, trying hard to smile. 'It is incredible.'

'Anyway, Annie said, handing the water bottle back to Alec. 'We should be getting back. Come round some time, Tom. Maybe . . .' she almost managed a joke, 'when your hair grows back.'

'I will,' Tom said, knowing it would be months before he could face it.

'Bye,' Alec said, guiding Annie up the path while Merlin raced ahead of them.

Feeling his heart drag him down to the ground, even

after this brief encounter, Tom kept walking. If he could just make it to the creek, he told himself, he would be able to sit down and get his breath – as well as his head – together.

Annie had looked older, he realized, but also prettier – probably because she was happier, he thought, hating himself. And there was something else that was different about Annie too – maybe the fact that she had let the American man, Alec, take her arm. Whenever Annie had gone walking to Lilly Creek with Tom in the old days, she had always pushed him away when he wanted to help her through the bush.

It was no good, Tom realized, leaning against a tree for a minute. He had come to Lilly Creek today to find peace, or even a resolution, but it had now deserted him. Perhaps, he thought, he should just turn around, head back out to town and hitch back to Hobart with his bike. He could always ring up Richard and Sarah later and say he was ill.

Following a black cockatoo with his eyes, Tom watched it land on a young yellow wattle tree and call in its mate. Perdita would love some of the wattle, he realized – and one cutting couldn't hurt. Reaching up to the tree, he quickly yanked off a low-hanging branch, and tucked it under his arm, making a note to find a plastic bag for it in town. Perdita had wanted to plant some Australian natives in the park for weeks – he couldn't wait to tell her, he thought, suddenly cheering up.

'I'll ring her,' he told the black cockatoos, who were screeching at him from the top of the tree.

'No,' he insisted, as a kookaburra joined in, laughing at him, 'I will.'

Suddenly, he realized, there was nothing else in the world he felt more like doing. There was a phone box at the bottom of the hill – a phone box he had often used during his late-night phone calls to Sarah. If he hurried, he thought, he might catch Perdita before she went out for the day. And perhaps, he thought – just perhaps – she might even come with him to the party. Relieved, he started walking back, following the trail that Annie and Alec had just left behind.

A gathering of black cockatoos was also on duty overhead when Sarah and Richard finally arrived at the beach.

'Look at the car park,' Richard sighed. 'It's packed.'

'Packed?' Sarah shook her head. 'In England, Richard, this is what they call having the place to yourself.' She could see about twenty cars and two motorbikes.

'Oh, I forget,' Richard laughed, 'you're a foreigner.'

Kissing him, Sarah opened the glovebox and searched for the sunscreen.

'Oh,' she said, squeezing the bottle, 'I think we're all out.'

'Doesn't matter,' Richard shrugged, getting out of the car. 'Just a quick swim. We won't have time to catch the sun.'

'A quick, first anniversary swim,' Sarah agreed.

'And then we can get back in plenty of time for tonight,' Richard said. 'I think my mother was saying something about blowing up balloons at the pub.'

'God,' Sarah said, stretching up her arms to the sky in the car park, 'it's so good to be here.'

'When you do that, your towel falls off,' Richard said, admiring her pink bikini.

'I'm so lucky,' she said, smiling across at him, hearing the sound of the sea just over the sand dunes. 'Thank you, thank you, thank you, thank you.'

'Well,' Richard said, taking her hand, 'today hasn't even really begun yet. So that's a good start. And you don't have to thank me.'

Squeezing his hand, she led the way towards the beach, following the sound of the waves while the cockatoos squawked at them from the trees.

'Oh, I forgot,' Sarah said. 'Bronte was going to fly in early. She rang while you were in the shower.'

'She'll be at a loose end,' Richard yawned. 'Town's practically shut down and Mum and Dad are organizing the room at the pub. And I can't see her spending the day with Harry, somehow.'

Nodding, Sarah reached behind her to sort out her bikini clasp, which had twisted sideways, and smiled happily as Richard obliged instead.

'No,' she agreed, 'I think Bronte would rather spend the day helping your mother blow up balloons than be forced to spend it with your brother, wouldn't she? Poor Harry,' she sighed, watching the cockatoos leave the trees.

'Preparazione!' Harry announced, putting on the free plastic gloves that came with the Italian hair-dye kit.

Sitting on a chair in front of him, Bronte tried to relax.

'Seguire rigorosamente le istruzioni indicate sul modo d'impiego,' Harry warned, 'so we might both be killed in an explosion as your head spins around like the pea soup scene in *The Exorcist*,' he explained.

'Is that what it means?' asked Bronte, impressed.

'I have no idea,' Harry shrugged. 'But I tell you what, Bronte, I've got a bottle of cheap white in the fridge. It's not Möet but it might give us . . .'

'Continuity of alcohol intake,' Bronte encouraged him.

'And courage for the task ahead,' Harry said, ignoring the complicated part of the instructions that explained allergy tests and strand tests.

His Italian wasn't that good, he decided. And in any case, all he really had to do was squirt the plastic bottle all over Bronte's hair. He didn't think she looked like the sensitive, allergic type.

'Oh look, free conditioner,' Bronte said, finding another small plastic bottle in the pack. 'That's nice of them.'

'I'll give you a free massage as well if you like,' Harry offered, 'as part of the service.'

'Yes, please,' Bronte sighed as he started shaking the plastic bottle of dye up and down, mixing his other potions together.

'So, a glass of wine for Madam, and a scalp massage,' Harry said. 'But please, not to movemento your heado, Madam. Otherwise, the acido will drippo.'

'Harry?' Bronte asked as he went to the fridge to find the wine.

'Mmm?' he replied.

'It's something I was saving up to tell you,' she said, 'but I wasn't sure about how you'd take it.'

'Well, spill the beanos,' he said.

'The woman I used to work with – my old assistant, Laura,' Bronte explained, 'well, I rang her and they want someone in the accounts department. For my old magazine, *Australian Woman.* I mean, it's not what you want, it's not a problem page, but . . .'

'Oh my God, Bronte, your hair's turning red!' Harry said, suddenly watching her hair go from light brown to scarlet.

'Well, it will match my suspenders,' she said, hardly caring. It was funny, she thought, but when she was truly happy – and she was, today – almost nothing could put her off.

'Accounts,' Harry said, with his head on one side. 'Hmmm.'

'And I thought, if you wanted to fly up for the interview at the magazine, well – you could stay with me for a couple of days.'

'Really?' Harry shot back. 'You'd really let me stay with you?'

'Sure,' she nodded, trying not to let the dye drip down her face too much

'I mean, really – with you?'

She nodded again, smiling at the expression on his face.

'Well, if that's the deal, then I'll take the job,' Harry said quickly. 'In fact, as soon as you've had your *trattamento finale*, I'm on that plane. The promise of two days with you, Madam, is a small price to pay for signing a long-term contract of employment as an accountant with a multinational media conglomerate.'

'Idiot,' Bronte laughed.

'Look,' Harry said, sighing with relief. 'Your hair's starting to go blonde now.'

The day slid by, reaching a peak of forty degrees just after lunch, and then gradually cooling down as the sun, obeying daylight saving, finally started to disappear after dinner.

'Look at that,' Don the barman told some of the customers in the Compton Arms. 'The whole pub's turned pink with that sun.'

'When it's dark orange like that,' an old man warned, 'we'll get bushfires tomorrow. Or storms tonight.'

'And I'll tell you something else,' Don observed, 'we've sold so much Cascade today I'm going to have to ring the brewery in case we run dry.'

Collecting glasses from the tables, Don wedged a can of air-freshener under his arm, so he could spray a final blast into the back room before any guests started arriving. If he aimed carefully enough, he thought, he might also be able to hit Pippin and Witchy Wendy Wagner and get them out of the front bar. It was just poor Harry's luck, he thought wryly, that both of them had chosen this particular Saturday night to turn up for an all-night drinking session.

'What about the ozone layer?' Pippin muttered as Don walked carefully around them with the spray.

'The Gilby family's having a party here tonight,' he

said casually, giving the air above Wendy's head a quick extra blast before moving on to the next table.

'Big whoop,' Pippin said to Wendy, raising her eyebrows. But it was too late – she could already see Harry, striding in through the front door in his shirt with the horseshoes, and his sideburns shaved into the sharpest points she'd ever seen.

'Oh, my God,' Pippin muttered, catching sight of Bronte walking behind him. 'Look at the blonde.'

'Wow,' Wendy whispered into her wine glass.

'Wow,' Don whispered to a few members of the cricket team, who had turned up early.

Enjoying herself – it had been years since she'd turned heads – Bronte took tiny steps forward in her fishnet stockings and high heels. As soon as she was through the door, she reassured herself, she'd head straight for the bathroom so she could look at herself in the mirror again. But she knew she was looking – as Harry described it – fabuloso. Tomorrow morning with a hangover she might feel differently, she told herself – but just for now, just for tonight, it was right.

Waving a hand airily at Pippin and Wendy, and ignoring the fact that the sight of them together still had the power to squeeze his heart, Harry walked straight past the pool tables. He wished Bronte would teeter a bit closer behind him, so they could all see that she was with him, but then again, the high heels were deadly – she had already nearly broken her neck in them on the way out of the log cabin.

'Nobody recognizes me,' Bronte hissed, finally catching up with him as they found the back room covered in balloons.

'Told you,' Harry smirked.

'Oh, hello Bronte,' Mrs Gilby said, taking the Gladwrap off a plate of pies. 'I like your hair.'

'Bronte,' grunted Dr Gilby politely, standing on a chair with an armful of balloons.

Laughing, Harry jabbed Bronte in the ribs with his

elbow. 'What you have to realize,' he whispered, 'is that my parents are aliens. They have extra-sensory powers of perception.'

'Oh, well,' Bronte shrugged, 'for a thrilling moment I thought I was going to fool them. But you're right, they are aliens.'

'Hey, Bronte,' Harry said, peering through the doorway of the back bar. 'Did you see those women out there?'

'Well, I saw you trying not to look at a couple of people. Local trollopes, are they?'

He nodded.

'And do they represent a problem for you, Harry?' she asked, 'Is that what you're trying to tell me?'

'That's Pippin and Wendy,' he sighed.

'Ah, the other two points in the Toblerone Triangle of Love. Well, you'll be pleased to hear they're being fumigated,' Bronte laughed, leaning around the doorway to catch Don brandishing air-freshener at Pippin's table. 'So whatever they've done to you, it won't be catching.'

Smiling, Harry stretched his hands lazily behind his head. He was beginning to feel good now, he realized.

'Oh look,' Bronte said suddenly, 'Tom's here.'

Following several other couples into the room, Tom and Perdita walked in, still holding the wattle cutting from Lilly Creek in a plastic bag.

'Greetings,' Harry said politely, realizing that Perdita was one of those women who actually came up to nipple level on his chest. Tom had told him she was short and cute, and he could see both those things – although she was a bit too homespun for his taste – but he hadn't explained properly about the lack of height.

'I like your haircut,' Bronte told Tom. In all the years she'd known him, his hair had always hung in his eyes.

'I like your hair too,' Tom said, feeling shyness overtake him as he realized everyone in the room was

343

staring at Perdita. It was the first time they'd been out together in Compton.

'Well, this isn't so much a haircut, more a drastic colour change – courtesy of Harry,' Bronte explained, patting Tom on the arm. She had forgotten how gorgeous he was. No wonder he had been snapped up so soon after leaving Annie, she thought, looking at Perdita.

'Harry dyed your hair?' Tom laughed.

'With this cheap Italian stuff from the markets.'

'Well,' he smiled, 'I think it's actually worked, Bronte. I mean . . .' he stumbled, 'I think you look great.'

Moving away to find a drink, Perdita and Tom found a quiet corner away from all the coloured lights.

'Harry and Bronte,' Tom said softly, almost to himself.

'Who's she?' Perdita asked. She had heard all about Harry, but she didn't know who the glamorous woman in the red dress was.

'His brother's first wife,' Tom smiled, hearing himself say the words. 'Richard's childhood sweetheart.'

And then, turning around, he saw Richard walk slowly into the room, followed by Sarah. He had been dreading this moment all afternoon, he realized as he had sat in the coffee shop waiting for Perdita to arrive. Now it had happened, though, like all dreaded moments it had lost its sting.

'Ouch,' Perdita said sympathetically. 'They're *really* sunburned.'

'Oh, my goodness,' Mrs Gilby said, rushing over to welcome them. 'What happened to you?'

Sarah had bright red patches on her nose, cheeks and forehead and two white stripes where her bikini straps had been. Richard, meanwhile, had the reddest nose she had ever seen.

'Look at that,' Richard grinned, rolling up a sleeve and revealing more burned skin. 'I mean, it's embarrassing, I'm supposed to be in the medical profession. I should know about these things.'

'Only cats and dogs, though,' his mother reassured him. 'You'll get away with it.'

'We were only supposed to go for a quick swim,' Sarah shrugged and smiled.

'And then someone wanted to have a nap in the sand dunes,' Richard raised his eyebrows at Sarah.

Standing in the shadows with Perdita, Tom watched as Sarah and Richard stood, side by side, letting Mrs Gilby pour their drinks. Even though they were sunburned and tired, they looked happy. He was glad for them, he thought. He had no idea where life with Perdita would take him, but he felt sure about Sarah and Richard now. And he was glad that Sarah had finally realized what he had instinctively known – that she cared more about Richard than she could ever admit.

Catching his eye, Sarah gave him a little wave. Waving back, Tom reassured himself that he had never told Perdita anything about her so far, and there was no reason to start now.

It's all working out, Tom, Sarah thought to herself, taking in the sight of Tom with another woman.

Richard had not spoken to her about Tom, or Harry's letter, since the day of his birthday party – and she suspected he never would. Instead, it was almost as if nothing had ever happened, she realized, watching Richard go over to him now. In a way, she suspected that was how the friendship between Tom and Richard had lasted all these years. Her marriage to him would be the same, she decided. Richard had a way of being strong enough to turn his back on anything that threatened either love or friendship, and that would be their insurance policy, even on the days when she got it wrong.

Wincing with her sunburn, Sarah made her way across the room to talk to Harry, and what appeared to be Bronte with a blonde wig on – except, as she got closer, she could see it was the real thing. She was wearing a tight red dress that Sarah had never imagined she would have chosen.

'There's something going on,' Richard whispered, cutting in front of his wife.

'What do you mean?' Sarah whispered back. 'With Harry and Bronte?'

Richard nodded his head 'I can't be certain, but . . . there's *something* going on.'

Sarah laughed. 'Maybe it's just the champagne,' she said. 'All that Möet that Bronte brought – I bet they've just been sitting there drinking it all day.'

'No,' Richard shook his head again. 'It's not just that. Harry's talking about flying up to Sydney to stay with her.'

'What?'

Before Sarah could say anything else, though, a low rumble of thunder drowned her out.

'It's starting,' Richard said, squinting up through the windows. The sky was as dirty and brown as coffee now and the sun had completely disappeared.

'Whooa! Lightning!' someone else yelled across the room as the windows lit up.

'It's a relief anyway,' Don said, coming in to collect more glasses. 'It had to break eventually. They've been forecasting storms all week.'

Smiling at Tom, Perdita craned her neck to watch for the lightning.

'You're thinking about the rain, aren't you,' Tom smiled back.

'I couldn't stand it if all the new trees died,' she replied. 'It's not that I only think about work, though.'

'No,' Tom agreed.

'I mean, there is time for other stuff too,' she said shyly, hoping that at last – at long last – Tom would take the hint.

'Here it comes!' Dr Gilby yelled, looking up at the

ceiling as the rain suddenly shot down from the sky and started hitting the corrugated-iron roof.

'What happened to the music?' someone from the cricket team yelled. 'Can't hear a thing above this rain!'

Suddenly snapping to attention, Harry found the volume control on the stereo.

Wobbling behind him on her high heels, Bronte decided she was going to have to take them off.

'Whoo, barefoot in the park,' Harry observed as she kicked off her shoes. 'Or, at least, barefoot in the pub.'

'Put something on we can dance to,' she sighed. 'I haven't danced for such a long time.'

'*Si, si, signorina,*' Harry said, switching back to his Italian hair-dye accent. 'Whatever you like.'

'This one,' Bronte said, grabbing *The Best of Henry Mancini*.

'Ah, yes, Mr Mancini, from your native Italy,' Harry agreed.

'Look – "Raindrops Keep Falling On My Head",' Bronte pointed. 'It's perfect.'

Nodding and smiling to himself in the dark – he thought the song would be perfect for other reasons too – Harry pushed the volume up to ten and slid the CD into the sound system.

'I love the start of this,' Sarah grinned, hearing the song start up through the speakers. 'That sort of plinkety-plonk bit at the beginning.'

'What's more, Harry's even managed to find a song that's appropriate for a change,' Richard said, squeezing her hand as the thunder rumbled along the back of the Compton hills for a second time and the rain kept coming down.

'Dance, *signorina*?' Harry said, offering his hand to Bronte as the music boomed through the speakers.

'Only if we stop doing this Italian thing,' Bronte said. 'But yes, I'd like to.'

Making room for them, people stood aside and

watched as Harry gently put one hand on Bronte's waist and took her hand in his.

'You smell of toxic chemicals from Milan,' he murmured softly into her hair.

'You need to change your shirt,' she murmured back, half laughing.

'Raindrops keep falling on my head . . .' Mrs Gilby sang along with the music, watching her youngest son move closer to Bronte as they did a half waltz around the floor.

'I always liked this song,' she told her husband. 'It's so optimistic. You know, Henry Mancini was absolutely right. You *can't* stop rain by complaining.'

'Not that Harry seems to be complaining,' her husband said, raising his eyebrows as Bronte slowly put her head on Harry's shoulder and the rain against the pub windows turned everything outside into a blur.

THE END

Single White E-Mail

Jessica Adams

'SEXY, FUNNY, SMART. FOR ANY WOMAN WHO
HAS EVER BEEN SINGLE'
Cosmopolitan

**Saturday night is a nightmare when you're single.
Saturday night is for couples and everyone knows
it.**

Victoria 'Total Bloody Relationships Disaster'
Shepworth is single and knows **all** about Saturday
nights alone. A broken relationship with the guy
she thought was 'the one' has led to a string of
disastrous dates. Now she's fed-up with being on
her own and is once again in search of the man of
her dreams. But life begins to look decidedly more
interesting when she becomes involved in an
internet romance with glamorous Frenchman,
Pierre Dubois. Little does she know he could be
closer than she thinks . . .

'A VERY FUNNY NOVEL FOR THE 90s WOMAN –
READ IT AND RECOGNIZE YOURSELF'
New Weekly

'ADAMS' DEBUT INTO THE LITERARY WORLD IS
FRESH, FRENETIC AND FUN'
Elle

'SHE GIVES NICK HORNBY AND HELEN
FIELDING A DAMN GOD RUN FOR THEIR
MONEY . . . THOROUGHLY ENJOYABLE'
Daily Telegraph

0 552 99830 3

BLACK SWAN

Four Ways To Be A Woman

Sue Reidy

A powerful friendship has survived between four women since their convent schooldays. Once they had believed they could do anything they wanted. Now, rapidly approaching forty they are having to take stock.

AGNES: Hip photographer and party girl. Fiercely independent, she doesn't have a maternal bone in her body. So what is she doing becoming involved with an ex-Catholic priest who can't wait to settle down, make up for lost time and reproduce?

CLARE: Top public relations consultant. Smart and affluent, she is also disillusioned and eager for a change of pace. She wants to have a child, but her partner isn't interested. What is she to do?

ATHENA: New Age healer and single parent. She hasn't had a relationship for ten years and is now looking for a good woman. But how does she find her?

BRIDGET: Well known painter, married forever to steady, reliable Matthew, she has been trying, unsuccessfully, to have a baby. But little does she know that there are graver problems on the horizon . . .

Sue Reidy's clear-eyed depiction of how it is to be a woman living in the confusion and uncertainty of a century's end is a remarkable achievement. Funny, frank and poignant, this novel will strike a chord with women everywhere.

0 552 99697 1

BLACK SWAN

The Secret Dreamworld Of A Shopaholic

Sophie Kinsella

When the going gets tough – the tough go
shopping . . .

Meet Rebecca Bloomwood.

She's a journalist. She spends her working life
telling others how to manage their money.
She spends her leisure time . . . shopping.

Retail therapy is the answer to all her problems.
She knows she should stop, but she can't. She tries
Cutting Back, she tries Making More Money. But
neither seems to work. The stories she concocts
become more and more fantastic as she tries to
untangle her increasingly dire financial difficulties.
Her only comfort is to buy herself something –
just a little something . . .

Can Becky ever escape from this dream world, find
true love, and regain the use of her Switch card?

The Secret Dreamworld of a Shopaholic . . . the
perfect pick me up for when it's all hanging in the
(bank) balance.

0 552 99887 7

BLACK SWAN

A SELECTED LIST OF FINE WRITING
AVAILABLE FROM BLACK SWAN

THE PRICES SHOWN BELOW WERE CORRECT AT THE TIME OF GOING TO PRESS. HOWEVER TRANSWORLD PUBLISHERS RESERVE THE RIGHT TO SHOW NEW RETAIL PRICES ON COVERS WHICH MAY DIFFER FROM THOSE PREVIOUSLY ADVERTISED IN THE TEXT OR ELSEWHERE.

All Transworld titles are available by post from:

Bookpost, P.O. Box 29, Douglas, Isle of Man IM99 1BQ

Credit cards accepted. Please telephone 01624 836000,
fax 01624 837033 or Internet http://www.bookpost.co.uk.
or e-mail: bookshop@enterprise.net for details

Free postage and packing in the UK. Overseas customers: allow
£1 per book (paperbacks) and £3 per book (hardbacks).